THE PHILOSOPHERS AND THE MERE

THE PHILOSOPHERS AND THE MERE

A Modern Myth Without a Tower

BRIAN CAPLETON

Amarilli Books Onyx Edition

Amarilli Books Onyx Edition
ISBN 978-1-7392582-5-2
Cover image by Brian Capleton, acrylics on canvas.

First Printing, 2024

True philosophy, as evident from the etymology of the word itself, is the love of wisdom. And what is wisdom, if it is not the knowledge of what is beyond the mere?

Contents

POSTLUDE

Prologue

Pythagoras sat with Gautama and all the friends under the shade of the kalpa tree in the gardens of Puvk Paradisa. "Please, please tell us", Pythagoras pleaded, "The story of the great house Aumhurst, and of the Aumhurst masquerade, that is mentioned in all the stories about Pavi Bujdam, that occur sometimes in the stories about Pavi Sparkadu, stories that we also sometimes hear in stories about Pavi Daksa. Please tell us all about Pavi Bujdam, and its surrounding ocean, the mere".

Gautama smiled and looked around at the friends. So he began his story as follows, saying:

Prelude

Winter in Pavi Bujdam is the time for telling stories in front of the fire. Stories of fragrant springs and glorious summers. And so it was that one day, a little group of friends, led by Aedesius, sat in front of the fire, together with Augustus, the storyteller, poet, and Lord of Aumhurst, sitting in his rocking chair, with the friends ready to listen to his stories. Stories of how he came to be the Lord of Aumhurst, and how Sandhya came to be his Lady, why things were as they were in Pavi Bujdam, and revelations of its deepest secrets.

"Please tell us", pleaded Aedesius, "A full story, rich in details, of the days of Sebastian, Lord of Aumhurst, and how his love Sati became the Lady of Aumhurst, and of the meaning of life in Pavi Bujdam. Pease tell us about Pavi Bujdam, tell us about Sebastian and his friends, tell us of this great artist and former Lord of Aumhurst, and also about the meaning and beauty of the mere. Tell us of how Sebastian tried to cross the mere. Please also tell us about Seraphina, the architect of Pavi Bujdam, and how Pavi Bujdam came to be created".

And so Augustus, the Lord of Aumhurst, surrounded by the friends, began his storytelling, as follows:

I

The Persons

It was the most wonderful morning at Aumhurst. Sebastian gazed up at the encircling sapphire sky in amazement. Was this not exactly what he had been waiting for? Here, now, was that pristine certainty, or so it seemed. A depthless infinity of clear blue, uninterrupted by even the merest hint of cloud.

In the cool, completely still air of the early morning, it promised to be the finest day since the end of the winter and the beginning of the good weather. He looked upwards and all around this azure splendour, this celestial sphere around his whole life and being, a beautiful blue void that seemed so full of potential.

And oh, what ecstatic stories there were hidden in the morning sunlight as it streamed down onto his face! Stories of endless joys, but especially of timeless love with Sati, stories in which they were always in the blissful forest together, or exploring the groves, or the gardens of Aumhurst, and the great house itself. But they were stories that he couldn't see any further into.

Perhaps he had been listening to too many of the stories told by Augustus, whom he knew would one day be his successor, and the new Lord of Aumhurst.

He waited for a moment longer, absorbed in the blue covering of the terrestrial globe on which he stood, and thought he could feel the turning of the Earth's mass around itself. He even fancied he could feel the call of the Sun to the body of the Earth, as she persisted through her magnificent yearly motion around her sire, the Sun, exploring her own time, her own stories, including Sebastian's, all at the behest of the Sun's own Self.

Sebastian had come up through the kitchen gardens (affectionately known by some of his friends as the garden of evolution) and out through the old black iron gate in the brick wall, onto the raised lawn overlooking the great house Aumhurst, and now stood, as it would seem to any onlooker, so inexplicably rigidly upright and as perfectly still as any well drilled soldier awaiting the next order, that he might himself, were it not perhaps for the colours of his clothes, be one of the sculptures.

They all stood, in their considerable numbers, with quite the living countenance of real people, frozen in time, here and there, bronze and stone presences in the spaces of the gardens all around him.

Affectionately known as "the persons", they were just one of the many eccentric augmentations all around Aumhurst. As sculptures, as works of high art by Sebastian himself, they fused and dissolved the distinction between human acts of artistic creation and the beautiful spaces of nature that had been created as Aumhurst's gardens.

And now Sebastian stood in the early morning sun secreted amongst them, as one of them, except that he, not being sculpted from stone or bronze, was perhaps himself somewhat of an imposter. Nonetheless, being so still, an unobservant eye might not have even noticed him.

His very good friend and neighbour Quentin Rosary, who lived further around the mere in the great house known as Merehurst, had, over the last year, on more than one occasion observed this behaviour when Sebastian entered this part of the gardens. He had never commented on it, either to Sebastian or to any other Bassenthwaite. It would not have been the done thing.

This was not at all because Sebastian was the Lord of Aumhurst, and had inherited the key to the Tower. It was not because Aumhurst was the puissance of the Mereage, and had restored the Omphalos of Pavi Bujdam, revered by the clans, and put it in the Tower and made it available to all, but simply because no one would ever question what might seem to be such unexplained behaviour of an incumbent of Aumhurst. Eccentric ways, or perhaps behaviours that were difficult to understand, seemed always to go hand-in-hand with those who inherited the key to the Tower.

The Mereage of Pavi Bujdam was that part around its coast that had the closest association with Aumhurst, and at its head, of course, was Sebastian. No one in Pavi Bujdam doubted who he was. Nonetheless, whenever he was questioned on it by his friends in the ever present pursuit of their philosophy, he would be the first to say that even as the Lord of Aumhurst he was only half his own being.

How could anyone say such a thing about the Lord of Aumhurst, let alone Sebastian himself? But it was true. The other half of his being, was, as he always insisted, Sati, whom some would say, seeing her when she was there with Sebastian at Aumhurst, was the most beautiful Lady of Aumhurst who had ever been.

Except that she was not the Lady of Aumhurst. Nor would she ever want to be, unless Sebastian made her so. Somewhere deep inside her, she had always felt her own gravity, like the provenance of her own descent. And somehow, she knew Sebastian and the Mereage of Aumhurst to already be part of it. It was as if, unless he invited her to dance, she had no reason to dance, for the dance was already hers.

Now in the grounds of Aumhurst Sebastian stood, as this half of his being, timelessly amongst the persons. And the persons stood all around, serenely facing this way and that, all of one creation, all of one mind, all of the same moment, in still, silent, group meditation of the various, lovely green spaces in the gardens.

As the clear, golden song of an early morning blackbird rang out from the trees, the persons were undisturbed, unmoved. And they remained so even as the quiet of the morning air was temporarily interrupted by the gentle chiming of the old cupola clock.

It was the cue Sebastian had been waiting for. As if by a magic spell from the clock's serene chimes, his own person now awoke from its frozen position of person amongst persons, into a brisk walk towards the mere.

§

The water's surface this morning was a vast, glorious, perfectly polished mirror. Such perfection seemed impossible, and yet here it undeniably was, in all its immaculate beauty. The many emerald green and red-umber islands rising up above the water were now flawlessly reflected in the liquid mirror, doubling the landscape seemingly below the surface of the water.

The beauty of it all was breathtaking. Opposite Sebastian, a rugged-topped, small mountain, rose up from the shoreline of an island, its deep colours further tinted in its reflection in front of him. To the sides, between the numerous islands, a distant and enigmatic mountainous landscape was stretched out in blue-grey along the horizon, above its own reflection.

Sebastian stood by a small inlet at the edge of the water, with the old scraggy woods just behind him. He contemplated the line of mountains in the far distance, fully absorbed, his senses occasionally lost in the upside-down world of the pristine mere. After a while, his gaze just fell weightlessly into the inverted purple and ultramarine sky.

The flat, silvery mirror of the water ran between the islands and extended as far as the eye could see, like an infinite shining surface towards the far-off mountains. Although appearing small from where he stood, they betrayed almost unimaginable heights rising from some-where so far away on the curve of the Earth that it was beyond and beneath the horizon.

Who could know, from where he stood, that beyond these mountains was another mere? Some would say, if they knew it, more beautiful than this one. Who could know? Quentin might have suspected Sebastian knew. He knew Sebastian well enough to know he knew all kinds of things, but that he rarely spoke of them freely.

On the stillness of the morning air occasional birds flew silently across the mere, above their own clear reflections. They were busy in their own lives and loves, the seeking of their mates, the breaking out of their eggs, their flights of joy and their migrating from one world of being to another with time and season.

From time to time others called out and shrilled from the trees behind Sebastian. He stood, arrested by the spellbinding beauty of it all. There was not a thing to be seen on the perfectly flat, shining surface of the water. Not a single ripple. Not even the little expanding concentric circles that Sebastian was used to seeing when the mere was still, betraying the unseen presence of some insect, or some fish seeking to encounter the surface of its world. It was an extraordinary, mesmerising scene, of magical stillness. As he stood absorbed in it, there was, however, something of a loneliness or a longing in him. This morning Saṭi was not here. She was at Merehurst. It was her way, sometimes, to stay over.

The mere was always arrestingly beautiful, but it wasn't always like this. Right now, it was as though the whole scene was suspended somehow in time, with the only movements, the occasional flights of the birds across its surface, seemingly unfolding in their own eternity. But Sebastian knew the mere and its ways. Nothing was ever fixed. It was forever new, and completely unpredictable.

Some would call Pavi Bujdam a continent. It was, in essence, a great island, understood by most to have been formed after the time of the Old Cataclysm. This was as far as anyone knew. The population included a diverse mix of clans, each cemented by the nature of their own particular mind and culture, and yet all living in harmony with each other.

An archipelago of smaller islands stretched into the distance all around Pavi Bujdam. No one knew how far away the furthest islands were. Far away from Pavi Bujdam the islands seemed to become more sparse. Island hopping in the direction of the far off mountains always revealed some islands still yet further away, but everyone knew the very good reasons why no one had ever completed the distance to the far-off mountains whose land was below the horizon.

Some of the islands in the inner archipelago were populated, and they found themselves obviously surrounded by other islands. But Pavi Bujdam, being apparently the largest, encouraged its people to believe that they were at the centre. They knew that the mere, like the far-off mountains, encircled Pavi Bujdam, and their observations seemed to place Pavi Bujdam at the centre. The intellectuals believed the population to have arisen on the island, whilst others, notably including Sebastian and Quentin, favoured the idea that they were descendants of Visitors who had come from across the mere after the Old Cataclysm.

Many believed there was a renaissance on Pavi Bujdam that was very much alive and ongoing now, and growing in ways that would probably have been unimaginable to the people of the Old World. New learning was coming not from the past, not from the Old World, but from the Visitors who came from beyond the mere.

Many stories about the Old World existed, and Aumhurst was rich in antiques inherited from it, but there was no single, agreed understanding of it. It was quite widely believed however, that it was nevertheless the finest achievements of the Old World that had set the foundation for Pavi Bujdam, and it was generally held by the scholars that in the stories of the Old World, it was the Old World's very lack of the kind of knowledge now held in Pavi Bujdam, that contributed to, or some would say even brought about, the Cataclysm.

The population of Pavi Bujdam was largely self-sufficient, but sometimes vessels would arrive across the mere, carrying Visitors from beyond the mere, and cargoes of worth. In addition to the new transformable and enabling technologies, the incoming cargoes often contained rare and sometimes exotic fruits, spices, fragrant natural oils, unknown seeds, musical instruments, and all kinds of life enhancing supplies, and as a result, life on Pavi Bujdam, generation after generation, had been slowly and surely changing.

It had been growing in refinement, through the enjoyment of new crops, a natural flourishing of the arts, and a growing cultural maturity. The new sciences too, had been coming to fruition. The Visitors who arrived from across the mere invariably brought new knowledge and often stayed for their duration, as teachers.

Occasionally, there had also been visitors from one of the other islands in the archipelago. When the people of Pavi Bujdam had spoken of the Visitor's home island as being closer to the outer shore of the mere, with a greater chance of reaching the far-off mountains, the visitors had laughed. They seemed to think that Pavi Bujdam was closer.

The mere certainly surrounded everyone's life. But only a few regarded it as the centre of their life. Other, that is, than perhaps the fisherman for whom it was important for practical reasons.

Today, as Sebastian stood looking out across it, in silent contemplation of the remarkable, perfect stillness of the water, immersed in the astonishing depth of the reflection, he was well aware of the mere's unpredictability.

The weather over the mere was infamous. The conditions far away towards the distant mountains were apt to such dramatic changes that great storms could be seen forming and raging there, obscuring the mountains, even whilst the mere close to Pavi Bujdam remained beautifully calm under still air.

The storms never seemed to cross the water towards Pavi Bujdam. The winds invariably moved around the mere, along what seemed to its people, to be the circle of the mere that surrounded their continent. Fisherman out on the mere would still sometimes have to avoid certain conditions closer to land that might also sweep them around the mere, and certainly the water could sometimes become rough. But they could be well aware of the building of the distant mere storms, with no fear of their approach.

There had been some islanders, notably the scientists, who had put their heads together to try to solve the enigma of the weather over the mere, but no one had ever succeeded in producing anything like the ability to reliably predict it. It was not that no one understood the weather patterns. The intellectuals and scientists understood. But nonetheless, they couldn't predict it.

Sebastian and Quentin had even attended lectures together, entertaining some vague notion that they might arrive at some clue that would enable them to make reasonably certain predictions, and perhaps achieve a crossing of the mere. But they had come away empty-handed. Uncertainty seemed to be part of the way things were, the way they worked.

The intellectuals had talked about state vectors and waves, and probabilities, and all kinds of abstruse concepts, but it seemed to both Sebastian and Quentin that the intellectuals were like dogs barking at an imagined squirrel in one of the kalpa trees in the gardens. They seemed to be suggesting that theoretically, the mere could never be safely crossed, and the farthest mountains never reached. And yet the Visitors who came across the mere, from beyond the mountains, had always succeeded in making the crossing.

They were popularly said by the islanders to possess what folklore called the Comprehension of the mere. But the Visitors themselves never spoke in such terms. As far as anyone knew, they also never spoke of their own land. Except, perhaps, occasionally, in somewhat cryptic terms. Certainly none of these Visitors to Pavi Bujdam ever returned for a second visit.

Of course the Islanders had asked their advice on overcoming the uncertainty in the weather over the far off waters, but they had always been told that the islanders already knew all there was to know. Nevertheless, the people of Pavi Bujdam had never succeeded in reaching the opposite shores, or if they had, they had never returned.

For just a few of the islanders this was a matter of consternation, but most of the indigenous people of Pavi Bujdam simply accepted the obvious ability of the Visitors to have crossed the water, and they never thought much more about it. Quentin had once pointed out to Sebastian the simple logic of the fact that in order for Visitors to have arrived, they must have crossed the mere, and those that failed, if indeed there were any, the people of Pavi Bujdam would have no knowledge of.

There *were* some predictable patterns, however, in the behaviour of the weather. It was predictable that if the giant mere storms were whipped up, they would always be far away towards the opposite shore where the mountains were. People would sometimes gather at the edge of the mere to watch afar the sheer beauty of the spectacle. A mere storm, even though so far off, was one of the most breathtakingly beautiful of all the natural phenomena known to the islanders.

A turbulent dark atmosphere with billowing purple-hued clouds or mist, or perhaps it was spray from the mere, no-one really knew, would swirl around a dancing play of coloured lights and flashes, and the watchers would enjoy listening to the long, drawn out, deep sound of the far-off storm. It distorted itself as it travelled across the surface of the water, creating the strangest of musical, sonic disturbances at this side of the mere. It seemed at least in appearance that the far-off water of the mere would rise up in some incredible churning, to meet the falling sky.

Everyone knew that the weather over the mere, on all but the most pristinely perfect day like today, with its beautiful clear blue sky, and its gentle, windless warmth, could, far over the mere, change dramatically in just a few minutes, and easily conjure up one of these storms without warning. But on days like today, there may be no storm to see, or there may be a few hours between storms.

On the one occasion when an attempt had been made to follow a Visitor back across the mere, the Visitor's vessel had inexplicably continued on course, whilst the pursuing boat has been swept by the currents around the mere, to where it was necessary to return to Pavi Bujdam in order to avoid developing mere storms.

Not so long ago a group of islanders had analysed the records of the storms, together with the records of the Visitors' crossings, and believed that they had found a way to ensure an outward crossing from the island. The plan had involved unmanned vessels venturing across the mere, together with a relay of manned ones, setting off at different times from various islands.

That was when the discovery was made that the mere was more dynamic than anyone had ever suspected. It was soon realised that further out, where the islands were sparse, even when the water appeared still, strong currents often existed in those deep waters that even without the need of the winds that circulated around the mere, would mercilessly sweep vessels away from their path of crossing, sometimes one way, sometimes the other, often over great distances around the circle of the mere. And always somewhere over the far side the mere, perhaps out of sight across the other side of Pavi Bujdam, a storm might be raging.

Any Visitors who came from beyond the mere, who subsequently left Pavi Bujdam, were never seen again. Some people thought they too, must be taken by the storms, which effectively ensured that only a one-way crossing of the mere was possible, from the land beyond, to Pavi Bujdam. And yet no Visitors ever brought stories of any of their kind who had travelled to Pavi Bujdam but not returned to their own land.

"How do you know you will be able to return to your own land"? Quentin himself had once asked one of the Visitors. He had received a serene smile in reply. "We are not afraid of the mere", he was told. The Visitor seemed to see inside him, behind where the question was coming from. He even seemed to be encouraging Quentin. "If you want to try to cross it, then you should do so", the Visitor had said.

Quentin knew only too well the stories of the islanders who had set out with that very determination, and had never returned. On one occasion he himself had been with a large group of observers on the shore not far from Aumhurst, and they had watched in dismayed silence as a number of vessels from Pavi Bujdam disappeared into the poignant, ironic beauty of one of the distant storms.

Attempting to cross the mere by air would be a mistake. Sometimes people would go out over the mere in powered balloons, for the sheer joy of the scenery. But it was well known that beyond a certain distance from Pavi Bujdam, not so far above the water, winds swept around the mere, and higher up, powerful jet streams followed the same course. All these movements of water and air seemed always to carry straight towards a storm somewhere around the circle. It was always the way the weather system worked.

There had been attempts to go under the water, too, but it was a similar story. Somehow the distant storms would always be an insurmountable obstacle. Legend even had it that far away from Pavi

Bujdam, somewhere in the middle of the mere, its depth was infinite. But then, it was only a legend.

Most of the population of Pavi Bujdam never questioned any of this. They never really even thought about it, particularly. It was mostly only certain clan leaders, a few intellectuals, and some scientists, who speculated about what was beyond the opposite shore of the mere.

Telescopes had given the investigators a good knowledge of the mountains there, and they knew they were very different to the mountains found on Pavi Bujdam, but they couldn't see beyond them. It was estimated that the far mountains reached up into the jet streams, or perhaps higher. Most notably, the observations, some would say, also cast doubt on the storms themselves. There were some amongst the scientists who speculated that the so-called storms, in fact, were not storms, but rather, were some other phenomena that was not yet understood. A few even suspected that the mountains themselves were not what they appeared to be.

On land, the very centre of the interior of Pavi Bujdam was well known to many. It was there that stood the Tower of Pavi Bujdam, a symbol of the Mereage, built at the same time as Aumhurst, and now under the auspices of Sebastian himself. The Tower was the tallest building on Pavi Bujdam, itself erected on the top of a mountain, and surrounded by forest. Many visited this place, but the only people who actually lived there, were hermits.

The story promoted by some intellectuals was that before the building of the Tower, the mountain had, in more than one sense, been a pilgrimage site and the meeting ground of the various clans of Pavi Bujdam, for as far back as the collective memory went. The mountain on which the Tower was built was revered equally by all clans.

Today, the Tower itself stood as the shrine and place of pilgrimage of all the clans, and had effectively been simultaneously adopted by all of them. So it stood as the symbol of the meeting of the clans in some deeper way, a way that had ensured the harmonious coexistence of them for generations, and would no doubt continue to do so for generations to come.

The intellectuals claimed that at the time of its building the Tower had been intended as a symbol of the dominion of the original builders of Aumhurst, the ancient Bassenthwaites. Some believed they were establishing the Mereage as a social system, and had built Aumhurst with the benefit of being on the edge of the mere, whilst its tower, being at the centre, was the statement that Aumhurst was nonetheless the puissance of the whole of Pavi Bujdam.

But then, the story claimed, something remarkable happened. The lost Omphalos had been found, which was universally believed by the clans to be an Oracle. It was placed in the base of the tower, and the consequential effect on the clans was unexpected. Without even trying, the Bassenthwaites became effortlessly elevated to the status of the universal authority in Pavi Bujdam.

This was the way some of the intellectuals rationalised. But there were others who insisted this was just a rationalisation of stories that were themselves myths. As Sebastian himself had pointed out, it was indeed known that all the Vicinages around the island, in fact, what was recognised as Pavi Bujdam itself, had been originally built by the creator of Aumhurst. That was the only fact. In contrast, the history of the clans, and the cause of the ongoing harmony between them, the origins of almost universal happiness itself, in Pavi Bujdam, and the absence of any noticeable disharmony in all but one area over the other side of the island, the origins of all this, was rather more a matter of myth.

§

Sebastian now looked down to his feet, seemingly distracted by thought. He absently kicked a couple of times against an old tree root that emerged from the ground. He breathed in and out deeply, and looked back up towards Aumhurst, high up on the hill, almost as if he was expecting to see someone looking down at him. Perhaps Sati was there, looking at him through a telescope from one of the towers. But if she was, it would not have been possible to see her, from where he was. He looked briefly back across the mere, gazing at the mountains, before turning his head and staring at the old Harborage a little further along the shore.

The Harborage was as old as Aumhurst itself. The lower story of the building intersected a quiet, watery inlet allowing the launch of small vessels from the boathouse underneath it. On the first floor above the arch, and to each side, were several impressively ornamented oriel windows looking out over the mere. They extended from rooms that were internally of remarkable elegance and beauty. They were the favourite venues in which Sebastian and Sati and Quentin regularly held gatherings with a close circle of friends.

Aumhurst itself, of course, also overlooked the mere. It was built in the most advantageous of positions, its upper rooms in the towers with truly spectacular views over the mere and its islands, all the way to the far-off mountains. But there was something quite intimate, even bewitching, about the Harborage, despite its still rather formal charm. It had a certain ease and grace about it that always seemed to warmly embrace its guests. Sebastian felt it was the Harborage itself that ensured the success of these small meetings.

The small group of friends would often meet together through a shared love of each other and their philosophy. There was Sandhya, Quentin's partner, and Sati, quite different to each other, but each arrestingly beautiful in her own way, both musicians and dancers, and both seemingly with hidden powers of silent wisdom that others perceived, whilst Sandhya and Sati themselves seemed unaware of it.

Then there was Timaeus, a mathematician and musician. And then, there were the perfectly identical twins Amba and Ambika, who, confusingly, would often call each other by each other's name, so that others would be confused as to which of them was Timaeus' partner.

Sometimes the friends would be joined by Marsilio, ever devoted to his love of truth, a theologian and renowned astrologer, and, some maintained, a magician. This was not least perhaps due to the way he sometimes dressed.

Together they were the inner circle of the larger community of philosophers in Pavi Bujdam, who met regularly at Springmere, the home of Marsilio, a little further around the mere, and the adopted venue of the Pavi Academy.

As Sebastian stood by the water, he knew that this very afternoon he and some of his friends would be meeting at the Harborage. For all the perfection in the weather, he would have to let the opportunity to exploit it, pass. But first, there was something in the Harborage that he just wanted to see.

He started walking down towards the Harborage. As he walked, the water of the mere glistened peacefully. He looked up towards the hill behind the Harborage, where the Aumhurst observatory stood, and then he looked out across the mere again. The observatory was well loved by Marsilio, who was an adept in observatory skills. His knowledge of astronomy was good, and he had often spent long, dedicated nights alone there, contemplating data, plotting charts, and creating beautiful images of the night sky. It was part of his overall devotion to his cause, and his pursuit of knowledge.

Unknown to Marsilio, about a year ago Sebastian too, had been at the telescope one day, and had lowered it to look across the mere. A perfectly straight band of water ran across the mere from the Harborage below, without obscuration by any island, making the opposite shore visible through the telescope. It was then that he observed one of the great storms, and what he had seen was of such beauty and wonder that it had changed him.

It was as though even just visually being there, as it were, looking at it through the telescope, he had somehow been taken out of time, away from Pavi Bujdam, away from the whole story of it, and then returned to it, and now, it wasn't the same. It was after that, that he had become preoccupied with the notion of time, and had taken to standing amongst the persons in the gardens, his own creations, temporarily imitating their relative timelessness, as if he was searching to experience what it was like to be one of them.

It was also after that, that he had become determined to take time away from his pursuit of fine art, and engage himself earnestly and conscientiously in something new. He began learning the necessary practical measures that accompanied the new popular art of creating things with the new materials and technologies that were brought to

Pavi Bujdam by the Visitors. Somehow, by doing so, he felt that as the privileged incumbent of Aumhurst, which he was only by virtue of his birth, he might actually be worthy of the key to the Tower.

He soon reached the Harborage, went down the stone steps, and into the lower boathouse that was always kept locked. Even down here in this functional part of the building, the fabric of it had been created with tremendous dedication and skill by unsung craftsman, creating in all its visitors a sense of privilege at just being there.

He closed the door quietly behind him.

There, still and sleek, in the silence of the boathouse, poised above the water, was the *Satya-Vajra*, her name displayed along her side, built with dedication over the whole of the past year, by Sebastian himself. Sebastian knew that theoretically, with the speeds she could achieve, he could reach the opposite shore across the surface of the water, beneath the winds, and above the currents, and return, easily within less than three or four hours. He knew that the intervals between the storms in any one place were generally longer on a day like today, and that such a journey should definitely be possible.

The *Satya-Vajra* was an uncompromising work of art using the very latest new sciences, and for its design, Sebastian had enlisted the help of Timaeus, but in secret. As far as weather conditions were concerned, today was the ideal day. But whilst the tests had confirmed the necessary speeds were easily attainable by the *Satya-Vajra*, attempting anything resembling the whole crossing had not yet been tried. In any case, later today, he knew, was the meeting with his friends. And besides, there was another factor to consider.

Such extreme speeds over the water were not to be taken lightly. Sebastian's research had revealed that accounts of extreme water speeds existed even in some of the books from the Old World. He knew well the language of water speed used both in the Old World and still in Pavi Bujdam today. There had been several previous attempts in Pavi Bujdam to travel at extreme speeds on the waters of the mere. Some regarded those who attempted it, as mad. For all their impressiveness, no one had yet come anywhere near sufficient speed to attempt a full crossing between the mere storms.

But this was different. By now, Sebastian knew that the speeds the *Satya-Vajra* could achieve, were, amazingly, simply unheard of. Timaeus had insisted that with the new design, the crossing would be safe. But there was no doubt that the necessary speed would easily reach and exceed the kind of speeds that were commonly referred to as being in the "death zone".

2

The Library

The next day dawned as clear and as beautiful as the previous day. It was not yet seven o'clock, and the shining walls of Aumhurst were already warm in morning sun, its towers bright against the land, watching over the glistening mere.

Inside the Library, surrounded by the serene ambience of ancient walnut, oak, and mahogany, Sebastian stretched out on an excessively large sofa beneath the history books. Above him were numerous rows of shelves all the way up to the high ceiling, home to hundreds of volumes including entire sets passed down through generations, inherited from the Old World.

Extending out along the walls to both sides of him, the number of volumes increased to thousands and thousands, in countless subjects, spreading out all round the room, completely covering all the vertical spaces from floor to ceiling. Their collective mass softened all sounds in the Library, adding to the sense of peace that was always present within its walls. The mellow regular grid of the wooden shelves framed endless golden-brown spines, and sometimes dark green leather, quietly re-peating their orderly horizontal and vertical rhythms over entire walls, interwoven sometimes with rows of lighter coloured volumes.

Only the old oak door with its pointed arch, almost uncomfortably squeezed between and under some shelves, together with the occasional standard lamp or library ladder, interrupted the flow of silent pages that enclosed the interior of the room. The old tables, chairs and cabinets, stood timelessly on the dark wooden floor, and over on one side, an Old World long-case clock quietly and tirelessly counted uneven seconds, one by one, with its deep, mellow ticking.

The door handle clicked gently, and opened, and there was Quentin, looking into and all around the room. He paused in the doorway. Then he saw Sebastian, still horizontal on the enormous old sofa.

"Ahhh.. *Sebastian*, sir"! he declared with an air almost of despair. "Well, well... why isn't this a surprise at all"?

Sebastian stirred on the extremely comfortable, if unreasonably large sofa, which together with Sebastian himself somehow seemed a key part of the library's character. He slowly sat up. He stretched and looked over towards Quentin. "Ah.... *Quentin* sir", he said in reply, his arms still in the air, smiling but returning an acted out air of despair. He seemed to pull himself together. "Now Quentin... you're *not* going to reprimand me again, *are* you? For spending the night in the Library"?

"Wouldn't *dream of it*, my friend", Quentin came back. "It's just that I happen to know there are two of the most beautiful sleeping places that I have ever seen - I believe they are called *bedrooms* you know", he looked up towards the ceiling. "Up there in the round towers above you. *And* they overlook the sunrise over the mere. I'll wager you didn't see it this morning did you? It was spectacular".

Sebastian finished his stretching and sighed. "Yes, you're right Quentin, I should have seen it", he admitted. "But the thing is, Quentin, you see, I can actually sleep in here. Amongst the books".

"You mean you can't sleep with Sati"? Quentin said, "If you don't mind me saying".

"But she's not here, is she"? Sebastian replied. "She's at Merehurst".

"Ah... you're right, of course", Quentin said, "I forgot. Yes, I remember now she was staying over in the East wing, wasn't she? I believe she and Sandhya are riding out early this morning".

Sebastian waved to Quentin to come into the library. Quentin walked into the room looking at the shelves and their contents. "Well, I suppose these books are like old friends, to you", he commented.

Sebastian was stretching again now. "*You* might see them as old", he yawned, "But to me, they're timeless. In the middle of the night they're timeless".

"The middle of the night"? Quentin said. "I thought you said you came in here to sleep? It doesn't sound to me like you're getting much sleep".

Sebastian spoke gently, almost dismissively. "No no, you don't understand. You can be in two places at once, you know".

"What? asleep and awake at the same time"? Quentin said. He was already walking over to a small set of mahogany drawers, intent on something besides the conversation he was now having. Being himself a musician with a particular interest in the music of the Old World, he felt quite at home at Aumhurst, with its many antique musical instruments, and its interior ambience which very much celebrated some of the Old World culture. "Two places at once, eh?" Quentin repeated, "You mean like in two bedrooms at once, perhaps? One on each side of the stair"? he said, looking upwards again, and grinning.

He gave Sebastian an ironic smile. Then looking down at the drawer now in front of him he paused for a moment and said "No, actually, perhaps I *do* know what you mean".

He turned the tiny metal key, slowly pulled open the top drawer, took out the violin from within it, and started turning over the instrument from front to back, admiring it lovingly. Then he lifted a bow out from the same drawer. He tensioned it, then put the violin under his chin. He smiled. "Like *this*, for example", he said, and began playing.

The profound soul of just a small part of a piece of music from the Old World, a timeless music from a world now lost in time, began to fill the Library. Sebastian recognised it as a partita by a composer he knew of, who in part, shared his name. Sebastian was immediately drawn deep into the weave of the harmonies. A whole sonic world of counterpoint between different musical spheres, two apparently separate melodic lines, now fluidly emanated from Quentin's skilled double-stopping.

He was an accomplished player. Two separate, poignant tunes, like independent beings, but in truth not, were manifesting something deep and profound as they came to life together under Quentin's bow. Then Quentin suddenly stopped, took the violin from under his chin, and started admiring it again.

Sebastian stood up. "Yes, exactly like that", he affirmed. "I'm talking about two things that only start to reveal what they mean when they come together. Like certain colours on the canvas. Or perhaps two beings".

Quentin very gently put the violin and bow back into the drawer, and carefully closed it. Then he walked over to the chair, sat down, and crossed one leg over the other. "What do you mean, Sebastian"? For a moment there was silence."Were you playing the violin in the middle of the night"? he asked.

"You know I don't play", Sebastian said. "At least not like that. Would that I could though".

"You're very good player", Quentin said.

"You're just generous", Sebastian smiled back.

It was obvious from Quentin's expression that he was prompting for more. Sebastian got up, stretched again, and walked over to the light coming through the small diamonded panes of the little crystal glass window. He peered out towards the mere. "You know I used to sleepwalk as a boy"? he said.

"Yes", Quentin said. "Probably more people know about your sleepwalking than you think".

Sebastian didn't react. "I used to walk out to the edge of the mere". He paused. "But of course I was sleepwalking".

"You never went in though, did you"? Quentin asked.

"I probably wouldn't be here now, if I had, Quentin".

Quentin prompted Sebastian again for more. "And..."?

"Well now I'm not sleepwalking anymore", Sebastian said.

"Did you go out to the mere last night"? Quentin asked with a sideways glance.

"Well, that's not what I mean", Sebastian replied. "I didn't need to. Like I said, you can be in two places at once".

"Oh, I see. Perhaps you were dreaming"?

"No, Quentin, the opposite".

Sebastian wasn't making any sense, so Quentin took a deep breath in, and then exhaled. This was just typical Sebastian.

Sebastian turned around and looked at Quentin. He spoke now with a new, enthusiastically fresh tone of voice. "Quentin, have you ever actually looked in any of these books"? He gave Quentin a friendly smile. "Do you know what's in them"?

Quentin proposed what he thought was a good answer. "Knowledge"? he said, grinning back. "Tacit knowledge"?

"Well that's just it, Quentin, you see, you would've thought so wouldn't you"? Sebastian went on, "But you see, what's around these walls, Quentin, is not knowledge. That's not how I think of it. Not anymore. It's *experience* Quentin. It's a record of experience". There was more new life in Sebastian's voice.

Quentin looked unconvinced. He nodded towards a section of books on one of the walls. "Those mathematics books that Timaeus likes, they're knowledge, aren't they"?

Sebastian already had the answer. "They're a record of people's experience of thought. Of mathematics", he said.

"I suppose you could put it like that", Quentin reluctantly agreed. He realised he had only been here a few minutes and they were already getting into one of their conversations. But then, this was how philosophising often seemed to proceed, amongst the friends.

Sebastian continued. "And wouldn't you agree that the same is true of the history books, the philosophy books, the records of the Visitors, all those volumes of the Journal of the Proceedings on the Investigations of the Storms, in fact, isn't it true of all of them? It's all just a record of experience of one kind or another, isn't it? Even if it's just the experience of thought"?

Quentin considered, and nodded. "Yes, I think I would have to agree", he said.

"So the whole Library is just a record of experience, isn't it"? said Sebastian.

"If you put it like that, yes, I suppose it is", Quentin agreed.

"And whose experience is it"? Sebastian asked.

Quentin was happy to answer. "I suppose it will be all the authors, and everyone they have learned from. Quite a big network of people I would guess".

"You would be completely right, Quentin", Sebastian said. "Quite a big network, indeed. And if you pick up the books and start reading them, you too, become part of that network, wouldn't you agree"?

"I would indeed, Sebastian. So what are you saying"?

"I'm saying, Quentin, when did all this experience happen"?

Quentin looked around the room, at the books. "A very long time ago, I would say, most of it, looking at most of these volumes. Most of this is from the Old World, isn't it"?

Sebastian was already walking over towards one of the library ladders. "Quite so, Quentin", he said. "That's when it started. Except that it didn't, did it? When did it really all start"?

He reached the ladder and started pulling it backwards along the wall. At some point it stopped and he put on the brake. He began climbing up the ladder. About halfway up he reached out to one of the higher volumes, withdrew it from its companions, and descended quickly down the ladder with it. He walked across to Quentin and handed him the volume. "It's rather like art", he said. "It's all a record of experience", he said. "And it's timeless".

Quentin took the volume. "If you say so, Sebastian. But why sleep in here"?

"I told you Quentin. Because I *can* sleep in here. Because the books are timeless. It doesn't matter whether I am asleep or awake, in here, I can be either, or neither, or both, it doesn't matter. I'm not disturbed". He gestured to the walls. "All this", he said, waving towards the books, "It's all wisdom and kindness, in here, as far as I'm concerned, because to me, it's all timeless".

Quentin looked around the walls. "Yes. I think I kind of know what you mean", he replied, sensing something. "I think I can kind of feel that, too".

"So you see it's not really just about knowledge is it"? Sebastian said. He gestured around the walls again. "This is all a record of human experience, and experience of thought, in which all that experience has become timeless, hasn't it? Do you see what I mean? Rather like a painting of something".

"Yes I think I perhaps do see", Quentin said. "I can certainly see that as an artist, you might see it that way. But the knowledge is still valuable isn't it"?

Sebastian looked serious. "What knowledge"?

"Well", Quentin laughed, as he looked at the spine of the book he was holding. "What have we here, for example? Ah... well I see it's from the philosophy section", he smiled. Then he looked at the title and for a moment he frowned. "Hmm. I haven't come across this before".

He proceeded to read from the gold embossed words on the spine. "*The Great Expansion, Volume I*", he read aloud. He laughed again and raised his eyebrows, turning around the book, which was quite a heavy tome. He then opened it, and looked a little puzzled. He flicked through the pages a couple of times. "What is this"? he smiled.

Sebastian answered. "It could be a mistake, Quentin. But I think not. The other explanation is that it's a work of art. An intended part of it. Or it might be a mistake, in a work of art. That is, if it's possible to have a mistake in a work of art. And if you really understand art, I'm not sure that's truly possible. Quentin, there are twelve volumes of it, in all. They're all different".

Quentin could see that all the pages were blank. It was a big volume, and they were all blank, from cover to cover.

"It's not the only one, you see", Sebastian continued. "I mean, it's the only one like that, but look at this", and he was already on his way back to the library ladder. He skipped up the ladder and in no time had retrieved another volume. He came back down and walked over to Quentin, and handed him the book.

Intrigued now, Quentin read the title on the spine, which said the same as the first volume, but declared itself to be Volume II. He opened the book, studied the first couple of pages, and then started flicking through. These pages were not blank. Rather, they were full of words. At least, he assumed they were words. The individual letters, if that's what they were, were not anything that he recognised. They were essentially just symbols.

"What language is this"? Quentin asked.

"Hmm...", Sebastian murmured. "How do you know it is a language"?

"Well I'm assuming so, after all, it is a book", Quentin replied.

"Precisely", said Sebastian. "You're putting two and two together, based on appearances"?

"Well, yes I suppose so", Quentin replied again.

Sebastian went on. "It doesn't look like a mistake does it? Although it could be. But what if it *is* all part of a work of art? I don't think there's any doubt about it".

"Well, I kind of see what you mean", Quentin answered. "I suppose it does't necessarily have to have any real meaning, in that way, I can see that. Not as a language, I mean. That's what this work of art, if it is a work of art, might be saying, I suppose. Perhaps that things are ultimately meaningless".

"There is another one I should like you to see", Sebastian said. He went back again to the library ladder, and up again to the set of volumes, and pulled out another book. In no time he was back down and handing Quentin the volume.

Quentin put the book he was already holding down on the table, and taking hold of the third book, looked at Sebastian and said "I'm guessing this is Volume Three"?

He looked at the spine which confirmed his guess. He opened the book and started flicking through. The pages here, too, were covered in print, but now, the letters were recognisable, and the words were comprehensible. However, the strings of words in the sentences, or whatever they were, appeared to be gobbledygook.

"Yes, I think I'd say this is some work of art by some artist", Quentin said. "I'm not sure what it's saying. Something about language perhaps? Something about meaning?" Then a thought occurred to him. "Sebastian, is this one of yours"?

"No, it's not a work of mine", Sebastian smiled. "It's not my kind of thing. As you know, I'm more painting and sculpture. Although it's true, I'm branching out now".

Quentin looked thoughtful. "So this was already here in the Library, was it"?

Sebastian nodded. "I've known about it for some time", he said. "I didn't put it here, I can assure you. I think it's been here for as long as the Library has".

"How can we find out who the artist was"? Quentin asked, flicking to the front and back of the book in search of a clue.

"Well just look at the name of the author on the cover", Sebastian said. "It's not a fictitious name. Well it is, in a sense, because the whole thing is not what it appears to be. But the name is real enough".

"Seraphina Bassenthwaite", Quentin read aloud with surprise. "I didn't know she was an author", he said.

"No", said Sebastian. "She is the architect of Aumhurst. It's all part of her creation".

"She is the architect of most of Pavi Bujdam, isn't she"? Quentin said.

Sebastian nodded. "All of it, actually", he said. "I would say the very presence of the books in the Library is part of her art. You see, for some time now, even before I found this, I've been thinking that everything is a form of art, and that we could start to engage with it in that way, and I suspect now I'm not the first Bassenthwaite to think so. I think Seraphina thought so. And it's not just this set of volumes that is the art here. I think the entire Library is part of the same artwork. The whole of Aumhurst is, in fact. I'm living in a work of art, Quentin. What I do is part of that art. We all are in the same situation. And Seraphina's influence doesn't stop at Aumhurst".

Quentin smiled at the idea, somewhat amused by it, and looked up and around the room. He thought for a while. "So the whole house is this art"? he said, realising that the whole house, including the library, all the work of Pavi Bujdam's most famous architect, was a setting for everything that happened within it, as much as it was an artistic creation.

Sebastian laughed as he was looking around too. "Yes", he said, "I think the books are part of a larger work of art, and are kind of pointing out that the whole house is a form of art. That's its message, I think. But I also think that this whole art, which extends beyond the house into the gardens, and beyond, is not necessarily consciously created, if you see what I mean".

Quentin looked even more amused. "I don't think the architect of Aumhurst, poor old Seraphina, would agree with you there, Sebastian", he laughed.

"No", Sebastian said. "That's not what I'm saying. I'm not saying Seraphina Bassenthwaite didn't know what she was doing. You only have to look at the house, to see the answer to that. How many houses more beautiful than this, are there on Pavi Bujdam? And the gardens, too. And then look at Merehurst too. And Springmere. In fact all of old Pavi Bujdam. No, it's not that".

Now Quentin looked puzzled. "What did you mean then"?

"I mean", Sebastian replied, "For example, that as an artist, I created the persons and put them in the gardens, knowing that they would become part of an ongoing art, in the way visitors see them, and because actually, they are not always in the same place. But I did it without even realising at the time, that what I was doing was already part of an ongoing art that already existed. Seraphina herself, I mean, her life, which brought her here of course, and which made her who she was, as a person, all that, is the art. It's ongoing but it's not being consciously created, you see, until we realise it and we engage in it in that way. It's possible for art to be unconscious, you know".

Quentin was just nodding, slowly getting into what Sebastian was saying.

Sebastian went on. "You and I are part of it too, you see. It's unbroken, and ongoing. It's always *becoming*. It's always evolving into something else. But mostly, it's not conscious. It's an eternally unfolding, unconscious art. That's how I see it. It's a constant *becoming*".

"Yes", Quentin joined in. "If you look at it like that, it does kind of change the way you see things".

The action in the old long-case clock by the wall now whirred into life and the clock began chiming.

"Coffee"? Sebastian suddenly interjected. No more than a few moments later the door clicked open again and Belvoir came in carrying a tray with a beautiful silver coffee set. He quietly put the tray down on the table and just walked away.

"Thank you Belvoir", Sebastian said. He poured the coffee, waited for Belvoir to exit and the door to click closed, and then spoke quietly. "He is just as knowledgeable as Marsilio, I think. But you wouldn't know it, would you, because he never says anything. Well, not usually".

Quentin came over. Picking up a cup of coffee he said "Why is it that he never says anything? At least not here, I mean. After all he does sometimes speak at the Academy meetings at Springmere, doesn't he"?

Sebastian answered "We do talk at length, sometimes, actually. But he seems to be vowed to silence for most of the time. I like the arrangement. He offers his services in exchange for nothing, except of course his rooms and living here. We never question him, and he never questions us. The things he does here are pretty limited, but we have a satisfactory arrangement, and I like him. After all, as you know well, in all the residences around the mere we do have the customs to keep don't we"?

Sebastian took a sip of coffee and then continued. "At the moment he seems to spend most of his time in the Bethel. But he allows himself to speak sometimes, in the evenings. I've spent a good deal of time, here in the Library, with him, as it happens. You should come over and join us, sometime. Actually if we invite Marsilio as well, things could get very interesting".

Quentin sipped his coffee. "I'll make a point of that Sebastian. I will", he said, taking another sip. "So, Sebastian, tell me, if you want to say *all this* is a work of art, or a kind of work of art in progress, but an unconscious one, and if you think Seraphina thought that too, then who was the original artist, if it's not Seraphina? That's the question isn't it"?

Sebastian took a sip of coffee, too. "*You* could be, Quentin", he smiled, "For example, if you have painted yourself into the picture, so to speak".

Quentin laughed aloud. "I don't think so, Sebastian, not even unconsciously". Somehow, I think, I would still know about it. And I can't say I do".

"You are the artist of your part of it, though", Sebastian said. "Just as I am of mine. And it might well be that you don't know it, wouldn't it? After all, I said it was unconscious, didn't I? Rather like sleepwalking as it happens. Rather like the way in which, sometimes, for me, paintings seem to paint themselves".

The two friends continued to drink their coffee. After a while, Sebastian walked back over to the little window. He gestured for Quentin to follow. He pointed outside, through the crystal glass again. "Look", he said, "What do you see"?

Quentin peered out of the window towards the mere. The Sun was shining and the scene was one of sheer loveliness. In the distance, beyond a number of beautiful green islands quite close to Aumhurst, their reflections shimmering in the water, the far off mountains were visible. "I can see the mere", Quentin replied.

"It's a question of finding yourself", Sebastian said. "That's what art is really about, you know. How far would you have to go to find yourself"? Sebastian pressed Quentin further. "How far *can* you go, here on Pavi Bujdam"?

Still looking at the mere, Quentin replied "Well, you can only go so far on Pavi Bujdam, until you reach the mere. I know that much. No matter which direction you choose. We can't change that, can we"? He looked at Sebastian. "Where would *you* go, to find yourself, Sebastian"?

"The thing is, Quentin", Sebastian began, "I've already been all over. You know that. More than most. I've been to the Tower, I've seen the Omphalos that my ancestors found and restored. I even have the key to the tower, Quentin, and I'm one of the few who have been to the top. I've actually seen the view from there. From the very highest point in Pavi Bujdam. And from there, you still can't see beyond the mountains around the mere. So, as far as I'm concerned, as far as finding myself is concerned, there's nowhere here, Quentin. Pavi Bujdam is just somewhere I've been kind of sleepwalking".

"But you said you're not sleepwalking anymore"?

"In a way, I still am. Because I'm still here. I mean, you can see me can't you"? Sebastian said with a grin. "So something about me is still sleepwalking, as far as I'm concerned. I don't think I've brought my art to its natural conclusion".

Quentin smiled. "Yes, Sebastian, there is no doubt you're here".

Sebastian went on. "Anyway, we were talking about *you*, Quentin. And we were saying that all *this* is the art. Somebody, whether it was Seraphina herself or someone subsequently, whoever the artist was who made those books, knew this, and put them here in the Library, so that someone like me would find them, and realise what they meant. And realise that all *this* is the art. The art that the original artist began. The art of Pavi Bujdam. And I now think that's how Seraphina saw it all".

Quentin walked over to the chair and sat. Sebastian followed him, and sat opposite him. They each relaxed back into their chairs.

Quentin decided to continue on with some alternative, congenial conversation. "Has the key to the Tower had much use recently"? he asked.

"A few of the clans people have been to see the Omphalos", Sebastian replied. "One or two of the clan leaders have even been up to the top of the Tower, you know".

"Indeed"? Quentin looked surprised. "I've never really understood why they don't all want to go up"?

"Well", Sebastian said, thoughtfully. "I think they all *think* they do, and from time to time, you know, I have offered to lend some of them the key. There are not usually any takers. But I suppose when it comes to it, it's a pretty steep climb. Even if you take a lift to the top of the mountain, there's no way up the Tower, except on foot. And of course it goes round and round. It's disorientating I can tell you. You can lose all sense of everything. It's a very, very long way up. It's not a day trip.

It's dangerous sometimes, in some places, I think, as well, and it's not something you can really undertake lightly".

"What about the leaders you mentioned, who went up"? Quentin replied. "What did they make of it"?

"I think you would have to ask them", Sebastian said. But like I said, you still can't see anything beyond the mountains anyway, even from up there. It still doesn't give you anything beyond the speculations and the beliefs".

The two friends sat in silence for some time. And then Sebastian began again "I came up with a theory about it, you know. Last year".

"A *theory*"? Quentin smiled.

"Yes. About the winds, and the mere".

"Go on", Quentin prompted.

"Well", Sebastian began slowly, "You see, the top of the Tower, as you know, is the highest point in Pavi Bujdam. The thing is, when you are up there, there's never any wind. And yet as you know, if you were to try to send a balloon or anything else up to that height somewhere else over Pavi Bujdam or over the mere, you would be blown away on the winds or the higher jet streams. And almost certainly into one of the storms".

Sebastian paused, thoughtfully. "So it seems to me, that's consistent with the winds all circulating around the mere, as we know. So it makes sense that the whole weather system circulates around the very centre of Pavi Bujdam. That means, if you think about it, if it was possible to get a balloon or perhaps a drone, up to the top of the Tower, then we might get up high enough to see over the mountains around the mere. And it would do away with all the speculation, once and for all. That's what was going through my mind last year".

"Ah, I see, yes", Quentin said enthusiastically. "Yes, of course, if it succeeded, we could record the view and bring it back down again. But why would we need to take it up to the top of the Tower in the first place? Why not just send it up from the ground, to the top of the mountain, and then straight up beside the tower?"

"Ah, *Quentin*, Quentin... Quentin, best of men, I can see you are on fire", Sebastian laughed. "You are now where I was. The Tower itself, of course, although it's revered by the clans, is just a symbol, really, isn't it? A symbol they relate to. My ancestors put it there. In my view they need a visible symbol to hold them together. But of course, what really counts, is its position in Pavi Bujdam".

"Exactly", agreed Quentin. "And that doesn't depend on the tower does it"? He went on. "Its position is part of the island, and even if we theoretically destroyed the tower, that position, the centre, would still be there, wouldn't it"?

"Quite so, quite so, Quentin", Sebastian agreed. "You would think, wouldn't you, that as far as the clans are concerned, you must climb the tower, and then go *above* the top of the tower, in some way, in order to come to knowledge of what is beyond the mere? But it seems to me, because so few of them actually want to go up the tower and find out, they just believe you can just see across the mere from the top of the Tower".

"Perhaps", Quentin answered, "They would never want to go any higher, anyway, because that would involve going into the sky, wouldn't it? Which is forbidden because it's sacred".

"That's true", Sebastian replied.

Now Sebastian looked more enthusiastic. "But you and I know that all we need is to make the ascent, without involving the tower, see how far we can get, and see what we can see. We wouldn't directly or obviously be treading on the toes of the clans, then, as far as the Tower is concerned. And if you send something small up into the sky there, no one would see it anyway. It would be no bigger than a bird of prey".

Sebastian sat back in his chair. "Imagine making an art that is all about what is beyond the mere", he said. "Not just another speculation painting like all those in the galleries".

"I see", Quentin agreed.

Sebastian continued."We could send a drone up, next to the Tower, without interfering with the clans, and imagine the art I could make, about what is beyond the mere".

Sebastian seemed enthused and said. "Do you remember last year when I was away for some weeks on an expedition to the interior of Pavi Bujdam"?

Quentin Paused for a moment, as though something was sinking in. He now looked incredulous. "*No*"! he said in disbelief. He lent forward towards Sebastian, smiling. "You tried it, didn't you"!

Sebastian smiled. "Come and look at this", he went on, already getting up and walking towards the door. Quentin eagerly followed him.

3

❦

The Auditorium

The favoured route to the auditorium from the Library was to go up the secret stairway, as it was informally known, along the Long Gallery, and down the Great Stairs. As Sebastian and Quentin were just leaving the Long Gallery, they met Amba, a frequent resident at Aumhurst, who had clearly just come from her bedroom. She looked as though she might have stepped out one of the great paintings on the wall of the Long Gallery, in which muses and graces danced in pastoral idyls, and beautiful ladies in flowing attire not at all unlike Amba's, engaged in amorous adventures with knightly gentlemen.

"Good morning, Amba", Sebastian greeted her. "Good morning, Sebastian" she replied, and turning to Quentin greeted him amiably with "Hello Quentin".

"We're going down to the auditorium", Quentin said. "You are welcome to come and join us, if you would like to", he said.

"Probably not this morning", Amba replied, "But perhaps we can meet up later"? She looked at him steadily.

"I'd like that, Amba", Quentin said.

At the bottom of the great stairs Sebastian joked "How do you know that wasn't Ambika? I thought Timaeus and I were the only ones who could tell them apart"?

"It was Amba", Quentin said, with certainty, but said no more.

The auditorium was situated silently in the basement of Aumhurst. It was the main reason why the great house, so famed for its architectural beauty, was well known by all the members of the island-wide Society of Philosophers, or Pavi Academy as it was otherwise known. Relatively few of the members, however, knew the full extent of Aumhurst's ordonnance. Not even all the members of the Inner Circle knew Aumhurst completely.

There were many beautiful houses in Pavi Bujdam, especially around the mere, but none, with the possible exception of Marsilio's home, Springmere, emanated quite such powerful effects on their guests, as Aumhurst. Most who visited Aumhurst felt embraced by an overwhelming sense of ancient warmth and wisdom. They were easily transported by the atmosphere of the old house into a kind of relaxed, interested openness, perfectly conducive to the regular lectures given by Sebastian and the other guest speakers.

After a short excursion through Aumhurst's wooden-panelled corridors and galleries, Sebastian and Quentin were now making themselves at home in the large, luxuriously comfortable chairs of the Auditorium. They both looked at the now lowered screen, as Sebastian pressed the button on his handset, and the show began.

The drone's camera-work on the recording was excellent. The journey up the mountainside was long and beautiful, the scenery magnificent. The ascent went past the canopy of the forest that encircled the mountain, and on past small tarns and rocky terrain. Eventually, the Tower itself on top of the mountain, came into view.

Then, there was a rotating ascent beside the Tower, panning across the scenery, with the circling of the camera periodically bringing the Tower itself into view. Each time the surrounding scenery slowly swept into view, the beautiful mere was visible, shining in the sun like a band of precious metal, far below, the mountains on the far side visible. But the increased width of the ribbon of their pointed peaks, nonetheless still receded into misty obscurity.

Eventually, the very top of the Tower was reached. And slowly, even the top of the Tower fell away beneath, in the occasional sweeping views of the mountain and landscape below. As the altitude increased, the zone behind the mountains surrounding the mere seemed also to fall away from view, leaving only a strange, blue, etherial glow, and for Quentin, a sense of disappointment.

"It's the curvature", he said in quiet disillusionment. "We can't see beyond, because of the curvature". He did indeed sound very disappointed. "It's pretty much what some of the speculations say".

"Yes", Sebastian agreed. "You can actually see the curvature itself, from that height, can't you"? he said, "That's certainly not just speculation", he said with some amusement. He went on, "But to see what is beyond the mere, we would still have to cross above it. What we need is a satellite. Like the ones the books talk about".

"I was reading about this", Quentin said. "Apparently the Old World had vast numbers of them. But so many were weaponised in the end that they were all destroyed by the warring factions. Anyway, yes, we would need to go into orbit", he agreed. "We just need..."

Sebastian interrupted him. "The clans wouldn't stand for it it", he said. "You know that. Putting space before the planet. Trespassing into the sacred sky, and all that. You know what their view on that would be".

Sebastian was sitting back, relaxed now. "You could hardly do that in private, anyway, without anyone knowing", he said. "But there could be ways of getting up high enough, that you could do without anyone noticing".

"The clans would still object if they found out", Quentin said dubiously.

"But only if they *knew*", Sebastian said. Then he smiled enigmatically. Quentin could not tell whether Sebastian was joking, or not.

Now Quentin suddenly looked very surprised. "*Sebastian...*", he began, with an air of reprimand. "You are Lord of the Mereage, you are at Aumhurst. You hold of the key to the Tower, no less, you are one of the keepers of the Omphalos. You simply cannot just go deceiving the clans like that. You could destroy the whole constitution of Pavi Bujdam".

Sebastian seemed dismissive. He laughed a little. "*Quentin*, it would be *art*, you see. Have we humans learned *nothing*? So many great works of art have been controversial haven't they? It's often the case that great art will upset *someone*, somewhere. You can't stop art, for that reason. You can't just restrict an artist's freedom of expression. I don't think Pavi Bujdam as a whole would stand for that, either. Not even though the clans say the sky is sacred".

Quentin still couldn't tell whether Sebastian was joking or not. He knew that Sebastian was in a rather elevated position, in more ways than one. Not only was he incumbent at Aumhurst, and Lord of the Mereage, but he was also clearly the most revered artist on Pavi Bujdam. And art, all the arts, in Pavi Bujdam, were held in higher esteem by the clans, than the new sciences, which in any case mostly came to Pavi Bujdam from the Visitors.

Who would question Sebastian if this was art? But then, Quentin wasn't sure. Perhaps it would result in a clash of beliefs. A clash, at least, between one faction and another. Also, it might result in a split of the clans. And who knows where that might lead?

Quentin was sitting contemplating all this.

Sebastian prompted him, smiling widely. "What are your thoughts, then Quentin"?

Quentin stirred from his thinking and addressed the question. "Well I think you may be right", he said. "But I don't think it would be worth the risk".

"Of course you are right", said Sebastian, "I'm only teasing, you know. As it happens, after the summer, last year, I considered all this. But then I got talking to Timaeus".

"Ah, *Timaeus*", Quentin said. He had a great deal of respect for the wealth of Timaeus' knowledge, and an equal amount of affection for his rather endearing, formal way of being. "Go on, you have my attention", he said.

Sebastian continued. "Well, you see, it turns out that I wasn't the only one to have thought of it. It seems this has already been looked into by the scientists. A long time ago. But then, you see, I'm an artist,

Quentin. Like so many others who are inquisitive, I can build with the new technologies, and I can do it as well as I can sculpt in bronze, but I'm no scientist, no mathematician. I never delve into those kinds of books. I'm really quite ignorant when it comes to science".

Sebastian went on. "No, apparently it's been known for quite some time, in fact. The mathematicians and scientists got there first, you see. With a little help, I understand, from the balloons and drones".

"How so"? Quentin asked.

"They have already shown what would happen", Sebastian said. "Apparently, and the reasons are complicated, but basically, if you try to go up from any of the islands in the mere, in fact anywhere except from the centre of Pavi Bujdam, then before you can get anywhere near sufficient height you get taken by the jet streams around the mere and back over Pavi Bujdam. And then if you fall, the winds take you back into the storms lower down. And no one is going to send anything into the sky that's big enough to get above the jet streams, from right in the centre of Pavi Bujdam where the tower is".

Quentin was persistent. "There has to be a way around it, surely"?

"There probably is, for all I know", Sebastian replied, "But no one is going to try it".

Quentin let out a long breath. "So, Sebastian, what *is* all this? What's all this really about then"?

"Well, Quentin, we were discussing it in the Library, weren't we"?

Quentin lent back and laughed. "Ah, yes", he said, "You are going to say the *art*, of course. All *this*, Aumhurst, Pavi Bujdam, the mere, the Tower, everything, the whole world, is *the art* isn't it"? Quentin grinned widely. "Including, if I remember, Seraphina Bassenthwaite herself. Who built this house, and Springmere, as I understand it. Well I suppose whatever this art is, that Seraphina has created, it's still kind of contained by the mere, isn't it? How can art of any kind get you to see what is beyond the mere? And by the way if it was Seraphina Bassenthwaite who is the artist, as you say, then I would say, then whose work of art is *she* a part of"? He laughed again. "I think there may be a weakness in your thinking".

Sebastian just smiled, but didn't answer.

Now Quentin looked a little puzzled. "Oh", he said, "And by the way, talking of Seraphina Bassenthwaite, something really struck me when we went past the top of the stairs, on our way here".

"What was that", Sebastian asked, in a tone as if he already knew the answer.

"Well, I had a closer look at that portrait of Seraphina at the top of the stairs", Quentin said. "And I was rather taken aback to be honest. It is rather dark just there, and I never really looked at it before. In fact, I didn't realise it was a portrait of Seraphina. But that's what it says it is. I thought it was...". Quentin didn't finish his sentence, but started frowning.

"Go on", Sebastian said, prompting him to continue.

"Well, don't you think she is the absolute spitting image of Sati"?

"I do", replied Sebastian, much to Quentin's surprise.

"You never mentioned it before", Quentin said.

"No, perhaps not", Sebastian replied.

Quentin knew he had no idea of all the things Sebastian knew, but he knew Sebastian knew all kinds of things that he didn't always talk about. Nevertheless, there was something about the portrait, and the fact that Seraphina in the painting looked just like Sati, that struck him very deeply.

Sebastian, however, didn't seem to want to go into the matter any further. "If we could go back to the Library", he said. "I can show you the rest of those books".

Quentin agreed, and both friends left the auditorium to its now returned silence, and made their way back through the galleries and passageways of Aumhurst.

On the way back, they went past the top of the stairs again. Quentin now observed the portrait very carefully indeed. Seraphina, or Sati as it might have been, was indeed strikingly beautiful. The painting was signed but he didn't recognise the name. The thought now crossed his mind that the painting might not be as old as it seemed to suggest. He toyed with the idea that it might be not what it appeared to be, and that Sati was actually, indeed, the sitter. After all, Sebastian was a highly skilled artist. And it was possible that Sebastian would consider the fact that the painting was in effect an illusion, to be part of the art. It was exactly the kind of thing that Sebastian might do. He was known for his work with the principle of illusion. It didn't look anything like Sebastian's work, but then, Quentin knew Sebastian was perfectly capable of creating that appearance.

He was startled by Sebastian behind him, appearing to read his thoughts. "I didn't paint it", Sebastian said. "It is Seraphina Bassen-thwaite, I can assure you", he went on. "There are other portraits of her, around the house. I'm surprised you haven't already noticed them".

"It *is* a striking resemblance", Quentin observed.

"Yes, too much to be just a coincidence, I think", Sebastian replied, enigmatically.

4

Like the Wind

Sandhya leaned over the balustrade at the top of the beautiful, wide sweeping staircase in the grand entrance hall of Merehurst, and announced that she was "going to ride out before it gets too hot".

The message spread around the white walls of the high space, bouncing off elegant blue and white porcelain vases, some of the sound being absorbed by the long flowing curtains and tapestries. Her voice reverberated all the way down to the checkered floor beneath, like a trapped bird trying to find its way out, finally and successfully reaching its intended ears which were already emerging through one of the doorways into the hall.

A brief enquiry from Sati confirmed they were to ride the two mile long Silver Gallop along the edge of the mere this morning, in the direction of Aumhurst.

In just a short while Sandhya and Sati were already on the cobbles of the old stable yard, selecting their favoured steeds from Merehurst's noble thoroughbreds. By the chiming of Merehurst's cupola clock they were already out and away, and trotting down to the edge of the mere.

The morning was wonderful and fresh. The combination of the cool morning air on their faces with the warmth of the Sun and the light reflected off the mere, was exhilarating, even before they had begun their gallop.

And now side by side, from a quick bridging of the reins and the firmest of nudges, canter broke into gallop, and the two beautiful steeds were racing each other along the Silver Gallop, faster than the wind, the bright shining mere all along their off side, the sun blessing their path, the sleepy green islands reflected in the water, framing their breathtaking, breakaway speed through the cool mereside air.

Further along the stretch, approaching the middle and overlooking the gap in the boundary fence between the Merehurst and Aumhurst estates, a small boy somewhere up on the hill behind, stood astonished at what seemed to him, the open recklessness of their daring. The two horses and their riders who had been amiably galloping side by side, were now racing each other with such speed, such explosive determination, that their obvious competition had reached out and firmly grabbed the boys attention.

He wondered if they had made some duel between them, or was it perhaps that having bolted they had now lost their minds in a mad frenzy of challenge and had abandoned all reason? For they now seemed to be racing for dear life, or perhaps, it seemed to the boy, even in a death wish.

As he watched, his own instinct told him this was more than just bravado, more than tomfoolery, more even than what any fool being a fool would have the imagination to engage in. The boy knew the stretch of the silver Gallop well enough from his watching of the many horses he had seen galloping it. But these two seemed possessed, they seemed taken by some mania, some frenzy, and to boot, they were on the wrong path to complete the Gallop's two halves in one.

He was palpably feeling the rising tension between the two steeds with every slight contraction and expansion of the contested distance between them as they thundered towards the boundary fence. He watched them as they raced neck and neck across the surface of the Gallop like living bolts from some unseen cannon, some sudden starting that must have unleashed them into this ecstasy of sheer, manic, equine power.

The rapid, rhythmic thudding of hooves, pummelled the air, again and again, frenetically beating like clapping and thundering musical beats of a drumming percussion that raced like a mad thing, along the edge of the mere. In horror, the boy watched, wide eyed, as the two horses hurtled not towards the obvious gap, but straight at the tall boundary fence marking the halfway mark along the length of the Silver Gallop.

And now, his worst fears were realised. Instead of their pulling up sharply as he had fully expected, which would have given them some chance as they flew towards the great fence, a still greater insanity seemed to be unfolding right in front of him. The riders were so entangled in battle that they suddenly urged their steeds on and on with even more excited actions, as they now raced towards the impossible fence with a sudden burst of accelerating speed. All rational hope seemed now to be lost in front of his very eyes, as the two reckless racers, shooting ahead of their own clouds of dust, through their very last moments towards the impossible fence, were stupidly, impetuously, hurtling towards unavoidable, crashing, horrific disaster.

Terrified to watch, but now rapt and thrilled by the sight of the charge, to the life to the death, to the one to the pair, to the race to the end, as they hurtled together head to head with billowing dust from their thundering hooves, now at the fateful moment the boy's eyes and mouth opened wider still. He saw the amazing pair of beautiful beasts like some stupendous sacrifice fly at the jump of death, mindlessly it seemed, through to their end, but courageously turning it into a leap for life like dancers born on magnificent invisible wings. The *prestissimo* pace of their race abruptly changed into a glorious *largo* of two combined beings, sleek of body, suddenly now exquisitely flowing high on an arc of beauty, in seeming defiance of the very law of gravity itself.

Never had the boy - who was not unaccustomed to watching the horse races in Pavi Bujdam - witnessed anything like it. He was not sure whether he was dreaming or was actually awake on the hill that really does overlook the Silver Gallop by the mere.

The two thoroughbred bodies rippling with muscular power, one closer to the mere than the other, were now engaged in a dance of celestial motion upwards through the space of the air above the fence, the shining mere behind them attempting to silhouette their graceful forms as they approached the zenith of their arc.

Now gravity succeeds in overcoming their audacious flight, but for gravity it is too late in the battle, as the horse's mastery of motion triumphs, their forward momentum is unbroken, and all hooves miraculously just clear the fence as the two brave steeds plunge steeply down and down, front legs stretched gallantly ahead, back onto the Gallop's green turf, in explosions of grass, dispelling doubt, re-engaging immediately in the battle now for the end of the Gallop.

And now the two streaking chargers harden more in their resolve, pushed on relentlessly and excitedly by the two riders as they hurtle even faster into the final frenzy towards the finish of the Gallop. The boy watches, enthralled, unbelieving at both the riders' and the horses' mettle and fearlessness in taking on the impossible - yet apparently not impossible - boundary fence between the Merehurst and Aumhurst estates. But take it on they did, without forethought, without doubt, and without knowing they had been observed.

The homestretch to the end of the Gallop of course had no finish line, and instead, the incredible speed of the two horses simply fell away as they were brought to a halt by their riders, who were both breathless with joy.

Now, from this end of the Gallop it was possible to see Aumhurst, its towers overlooking the mere. The frenzy was over, the exhilaration of their consummate expression of the physical, done. Somewhere, a higher inspiration had come down to meet with Sandhya and Sati by their very engaging in what was, after all, the mania of it.

Sati saw it had been a performance, an ecstasy, even a rite of purification. It was once only, and it would never happen again. As they looked across to Aumhurst, she somehow knew inside her, in her deepest self, perhaps it was in a moment of prescience, that she was looking at what would become the setting of another great frenzy. One destined to be much more powerful, something even beyond the thrill of their race along the Silver Gallop at the edge of beautiful mere.

5

The Market

The marketplace at Pavi, not far from Aumhurst, was traditionally arranged in concentric circles of stalls, placing the market goers in what seemed like a labyrinth, if it were not for the many passing points through from one circle to another. Everyday living necessities, produce and goods, the ones that were most abundant, were found on the outer circle, with merchandise of increasing value and rarity progressively found towards the centre.

Timaeus was walking around the innermost circle, considering the merchandise, with his beautiful Ambika by his side. There were all kinds of jewellery, fragrances, incenses, transporting potions, and even cintamani stones. He passed one stall displaying numerical talismans in the shapes of numbers. Many of them were in the shape of threes, there were also sevens, and a few of the other numbers, fashioned from beautiful blue touchstone. But the stall also displayed rosin candles made from the resin of the kalpa tree, in shining deep red, placed in beautiful, prismatic glass stands. They stole his attention.

Timaeus was observed by the stall-holder. "They are made from kalpa rosin, my dear", said the dusky-skinned woman, swathed in gorgeous colours. He examined one more closely. The stall-holder watched him. "I can tell you their secret", she said.

"That would be most kind of you", said Timaeus, ever the perfect gentleman. "What is their secret"?

"They are able to bring you what you wish for, from the Sun, my dear", she said, mixing myths from the various clans. "The kalpa tree spends its life reaching for the Sun, drawing its energy from the light, and storing it, until its resin is imbued with it. Then we draw out the resin, and make the rosin, and when you light the candle, some of the Sun's Divine light of happiness and good luck is released again, just for you, to light your room and your life".

"Is that so"? replied Timaeus.

The woman in the gorgeous colours continued. "It's amazing, isn't it"? she said. "The light is full of good luck, if you know how to capture it, which we do. The Sun's light itself is based on the Holy Three, you know". She gestured to some of the beautiful touchstone talismans. "Did you know that the Sun's light is sent ninety-three million miles before it reaches us, which is a nine and a three, and the nine is three times three? It's wonderful isn't it, how everything fits together"?

"It is, I've always thought that", said Timaeus, genially.

"I can see you are sensitive to these things", the woman said.

Timaeus carried on admiring the very beautiful candle that had most taken his interest.

"I see you have good taste", she continued. "We collect the resin and mature it seven times over, each time for as long as it takes the good luck light from the Sun to reach us. That's how we send our obeisances to the Sun. Seven times as long makes it burn better. That's quite a time. So the rosin you are getting here, has a good mature age. It is excellent value.

Timaeus, still looking closely at the candle, turning it carefully around in his hands, and examining it closely, said quietly and almost absentmindedly "Hmm... fifty eight minutes and fourteen point seven seconds, to be precise", in a somewhat automated tone of voice.

The woman looked at him quizzically. "You're not a clansman are you"? she said.

Timaeus looked up and said "It's beautiful, I'll take it. Oh, and er...

no, I'm a mathematician. Ninety-three million miles at a hundred and eighty six thousand, two hundred and eighty two miles per second, works out at three minutes and fourteen point seven seconds for each maturation. I think seven times that is long enough for it to burn well".

"Well", she said, packaging the candle for him, "You do learn something every day, don't you"?

"I endeavour to", said Timaeus.

"It's beautiful", observed Ambika. As they moved away from the stall Timaeus said, with a gentle sense of irony, "Do you think it will bring us luck"?

Ambika smiled with kindness. "She's not entirely wrong", she said.

"You mean about the resin storing the Sun's energy"? Timaeus replied.

Ambika smiled. "Well, that too, but that's not what I meant".

"What did you mean then"? Timaeus said.

"Well", Ambika said, "About the Sun and the Sun's light. It *is* full of energy".

"Ah...", Timaeus began, smiling with his knowledge of Ambika, "But I suspect you're not talking about the energy that the scientists speak of".

"No", Ambika said. "I'm speaking of the energy that Marsilio and Sebastian sometimes speak of, the energy of the Good and the Beautiful, which Marsilio calls the Being, which he says comes from the One, and is the One, and is the origin of Pavi Bujdam. Which he says is also really the Being. Although I must admit more recently Sebastian seems to have become somewhat more obsessed with Seraphina and her art, as being the creator Pavi Bujdam".

"I don't think the stall-holder mentioned anything like that", Timaeus said.

"I think you may be viewing her a little too harshly, Timaeus. She did in her own way. She was talking about happiness, after all. That's her way of talking about the good and the beautiful".

Timaeus shrugged. "Yes", he said, "But she seemed to think it was something you could get by lighting the candle. I can't think about a candle, not even a kalpa rosin candle, as some kind of store of happiness, in that way, Ambika".

Timaeus and Ambika carried on weaving their way between the crowds, temporarily in single file, and then Ambika came alongside Timaeus again and they managed to continue their conversation.

She said "Will you not feel a sense of happiness, or joy, or the good and the beautiful", when you light the candle? You don't need it to see by. That's not why you acquired it, is it? Will you not be indeed lighting it for the sake of the good and the beautiful in your own experience of being? Why else would you have acquired it"?

"Ah, I see what you mean", Timaeus replied.

"Where do you think the good in your own experience of being, comes from"? Ambika said.

Timaeus considered. "Well, that would depend on how you look at it", he answered carefully.

They walked on a little further, until Ambika answered simply "How so"?

"Well", said Timaeus, "The scientists of course would say it is a matter of the brain. And I am inclined to agree. But I suspect you are onto something different, here".

"Yes", Ambika said. "I am talking about where the brain and its ability to create this experience, comes from".

"Well I cannot see that it came from Seraphina", Timaeus said. "I concede that when we are talking about the Sun or about the candle, then if we are talking about our our experience of the good and the beautiful, then we might also want to be talking about our being. But I would still go along with the scientists and say that our perceptions of the Sun, and the candle, and so on, and what we feel, and experience, are all a matter of the brain".

"Indeed", Ambika agreed. "I can see you are with me, so far".

Timaeus seemed a little surprised, because he rather thought that he had just contradicted her. But he knew Ambika too well, to be overly surprised.

"Well then", Timaeus continued, "I should like to hear your entire view of this. Although I think it is a pity that Sebastian and Sandhya and Sati are not with us to hear it, and indeed your sister Amba and Marsilio even".

"Perhaps another time, for them", Ambika agreed, "And perhaps by then, my view may have developed a little further".

"Yes, perhaps another time", said Timaeus. "But please, do tell me your philosophy on this".

Ambika continued. "Timaeus my dear, I was speaking, as Marsilio sometimes does, and as Sebastian was in his lecture, about the Good and the Beautiful, which they, and I too, call the Being. Really, I am following one of the most ancient philosophers of the Old World, I believe his name was Plato. Marsilio was saying that the Good and the Beautiful is the Being, and that the Being is always Being, and never becoming. Whilst human beings, and their world of being, which is Pavi Bujdam, is a world that is always becoming, and never Being. So I was not so much speaking about the brain, whose state, and whose functioning, is always becoming, and never stops becoming, as long as it is alive and functioning, but rather, I was speaking of the Being that always Is".

She continued on. "We know the Sun by its light, don't we? But what is this light from the Sun? I mean, what actually is it, if we are talking about the Good and Beautiful, or about the Being, and not so much about the brain, or what the scientists talk about"?

"If we are talking in that way"? Timaeus said. "Well then, I would say the light from the Sun is indeed an experience. And our experience of it is already part of our own being, I would say, so in these terms, what we say it *is*, I suppose you could say is a question of being".

"Indeed, Timaeus. I am asking, what is the nature and quality of this experience of being, when we experience and enjoy the light of the Sun"?

"Well I would say", Timaeus began again, "It's something I do myself indeed experience as beautiful, and good. That much is true. In fact, I would go as far as to say that I do actually love it, especially after the winter. I suppose in another sort of way I love it as much as I love the understanding of things in terms of mathematics".

He considered thoughtfully. "And the same is true, even in my appreciation of the candle. And no doubt my appreciation of it even more, once it is alive with the flame and the light, when we light it after dark. That, I would agree, after all, is why I have acquired it, just as you say".

Ambika replied, "Excellently put, Timaeus, thank you. Do tell me more then about your experience of the Sun".

Timaeus continued. "Well when it comes to the light from the Sun, yes, I agree, there is a certain joy, that seems to me, to be inherent in the way it shines on the land and the mere, and especially on the mere, and how it makes the water seem to glitter and sparkle so beautifully. It is joyful, it's true. And I also enjoy sun bathing sometimes, I must say. Provided it is not too hot! I know that many people feel the same way about all that, as I do".

Ambika smiled and nodded. "Yes, it is the same for me, Timaeus. And is this not all in the brain"?

"It is indeed. I think that was my point, Ambika".

Ambika continued, "Well then, how does this relate to the Being, the Good and the Beautiful that Sebastian spoke of, and that I am speaking of? This is the question. As I remember Sebastian saying, the Being always Is, and is never becoming. Because it is eternally Being. Whilst our world is a world that is always becoming. It is all changefulness, and evolution, isn't it?

"So let me ask you, Timaeus, the joy we both feel when we see the light from the Sun, is it not a part of the good and the beautiful that we both experience? A good that needs no understanding, say, of a mathematical or scientific kind, in order for us to know and experience this joy"?

"That's certainly true", Timaeus agreed.

"Indeed", Ambika said. "And isn't it so that Marsilio says the good and beautiful comes from the Being that always Is, and is never becoming? Except that we are experiencing it in our own way, in terms of our own limited experience of being, which is delivered through the brain whose functioning is always becoming".

"Yes I would agree it is provided by the brain", said Timaeus. "So please, do continue".

"Well, so it also is, Timaeus", Ambika said, "That the Good and the Beautiful of the Being can be experienced in even greater depth. I myself, have this experience, you see. But now, I have to ask you, do you want me to continue explaining this"?

"Ambika, you have my full attention", Timaeus said.

"Then I will go on", Ambika said. "I am saying that our joy in seeing the light of the Sun, that so many feel, is an experience of the Good and the Beautiful of the Being. But it is not a direct beholding of that Joy, the Joy of the Being. Our joy that we have been talking about comes from seeing the light from the Sun, the same Sun that the scientists study. So in this way, we could say the Sun is like a visible symbol of the Being, could we not"?

"Well I at least see what you mean", said Timaeus.

"And our enjoyment of the Sun, which we experience, the experience itself, is therefore also like a symbol, but an experiential symbol no less, of the more direct enjoyment of the Being, that I am speaking of".

Timaeus answered "Again, Ambika my dear, I can see what you are saying. Although I can't say I have that experience. And I think the Sun can also burn things in an undesirable way".

"That's true, Timaeus, my dear", Ambika said, "But that's only in the material world. That too, is a symbol of the relation of the higher to the lower".

"So you are saying the Sun is just a symbol"? Timaeus said.

"Yes, my love", Ambika continued, "Even just beholding the symbol, even in just the light from the symbol, is a little of the Joy of the Being that always Is, and is never becoming, but it is a symbolic joy, an experiential symbol, a mere symbol of the full Joy of the Being, as we could know it if we were to directly behold That Being that the visible Sun symbolises. Are you with me, Timaeus, my dearest? I do hope you are".

"I think I am, Ambika", Timaeus replied.

Ambika continued, "Allow me to explain it another way. I am saying our enjoyment of the Sun is a pleasure. Is that not so"?

"I would definitely agree", Timaeus answered.

Ambika continued, "So somewhere, we have within ourselves this very pleasure potency within us, do we not"?

"I would agree with that, too", Timaeus answered again.

"So would it also not be", said Ambika, "That in accordance with what we have been saying, this pleasure potency itself, within us, is as it were an experiential symbol? A kind of imitation of the true pleasure potency of That Being"?

"Well, again, I can at least see what you are saying", said Timaeus.

"And so what I am saying, my dear", Ambika continued, "Is that when we come to knowledge of the Good and the Beautiful of the Being, the Being that is eternally Being but never becoming, what we experience in even just the light of its symbol, the light we see with our eyes, through the brain that is always becoming, even in that, deeper aspects of the Good and Beautiful of the Being, the delights made from the creative pleasure potency of That Being, may also perhaps be sometimes known and experienced. Even just through the light of the imitation".

Timaeus simply smiled. "Tell me what these delights are, Ambika", he said.

"Well, Timaeus, it is part of that, that I call the ocean of the streams of stories of love and the ocean of beautiful places, and the ocean of streams of stories of love in beautiful places. But even in this, I have to say, Timaeus, things have already started to enter this becoming, that emanates from the Being".

Timaeus answered, "Ah yes, I know you do often speak of that, my dear. And I have heard both you and Marsilio speak of it on many occasions".

Ambika said, "Well, Timaeus, just as the light from the visible Sun that we see, which is the symbol, just as that light expands away from the Sun, and as you rightly say, so that in three minutes and twenty seconds of time on Pavi Bujdam, it reaches us, so too, the Being is always expanding in a very different way, so that even though the Being always Is and is never becoming, it creates the world of becoming in which we live, which is our world of time and our experience of being".

"Go on", said Timaeus.

Ambika continued. "I am saying that just as the Sun is splendid with light, so the Being in splendid with Being. It is the higher splendour. And it is the ocean of Being that emanates from the Being, that I am calling the ocean of streams of stories of love, and the ocean of stories of beautiful places. Just as light comes from the Sun, and depends on the Sun, and has emanated from the Sun and still belongs to the Sun, and yet the Sun has no dependence on it, so also in the case of the Being, that Radiance or emanation that always Is, becomes and expands into many oceans of being, long before we reach what has become us, and our brain, and our experiences of being, which are all still becoming".

"I think I see the general tenor of what you mean", Timaeus said. "Although I would have to take your word for it. What are these beautiful places that you always speak of, Ambika"?

Ambika answered, "These are not like the places in Pavi Bujdam, Timaeus. I say that the good and the beautiful in the places of Pavi Bujdam is an imitation, as it were, of the Good and the Beautiful in the places I am speaking of. *They* are completely in the Joy and ecstasy of the Being. And yet, even within our experience of the light of the Sun, which is only the symbol, only an imitation, we can still intuit, and sometimes experience, glimpses of these most beautiful stories of love in places of beauty".

Timaeus contemplated what Ambika had said, and then replied "I would like to say, Ambika my love, that I think I do have something like the experience you are talking about, except that I experience it sometimes, rather, through music. But in what way does this relate to the candle"?

They both now laughed at Timaeus referring everything back to the candle. Ambika answered, "The light of the candle flame, although it does not directly come from the Sun, is nonetheless light, isn't it? Even the candle flame is therefore a symbol, or an imitation, too. The candle flame too, creates light, and as you know, we also experience it through the brain, whose functioning is always becoming. But the stories in its light that it might induce in us, if we are sensitive to it, are not directly from the Sun. They are of a lower nature, associated with our self, and our experiences on Pavi Bujdam, rather than with the transcendental emanations of the Being I have been speaking of, that always is, and is never be coming, whose symbol is the Sun".

"Ambika", Timaeus laughed, "You are being very articulate, I can hear that, and I know this is what you do, when you start to become frenzied, but there, I think you might have gone beyond me".

"No matter", said Ambika. She continued on, but now perhaps unwisely. "Some of the clans speak of *abhimāna*, you see. It means your idea of who you are. And my idea of who I am. It is like the light of the candle, this idea, this *abhimāna*, whereas the light of the Sun, as it were, comes from the loss of *abhimāna*. That light of the Sun is the symbol of the Being that we already really are, beyond our *abhimāna*".

Timaeus now held up his hand. "Ambika, my dear, I do think you may be entering some kind of frenzy. But you are still completely beyond me, I'm afraid", he said.

Ambika now came gently back down from her cloud of philosophy and contemplation. "But you do see, Timaeus, don't you", she went on, "That Tana wasn't entirely wrong, was she"?

"Who is Tana"? Timaeus asked, puzzled.

Ambika smiled. "The woman in the gorgeous colours".

"Ah, the stall-holder you mean? How do you know her name"?

"You seem to forget, Timaeus, I know all the stall-holders on the inner circle".

Timaeus considered. "Yes, of course", he said. "I can see now she saw things in her own way. She didn't see what you can see, but she saw something".

"But isn't it like that with all of us"? Ambika said. "So much depends on the nature of our mind, the nature of our brain, doesn't it"?

"That's true", Timaeus answered, now thinking to himself that perhaps the correct way to understand everything was through numbers. But he didn't say it. Instead he said "Except that there are some things that don't depend on any of that, at all".

"Really"? Ambika said, sounding, at least in appearance, surprised. "What things"?

"Well *numbers*, for a start", Timaeus couldn't help himself saying. "The way in which numbers *really* relate to each other, and truly fit together, rather than just how people like to think they do. Such as in all those numeric talismans on her market stall, and all that business Tana said about the time it takes the light to come here from the Sun".

"Ah, yes, you're very adept at that side of things, of course", Ambika smiled. "But that's only one side of things. Although you are right, of course, in saying that it doesn't depend on anyone's own opinion or ideas".

"That's what I like about numbers and mathematics", Timaeus said. "It transcends all that personal nonsense. It's not an opinion, or a belief, it's a genuine discovery".

Timaeus and Ambika walked on a little further, in silence. But then Ambika replied, "Your mathematics and the sciences you understand are not the only thing that transcends mere opinion, you know, or what you are calling *all that personal nonsense*".

"How so"? Timaeus asked.

Ambika answered easily "Do you remember what we said about *why* you bought the candle, Timaeus? And what you said about how you enjoy the Sun? And how you will enjoy the light from the candle when you come to light it"?

"Of course", Timaeus answered, walking on. "It was only a few moments ago. I suppose you are going to say that what you are talking about, the Being, and your various oceans, also in some way transcends all that personal nonsense"?

"Well, Timaeus", Ambika replied, "When I talk about the ocean of the streams of stories of love, and the ocean of the streams of stories of beautiful places, and love in beautiful places, then I would say that certainly transcends opinion, and it transcends what you are calling *all that personal nonsense.* The ocean of the streams of stories of love and the ocean of beautiful places, that I talk about sometimes, isn't personal, you see".

"Isn't this very philosophy, of which you speak, personal though"? Timaeus said. "I mean, is this not something you personally believe"?

"No, Timaeus, it's not something I personally believe, it's something I experience. Like I experience this market, but I don't believe it".

"Really"? Timaeus smiled, surprised at her answer. "I believe you, but I don't know why", he said, smiling in some kind of amusement.

They walked on a little further. And then Timaeus felt he wanted to know what she really meant. "Well you must tell me, then, Ambika. I am intrigued to know why you say you don't believe this market, since you and I both clearly experience it".

"Do you have to believe what you experience"? Ambika answered.

"Hmm... Yes, I see, I suppose you don't", Timaeus replied thoughtfully.

Ambika smiled and answered "If you were dreaming, wouldn't that be the difference between not knowing you were dreaming, and knowing that you were? If you knew you were dreaming, you would still experience the dream, wouldn't you? But you wouldn't believe it".

"I suppose so", Timaeus answered. "So are you suggesting in the market here, we are dreaming"?

"Not exactly, my dear", she smiled.

"Then what are you suggesting"? Timaeus replied.

Ambika answered. "I am not saying our walking in the market together now is a personal dream belonging to me or you. Neither of us are in our beds, asleep. But like a dream, it is just an image. After all, you said yourself that what we experience is just brain function, didn't you? Sebastian of course, I think, would probably say that it is all the art of Seraphina. He would probably say it is the manifestation of her dream, or idea, in this form of art, just as one of Sebastian's paintings is the manifestation of his idea".

Timaeus smiled. Then he laughed a little. "Yes", he said, "I think I'm beginning to see where you are coming from, here".

They walked on quietly now, for some time. And then Timaeus was stirred to speak again. "I'm wondering then", he began, "How numbers and mathematics, which I love so much, are related to what you are speaking of? Since neither what you are speaking of, nor numbers, depend on what is personal, and yet each are a quite different kind of thing".

"That is a very good question, Timaeus, and I do think you should certainly look into it", Ambika said. "Especially since you speak of your love for mathematics and numbers. Whilst I, in speaking of the ocean of the streams of stories of love, and the ocean of the streams of stories of beautiful places, am certainly speaking of what I love. And when you mentioned what you experience with music, I experience that too. I too, when I am singing, experience something of these streams of stories of love, and place. So we are both speaking of what we love, and when it comes to love, I certainly think we should seek to overcome any ignorance we may have of it".

"I entirely agree with you, Ambika", Timaeus said, smiling, and looking closely at her. "And I do think we should perhaps look more closely into the question of music, and indeed its relation to numbers".

"I think we should", Ambika agreed. "But your knowledge of the keyboard, and the lyre, and of the science of music, is greater than mine".

Timaeus now turned to Ambika, feeling more strongly his love for her, and he smiled again, very conscious of her beauty, which now seemed to him to be suddenly completely radiant. "Well, Ambika", he said, "I have learned something, although I cannot say I have followed you entirely".

They walked on together a little further, and then Timaeus laughed and said "But no matter, I think we should perhaps make our way to Aumhurst, where I should think Sebastian would be very pleased to know how much you appreciated his lecture".

6

Tea with Music

Quentin was sitting in the Library with Sebastian. As was its regular way, the action of the old long-case clock by the bookshelves autonomously whirred into life, and its mellow, musical chimes rang out. Almost immediately the library door gently clicked open, and under the arch entered Belvoir.

He was quietly wheeling in front of him a small silver trolley. Despite its ever-so refined and reserved appearance, it positively heralded the arrival of high tea with its four-tier silver stand of wonderful cakes, some of which were themselves several tiers high. The whole display's quiet entrance on the silver trolley pushed by Belvoir, was just as effective as had it been accompanied by a band of ceremonial trumpeters. It was a temptation that even the most studious of readers in the Library could not possibly have ignored.

"Ah! Belvoir, you're such a gentleman, thank you so much", Sebastian smiled, greeting him. Belvoir positioned the trolley comfortably close to the table, and in his usual manner simply turned and left without saying a word.

The two friends sat down and began to partake of the tea and cakes. It was true that there was little in Sebastian's daily agenda that fitted into the wider conventions of life on Pavi Bujdam; his ways of being and living were generally what some would regard as eccentric, but the almost ritual-like performance of the morning coffee and afternoon tea were obvious exceptions.

Quentin regularly joined Sebastian for these events. Quentin himself was as much revered as a musician in Pavi Bujdam, as Sebastian was as an artist, and he often came over to Aumhurst just for musical reasons, sometimes together with other members of the circle of friends, given that the house was home to a substantial collection of musical instruments. He had become familiar with the play of morning coffee and afternoon tea, and enjoyed taking part.

So now, while they are having tea, we might mention that the circle of friends we have so far met, is incomplete. As the ancient philosophers knew well, a perfect circle must be divided into twelve parts if it is to embody the very secrets of the symbols that are those our circle of philosopher friends are mutually seeking. And embody them their circle must, because theirs is no less than the inner circle of the Pavi Academy. The wider circle of philosophers of Pavi Bujdam would meet regularly together, and referred to themselves as the Pavi Academy, a name they liked the sound of, although it didn't really have any further meaning. Their philosophising invariably circulated around the question of the mere.

As we have already found out, Quentin, when he was not at Aumhurst, resided at another great house known as Merehurst, further around the mere, together with Sandhya, another musician and dancer. The twins Amba and Ambika, together with Sandhya, Quentin and Timaeus were the members of the Pavi Consort, their musical performances often included as an integral part of the meetings of the Pavi Academy. Sebastian was one of the founding members of the Academy, however, the Leader of the Academy always was, from its very beginning, Marsilio, whose residence Springmere, down by the orange groves, was regularly used for meetings.

Marsilio had a close connection to Belvoir, who as we have seen, now lived at Aumhurst, contributing occasional voluntary services in gratitude for accommodation and a very comfortable daily living at the great house, an arrangement that was part of an ancient tradition of alms, applying to all the great houses around the edge of the mere. Belvoir had once been a fellow monk with Marsilio at the old Atoll Priory, before it was flooded in the rising of the waters of the mere.

§

Having sampled one of the large, soft pink cakes, a favourite of his, Quentin took a last sip of tea, replaced the cup delicately on the saucer, and then asked, "I say, Sebastian, do you have the copies of the music you were talking about, the parts you said you found"?

Sebastian walked over to an oak chest of drawers in the corner, and took out a set of parts. "These I found hidden away in the Long Gallery", he said, "Along with some books I've been looking at, and I now think it all belonged to Seraphina. I think this, too, is part of her art. Do take it, Quentin, and have a good look at it. The music is talked about in one of the books, and I have a feeling from what I've read, although I must confess I don't understand everything about it, I think it's going to be ideal for a meeting. When do you think I might be able to get to hear some of it"?

Quentin perused some of the sheets of music. It was scribed in brown ink, in a florid hand, with long lines of notes connected by gracefully curved and flowing beams."This looks *very* interesting", he said, peering closely at it. "I should think we can get some rehearsals in, over the next week. I'll let you know".

Sebastian shut the drawer.

"If it's what I think it is", he said, "Then it could be interesting to perform. Some of it looks as though it's dance music. Perhaps you could transcribe it for your lyre"?

"I would be delighted", Quentin answered, a part sheet already in his hand, and he was already moving towards the little table where the violin was kept. He put the sheet down on the table, opened the drawer, and carefully withdrew the violin and bow. After a few brief moments of bow tensioning and tuning, the line of notes was coming to new life through the violin, a striking solo stream of poignant beauty, heard for the first time since the days of Seraphina Bassenthwaite.

Sebastian stood and listened. He was momentarily transfixed. It was enough for him to realise that this music was indeed somehow connected with what he and Marsilio had been talking about in their last private meeting together. But then, only a short time ago, the question of whether copies of such music still existed was only a matter of speculation. Now, he was sure, here it was, within the walls of Aumhurst.

Somehow, through the foresight or wisdom of Seraphina Bassenthwaite, Sebastian now thought, the very thing Marsilio was talking about as only a possibility, had manifested. The music was here, now, in Aumhurst, it had been preserved and now passed on by Seraphina into Sebastian's possession. Unknown to her, of course, thought Sebastian. But then the thought occurred to him that perhaps it wasn't so unknown, after all.

7

The Vicinages

The Vicinages were all around the coast of Pavi Bujdam. On one side of the island were the seven that the clans considered holy places. These were the main busy centres, each with a town with its own bustling market, and each with its own history and character.

The population everywhere was a mix of the seven clans, which, although each had noticeably different characteristics, intermingled amiably together, and worked effectively in the busy world of Pavi Bujdam, in harmony.

With their different belief systems and customs they nonetheless all shared the same centre, literally, the Tower of Pavi Bujdam, which housed the Omphalos revered by all. It was thought, however, that these seven holy Vicinages had originally been the territories of the seven separate clans, and that somehow, over time, they had dispersed themselves.

Stretching between and connecting the seven holy Vicinages were seven perfectly straight, main roads, each the shortest distance between two of the towns. It was possible to follow a never ending route along the line of the roads, passing through all the Vicinages, one at a time. However, all the roads cut inland across the island, connecting

Vicinages that, if you were following the path along the edge of the mere, would be separated by other Vicinages.

This arrangement had somehow naturally evolved over the history of the island. Every year, the Festival of the Harmonies took place in the springtime, in which all the clans would embark on their peregrination or walkabout through the towns, proceeding along the roads with much music and dancing, of a kind characteristic of each clan.

Each clan had its own favoured starting town, perhaps, it was thought, the location of the original home of that clan. At that time of year, the population would largely separate out into their respective clans, each camping close to the mere on the outskirts of their favoured town. Then all the clans would begin their peregrination in the same direction along the roads. Having passed through all the towns, and back to where they began, some would then begin their pilgrimage to the centre of the island, to see the Omphalos. This festival had taken place each year for as long as anyone could remember.

On the other side of the island were another five Vicinages, not frequented by the clans, which were generally regarded as a remote. It was not that there was no population there, for a smaller population there certainly was, but the people there did not intermingle in quite the same the way that the clans did on the first side of the island.

In general, the Vicinages around Pavi Bujdam who were immediate neighbours to each other, maintained very harmonious relations with each other. However, there was one Vicinage on the remote side of the island, known locally as Gsoaf, that constantly wavered in allegiance between the Vicinages on either side of it, Ceshmere and Eflmere.

Sometimes it had a harmonious relation with one, and sometimes with the other, but never with both. On the contrary, when its relations with one were good, then with the other they were always very disharmonious.

Historically, and quite fortunately, the only other real tensions that arose between Vicinages always occurred, for some reason, between those Vicinages that were separated by three other Vicinages. The nature of this order of things was known by everyone but not really understood by most of the population of the island. However, because as a result of this remarkable rule, tensions generally were arising only between Vicinages that were not direct neighbours, this principle maintained stability in Pavi Bujdam.

The notable exception was Gsoaf, which as we have already mentioned, was on the remote side of the island. But there, another remarkable rule would arise, whose the reason for being, again, was not really understood by most of the population.

The salient fact was, that whenever Gsoaf was in disharmonious relations with one of its immediate neighbours, either Ceshmere or Eflmere, which it always was with one or the other, then its relations with the town that was three Vicinages further on around the mere beyond that neighbour, became very harmonious, when otherwise, it would have been very disharmonious due to the general rule we have already mentioned.

Not only this, but harmony then also arose between all four pairs of Vicinages between which fell Gsoaf and whichever of its neighbours it was currently antagonistic towards. In all four pairs, their relations then became extremely harmonious. But this harmony was at the behest of whichever of Gsoaf's neighbours it chose to be in favour with. All this, though remarkable and strange, seemed to be the natural order of things on Pavi Bujdam.

There were of course many who would have loved to have seen permanent harmony between all the Vicinages, not least Sebastian himself, as Lord of Aumhurst. But it seemed that everything hinged on the allegiance or otherwise, of Gsoaf, to either Eflmere or Ceshmere.

And so it was, that despite Aumhurst being the puissance of the Mereage and at the head of the whole of Pavi Bujdam, conditions in Pavi Bujdam depended not on Sebastian, or Aumhurst, but on Gsoaf. The tensions and harmonies on Pavi Bujdam played themselves out, season after season, year upon year, only changing significantly when Gsoaf changed its allegiance.

The disharmonious relations had never been known on Pavi Bujdam to have resulted in war. Nevertheless, the existence of less than perfect harmony on the island was a matter of great interest to a number of the members of the Pavi Academy.

Some held that with intervention and negotiation with the rogue Vicinage, it might be possible to stabilise Pavi Bujdam into a condition of complete harmony. Others, notably Marsilio, Sebastian and Timaeus, would smile quietly at their arguments, and maintained that it was already and unavoidably in the very nature of the Vicinages themselves and their relations to each other, as part of Pavi Bujdam, that complete harmony was impossible.

Sebastian and Marsilio had on many occasions discussed the matter privately, and although they had not yet made their views known to the Academy, they concurred with each other that in truth, the tensions that were perpetually somewhere over the other side of the island, were actually due to the situation of Pavi Bujdam, specifically, that it was surrounded by the mere.

The presence of the mere was certainly something that was revered by the clans, but very few of the population, in the opinion of Sebastian and Marsilio, were truly aware of the influence of the mere. It was not that the mere caused the disharmony, they thought. Rather, they had to come to the view that the disharmony went hand-in-hand with Pavi Bujdam being surrounded by the mere, and not knowing what was beyond it.

8

Rapture

From within the gardens, flowing around and amongst the persons, came the most sublime and beautiful polyphony, two crystal female voices, intertwined, moving between the persons, here behind, there beside, hiding here, moving there.

Where was it coming from? It was emanating from an open window somewhere high in the golden stone walls of Aumhurst. Was it coming from the tower overlooking the mere? Or was it over there, by the open oriel window? Who knows? Who could possibly tell?

The sound fell down into the gardens like two intermingling liquid threads, silver and gold, floating through the air, sometimes parting, sometimes conjoined in extraordinary moments of beautiful, diaphanous harmony, always perfect, together, and yet apart. Combined, the two exquisite voices cast a spell even on the ears of the inanimate stone and bronze statues standing amongst the leaves. A magic as strong as Venus and Cupid together, pulling so strongly on the heart that even the persons might well have come to life in search of its Divine source.

The Divine source, that it certainly was for anyone whose heart was so affected, was indeed somewhere high up in the tower overlooking the mere. Where else would Ambika and Sati have chosen for their rehearsal of the newly found music, on a day like this, with the glory of the Sun over the mere?

Marsilio would have been in no doubt about the significance of the scene in that room in the tower, and the rapture it embodied. There, framed by the sparkling glass in the mullion of the open window, Sati and Ambika stood facing each other, their music in front of them, like two angels chosen by providence to bring celestial harmonies down from the spheres of Angelic Mind into the substance of the world. All of this Marsilio would have recognised. And indeed, so it was. And as it would happen, perchance, Sebastian, having come up through the kitchen garden, was now already amongst the persons, and now, finding himself quite suddenly and unexpectedly flooded by the light of that Divine music, stood utterly transfixed, like one of the persons. But unlike the persons, he was enraptured. And in a worship he didn't understand, silent tears spontaneously came to his eyes, and fell down his cheeks.

He knew what it was. He had never heard it before, indeed, most likely no one had heard it since the days of Seraphina Bassenthwaite. But yes, he instantly knew what it was. And he knew it was, even, only an incomplete part of the music he had found in the Long Gallery. It was usual for the Consort to rehearse parts in various smaller ensembles, before putting their work together for rehearsals with the whole Consort. It might well be, Sebastian knew very well, that other members of the Consort were rehearsing this very moment other parts of the music, if not at Aumhurst, then at Merehurst.

He continued standing, effectively hidden amongst the persons, at first spellbound, then lost in rapture, and then inexplicably and painfully pulled towards something that he already knew he somehow recognised so strongly, and yet didn't know what it was; it was something this music somehow embodied, something just even in the simple beauty of Sati's and Ambika's pure voices, something that he knew he longed for, even though he didn't know what it was, and for a moment fancied he might know the meaning of those ancient myths from the Old World, about sirens and ships. But then, there was nothing sinister at all about these voices, or their music. It was the opposite. He realised he was in love, in some way, he knew he was listening to a sublime beauty that was nothing less than the Good and the Beautiful that he himself had previously lectured on at the last meeting of the Academy, without even realising the truth of his own words. For he had understood then, only with his mind.

Often when he was listening to Timaeus or Quentin playing music from the masters of the Old World, it was the interplay of deep visceral feeling with that indefinable crystal mirror of intellect, like some transcendental mathematics in motion, or perhaps, he once thought, the emotions of mathematics, that had struck him so deeply. And yet here, as he stood immersed in this gift emanating from the window above, the mathematical shape of music, the importance of it, had somehow dissolved away into the sheer rapture of the of harmony itself. It was beyond the understanding of the mind, but not beyond understanding as being.

Sebastian knew from the lectures of Timaeus at the Academy, and from things that Timaeus had said in meetings in the Harborage, that harmony was also mathematics, for harmony was numbers in proper ratio, but as he stood here now, intoxicated by these harmonies, expressed through the beautiful voices of Sati and Ambika, he perceived no numbers. Rather, it was an exaltation, a flight of the soul upwards beyond anything that could be understood in that way, a flight towards the incomprehensible, beyond all quantifying. It was in that very flight into the inexpressible yet profoundly knowable, that his very self had somehow been dropped from the talons of the bird as it soared, leaving it to rise upwards unencumbered.

He felt a sudden urge to get all the members of the inner circle of the Academy together in the same room, perhaps at the Harborage, to try to further the emergence of this, whatever it was, that was within him, as much as it was here also in the gardens of Aumhurst, into some sort of more conscious flowering. Perhaps it might become an idea for a new painting that for some time now, he had been feeling the urge to undertake, on the subject of the mere and what was beyond it. But whilst before, emergence in himself had generally come through the process of painting, this was different. It was something more extensive, more expansive, something that he really felt must involve the other members of the inner circle.

As suddenly as he had discovered the voices from the open window of the tower, and had fallen immediately into their Divine sphere, so now they simply stopped. He waited for a little while. And sure enough, they started again. And then stopped again. And now there was continued silence. This, Sebastian knew, was the ordinary way of things in rehearsals.

9

The Studio

Sebastian's studio was a place of indefinable order and chaos. As an artist's place of work no one could say it was untidy, but there was no way of making sense of things such that one could say one honestly understood it.

Several forests of jars and paints, sets of brushes and tools, and who knows what, covered various surfaces around the studio. Large and small sculptures, many of them with an almost living presence, looked on into the room, sharing spaces with framed canvases whose reason for being was for the most part, hidden by cloth or by their being stored in ranks and files of many, placed along the walls, with their backs turned to the room.

Other paintings seemingly randomly placed stood around like onlookers into the room, some human, some hymns to nature, some abstract. But unlike paintings in a gallery, to have inspected them closely would have somehow seemed to be invading their privacy.

At one end of the room Sebastian was at work, painting his subject. She was sitting, hands in her lap, her gaze occupied through the crystal glass of the window at this end of the studio. Here, the walls were free of any clue that this was in fact an artist's studio. On the contrary, here in the carefully arranged set, were panelled walls, a beautiful tall vase and an ancient long case clock which had been imported from elsewhere in the house. Beside the beautiful crystal glass window, all was sufficient to give the convincing impression of a wholly different environment.

Right beside the sitter was another easel, with a very large, life-size painting, positioned on the floor, resting on it. A painting, in fact, of the sitter herself, in no less than precisely the same scene, in which she appeared again with the easel beside her with the painting itself. In which, in turn, appeared yet again, the sitter, and the painting. Again, of the same scene, with the sitter and the painting. Any onlooker in Sebastian's studio would probably have been intrigued to have examined that painting much more closely. How far would this recursion go? Was it really always the same scene, recurring each time with each painting of the painting?

The light coming in through the window illuminated the sitter from one side, with a poignant sense of mystery. Gentle hints of rainbow colours played here and there, in the background, and even across her face, coming from the natural refraction of the light through the uneven crystal glass. The sitter, stunningly beautiful in her flowing green silk gown, was the very picture of contemplative stillness. It was Sati.

The session had already been in progress for a good hour. Sati's natural discipline of character prevented her from initiating a distraction by starting a conversation, but now, after an hour of working intensely in silence, Sebastian himself spoke.

"I now have the essence of the light", he said, with a sense of satisfaction, "Which is just as well because it will be gone in another half an hour at the most. But I have enough to work with, now though".

Sati remained as she was, still saying nothing.

"Extraordinary", Sebastian said, observing both the painting and Sati.

Still Sati said nothing, and anyone who knew her, would know that she was not likely to do so, until she was specifically asked.

"Truly, extraordinary", Sebastian remarked again.

The brush in his hand was still moving as he spoke, but now it was held in suspended animation as with his other hand he reached out and picked up another brush, and after charging it with paint, brought it up to the canvas, resumed, and began to paint with both hands, as was frequently his way.

The long-case clock ticked on and on, until eventually Sebastian stepped away from the canvas.

"A-ha", he said. "Yes, I think we have it at last".

Now that Sebastian was away from the canvas, Sati smiled.

"What do you really think about the resemblance"? Sebastian suddenly asked.

"Do you want me to look at it"? Sati said in her usual gentle way, still seated.

"No no. Not this. Your resemblance to Seraphina".

"Ah", Sati smiled. "*That* resemblance. Well, Sebastian, I've told you before, haven't I? I don't think the resemblance is particularly strong".

Sebastian was still oscillating his gaze between Sati and the painting in front of him. "The resemblance is perfect", he said, contradicting her.

"Perhaps, in your eyes", Sati replied. "But not to me".

"Quentin thinks so too", Sebastian insisted.

"Well he would", Sati replied. "He doesn't know me that well".

"I think he knows you perfectly well", Sebastian said, as he now continued painting. "In any case, what has that got to do with it"?

"Sebastian, I'm really surprised to hear you say that", Sati exclaimed. "Given your interest in perception and illusions and such things".

"Hmm", Sebastian murmured, "Well, I wouldn't even really say it's even just a resemblance. I would say Seraphina could be you. Perhaps she *is* you", he smiled. "Or you could be her".

He looked at the painting, and now started to cover it over, deciding he had done enough for now. "Do you know what? I've been painting Seraphina", he smiled.

Sati elegantly rose from her chair, and turned to look at the painting on the easel beside her, with its recurring scene and multiple Satis or perhaps Seraphinas receding into the diminishing canvases in the picture. She smiled and said "I expect she's in there somewhere".

She couldn't remember how many times she had sat for Sebastian, for this project, each time with the last portrait he had completed, beside her on the easel. She could not remember how it had all started. Did she have the easel beside her, for the very first painting? She couldn't decide. Goodness knows, she thought, where he was keeping all these other portraits. And *why*, was a question she had refrained from confronting him with.

But there comes a time when the eccentricities of the ones who hold the key to the Tower do have to be questioned. Not criticised, but just questioned. And now, it seemed, was such a time, for Sati. She turned away from the painting on the easel beside her, and looked straight at Sebastian. "Sebastian", she began, "Do you mind if I ask, why is it that we are doing this"?

Sati thought she had been met by silence. But then, "I don't know", came the answer. "But I know that it's important".

Sebastian came over to her, and took her hand, and led her to a nearby chair. He sat down too, facing her. He looked serious. "In between our sittings, I almost completely forget it, you know, and it seems unimportant. I could just walk away from it. And probably never look at any of them again. But then it comes in again, and I know that I have to continue", he said.

Sati smiled, wondering if he perhaps it was time to move on. "How many times has it been now"? she asked gently. Sebastian got up and walked back to his canvas, and took off the cloth. He peered into the picture, and after a time, he answered "Twelve paintings", including this one". He carried on looking into the painting. The clock continued ticking its serene seconds. Sati began to wonder what was going through his mind. And then suddenly he said quietly "In the painting you look as though you are the Lady of Aumhurst".

Sati replied gently, "Yes, Sebastian. That's only in the painting though. As you know, I am not the Lady of Aumhurst. Although I could be". Sati had not tired of it, all this time. And she would go on, if she was asked. But then Sebastian, still standing at his painting, now said "This will be the last one". He came back over to her, sat down again, and held her hand.

Sati looked hard at him, searching him for more. "Where do we go from here"? she said quietly. There was a longing within her rising like a fountain, like the knowing of the whereabouts of some missing piece of the truth, without yet having discovered it. She knew that if he wanted a real Lady of Aumhurst, she could be that one.

Sebastian looked at her, saying nothing. She continued to look at him. He still said nothing. After a time she said "If you want to continue to see me, like this, then we shall have to do something, shan't we"? She smiled at him.

"Ah, Sati, my beautiful Sati", Sebastian said earnestly, still holding her hand, "We *are* going to do something", he said, "But there *is* also more to this, than our meetings together. Although I treasure that".

Sati looked steadily at him. "*Is* there more"? she said. "You just told me you didn't know why you are doing it".

"I don't have to know why, in that way", he said. "And it's not just the paintings, anyhow. It's in the doing of it. The experiencing of it. Art is a metamorphosis of the artist. And it's a metamorphosis of you, too. The painting is the record of a doing, isn't it? It's what we are *doing* here that counts. *This* is the art, Sati. What we are doing together. And we haven't yet discovered everything it means".

"Yes", she said. "I feel that", now looking away from him.

"I'm going to create an exhibition", Sebastian suddenly announced. "Part of it is going to be all twelve of these paintings".

Sati's face lit up. "Ah, yes", she said enthusiastically, "Yes, I absolutely see it now. It's brilliant".

"But that's only part of it, Sati", Sebastian said. "Although I'm not sure what the rest is going to be, yet".

"I expect it will come to you, my dear", Sati smiled, confident that it would.

Even as she spoke, the end of the room where she had been sitting was now devoid of the light that had earlier been coming through the crystal glass window.

The wisps of rainbow colours had gone. The long-case clock was clothed in shadow. The tall vase had become inconsequential. The light had been lost sooner than Sebastian had predicted. Clouds had come in over the mere. Sati and Sebastian both fancied they could hear thunder in the distance.

"The art goes on", Sebastian said. "I can't stop it. Nobody can stop it. And there's a reason why I asked you what you thought about the resemblance".

"What is it"? Sati asked.

"It's the art, Sati. It's ongoing. It never ceases. Everything here is *it*. It's all the art. And somehow, Seraphina was at the beginning of it".

He looked hard at Sati. "And I think she's still here", he said, still looking deep into Sati's beautiful eyes. In that moment, it seemed to him the entire cosmos was within her.

Sati smiled sweetly. "You think I'm Seraphina"? she said gently.

Sebastian continued to look steadily into her eyes.

Still smiling, Sati said simply "Oh", and then she playfully put on a look of disappointment. "You've found me out", she said, jokingly. And then she smiled again.

10

Marsilio

Just a little further around the mere, Springmere, the beautiful residence given to Marsilio by Sebastian, stood with its multiple golden arches in the full aspect of the sunshine most days. There was something about Springmere, that despite the size and stature of the house, was forever playful, almost childlike. It welcomed its visitors like a child welcomes friends into an imaginary world.

Being surrounded by orange groves, in the spring and summer the most beautiful birdsong pervaded Springmere's architectural spaces, daily echoing over the cobblestones of the courtyard within, and reflecting off the surrounding golden stone and lemon yellow walls.

Visitors to Springmere invariably found themselves overcome with feelings of timelessness and happiness, not unlike a return to a blissful childhood. The very walls of Springmere bathing in the sunlight seemed to emanate kindness, and the birdsongs became part of the very fabric of everyone's experience when they were at Springmere.

Something in the very architecture of the building seemed to invoke this change of heart even in the most melancholy person. Those who came to Springmere in search of an enhancement to their philosophy under the guidance of Marsilio, would find something here that evoked joyful thoughts and experiences entirely beyond their more familiar self.

Whilst Sebastian liked to host his intimate meetings with his closest friends at the Harborage, directly overlooking the mere, in order to mutually further their philosophies, it was Marsilio's home, Springmere, that Marsilio himself, as the head of the Pavi Academy, had decreed to be the regular place of meetings of the Academy's inner circle.

A little further around the mere from Springmere was Holm Island. It was not far off the edge of the mere, roughly halfway between Aumhurst and Merehurst. From the shore, the little Holm island looked completely covered in dark green trees, somewhat mysterious, and with a landing jetty visible on the middle of its shoreline.

Most Tuesdays Marsilio would set off from Sringmere's own little boathouse on the bank of the mere adjacent to the edge of the orange groves, and he would row out across the quiet of the mere to Holm Island.

It was a leisurely row this morning, during which Marsilio would think of nothing, but rather, would just be absorbed in the surrounding natural stillness, the dancing reflections of the sunlight on the water, and feel the embrace of the hills and mountains, and of the islands all around. As usual, the etherial glow of the distant horizon was visible between some of the islands, with its blue-tinted far-off mountains.

Today, the water was calm, and the occasional bird would skim silently across the surface of the water. Only the regular, slow and gentle plopping of the oars into the surface of the mere, with Marsilio's slow and constant rhythm, could be heard above the deep peace of the morning.

As Marsilio approached the island's jetty, he noticed there was already another small boat moored there. He was partly disappointed that he would probably not be alone, for his intention was to meditate in private, but he was also partly intrigued.

In a little while, he came into the shore and was tying his boat to the jetty, and then beginning to make his way onto the island. He followed the usual path up to the clearing that he knew offered the most splendid views. As he approached his destination he saw he was indeed not alone.

In the clearing was a little seat, overlooking the most beautiful view, and on it was sitting a little man with a little face as red as a beetroot, but which glowed like the moon. Beside him was a great pile of papers and a few books, and on the ground by him was what looked like an empty bag.

Marsilio approached along the path, and when he reached the man, extended his hand in greeting, introducing himself by saying simply, "Marsilio". The little man got up and shook hands, and then in a moment of what seemed like recognition, completely forgot to give his own name, and instead gave a little bow, saying almost breathlessly, "My goodness me, this must be providence, or fate".

"Why is that"? asked Marsilio.

"It's *the* Marsilio, isn't it? The leader of the Academy"? the little man said.

"If it is the Pavi Academy you are referring to, then you are indeed correct, sir", Marsilio said. Then he gave a little bow himself, to the little man, and said "Marsilio is honoured to meet you".

The man's round little face beamed even more brightly. "No, no, the honour is mine, sir", he said. "You see, I am here to work on my charts", he went on, gesturing to the pile of papers and books on the seat.

"You're an astrologer"? Marsilio ventured, catching sight of the charts.

"Indeed I am, sir", the little man answered proudly.

"Then I hope you will not be too upset at meeting me", Marsilio smiled.

The man's face looked almost shocked."Why should I be upset"? He asked. "I am delighted! I came here to work on my charts, and now, here I am, speaking to the most famous astrologer in all of Pavi Bujdam"!

"Ah", Marsilio said, sitting down on the seat, and as he did so the little man sat too, beside him.

"Well then", Marsilio continued, "Of course I know that you will not have read my private letters, but am I to take it that you have not read the disputations that I have published"?

"Disputations"? the little man answered, his face now wearing a frown, and glowing redder than ever.

"Yes. My disputations against the claims of astrologers".

The little man looked shocked, now. It was as if a lunar eclipse had started to come across the red moon glow of his face. He clearly didn't understand. "I don't understand", he said, and even as the words came out of his mouth, he suddenly felt how he was just confirming to himself how little he knew, rather than communicating anything meaningful to Marsilio.

But then the lunar eclipse passed, and his face glowed again, although now with an altogether more uncomfortable kind of redness. The little man pulled himself together and managed to say "I thought you were Marsilio the astrologer"?

"Please", Marsilio replied, "Don't be surprised. You are not mistaken. Tell me, what are you working on"?

Feeling now a great magnanimity and kindness emanating from Marsilio, the little man's round face seemed to relax more, even though he was still somewhat confused. Having moved into a more comfortable aspect, and now finding himself in a favourable conjunction with the great star Marsilio, he felt immediately inclined to talk about some of his interpretations of the charts.

"Well", he said, enthusiastically shuffling around through the papers and pulling out one of them, "Perhaps I could show you this"? He said. "It's the chart of Lord Aumhurst".

"Is it indeed"? Marsilio replied, as though he was not already completely familiar with it.

"Yes", the little man went on, "And there's something very striking about it, indeed, perhaps worrying about it, that I should very much like you to see", he said.

He thrust the chart in front of Marsilio, his finger pointing to a part of it. "Look at this conjunction", he said, and sliding his finger around the chart, said "And look at these aspects, and this, and this".

He looked at Marsilio to see his reaction. Marsilio took hold of the chart, and looking at it, just nodded. "Indeed", he said. "And what do you think about it"? he asked the little man.

"Well", the man began, "I think anyone with considerable experience in these matters, as I have, would begin to wonder about *this*, wouldn't they?" he said, pointing to the chart. "Look at this multiple conjunction in the eighth house. And the thing is this", he said, looking at Marsilio. "It's rare, but it will occur again this year. And it has something to do with the mere".

"I know", said Marsilio, calmly.

The round moon face of the man shone again, with wider eyes now. "So you know about this"? the man said, excitedly.

"How could I not"? Marsilio answered. "Sebastian is not only my very good friend, he is also my patron".

The moon face shone very red indeed. "Of course", he hastily reprimanded himself. "But what is to be done about it"?

Marsilio smiled and said "My friend, you have not told me your name".

Matter-of-factly, the man said "Ah, yes, Corbius Turnstone, at your service, sir".

"Well, Corbius", said Marsilio, "In what way is it you suppose there is anything to be done about anything"?

Corbius looked most surprised. "This is a bad portent indeed, is it not"? he said. "And Lord Aumhurst is young. For someone with a chart such as this, the forthcoming conjunction later this year doesn't look good does it? I know of many other astrologers who would see this as Lord Aumhurst's end".

"Indeed", said Marsilio. "I know of many, too. But they are mistaken".

"How so"? Corbius asked, astonished. "The signs are clear are they not"?

"Yes, Corbius, but as you said yourself, they are only signs. Far more important is the question of what they are signs of".

"Well, with something as clear as this, isn't that obvious to any astrologer"? Corbius answered.

"I don't think so, Corbius", Marsilio said. "You see, if a man looks at you with a frown on his face, and fire in his eyes, then similarly, these are signs, are they not"?

"Well of course", Corbius said, already sensing that he was beginning to be slowly immersed in something that was not what he expected.

"And if that man", Marsilio continued in the most passive way, "If that man were to commit a murder, then would you say that the cause of the murder was his frown or his eyes"?

"Well, no", Corbius admitted.

"And yet they are signs, are they not"? Marsilio continued.

"They are signs of his intention, I would say", Corbius said.

"So would you say it was his intention, that was the first and root cause of the murder"? Marsilio went on.

Corbius thought for a moment. "Well I don't think we could separate the intention from the man, could we"?

"Indeed not", Marsilio agreed. "But his frown and his eyes are indeed signs of what the man is intending, are they not"?

"Well I would agree with you there", Corbius said.

Marsilio continued, "But are they the *cause* of what the man is about to do"?

"No, they're not", Corbius found himself saying.

Marsilio went on. "And if they are not the cause, then it doesn't necessarily follow just from these signs themselves, does it, that a murder will be committed"?

Corbius' moon face was certainly red and shining now, as he realised himself to now be swimming in something that was quite unfamiliar, but that he quite liked the sensation of.

Marsilio continued. "Because perhaps the fire in his eyes is something other than anger, perhaps some other kind of frenzy, and perhaps the frown, a frown of concentration on the frenzy, or perhaps even some kind of ecstasy"?

Corbius found himself breathless. "Yes I suppose that could be", he said.

Marsilio now gestured gently towards the chart again. "So would it not similarly be a little hasty to pass judgement on these signs here, since these too, are just signs"?

"I... see what you mean..." said Corbius. Now Corbius' face seemed to pass from waxing to waning. "You mean", he said "That these stars and planetary alignments won't cause anything"?

"They are signs", said Marsilio.

"Well yes I *know* they are signs", Corbius replied.

"But what are they are signs *of*"? Marsilio said.

"Excuse me...", Corbius replied with some indignation, for a moment forgetting he was speaking to the man he himself considered the great Marsilio. "I think I know my astrological signs pretty well", he said.

"That's clear", Marsilio said, "But what I am referring to is not what you are referring to".

Now Corbius' face positively lit up and began to shine again, and with a renewed keen interest he said "I see, this is perhaps an area of astrology that I haven't come across. I don't think anyone I know has come across it! How exciting"!

Corbius considered the possibilities. "Do tell me what they are referring to", he said. If he could learn it, it could really make his name. But Marsilio's answer came from beyond his sphere of thought.

"We are speaking of the soul", Marsilio said.

Corbius felt mentally breathless again. It was as if he was trying to hold together a loosely made straw structure whilst skating on ice. His head was now beginning to spin. His encounter with the great Marsilio seemed to have brought him into an unexpected experience, but he nevertheless felt a kind of deep light that emanated from Marsilio, one that he was enjoying, but felt he couldn't keep up with.

"But it is our human affairs that we need to keep abreast of, isn't it"? Corbius managed to say. "By being able to predict our forthcoming difficulties and advantages"?

"You cannot understand the meaning of the stars in terms of human affairs", Marsilio said. "This conjunction in the eighth house, for example, what is it that determines where the eighth house is"?

Now Corbius was excited that he was under instruction from the great Marsilio. And he had been asked something he knew the answer to. "Well", he began, "It is determined by the exact time and place of Lord Aumhurst's birth", he said.

Marsilio said "But is that not determined by the rotation of the Earth around its axis, in relation to the Sun, and the position of Lord Aumhurst's birth on the planet Earth, within that picture. Is this not so"?

Corbius thought a little, he thought about how to work out where the eighth house is, and about time, and about the rotation of the Earth, and then saw that Marsilio was indeed right. "Yes, that is so", he said.

Marsilio continued to speak gently. "And the time of Lord Aumhurst's birth amounts to nothing more than the positions of all the celestial bodies, as he is born, does it not"?

Corbius frowned and thought hard again, he thought about clocks, and minutes and seconds dividing up the day, and days, and years, and conceded that Marsilio must be right. "I think that is so", he said.

"And does the Sun move or is it stationary"? asked Marsilio.

"Well", said Corbius again, "It appears to move from the Earth. But scientifically speaking, it does not move".

"But everything moves", Marsilio said. His answer was quite un-expected by Corbius, and he raised his eyebrows. Marsilio continued, "How fickle we are! "First we thought the firmament is fixed and moves only on its sphere which is moving around the Earth", said Marsilio. "Then we thought the Sun was at the centre, and we said that the firmament does not move at all", he went on. "But Corbius, the truth is that the whole universe is moving, it is all expanding. Our solar system is just one of many in our galaxy. There are more planets in our galaxy than there are stars. The stars in our own galaxy are all together rotating around a black hole at the centre of our galaxy. And the same is true for other galaxies. And the galaxies are rotating in clusters, and the clusters in superclusters. Everything is attracted back to its attractor, its Source, Corbius. It is all Divine providence".

Corbius could not answer. He remembered now that Marsilio was not only an astrologer, but also, a philosopher and a theologian.

Marsilio was looking at the chart. "It's not about predictions for Lord Aumhurst and his personal affairs, Corbius, because it is not about his person".

"But what is it about then"? Corbius asked.

Marsilio answered "What is important is how Lord Aumhurst is attracted to his Source. These celestial souls and spheres", he said, waving at the chart, "Are all simply seeking their Source, Corbius, in order that they may return to perfection and become one with God, for they have been created through God's providence, from His preeminence".

"I see", Corbius said, without seeing at all.

Marsilio pointed to the sparkling mere. "See the light from the Sun", he said. "See how it sparkles as a million tiny, reflected suns on the surface of the mere".

Corbius looked out onto the water, and there were indeed millions of tiny suns playing on the surface of the water, as it rippled.

"How many suns do you see there"? Marsilio asked.

Corbius swallowed and managed to answer "They are innumerable. I cannot count them".

"Indeed so", confirmed Marsilio. "You couldn't count them, even if you tried, because they are constantly moving, dancing, always in play, coming to be and ceasing to be. Each is only the reflection of the one Sun. The whole arises because of the action of the Sun on the water. This is like the providence, Corbius, it is the Good, and the Beautiful. Is not this interaction of the Sun with the things of its own making, beautiful"?

Corbius gazed into the illuminated water. "It *is* beautiful", he said, overcome with the ever flickering, dancing play of it, and yet also the stillness of it.

"Just as you, and I, here, are also of its making", said Marsilio.

Corbius was still absorbed in the beauty of the dancing play of scintillating light on the water. Something about it had seemed to come out of it to pull him into it. He just said, still staring into it, "Yes", it is indeed beautiful".

"Who is this one who sees this"? Marsilio asked.

"It is Corbius Turnstone", answered Corbius.

"And how well do you know this one"? asked Marsilio.

"I have a very good knowledge of my birth chart", came the answer.

"And do you not long to know your creator"? Marsilio asked.

Corbius was struck dumb.

"Perhaps you have not yet discovered", Marsilio continued, "The ocean of the streams of stories of love, and the ocean of beautiful places, through which you come to be sitting here, now, looking at the play of the light of the Sun, upon the water of the mere"?

Corbius remained contemplating, looking out across the water, pondering deeply the sparkling sunlight on it. There, as he gazed, he watched the seemingly everlasting myriad of tiny, miniature suns, following on and disappearing from each other in an endless play of coming and going. He seemed to enter a deep state of contentment, happiness, and not needing to know anything. He now seemed to be deeply happy just to be sitting with Marsilio. And as he became deeply immersed the sparkling reflections any problem he had thought to be associated with Lord Aumhurst's chart, seemed now to evaporate.

The two sat in silence. After a little while, and after a number of birds had flown silently across the sparkling reflections, some restlessness then arose in Corbius again, and he was about to ask a question. But before he could muster the words, both astrologers were drawn away from their philosophising, as their attention was directed to the shore just across the water, towards the sound of thundering hooves racing along the edge of the mere.

Two beautiful and powerful thoroughbreds were charging in the direction of Aumhurst, the manic cloud of dust from their frenzied hooves billowing behind them. Marsilio was perhaps more familiar with the terrain there, which he knew to be the Silver Gallop. For a moment he thought the horses had bolted, and were out of control, for they appeared to be heading straight towards the tall boundary fence, rather than the gap.

Corbius was no horseman, but even he could see the situation. He was convinced he was about to witness the result of a terrible transiting aspect, and his gaze froze in horror as he watched before him the unfolding of a seemingly inevitable fate which must have been brought about through the most unfavourable of stars.

Both Marsilio and Corbius watched. They watched in silence as the two horses and their riders went hurtling towards the boundary fence and their apparently inescapable demise, but then ascended into the air over the fence with super-equine grace and power, and somehow, recovering from the terrifyingly steep descent that followed, raced on to the end of Silver Gallop.

11

The Harborage

Sebastian, when painting, had more than once thought how often underestimated is the power of light to transform our state of being, perhaps because its effects are not always felt in the same way by everyone. But for the friends who would meet in the Harborage its effects were certainly always appreciated.

Being so close to the water, there was often a very pure quality to the light in the Harborage rooms overlooking the mere. This morning was certainly no exception. The sun was shining directly in through the beautiful oriel windows. The incoming light direct from the Sun joined the reflected sun coming straight off the rippling surface of the mere, so that the walls and ceiling of the room were flooded with an extraordinary, gently moving light. Its patterns rippled on the walls and ceiling of the beautiful interior of the room like a tinted play of tacit stories, perhaps of love and place, somewhere from where the light was coming, which was of course only the surface of the mere.

Timaeus was just finishing the task of tuning his twelve-stringed lyre. Amba and Ambika together with Sandhya were standing at the desk behind Timaeus, examining some sheets of music, whilst Sebastian had been preparing an easel and some paintings which he had placed on the small podium.

The chiming of the Old World clock soon signalled the start of the meeting and Sebastian stood to address the little assembly. On these more informal and intimate occasions the friends were accustomed to simply beginning the meeting without any prelude. Members of the group would have speeches prepared, which they then delivered to the group as a whole. Today, Sebastian himself was to start the proceedings.

The rest of the group made themselves comfortable as Sebastian stepped back onto the little podium next to the easel beside the paintings currently turned with their backs to his audience. He began his speech.

"I wanted to talk today about light", he said, and then, smiling, went on "At least, that's how we'll start, because I know from experience how our philosophising explorations tend to develop". He smiled in amusement.

There was some quiet laughter in recognition.

He reached down to one of the paintings and put it onto the easel for all to see. It was a painting of the mere, with some of the islands.

"You might recognise this from the exhibition I had earlier this year", Sebastian said. "If you remember, the exhibition was called *painting in light*. You may also remember I had published a letter in which I said that I myself and a number of other painters I know consider that the world is made of light. And I wanted to say a little bit more about it now. Because some people who spoke to me wanted to know how it is, that as an artist, you can so easily see the world as made of light. One quite mundane way, of course, is that in painting you do have to portray light through paints that in fact absorb light, as well as reflect it, but it must be done as though the light in the painting is radiant in the way that it is in the world itself. But there is more to it, than this".

At this point Amba raised her hand, and Sebastian invited her to speak. "I like the idea", she said, "That the world is made of light. But perhaps it would be good to say something about how this might be in a way that is not just dependent on how an artist looks at it visually".

"Indeed", said Sebastian. "A very good point. This is what I was coming to. After all, we're not all visual artists, here, but we *are* all artists, of one kind or another". He seemed to be contemplating for a moment. "As you probably know I have come to be convinced recently that we are all taking part in a great art that we are not necessarily conscious of. An art that I now think sources back to Seraphina Bassenthwaite. In a way, you could say, in as much as her art was a manifestation from her own mind, so it is that we, too, and our world, are not just her continuing artwork, but she is in some way who we are. And since that would also be true of anything she created, perhaps we are, as it were, mixed from everything she has created, similarly to how everything in a painting is mixed from everything that comes to make the painting, both the paints, and the picture itself. In a way, I am saying, if we are talking about the world being made of light, then Seraphina Bassenthwaite could be called an original light. Perhaps not the origin of all, perhaps not the One that Marsilio speaks of, but nonetheless a light of inspiration and a light of understanding. And from her came a flow of creativity.

"If you can bear with me, I would just ask, can you allow that everything is made of light in a way that is not just related to our seeing, but also to our understanding? There is, after all, a connection, which is why we sometimes speak of understanding as seeing. And we often speak of the light of understanding, do we not?

"So we are saying that everything is made of light. This is in the sense that everything we can see and understand essentially involves light, even at night time, or if we are not talking about light we can visually see, then it involves some kind of understanding, even where there is very little understanding. Without light of either kind we cannot see or understand anything. And whilst this certainly applies to what we can see with our eyes, it is also metaphorically true of what we see with our understanding.

"You see, in my view, the light of understanding itself is only as much what we might call light, in this way, as it contains in some way light itself. And ultimately, I believe, this is the light - to call it that - from which everything comes and is made. If and when there is only this light, then what is there to understand?

"I am saying that everything we understand as something separate from the light of our understanding itself, is something that then appears itself, to us, not to be that light. There is a kind of separation. But I am saying this separation is only an appearance.

"The way in which it is made from the original light is something that the understanding we are using now, cannot itself, throw any light on, so to speak. So what is the original light? It is what I believe to be none other than the Good and the Beautiful that we sometimes hear Marsilio speak of.

"And so you see, that light itself, whether we are talking about the light we can see such as I directly represent in my paintings, or the light of our understanding when we understand anything including a painting in whatever way we understand it, whichever light we are talking about, the light is a symbol. I am saying that even the light of scientific understanding is a symbol.

"I am saying that light as we see it with our eyes, or the light of our understanding, is not just a symbol of an original light, but it is also a symbol of something that is in-between the original and the way in which we see or understand. And what I am calling the in-between is the way in which what we have here, as our own existence in Pavi Bujdam, and our being here, comes about. This, I believe, is none other than the artwork of Seraphina Bassenthwaite. Some people have said to me that this doesn't make sense. But this is only the case if you think of Seraphina Bassenthwaite, as it were, as "one of us", or as a resident of Pavi Bujdam. But she is not, she is not that kind of being. She's not so limited. And in that way, everything we have here, the whole of Pavi Bujdam, is her, inasmuch as it is her ongoing work of art".

Amba now interjected. "But there are portraits of her on the walls of Aumhurst. I wouldn't say she doesn't look like one of us. In fact, she looks just like Sati".

Sebastian laughed. "Yes, well spotted, Amba", he said cheerily. "That's true, but if you look at the pictures in the Long Gallery you'll see there are also some paintings of horses with wings. In the paintings those creatures look perfectly reasonable, and realistic, to me, but as you know, they don't really exist, at least, not in that way. The pictures stand for something. They are just a depiction. Why shouldn't Seraphina be depicted like one of us? This doesn't mean that she is necessarily such a limited being".

Amba replied immediately, "But why does she look like Sati"?

"Well", Sebastian said, "That's a very good question, but it's not really what I wanted to talk about in this meeting".

Sebastian turned back towards the painting on the easel, and gestured towards it. He continued with his talk. "When we look at a painting, then, visually, or corporeally", he said, "We are just looking at light. To go beyond, we have to understand the nature of light itself in a most immaterial way, as I have been saying".

Ambika now asked "But how does everything you are saying apply to your sculptures"?

Sebastian continued. "I'm not just concerned with making likenesses that, as it were, remind you of whatever it is I'm making a likeness of. Because that is all just about the corporeal or material light that we can see. And the same is true when we are talking about the light of under-standing. If you look at the persons here in the gardens of Aumhurst, the point of them is not just to look like persons, visually. It's not just for understanding that way. If that was the case, then what would be the point? After all, there is already a plentiful supply of persons in Pavi Bujdam, isn't there?".

Sebastian's little audience laughed.

"So that brings me to the next thing", he continued.

"You've all seen them, the so-called persons. They are all a work of art, and it is ongoing. It's not that I haven't finished the sculptures, I have. But where they are in the gardens, and people encountering them, is all an ongoing work of art.

"Are they beings, or not? You might say they are made of stuff that is not-being. The bronze, and the stone. But I'm not concerned with them as something that is not-being. Whenever I'm engaged in any art, I'm only concerned with being. But I don't think that's necessarily true of all artists.

"You see, as I see it, there are two kinds of artist in Pavi Bujdam. The philosopher and the sophist. Which one do you think I am?

"Unless you realise that it is part of an ongoing art, then stone or bronze is not-being, you see. But it is being if you understand it as part of an art. Just as I said I am concerned with being, so I think that what the sophists are really concerned with is the nature of not-being and what you can do with it, what you can recreate with it, or what images or sculptures you can create with it. Or what complicated things you can say about it. That is their artistry.

"You might say that stone or bronze, like I have used for the persons in the gardens, is not-being. Unlike a human being, who is being. And in as much as you just see it as bronze or stone, you would be right. But I'm not concerned with that. I'm only concerned with being. Because I'm the first kind of artist, like all of us here, I am a lover of truth, I am a philosopher. It's not the sophistry that I can come up with, as a person, that I am interested in. What I am interested in is a different kind of artistry, a Divine artistry, if you like, as I would call it, a kind of frenzy, or the continuation of an art that is already alive and ongoing. And as I have said, I believe it is all a continuation of the art of Seraphina.

"I sculpt with bronze and stone, and I paint with paints. Which I make from ground up mundane substances called minerals. Which you might say are substances of not-being. But as a philosopher and an artist I say that everything is made from light, and I call that light, as part of the ongoing art, being. Even when it has become what appears to be not-being, like the stone, and the paints.

"And you might want to say *how has it become so*? How can being become not-being? Except perhaps by some kind of death. But I say it is the other way around. I say it is through some kind of death, or death zone, that not-being is transformed into being. I don't yet know what that is, but I do believe that Marsilio and Belvoir know something about this".

Sandhya now raised her hand, and Sebastian invited her to speak. "Where does the being in us, our own being, our own light, and life, or even light of understanding, really come from? Does it come out of the stuff from which we are made, the stuff of chemicals and so on, that appear to be the stuff of non-being? As the scientists say it does"?

Sebastian answered her. "It may surprise you to hear that I say it does. But unlike the scientists I also say that this is only possible because what appears to be non-being is only like darkness relative to light. It is like shadow. It has no meaning other than in relation to the light. Because everything, ultimately is still made from light, as I said at the beginning, even if it has become darkness, which really, is just the artistry having become nothing but sophistry".

Now Sebastian paused. He looked around his little audience. "I have perhaps gone a little too far now. Would anyone like to contribute? He enquired.

"I should like to say something", Ambika said. "I feel I agree with what you've said, but then, what you are talking about is not the kind of thing we commonly encounter people talking about when, say, we are walking through the Pavi market. Most people, I think, understand Pavi Bujdam, as the place in which we live, without any conscious knowledge of this Divine artistry that you are talking about, and the point is, that in order to live well, or at least try to live well, that's all they need to understand. They only need to understand Pavi Bujdam, in the way that they do, and that, they do well enough".

Sebastian nodded. And then he gave his answer.

"I am inclined to say", he began, "The opposite. I am inclined to say that almost nobody in Pavi Bujdam really understands Pavi Bujdam at all. Because almost nobody is interested in raising their understanding, let alone going beyond it into what I am calling the light. Present company excepted, of course.

"We don't just live in a world we call Pavi Bujdam, we also live in the world of our own understanding. Is that not so? Each of us, individually, and also collectively. And we don't generally see that the way we understand our world, is just an expression of the limited nature of our own understanding".

Sebastian waited for Ambika's response. "So...", Ambika now interjected quite enthusiastically, "It seems to me that because we also have a hand in making Pavi Bujdam, as a place to live, because to some extent we build what it is, and the way it is, then... I think what you are saying is that because the nature of our understanding is limited, then we must be limited in what we are making out of Pavi Bujdam. We build the places, we build our society, and the way it works, but what we are doing is limited because of the limited nature of our understanding. Is that what you are saying"?

"Exactly so", Sebastian confirmed.

Amba now joined in. "But why do we not all just band together and overcome this limitation? I would say even the people you are calling sophists have a good understanding of things, in their own particular way. I am sure we would all work well towards the same end", she said.

Sebastian waited for an answer to be forthcoming but the little group remained silent. So he now continued "Well, we have talked about philosophers, like us, and we have talked about the sophists. They are artists who make artistic creations, but who, I say, are doing so without any real knowledge of the light. So they are often people who say beguiling things, that appear to be very clever, but truly, is without any real knowledge of the light".

His little audience nodded.

"Well, there is a third kind in Pavi Bujdam, also. A kind we could call the un-sophists. And they are by far the greatest number, I think. They are certainly not philosophers, like we are, but nor are they sophists. Rather, they see Pavi Bujdam according to how they are brought up to see it, and only according to how they have been taught, by others of their kind. When they come to my exhibitions they judge my work merely according to whether they personally like it or don't like it. And they love to group themselves into networks of like-minded people.

"They tend to see things in terms of simple questions, such as is something *this*, or *that*? Do we agree, or disagree? Should we follow, or not follow? Do we like, or not like? Shall we give this the thumbs up, or the thumbs down? And they are encouraged to continue to be like this by the nature of Pavi Bujdam itself, because it has largely been built, essentially, in a way that can be understood by, and appeals to, the un-sophists".

Now Timaeus, who had been listening quietly, decided to speak up. "I must say I know many people in Pavi Bujdam whom I would not say are philosophers like us, but also certainly not the kind that you describe as un-sophists. Their ways of thinking and understanding are certainly sophisticated. And yet I also don't think they are sophists, as you describe. They are invariably scientists, and I work with some of them. So they are not really philosophers like us, nor are they as you describe sophists, but they are also not as you describe un-sophists. I was just wondering how we might relate what you are saying to scientists and science, which seems to me to be so important"?

"That's a very good question, Timaeus", Sebastian answered. "Because this is very much related to science. And not just to the arts. But my answer might be quite involved, so you would have to bear with me. Do you really want to hear it"?

12

Sebastian on Science

"Go ahead by all means", Timaeus said.

"Well it seems to me", Sebastian began again, "That right across Pavi Bujdam we live in a world of understanding in which it is commonly thought that a thing either is or is not. That it either exists or does not exist. People seem to think that something must either be or not be. That it is either true or false.

The masses of people here in general believe for example, that something is either right or wrong, or that something is either the truth or not the truth. Or that someone is either lying or telling the truth.

So we see all the endless occurrences of expressions of opinion in terms of *like* versus *not like*, or thumbs up versus thumbs down. The un-sophists value binary opinion very highly. And they think truth can be decided on the basis of majority opinion, of precisely that kind. They vote for, or against. And in every vote there is either a majority, or not. And so largely, this is how life as I see it around me, proceeds, on Pavi Bujdam. And when they are voting, if they cannot get the majority, there is some kind of coalition, which they then think is bad, rather than good. Or perhaps there are some who think it is good, rather than bad.

This is how the un-sophists think. And as a result, they are very easily divided, one faction against another, and then led by the sophists, who themselves pretend to be un-sophists, in favour of this or that, in order to divide them and lead them, in this way.

And then this principle becomes convoluted in a way that no one really sees, because there are so many different issues that the un-sophists can be for, or against. Eventually, sophists can become leaders, not just of their own particular following, but of a whole Vicinage. I believe this is what has happened over the other side of Pavi Bujdam, around Gsoaf.

Each leader, or group of leaders, that the un-sophists call politicians, or parties, exhibit to the un-sophist crowd, their own collection of stances that the un-sophists see as what the leaders are for, or against. And this has been going on for so long now that many un-sophists themselves now also become leaders. And mixed in with the un-sophist leaders are also sophists, whose stances the un-sophist crowd cannot understand, when, being sophists, they shift their position. And so the un-sophist crowd judge the sophists, in the usual way, as either lying or telling the truth.

In the world of understanding in which the un-sophists live, it is not possible to do the right thing, and also be making a mistake. So they cannot conceive that it is actually possible for the right decision to also be the wrong decision. Or for the wrong decision to also be the right decision. They cannot conceive that there might be no right or wrong in the bigger picture. Especially if they already have an opinion about what is right, and what is wrong.

They live according to an idea that boxes them in, and protects them from having to raise their understanding. They uphold the idea of right and wrong as something they can try to follow, and believe others should follow. They believe that this right and wrong exists in such a way that if only everybody followed the right, then the world would have no wrong in it.

And because they believe that everyone in Pavi Bujdam is basically the same, in this way, they also believe that anything anyone says must be either be a lie or the truth. And they do all this without any inspiration to deepen their understanding, to begin with.

And so they are the quickest to vilify anyone they judge to be a liar, without ever seeing that what emerges from their own mouths only emerges from this very lack of understanding. And so it is never the truth, even when it is not a lie".

"I've never heard you speak like this before", Ambika said.

"No", Sebastian replied, "But recently I have come to see these aspects in the interior of Pavi Bujdam. Although they do also tend to be concentrated over the other side, around Gsoaf".

Ambika replied, "Do please continue".

"I was saying", Sebastian went on, "Being boxed in, as it were, in this way, most people in Pavi Bujdam have excluded the possibility that this whole world in which we are living comes from something that both is, and isn't. They cannot conceive that it comes about through principles of things that both exist, and yet do not exist".

"What things are you talking about, Sebastian"? Timaeus asked. "Are you referring to what is beyond the mere"?

"In one way I am", Sebastian said, "But in a more immediate way I'm talking about the way the scientists see things".

"Ah, yes", Timaeus said, "Please go on".

Sebastian continued "The un-sophists do not understand that there is something that can be true and exists, and yet is not true, and does not exist. They would consider that an absurdity. Whilst not realising that the way they themselves understand this world in which we live, through their opinion, and placing so much importance on opinion, and then on mass opinion, is, for the most part, an absurdity. And really, this is where we come to science.

We, the people of Pavi Bujdam, pursue our science, which brings us so much benefit. Except that we don't know what is beyond the mere. Do you see what I mean? We don't even know what is beyond the mere. And yet we think we know so much.

So most of the people in Pavi Bujdam, the majority, who are un-sophists, have already stopped the potential of their own understanding in its tracks. Because they believe the nature of the world in which we live, Pavi Bujdam, is something they already understand. It doesn't even occur to them that it may be possible to raise their understanding. And hence change their situation. Through a greater understanding of their own situation. They continue to see the world as based on the principle that something must be either true or not true, or a lie or the truth, and that something must always either exist, or not exist.

And yet from our science itself, we do actually understand, already, just as they already did even in the Old World, as I understand it, that everything in our world, which extends to this whole universe, is veritably made from that which is true and exists, and yet is not true, and does not exist. Until, that is, it is observed. This, the scientists of Pavi Bujdam say, is the nature of what they call the quantum particles, which are the foundation building blocks not just of the whole of Pavi Bujdam, but of everything we know of.

We have had for centuries now, the understanding in science, that something can exist and yet not exist, until it is observed, but still we are unable to see the nature of our world in the right way, because we still cannot understand what it *means* that our world has come about in this way, which indeed it has, even according to the science".

Ambika now spoke up. "But what does this mean in terms of how we relate to each other? What about love"?

Sebastian went on, "I have talked about this with both Marsilio and Belvoir. And we came to the view that the people in general, the un-sophists and even the sophists, know nothing of how love is entangled in this situation. The scientists, for example, think that they already understand love, and that love comes out of the evolution of the brains in our heads. Which they think definitely exists, rather than does not exist. Because what they take to be existence, is what we can know and encounter, and scientifically measure, even though it is in the painting, as it were, made by the painter in our head, so to speak, that they call brain function.

And they do not take into account that this very evolution they speak of is itself made from what both is, and yet is not. They do not know that the very way in which through this brain, we have our experience of being here, on Pavi Bujdam, is through the play and development of something that is, and yet is not.

And yet this play of what both is and yet is not, is at the basis of our whole existence. It is so fundamental, that it is even represented and symbolised in what science understands as the very foundation on which our world is built, that is, the quantum particle. Even in the Old World they knew this, they knew all about the nature of the smallest things from which our world is made, the things the scientists call quantum particles, and yet we still do not see what this means.

Most people in Pavi Bujdam don't see that everything is a symbol, or symbolic. But to those who know the light I have been speaking of, our world is veritably *made* of symbols. Look at any of my paintings in the galleries, and I can tell you, they are full of symbolism. As are many other works of art, by other artists. If you don't see the symbols, then what will you see? You will see the figures and the things in the painting. And what are these? They are an imitation, in paint, of something in what most people might call 'real life'. But I say this so-called 'real life' is itself a kind of imitation of something you can only perceive when you know the light that I am talking about".

"This is very interesting to me", Timaeus said, "Because as it happens, in my very deepest mathematical thought, at the very edges of what I and some of my colleagues study, I think I do often think symbolically, rather than in terms of whether something may be true or untrue".

"Yes", Sebastian said, "Exactly. I can understand that, even as an artist, rather than a mathematician".

Now, at last, Sandhya spoke. "Sebastian, you were saying about how love is entangled in our situation, and then you went on to talk about how the world is made from what both exists and yet does not exist. But you didn't really say any more about why love is not just explained by evolution, in the way the scientists say. Would you like to say something more about that"?

"Thank you Sandhya, of course", Sebastian replied. "What I was saying really comes from conversations I have been having with Belvoir.

It's quite a rare opportunity to get to talk to him, and it was some time ago, but we were talking about this very thing. And I must say straight away that what I am saying about it now, is based on what he said.

At the time, Belvoir convinced me of what he was saying. And it now seems to me that many people here in Pavi Bujdam are misled by beliefs about love, based on what is essentially a masquerade. A masquerade of scientific knowledge, and the technologies it leads to. They regard the evolutionary precursors to our love, as the explanation of our love or where it comes from. But the truth, if you know the light, is that it is just a symbol of what is going on in a great process, a great play of appearances, of what appears to be, but really, is not, that we ourselves, only identify with by mistake. It is because we mistakenly identify with this play, that we never allow ourselves to discover the truth of our own love, and what, and who, it is, we really love. But if you want to know more about this, then I think it best that you talk to Belvoir. He seemed to have the deepest knowledge of it".

Amba now said "How do you say this relates to our brains, then, since scientifically speaking, what we experience, including love, is a matter of brain function? How is this related to the light that you speak of"?

Sebastian continued, "I would say that this world that we are experiencing, in terms of the nature of the way it appears to us, which is the matter of it, is a creation, like a painting, made from a painter, so to speak, that our scientists call brain function. And everything I have said about art, and artists, and the light, applies to that".

Amba now said "I like the idea that brain function is like a painter or an artist. Perhaps we should say more about that".

Sebastian continued "Almost no one in Pavi Bujdam truly understands, you see. We think we understand Pavi Bujdam, and then we think we understand the cosmos and our place in it, and yet we cannot even see beyond the mere. How many of these great knowers and observers that talk so much in Pavi Bujdam, know what is beyond the mere? Some of the sophists of course, pretend to, but we are fools if we believe them. I am not criticising the scientists, by the way. We can, and we should be, grateful to the scientists. We should be grateful for the new sciences and technologies. I myself enjoy these, and over the past year have been creating something with them. But in general I find the scientists are not even interested, or only tangentially interested, in what is beyond the mere. They are simply convinced that it is not a real question, and that the Visitors are really just coming from the farthest islands. And I think that in truth, what the scientists bring us, does not come from them alone. It comes from all of us, and is inspired by the Visitors. *They* bring the knowledge of it, from what beyond the mere".

Sebastian now turned round and pointed in the direction behind the Harborage. "Just up on the hill there, behind the Harborage, is the Aumhurst Observatory. From there, you can look out and see what the scientists call the cosmos. But if you lower the telescope and look straight across the mere, you still cannot see what is beyond it. The scientists seem to forget that what they call the cosmos is just an ornament, and that the very word cosmos means ornament".

Now Sebastian's pace of speaking was quickening. He seemed to become a little frenzied. "And I'm sure, as Marsilio or Belvoir would say, if they were here, ornaments don't need to move, in order to be an ornament. But beneath it, here, in Pavi Bujdam, we are all engaged in movement, aren't we? Through our movement we can explore the whole of Pavi Bujdam. And some of the islands on the mere. But if we try to go beyond Pavi Bujdam, then everywhere, in any direction, we encounter the mere. Because we are trying to go further, only through movement. Rather than with sufficiently great speed, perhaps unheard of speed, at exactly the right time and in the right weather".

"Sebastian, Sebastian", interrupted Timaeus now, "What is this frenzy? I think now you are going a little too fast, except perhaps, for yourself. Certainly, for us".

"Am I"? said Sebastian apologetically. "I know I do tend to do that. Sometimes it's because there are several threads running in my mind, at once, and they kind of accidentally cross over. Well, I think we are now coming off the subject, so I think we should perhaps move on".

13

Pareidolia

Now Sebastian turned around towards the easel behind him and removed the cloth that had been covering the painting. As his back was turned to his audience, he said quietly, "And yet, I think, if we *can* go fast enough, in the right way, at the right time, in the right weather, we *can* get across the mere". No one could hear clearly what he was saying.

The cloth fell to the floor. And now there were murmurs of delight from his audience. The painting was like a magnet to everyone. The beautiful plays of colours, and forms, and ideas, all in something as seemingly simple as a wonderful landscape. With its ominous, billowing clouds, tall above the vivid green of the rolling hills beneath, clouds whose edges betrayed the diffraction of light, in rainbow colours. And beneath, the rolling bright green hills falling away towards an azure sea far in the distance.

Sandhya's voice was heard from the back of the room. "It's amazing", she said, "I feel I recognise that person, but I cannot at all think of who they are".

There was laughter from the other members of the audience. They were appreciative of Sandhya's wry sense of humour, or so they thought. But Sandhya looked a little bewildered at their response.

Sebastian, who had himself been looking at the painting, turned around to face his audience. "No no", he said firmly, "Sandhya is not joking, are you"? he said, looking at Sandhya.

"What's so funny"? she asked, bemused, looking around the others for an explanation of their mirth.

"If I might interject", Sebastian said. "Sandhya is quite right", he went on. "Perhaps, Sandhya, if you come closer and study the painting a little, you might come to see something", he said.

Sandhya got up and came to stand in front of the painting, contemplating it. And then she gasped. "Oh"! she said. "This is amazing"!

Now Amba and Ambika, together, let out similar exclamations. "It *is* a person"! Amba declared. "And yet it's a landscape"! And now Timaeus got up, walked forward, and soon gave a similar reaction.

"This is extraordinary", Timaeus declared. "In a way, it is demonic, but not in a bad way I would hasten to add". He looked up and grinned at Sebastian. "I am beginning to think you are a sorcerer, though, Sebastian".

Now from the covert position behind the table, Sebastian pulled out another painting, and placed it in front of the first. It was just a few brushstrokes, but it was also clear that it was a bird rising up into the air, above water. The simplicity and artistry of it was strikingly beautiful.

"You see", said Sebastian, "But it's not a bird at all", he said, "Is it"? He smiled. "Not literally, I mean. If you look at it, it's just a few brushstrokes, which in themselves, really, don't look anything like a bird looks".

He now quickly pulled out a photograph, and put it in front. It, too, was a landscape, and above it was a dramatic sky with clouds. "I took this just the other other day", he said. "There is no trickery, it is a straightforward, simple photograph. What do you see"?

The others laughed. Stretched out across the sky in the stuff of pillowy clouds, was the unmistakable typical form of a reclining, aloof cat.

"It's just chance, of course", said Sebastian. "It looks like some kind of magic, or design, when you see something like this in the clouds, but it's all in our brain, our mind, it's just the way we are pre-configured to interpret certain patterns or visual clues", he said. "It's what we call pareidolia".

"Your painting isn't just chance though, is it"? said Sandhya. "And in the painting there is more than one thing, that it can be".

"Indeed", answered Sebastian. "I am just exploiting the principle, you see. Actually, it's the principle of the brain".

He took both the photograph and the painting of the bird away and put them back on the floor. "What we see, and what we understand, is always a kind of recognition. And what we recognise is always something already in our mind, or our brain, or something that can be made up from what's in there".

"It is remarkable", said Timaeus. "It seems to me, after all, that if what we are seeing in the world around us makes sense to us in terms of what we already know, and how our brain processes are already working, and given that we have this tendency to always try to make sense of what we encounter, in this way, then surely we must be doing this with everything? So I now see what you were saying earlier, about how what we are understanding is not really separate from the nature of our understanding. The world itself, in a way, then, you could say, is almost just a mirror of our understanding".

"Exactly so", said Sebastian. "But not almost. It is, completely".

Sandhya now said "But I think you are both missing something here. You said yourself, Sebastian, that the world is like a painting created through the paints of our brain function, as it were. I am inclined to agree with you. But then, you see, we are not experiencing a painting of the world are we? Rather, the world itself, is the painting isn't it?

Timaeus now replied. "I would agree with you", he said. "Except that I can't see how the world is just a creation of my brain function, a kind of painting made by it, because I don't see that Sebastian's painting will cease to exist when I go to sleep, or that if I were to turn my back on your beautiful painting, Sebastian, that the painting would just disappear. Indeed, if we were to *all* leave this room, I do not believe the painting would disappear".

Now Sandhya suddenly seemed to be in some kind of frenzy. "No", she said. "Indeed. But I would say that this is because the painting made by our brain is part of the world, and the world continues to be as it is, whether or not we are perceiving it".

"I would say that is definitely the case", said Timaeus. "But then how is it that the world is also a creation, a painting, made by our brain function"?

"Because" said Sandhya, now more enthusiastic and perhaps with even more signs of frenzy, "As I see it, none of us, each with our individual brain, is the true artist. Rather, we are all apprentices. But we are not like painters' apprentices would be here, on Pavi Bujdam. Rather, there is one artist, and the artist is creating all of us. He or she is painting each of us, as a version of himself or herself. And then we are painting the world, each in our own way, and yet at the same time, it is painted by the artist who paints us. But rather like your painting on the easel here, Sebastian, each of us is painted by the one artist in such a way that we have two aspects. It is as if you were able to paint, as you have done, Sebastian, many more of these paintings, each one a different portrait, one for each person, but each one also the same land-scape of the world, albeit a different aspect, a different scene of it, each time. But this can only be seen by the original artist. Each of us, as the portrait, then proceeds to paint our own version of the one landscape, and this is the world we each see".

Now it was Ambika's turn to join in. "I think I can see what you are saying", she said, "But I wonder then how our private experiences of the world would relate to what is publicly experienced. I don't think that what is publicly experienced is just the sum of private experiences".

"It certainly isn't", said Timaeus. "I think it is the other way around. I think what we privately experience, that is, the way we privately experience the world, is a private experience of something we call the world, that itself does not depend on anyone's experiencing of it. Our brain may be painting the world, the world that we experience, but somehow, that painting doesn't seem to be entirely dependent on the painter in our head. I just don't believe the world depends on our experiencing of it".

Sandhya quickly replied. "It doesn't", she said. "And yet it does. As I said, it depends on the one artist painting it. The artist who has painted us all. But she has painted us all in such a way that our portrait, so to speak, the identity of each one of us as the person in the portrait, is inseparable from the landscape of the world that she has also painted".

Ambika spoke again. "That's all very well, but then, who is this one artist"?

Sandhya replied "That's for us to find out. After all, the one artist, if you remember, I said creates all of us, each as a different portrait of the artist. So it is a question of finding out who we really are, or of whom we are a portrait, isn't it? Really, we are all different images of the one artist".

Sebastian now turned to Amba, who had remained silent. "Amba", he said, "I should like to know what you think about this".

Amba smiled her beautiful smile. "I think that if Sati was here, she would settle the matter", Amba replied. "But as she is not, I should say that I suppose...". and Amba now began to think. "I suppose", she continued, "It is a matter of time, and the past".

"How so"? chimed several of the others, simultaneously, intrigued by Amba's turn of direction, but knowing her to be of deep insight.

"Well", she began, "If the brain, or our brain function, is the painter, so to speak, then there must be a way that it has become so, there must be a way that it is possible that this merely biological matter in our brain organ, that we are calling the painter, is painting what we experience as the world".

"Indeed", Sebastian said. "Go on", seeing that now Amba too, was in her own kind of quiet frenzy.

"And the way it has happened", Amba continued, "I believe is through time and the past. Because what our brain is now, has been built up through a great process of evolution, according to the science. We know this, from the scientific evidence. It has come out of the past, and is based on the past. Just as any painting that you might paint, Sebastian, doesn't suddenly pop into existence completed. I presume you have to go through a long process in time, of evolving the painting, in order to bring it about".

Sebastian smiled and nodded in agreement.

"I agree", said Timaeus.

Amba smiled again now. "But unlike a painter who walks into a studio that is separate from himself, in order to make a painting", she continued, "The painter we each are, is only the painter now, as the painter already *is* now, complete with all the necessary things, the paints, and the canvases, having, as it were, evolved. And this is the brain and the brain function that we have".

Amba continued. "The painter has had to learn to be a painter, and has had to create his or her own studio, and own easel, and own canvas, and own paints, and own brushes, and so forth. Gradually, little by little. Nothing was already created, it all had to *be* created. There was a time when this painter, in the earlier stages of this evolution, was not painting anything like the world as we now know it, and perhaps could not even be said to have been painting. Just as would be the case if you had to create your own canvas, Sebastian, and your own paints, as I know, in fact, Sebastian, you do".

"Well I don't create my canvases", Sebastian smiled, "But I certainly create my own paints. And yes, it's absolutely true that when I am creating my own paints, I am not even painting, or actually really creating a painting, at that point", he said.

"Exactly so", Amba said. "And so the great process of evolution is the distilling of something out of the past. Something that evolves. And what ultimately evolves is what we are calling the painter, our own brain function, whose painting is what we are encountering as the world. The evolution of the painting is the evolution of the painter and the materials and studio, they are all the same. They all evolve together. And this whole evolution is the work of the one original painter who paints us all".

"I think you might be describing Seraphina", Sebastian said. "And I think all that's true", he went on. "When I paint, the painting itself evolves. It even in some way sometimes seems to paint itself, and as it does so, I evolve. It's a transformative process, painting, even cathartic, sometimes. It is the same with making the sculptures. It was particularly true when I made the persons in the gardens".

Now Sandhya too, seemed to be a little frenzied. "Exactly", she said. "But Amba, you are saying that the world we experience and our means of experiencing it, is all one evolution, or comes about, all through one evolution. I feel you haven't emphasised enough that our own brain function, whose painting, as it were, we have agreed we are encountering as this world, is also the painter of what we ourselves are, in other words, it is also the painter of what we experience as our self.

"Go on", said Sebastian.

Sandhya continued "According to the scientists, what is in our heads is nothing but biological brain function. We know this. You have said this brain function is like a painter painting the world that we experience. But this painter is not remote from the painting, somehow painting it from a distance. The canvas is our brain. And this is where the painting is. But it is also where we, the painter, are. So I am saying that the painter and the painted are one. And yet the world that we can see around us is not inside our head. Rather, our head is in the world".

Now Sandhya really did seem to be on fire with the frenzy. She continued. "You might have thought this is an insoluble contradiction. But it seems to me that it is not. It is only a contradiction when we literally leave our self out of the picture that is painted by the painter. And we shouldn't do that, because this painter is also painting our self, and this is a self portrait, so to speak, that we are speaking of. What we are painting as the world, is in fact a painting of our self! Just as Sebastian's portrait that he painted, is also the landscape. That's what I think I wanted to say".

The others were listening intensely. Nobody said anything, so Sandhya continued. "In the case of each one of us, I think, this is only possible because of the one painter who paints us all, that we have talked about, as her own self portrait. Perhaps Sebastian is right. Perhaps it *is* Seraphina".

Sebastian now said "Yes, Sandhya, I think I would agree. We are talking about a painting within a painting. And perhaps there are many paintings within many paintings. The individual painting, that we seem to be painting, as the result of our brain function, is only a painting within a painting. Because we ourselves are painted by the one painter we spoke of, who paints us all. So when it comes to our individual painting of the world, through the painter in our head, so to speak, the painter and the painting that the scientists call brain function, we cannot help but paint it according to how the original artist is painting, or has painted. I believe this original artist to be Seraphina. But it now also occurs to me that perhaps there is another painter, who is painting Seraphina. I don't know how many painters there are. But it does occur to me now that perhaps the origin of all, as I have heard both Belvoir and Marsilio say, is what they call the One".

"But it sounds to me", Timaeus said, "As though there is some kind of direction in this evolution business, that is, I mean to say, it is as if we are saying that our very being here, as we are, is a kind of cause of the evolution that brings about our being here, if you see what I mean. And somehow, I am not inclined to agree with that. Because it seems to me, that if this were so, then we are both the cause of ourselves, and also the effect of that cause".

Ambika, who had been sitting quietly for some time, now spoke. "Perhaps that is the point, Timaeus. We often don't see how we ourselves are a cause. Is it not so, that so often in our lives, we ourselves lament things that happen, when in truth, if we were a little more observant, we would see that we ourselves have caused them, either directly, or by seeking situations and entering into situations which become the seed of the things we lament"?

"Ah, Ambika, I see you have lost none of your lustre", Timaeus smiled with admiration.

Ambika now seemed to be a little frenzied, too, and immediately replied "Perhaps you would know my lustre more clearly for what it truly is, if you too could see that you are indeed the effect of your own cause".

Timaeus now laughed out loud lovingly at Ambika's characteristic turn of phrase. "Ambika", he replied, "I don't think I ever underestimate your lustre, on the contrary, I delight in it, and I treasure it, but I'm afraid you have lost me there", he said.

"Although I must say", he continued, "From what you just said, am I right in thinking that you are suggesting not only that we are somehow our own causes, but that this is also somehow lamentable"? Timaeus looked somewhat dismayed.

"It depends", Ambika answered. "I think while we are here, we should as much as possible be in a state in which we can enjoy the good and the beautiful that is here. I don't think we should be lamenting. I suspect that really, there is nothing to lament. But because of the way we are, we do find things to lament, don't we? Even in Pavi Bujdam where there is more or less perpetual harmony. For reasons that as far as I can see, no one except perhaps Marsilio or Belvoir, understands. Certainly this harmony is here on our side of the island, within the Mereage. And all I am saying is that in that, whether we are in harmony or not, we are our own causes. Perhaps not always obviously in the immediate ocean of causes and effects that we can see all around us. But where does that ocean come from? That is the question. And where does the fact that we are in that ocean, come from"?

"I must say, if you put it like that, then in those terms, I don't have an answer", said Timaeus.

Sandhya spoke again now. "I do wonder what Marsilio would say if he was here"? she said. "I wish he was here".

"Well", said Sebastian, standing up. "It's funny you should say that, because it wasn't so very long ago that Marsilio was here. In fact, he came to see Belvoir. We got talking, And I must say he said something that set me alight, and it carried on burning for a few days afterwards, and I was minded to write to him about it".

Sebastian walked over to the cupboard where he kept all the correspondences that he thought were pertinent to their meetings in the Harborage. "And somewhere here", he said, looking through the papers, "I have his reply". He shortly produced the letter. "Yes, here it is", he said. "I think I should like to read you just this part here", he said, and proceeded to read aloud from the letter.

"My dearest Sebastian, it is because I love you, and that I want you to know the love that I know, that I am writing this. Let us be only concerned with harmony, and of finding the truth of harmony. Let us seek harmony, and the Source of harmony. For while we try to understand and solve disharmony, we will never come to the truth. That is why, around the walls of the courtyard in my house, I have inscribed the words 'Everything proceeds from the good to the good'.

Let us be glad we have increased our knowing of our own harmonious identity in the direction of knowledge of the one and only Source, the One, from whom our human experience springs. A fertile mind, no matter how fertile, cannot truly understand this. It is, nonetheless, the emanation of Providence from the One, into the fertile mind, that causes the fertile mind, when properly directed, to come to see and understand the world in terms of harmony, rather than disharmony. And thus, in doing so, as the being we find ourselves being here, we come further to know our Source".

Sebastian put down the letter. "I can't really say any more about it", he said, "And I wouldn't try to explain it, but somehow, it seems apt. Perhaps this is something to do with the difference between what is happening here, over this side of Pavi Bujdam, where we all live in harmony, and what is happening over the other side, around Gsoaf. I wonder if perhaps there is less of the Providence that Marsilio speaks of, there".

"If Marsilio was here", said Sandhya, "Then I'm sure he would explain".

"I'm not so sure", said Ambika. "I think there are some things that cannot be explained, and don't need to be. Like love, for example. I think there are some things to be known, by knowing. A knowing which is beyond all understanding. And I think it is sometimes the very fact that we are looking for an explanation, that prevents us from understanding. And I think that is an error that is sometimes made by the scientists".

"Well, thank you for listening", Sebastian now said. "I think I have had my time, and I think it is now time for Sandhya", he said, looking at Sandhya, "Because I believe you wanted to contribute something of your own, also, this morning"?

"Thank you, Sebastian", Sandhya said. "Yes, I thought I would say something this morning, but I don't intend to speak for very long".

14

⚘

Sandhya

Sebastian left the podium and Sandhya now stepped onto it.

"Well then", she began. "I wanted to bring up the subject of frenzy".

"Frenzy"? Sebastian said. "That's interesting. Because that's one of the things that came into that very conversation I was having with both Belvoir and Marsilio".

"Yes", Sandhya said. "That doesn't surprise me because I have heard Marsilio talk about it in relation to music, and that's where I have the inspiration from. But I wanted to extend the idea. I know that Marsilio talks of different kinds of frenzy as states into which we can be transported, in which our understanding is in some way raised beyond comprehending only through mental thoughts and concepts and learning and reasoning, and so on".

"Correct me if I'm wrong", Timaeus said, "But I have heard Marsilio talk about this too, and am I right in thinking that when he speaks of this, he is talking about something that although he calls it frenzy, is not just a common state of frenetic activity or emotionality"?

"That's perfectly correct", Sandhya replied. "It's something quite different. It's something that reaches upwards, as it were, towards what I think Marsilio calls the Being and the One. As I understand it, it is a state of inner energisation, almost a creative mania, an awakening of a higher state that takes over the lower, a state of ecstasy even, that I believe I have heard Marsilio call *rapture* or... now what was it? Ah yes, *ekstasis*, I think is the word he used".

"Ah yes", Amba said, "I remember clearly him speaking about this".

"So do I", Timaeus said. "I remember particularly he was talking about music".

"Exactly", Sandhya continued. "He was saying how we can actually enter this frenzy through the right kind of music. But there are other ways in which it manifests".

"You mean like dance"? Ambika said.

"I believe so", Sandhya answered. "But Marsilio didn't specifically mention dance. One of the ways, for example, was, I believe he said, through certain forms of ritual or rite".

Amba spoke now. "But you are saying that the frenzy Marsilio was speaking of, could apply to dance also"?

"I believe so", Sandhya replied.

Timaeus now said "You've mentioned music and dance, and certain rituals, so what are the other ways in which we might encounter this frenzy"?

"Well", Sandhya began. "Aside music or indeed poetry, another two ways he talked about had to do with the prophetic, and with the frenzy of love. At another time I have heard him say that the frenzy comes through the power of four things, that is, through love, prophecy, the mysteries, and the muses, by which I believe he means poetry and music. But I think it is more than that, you see".

"Might it be that all these connected"? Timaeus asked.

"I certainly think so", Sandhya said. "Remember I haven't yet spoken to Marsilio about this, but it seems to me that they could be combined, or one could flow into another. But that's not all. I am saying I think it could apply to other kinds of activities too".

"Indeed, I would be inclined to agree with that", said Timaeus. "If I might be allowed to say, there is a kind of frenzy, if that's what we are calling it, that I sometimes experience, when I am performing music with others, which is more like an entirely alternative place that I go into, indeed, now I come to think of it, it is a kind of ecstasy, if you want to call it that, in which I am conscious of amazing and beautiful things, I would even say beautiful places, and it certainly seems sometimes that I have been lifted into the most Divine company in some way. It seems to be connected with what we are doing in the musical performance, and yet is entirely beyond all description in mundane terms. That's the best way I can describe it at the moment".

Amba and Ambika and Sandhya were all nodding enthusiastically now in recognition of what Timaeus was saying, clearly in agreement.

Amba said "I know Marsilio himself carries out musical performances sometimes as a kind of ritual, specifically to bring about the frenzy that he speaks of".

Sandhya said. "I think musical performance or dance performance, for example, is a kind of ritual in the highest sense. And in a way, that's why I said I would come onto the podium, today. There is something I wanted us to try. Something that is part of a performance some of us have been working on. I don't know whether it will work or not".

"Perhaps we shall know more when we see what it is you have in mind", Sebastian said. He sat back in his chair and put his hands up behind his head. "And by the way", he said, "They are of course all connected", he smiled. "All these things are connected with what you call, or rather Marsilio calls, frenzy. They have to be connected, they cannot be separate. I think I could say more about it, but I also think we should keep it for another time. Sandhya, please continue".

Sandhya went on, "Well you may remember that last month, in the spring, Sati, Amba, Ambika and myself were meeting down in the Orange Grove at Springmere"?

"I do remember", smiled Sebastian, "And you wouldn't let anyone know what you were up to".

The others laughed and Sandhya smiled. "The reason was that we were rehearsing something", she said. "Something that is not yet complete, but is developing. Sati isn't here today, but that doesn't matter because we three who are here, make up, as it were, a discrete part of what we were rehearsing for. And Sebastian, this is really for you, you see".

Sebastian sat upright, looking very surprised. "Well, I'm honoured", he said, smiling. "But what about Timaeus here"?

"I'm afraid I'm in on it, already" Timaeus said, now smiling too.

"Aha! A conspiracy"! Sebastian joked.

"Not exactly", Sandhya said, "It's work in progress, and we rather hoped you yourself might become part of it eventually".

"Really"? Sebastian said. "I am intrigued".

"Well now that we are here", Sandhya said, "I just thought we might take this opportunity to perform something for you, just a little part of it, just to see what you think".

"I would be delighted", Sebastian said, looking very pleased. "Do go ahead by all means".

With that, Timaeus sat himself on a chair at one back corner of the podium, whilst the three women took up a standing position at the centre. They then assumed what was clearly, as Sebastian could see, the starting position for a dance. They appeared to form a circle.

Sandhya stood facing towards Amba and Ambika, herself and Ambika looking straight into each other's eyes, whilst Amba standing beside Ambika, was looking past Sandhya at some imaginary unknown person of her attention, behind Sandhya.

In her right hand raised to the level of their faces, Sandhya held Amba's left hand, whilst the fingers of Sandhya's left hand and Ambika's right hand intertwined, held high above. Amba and Ambika held each other's hands lower down, behind Amba, completing the unbroken circle of hands.

Timaeus then started to pluck the strings of his lyre, producing what seemed to Sebastian to be, for all its simplicity, the most profoundly beautiful progression of harmonies that immediately put him in mind of the music he had heard emanating from the tower when he was in the gardens with the persons, and had overheard Sati and Ambika rehearsing. He was sure they must have already transcribed it.

As he heard what seemed to him now to be the most exquisite

concords emanating from Timaeus' accomplished playing of his lyre, the female trio started to move, and danced, round and around, their perfect circle in time with the music, uniting their gazes in some kind of synchronised knowing, taking their steps to the *tempus perfectum*, a rhythm of three within rhythms of three, hand-in-hand, in a wonderful orbit of harmonised motion to the songs that poured from the strings of the lyre.

As they continued on and on, something in the musical repetitions from the lyre, something in the rhythm, something in the progression of harmonies, uniting with the flowing elegance of the three circulating females, began to draw his attention in, and began to resonate with something within him.

The dance continued on, and as Sebastian watched, becoming ever more absorbed, he found himself overcome with longing again for that something unfathomable, something here again now, woven right through the music's harmony and the beautiful movements of their bodies, Amba, Ambika and Sandhya, now altogether radiant with pleasure, as they circled with flowing presence, their dance seemingly no less than the embodiment of some form of celestial perfection.

And then the music from the lyre entered a natural cadence, and the changing harmonies became stationary, leaving the whole scene poised on something unresolved, as though the heavens had drawn to an unexpected close.

After a moment's silence, Sebastian began to applaud.

"Marvellous" he exclaimed. "I was enthralled". He took a deep breath. "And you were saying this is just part of something bigger"?

"It is", answered Sandhya, "But we don't yet know where we are going with it".

"Well you are definitely on the right path", Sebastian said, "Wherever it is that it is going. And how is it that it is going to involve me"?

"Well, that's just it", Sandhya said, "I don't know yet, I don't think any of us know".

"We shall have to wait and see then", Sebastian smiled. "In any case, what you are doing is beautiful. If I didn't know otherwise, I would have been certain that you were the three muses", he smiled. "And Timaeus, what *is* that Divine music you are playing"?

"Actually it's yours", Timaeus answered, "That is to say, it's part of the music that was passed on to you by Seraphina".

"I suspected so. Well that explains it then", Sebastian said. "Although I don't think we can exactly say that Seraphina passed it on to me, specifically. I think it's more a question of her leaving it where it would be found, in a way that as I see it now, was an act of artistry".

All the performers except Sandhya now left of the podium, leaving Sandhya to continue her speech. "Thank you, Sebastian, for your appreciation", she said. "I was talking about the frenzies, and I just wanted to say something more about that.

"Yes, do go ahead", Sebastian said.

"It seems to me", Sandhya went on, that as I have said, other activities too, can be part of the way this frenzy comes about".

Sebastian now said, "I think it is certainly possible with painting and sculpture, not only for the artist, but also sometimes for the appreciator".

Sandhya replied "But you see I think there is something else. I am a musician too, and I do sometimes experience it with music, and I also experience it sometimes with your works of art, Sebastian. But what I was also saying was that there is something in motion itself, and in the interaction between beings, such that say, dancers experience, but beyond that, too, in other activities, not necessarily ones we would call art, that can give rise to the frenzy, if we are calling it that. And whether we are talking about music, or dance, or the visual arts, or poetry, or some rite, could it be, that if it is something involving motion, we can raise a performance, to new heights, as it were, and perhaps, who knows, even bring about the otherwise impossible"?

Sebastian sat back and smiled. "The impossible? Perhaps", he said. "But still", he went on, "We live in the world that we do. And it has certain aspects of its nature that we cannot overcome. Otherwise, for example, we could all easily just cross the mere whenever we wanted to. However exalted we might be, or even however fast we might go, however determined we are, we shouldn't underestimate the limitations of our world".

"No", said Sandhya. "But then, perhaps Marsilio or Belvoir, had they been here this morning, might have said that whether or not we can jump over an obstacle, or as it were clear the highest fence at the height of our frenzy, without fear of falling, has more to do with harmony with what is above, than it has to do with what is below".

Sebastian laughed lovingly. "Sandhya", he said, "I see you are speaking in horse-riding terms, already, with your reference to clearing the highest fence! I know you love your horses. But when you speak of above and below, are you saying that we live in a world below, that has some kind of relation to a world above, as it were, in the spiritual way that Marsilio so often speaks of"?

"I suppose I am saying that", said Sandhya. "And I suppose I am saying that it is possible to bring about harmony in the world below, through harmony with the world above. And similarly, it might be also possible to overcome certain obstacles in the world below, through harmony with the world above".

"Ah", smiled Sebastian now, "Yes, this is certainly the way Marsilio sometimes speaks".

"But what about the impossible"? Sandhya said. "Do you think the impossible could become possible"?

"How do you mean"? Sebastian asked.

"Well, for example", Sandhya said, "Imagine some obstacle in your path. Perhaps it might be possible to pass over the obstacle, as it were"?

"Yes but I think there are limits", said Sebastian. And now almost as an afterthought he added "Even in the height of frenzy, for example, I shouldn't think you could jump the boundary fence on the Silver Gallop. Which is clearly why Seraphina put a gap there".

Sandhya answered "But what if the horse were to share the same frenzy"?

"I don't know that we can talk about animals such as horses experiencing the frenzy, can we"? Sebastian answered.

"But we have said that perhaps there is more than one kind of frenzy, haven't we"? Sandhya said.

"Yes, that's true", Sebastian replied. "And perhaps they can work together".

"Exactly", said Sandhya.

"Well I absolutely love the idea of jumping the boundary fence in Divine frenzy", Sebastian said. He grinned. "But Sandhya, please don't try it".

15

The Masquerade

Every year in late spring or early summer was the Aumhurst masquerade. For everyone who was part of it, the masquerade was the culmination of year-long, tacit preparation. A preparation that the participants of the masquerade were mostly unaware of.

During the course of the year the citizens of Pavi Bujdam would inspirit the emergence of unseen things that steadily grew in the light of the everyday, from attitudes to behaviours, from encounters to flirtations. All from hidden seeds that later sprouted in the corner of one's attention, never cultivated, yet always propagating through relationships.

Until, at length, when springtime came, the bud was there, clear but veiled, in each and every person's interaction with each and every other person. And then with the coming of summer was the full flowering of the masquerade itself, where the blossoming of suggestion coincided with the ripening of its fruit, just as it does to this very day, on the orange trees in the groves around Springmere.

It wasn't Seraphina, or Sati, or Marsilio, or Belvoir or Sebastian, or any other of the friends, who organised or created the masquerade as a whole. The masquerade created itself. It created itself out of the very idea of being someone whom you are not.

And the reason it was possible was precisely because of the freedom in Pavi Bujdam. Not the freedom of any individual mask who would turn up at the masquerade, but the freedom of everyone in simply being who they already really are in Pavi Bujdam. For such freedom allowed for the masquerade to take place, in which most of the masqueraders forgot who they were in Pavi Bujdam, for as long as the beautiful Old World clocks of Aumhurst were stopped.

Some would say that during the time of the stopping of the clocks, even the turning of the Earth around its axis, as known in Pavi Bujdam, gives itself up to the turning of the masquerade Earth. A few of the astrologers would say such sacrifice happens through the magnificence of the moon.

Whatever the truth of it, in every summer the masquerade fell, from dawn till dusk, and on into the nights lit with lamps to guide the way of the masqueraders on the paths through the gardens of Aumhurst.

And should the masqueraders wish to wander there, day or night, then the already beautiful Aumhurst became a place of magical exploration. It became the setting of pastoral delights in the gardens of Aumhurst, a veritable Arcadia for the joy of the *fête champêtre* and its delicious metamorphosis into the *fête galante*.

In truth, the Aumhurst masquerade was, for residents of the Mereage, the jewel in the life of Pavi Bujdam, and in truth it was the true reason for the Mereage. For it was only from the masquerade itself, only through the joy of the *fête champêtre* and the fall into the *fête galante*, and then from there into the intoxicated revelry of the beautiful bacchanalian, that the population of Pavi Bujdam came, who could then be drawn to the powerful lure of the masquerade itself, which now repeated itself year after year.

Almost no one in Pavi Bujdam knew the origin of the masquerade now, not even those who indulged in it, for it had been forgotten. Forgotten was the light of the great romance on the delightful lawns of love surrounded by the flowers of fragrant groves, or the quiet of the balmy night 'neath the moon and the stars, where plays the innocent touching of breath and rediscovery of the unknown. Forgotten was the most beautiful of all beautiful ones who loves and delights in dancing as so many beautiful ones, dancing the dance of the meeting of eyes and the touching of hands, encircling the stories of meetings of those delighting together in what might be. 'Till intoxicated with the joy of the possible the intoxication itself brings sleep and the dream of what was.

So now, in Pavi Bujdam, most people entered into the masquerade through the state of intoxication itself, and there they generally found what you might expect to find if you enter a masquerade already intoxicated.

So the masquerade today was the delight of a temporarily new world, inhabited by characters and persons of a new kind, all within the masquerade at Aumhurst, that in the play of the masquerade was no longer Aumhurst at all. Or so it seemed.

The theatre of it was so complete that even the very whilst and while of time itself became confused, as was inevitable in the goings-on that went on within the walls of the house and gardens of Aumhurst during the masquerade. No-one in the whole of Pavi Bujdam would imagine the scale and nature of the illusory nonsense and trickery that is possible in the game of convincing an audience. All this and more was not only possible but actually came into being in the play of things that worked itself out as the masquerade.

It was a time when the players were attracted into their roles like gravitationally pulled planets, sometimes stepping back into some un-completed play from last year, other times falling into some other role. Whilst always, every part and parcel of the play could only ever live as long as it took the masquerade to play itself out.

Some would say that over the years it was forever playing itself out. The long hot summers at Aumhurst might become winter in the mas-querade, but the summer of Pavi Bujdam could be enjoyed even as it became the masquerade winter. Or, for some in the masquerade, having unwittingly made their play, it could just become a cruel winter.

The masquerade went on for days of Pavi Bujdam time, or even, who knows, perhaps for weeks? Some of the participants as they became lost in the play of it, becoming weary, and perhaps leaning against one of the Old World long-case clocks that had been stopped for the duration, would declare that it felt as though it was all a dream. The colour and the spectacle of it all could lose its lustre for some. But in fact it was something that had itself been created by dreams. Dreams that were engendered often by those who in the course of the year were planting perhaps even unknown to themselves, their own hidden seeds in the garden of that year-long preparation of the masquerade.

To the inner circle of the Pavi Academy - with the exception of Belvoir who simply and perhaps more wisely would never take part - the masquerade was a time of coming to be, in that play within the walls and gardens of Aumhurst, a play of something that never really was, is, or will be, but which provided the opportunity for the fiction of it.

This year, after the stopping of the ticking of all those beautiful Old World clocks in the great house Aumhurst, Sebastian and Quentin could be found parading the gardens, like Lords of the manner, encountering the bronze and stone persons who by now where themselves dressed up and masked, like every other person in the masquerade.

Sebastian, an ogre of strange, golden face, and Quentin, his snub-nosed blue servant, would reprimand an impudent red magician for his poaching of a pheasant, and having forgotten the power to recognise the tell-tale sign of a true Marsilio through the apprehended offender's astrological words, would cast him into the custody of the mathematician's accomplices.

And somewhere in the masquerade was the weighty and impactful painted wooden mask of a judge who would convince or satisfy the whole masquerade with a pronouncement as sure footed as an elephant. A seemingly enviable animal until they try to jump the boundary fence between Merehurst and Aumhurst. Or if they were to attempt to walk on something that does not support their weight.

And so the weighty pronouncement called a sentence, was made. But the snub-nosed blue servant would miss his mark by a hair's breadth, and somehow, almost inexplicably, the red magician would be pardoned, and not only pardoned, but by none other than the ogre of the strange, golden face, himself.

Whereupon the red magician would introduce a handsome white magician dressed entirely in black. And at length the handsome white magician would deliver a wise preamble to all the grinning masks who stood around gesturing and signalling virtuous agreement to each other, but in truth, without understanding a word. Until finally the white magician declared the need of help from the black magician.

Now an identical handsome magician but dressed entirely in white would immediately enter the proceedings, who himself, despite his also wise appearance, says that he needs advice from the white magician. And then, whilst looking straight at you, tells you that because the white magician is innocent, you are free to speak as you wish.

And now the black magician tells us all, that he himself has come from a magical far off land where the king, approaching his death, wished to be buried in the tomb of a virgin, but when his servants had opened up the tomb, the influx of daylight brought the bones to life, which then changed into a black horse who immediately fled the scene, and ran off to the desert.

The black magician looks around again. He tells his audience that in hard pursuit at last, he finds the horse now grazing on a plain. And now with tempting tale the listening masks, desire to know the end of his account. With keener ears the masqueraders listen for the ending to the black magician's tale. So now the black magician ends his story. For where the horse was grazing on the plain:

He had found the lost keys of paradise.

The black magician clearly needs the advice of the white magician - for as is now clear to everyone, he does not know what to do with them.

Only in the splendid Aumhurst masquerade could such an archetypal Jungian fable repeat itself year after year, whilst the masqueraders remain none the wiser. But nonetheless, repeat itself it did. And year after year the masqueraders remained indeed none the wiser.

Apart, that is, from Marsilio. Who, somehow always finding himself in the masquerade as the red magician, and then later as who knows whom, remained always Marsilio nonetheless, and despite the mask and the costume, he knew it.

For it was not the case that masqueraders necessarily remained in the same character throughout. Oh no, most certainly not. Those who were in the masquerade often created by themselves, another masquerade, within the masquerade. They loved creating masquerades. Those who understood the masquerade a little more deeply than most, knew that there were masquerades within masquerades, all within the Aumhurst masquerade. And more. And they followed and swapped with each other from year to year, like threads in some exotic tapestry. How else would the Aumhurst masquerade achieve such unimaginable richness out of pure imagination? And so it was that deep within some inner masquerade the players would temporarily lose all memory of their having come to be who they seemed to be, within the masquerade.

Tonight, as the ogre of strange, golden face, together with his snub-nosed blue servant, followed the beautiful lamplit paths through the gardens of Aumhurst, rustling past blackened leaves and stealthily emerging into pools of half-light with ambiguous intentions, the still warmth of the night was suddenly and temporarily lost to a breeze of wind from the West. As they entered an orange grove, carried on the air together with the smell of orange blossom was an easily mistakable sound that might have been thought unmistakable evidence of a most inappropriate kind of hunting for such a civilised masquerade. The voice sounded like that of a frightened nymph, but the one who emerged from the beautiful thicket, all covered in flowers, was the pregnant figure of Flora.

How could such an exchange of identity take place in the masquerade? Such things, Marsilio would say, show the providence behind all becomings and happenings and changes. Such things are easy when all that is, comes from that towards which all that is, is always striving to return. For as Marsilio would often say, even in the masquerade, everything is directed from goodness to goodness.

And so it is that the magic wand of he who is a villainous red magician in the masquerade, could become the healing caduceus of the noble figure of Mercury himself, commanding a whole scene in front of the Orange Grove.

And circling in and out of trouble in the depths of some masquerade within a masquerade, we might find three of the most beautiful women in three of the masquerade's most attractive costumes, who later in the year are none other than the beautiful Amba, Ambika and Sandhya, dancing to the music from the lyre. And if it were only possible to cross the mere, as was always the aspiration of Sebastian, their dancing might fly finally upwards to meet the Orphic graces of which Marsilio would sometimes speak: Splendour, Viridity, and Joy.

This year in the masquerade was to be the performance of a most splendid concert. So many masks, so colourful and decorated, were woodenly clattering together as they moved and turned, and bobbed and swayed, on their brightly costumed bodies packed into the foyer. Above the hubbub of the loud sea of conversations colliding with conversations, the weight of a collective excitement hovered over the crowd like a magical blanket, warming the atmosphere.

At last, a very civilised low dong of semi-musical sound from somewhere, signalled the awaited opening of the auditorium doors, and almost the entire population of the foyer began to politely manoeuvre and form itself slowly into inward pouring streams of bodies shuffling through the doors.

The auditorium was well lit and generously furnished with the most luxurious of soft seating, wall curtains, and carpet, all of which provided a noticeably contrasting hush after the foyer. The rivers of masqueraders flowing in through the doors gradually filled the seats, and at length the auditorium was a mass of glittering masks and brightly coloured robes, maintaining what was now a more subdued but still excited hum of lowered voices. Then at length the lights were lowered and the audience was plunged into darkness. Silence fell upon the whole space.

Somewhere in the half light at the front of the auditorium the curtain was raised, and a beautiful, luciferous spotlight from somewhere above the masqueraders suddenly turned the centre stage into a zone of wonderful potential within the impenetrable darkness. But out from that darkness looked the masquerade audience, now no longer onto just more masquerade, but onto something higher, created out of the masquerade, through the masquerade, in the masquerade.

There, metamorphosed in the pool of atmospheric light, was the seemingly etherial presence of a grand piano, a magnificent musical instrument created through the fusion of science and art, intelligence and artistry, culture and technology.

The masqueraders, absorbed as they were in their masquerade, had little memory amongst them of that artwork of Sebastian, the maze through which they had wandered, intoxicated, before coming into the masquerade. A maze somewhere between the icastic beauty of Aumhurst in the original Pavi Bujdam, and the fantasy Aumhurst in the masquerade. So too, they had little knowledge of the wonder of the way in which the grand piano on the stage before their very eyes had come down into the masquerade from its home in the great house of Aumhurst.

And now as another small spotlight, this time moving, illuminates the musicians who emerge from the wings and walk across the stage, the audience roundly applauses. An applause which subsides as quickly as it arose. There are a few moments of musicianly adjustments, and the concert begins.

Somewhere between those musicianly adjustments of the kind repeatedly made in the concerts of Pavi Bujdam, and those now being made in the masquerade, and somewhere between the music that followed in the masquerade concert, and the unfettered concerts of more sublime performances in Pavi Bujdam, which were free of the restrictions and impediments of the thickness of costumes and heaviness of masks, somewhere there, in between, was the arising of the masquerade itself.

The pianist's fingers fly with genius across the mathematically arranged landscape of the keyboard. Inside the sweeping curved case of the instrument was many tons of tension spread over hundreds of strings, soundly supported by the weighty presence of a shining, golden frame.

Somewhere between the pianist's flying fingers and the birth of the music, an unseen marvel was taking place, a secret but essential part of the performance. Another concert of thousands of ingenious mechanisms, of levers and felts and springs and hammers, was translating the pianist's intentions into the striking of strings and the lifting of dampers.

The strings themselves now became the medium of the mixing of untold vibrations, cycles of the living and dying of otherwise unformed energy, all under the dominion of the same laws, the same principles that found their way all the way through to the pattern of blacks and whites on the keyboard. And all their way through to the patterns in the forms of the other instruments and the motions of their players' fingers.

The audience in their robes and masks sat enthralled; immersed in the sheer experience, the calm thrill, the emotion, the sublime messages, of the music. Messages that soaked into the interstices of whoever it was that lived within the masks and their costumes.

Somehow, somewhere in the great scheme of things, as Timaeus might see it, the aloof, monumental stature of pure numbers, and the harmonic mathematical ratios between them, created by nature in the fabric of nature herself, together with all their infinite variations, found their way down through imaginable and untold involutions and convolutions, finally coming to rest as musical meaning in the very beings of the masqueraders.

And why? How? If it was not because the numbers themselves were already created in the same way, from some more celestial magnificence of Being in which numbers do not matter?

Some splendour from which emanates not only splendour of being and world of being, and the oceans of streams of beautiful stories of love and oceans of beautiful places such as Ambika or Marsilio might speak of, but further, through both, and through Aumhurst, and through the maze, the splendour of the masquerade music in the masquerade concert.

And so it was that the imaginative creation of the masquerade took place every year in Pavi Bujdam. A masquerade that contained all things, from the villainous, to the highest arts. And it still takes place to this very day.

And so too, each year, it is only in the spectacle of the masquerade, that the lives and loves of the friends and philosophers of Pavi Bujdam, always free in the Mereage from any truly deep troubles, the lives and loves of the friends who generally live in harmony and happiness, do become entangled in the apparently insoluble troubles and strifes and pain and anxieties of human affairs and relationships.

16

❧

Cura Te Ipsum

Quentin walked briskly into the bright, sunlit courtyard of Spring-mere. There, Sebastian, who had to come to visit Marsilio, was standing. Quentin wore a new smile of triumph.

The lemon yellow walls surrounding him caught the sunshine and smiled brightly back at him. The little birds were endlessly flying in and out through the arches all around him and high above was the inscription *All things are directed from goodness to goodness. Rejoice in the present.*

The beauty of Springmere surrounded them both. The concert of the chirping birds and their songs rang and sang out musically, echoing off the yellow walls of the courtyard, as they flew in and out of its peaceful space in pursuit of their business. With every swoop they seemed to be carrying into the courtyard secrets on the wing from the surrounding orange groves.

"What is it my friend"? Sebastian greeted Quentin. "I can see you are bursting to tell me something".

"I believe I have solved it", Quentin declared.

"Solved what"? Enquired Sebastian.

The smile on Quentin's face broadened. "You won't believe it", he said.

"You won't know whether I do or not, unless you tell me", Sebastian replied.

"The trouble", Quentin said. "I believe I have solved the trouble in Pavi Bujdam, over at Gsoaf. The trouble between Gsoaf and its two neighbours".

Sebastian looked quizzical. "And how is this"? he asked.

Quentin just smiled, enigmatically.

"Well I think you are going to have to tell me more", Sebastian said, cautiously.

"I have just returned from Gsoaf", Quentin said, "On my usual, annual negotiations, to try to smooth things over. We met up with the leaders of Eflmere and Ceshmere, too. It seems it's not possible to reach a compromise between the three of them, without some change in the other Vicinages over this side of Pavi Bujdam. That's what they think. They are of the opinion that things in Pavi Bujdam as a whole, are simply not fair".

Sebastian looked a little confused. "So...", he said, "In fact you *haven't* solved it"?

Quentin smiled again. "No, you don't understand. You see, as we know, it isn't currently possible to reach a compromise between the three of them, Gsoaf, Eflmere and Ceshmere, to sort out the disharmony that is always arising between them. But the point is, Sebastian, those are not the only Vicinages in Pavi Bujdam, are they? Why should they be the only ones that change? All the Vicinages have dealings with each other. They all do at one time or another. That's the point. Nobody here exists in isolation do they"?

"Well I would say that is completely true", Sebastian confirmed. "In fact, I would say we are all here in one big connected network of one kind or another. It is one big ecosystem, if you could call it that". He thought for a moment. "I suppose", he went on, "If it wasn't for the fact that we don't know what is beyond the mere, we could even include the Visitors".

"I entirely agree", nodded Quentin. He continued "Anyway, the point is, that as you say, we are all in one big connected network. We all live on the same planet, as it were. That means, of course, that it is not going to be possible to sort out the problems between Gsoaf, Eflmere and Ceshmere, without all the other Vicinages somehow being involved, is this not so"?

"Well", Sebastian said, "Looking at it like that, I suppose the whole of Pavi Bujdam does work as one system, but it's complicated, and it might not be possible to properly understand it all as a whole".

"But you see", Quentin said, "We don't necessarily have to understand all the little details about everything. It's all in the overall principle. And actually, if you look at it, compared to what it possibly might have been, our situation here in Pavi Bujdam, with the Vicinages and all that, in a way, is quite simple".

"How is that then"? Sebastian asked.

"Well", Quentin replied, "We only have twelve Vicinages to consider, after all, don't we"?

"Well that's true", Sebastian said. "But they're not all the same. As you rightly pointed out, three of them over the other side of Pavi Bujdam are repeatedly creating trouble with each other in one way or another".

"Exactly so", said Quentin. "The Vicinages always live in harmony, except when you get over to the other side of the Pavi Bujdam, where Gsoaf is. This is how it is, with the trading, the arrangements, the relationships, and so on. But what we have here is twelve Vicinages, all with relations to each other, and the whole thing, actually, is working as a whole. Gsoaf, Eflmere and Ceshmere, where the trouble arises, are all part of that, too".

"Go on", said Sebastian.

"Well", Quentin continued, "What we have over the other side of the Pavi Bujdam, is these three Vicinages, namely, Gsoaf, Eflmere and Ceshmere, where all the trouble seems to be. But from my negotiations with them, I can tell you they think that what is happening, is that this trouble is only really arising because of the way harmony between the other nine Vicinages is maintained, given that Pavi Bujdam works as a whole, and fundamentally, all the Vicinages are connected in some way, and are affecting each other".

"Yes, I see what you are saying", Sebastian agreed. "We certainly all live in a connected world, in Pavi Bujdam".

"Right", said Quentin. "So what if the easy and comfortable conditions here in the Mereage, the harmony between the Vicinages on this side of the island, is only really being maintained at the expense of Gsoaf, Eflmere and Ceshmere"?

"Yes, I have heard some people say that", said Sebastian. "But I have another view, you know".

"Really"? Quentin said, surprised. "What's that"?

"Well...", Sebastian began slowly. "What if the trouble itself, that we see always happening between Gsoaf, Eflmere and Ceshmere, is actually something that itself is just inherent in Pavi Bujdam. I don't mean that trouble necessarily has to be in the region of Gsoaf, Eflmere and Ceshmere. Although, that's where we happen to find it. I mean, wherever we found it in Pavi Bujdam, would be what we are calling Gsoaf, Eflmere and Ceshmere. The names of the Vicinages really just reflect where the trouble is, and where it isn't.

"What I mean is, that perhaps the trouble begins just in the existence of Pavi Bujdam itself, and actually, has more to do with the fact that we don't know what is beyond the mere. Basically, as a whole, we don't know. Although I think there are some who do know. Belvoir, for example, and possibly Marsilio. And of course the clans have their beliefs about it, and we assume that the Visitors, when they come here, must have some knowledge of it".

"So let me get this right", Quentin said. "You're saying that there is some kind of trouble always inherent in Pavi Bujdam, that has something to do with the fact that we don't know what is beyond the mere? And so you are saying that this trouble also happens to be over the other side of the island, between the Vicinages we call Gsoaf, Eflmere and Ceshmere"?

"Exactly so", Sebastian replied.

Quentin now smiled again. "Well if that is the case, we could still surely, organise things more fairly. What you are saying means we can only get rid of the trouble altogether if we find out what is beyond the mere. I see where you are coming from. Nevertheless, I don't think that's the answer".

Sebastian didn't show any reaction. "But Quentin", he said, "You haven't yet told me what your proposed solution is".

"Ah, yes", said Quentin. "Complete equality", he said triumphantly. "That's the solution".

"How so"? Sebastian asked.

"Look", began Quentin, "I know that unlike the Old World, we don't have actual wars here, in Pavi Bujdam, for some reason that the academics argue about, but nonetheless, if you go over to Gsoaf and Eflmere and Ceshmere, where they are an unhappy *ménage à trois*, figuratively at war with each other, then you will find yourself in a place that, if I could put it like this, is pretty bad tempered".

"Ha"! Sebastian laughed, having had the experience of going there himself, "That's an understatement".

"Yes", Quentin said, "It's not the sort of place you would want to be for very long, if you are of a more harmonious kind of temperament, such as we are here, is it"?

"Certainly not", Sebastian agreed.

"Why is it though", Quentin asked "That there are not more people here, on this side of the island, who are disharmonious amongst themselves in the same way? Not that I want them to be. I just mean, you would expect things to be much more mixed up and evenly distributed in that respect, across the whole of Pavi Bujdam, wouldn't you"?

"I don't know that I would", Sebastian answered. "After all, this is Pavi Bujdam".

"What do you mean"? Quentin asked.

"Well", Sebastian said, "If you took thousands or millions of Pavi Bujdams and networked them together in some complicated way, like the Old World, then the trouble would appear here, there, and everywhere, wouldn't it? Even if you divided that world up into various zones".

"Hmm", said Quentin. It just sounded hypothetical to him. "Anyway", he said, "Whatever the case may be regarding that, it's very different here, over this side of the island, to how it is over at Gsoaf and its neighbours. And having been over there, and listened to what they have to say, I still think, putting the mere aside for the moment, that the problem is inequality".

"But you can't put the mere aside, can you"? Objected Sebastian. "It surrounds us, and we are ignorant of what is beyond it, even if people outside of the clans aren't interested in that".

"That maybe so", Quentin said, "But just hear me out on my idea".

"Certainly, Quentin, I want to hear it", Sebastian smiled, gesturing for Quentin to continue.

"Well, it seems to me", Quentin began, "That we have to find the way in which we can ensure that all the relations between all the Vicinages are essentially the same. We need equality. Perhaps by changing the trading arrangements, for example, and who is allowed to trade what with whom. And that might lead to things being a little less than ideal, as they are at the moment, over this side of Pavi Bujdam. But we would be making things completely equal and fair".

"Ah yes, now I see where you are coming from my friend", Sebastian said. "But what about the fact that the whole Mereage has its head, its puissance, here, and not over there? Where do you think we should put the head of the Mereage in this equal system of yours"? Sebastian smiled. "Or perhaps you think we should not bother with it, and get rid of it"?

Quentin considered what Sebastian was saying. "I think if we got rid of you, Sebastian", he said cheerfully, "I suppose there might be unforeseen consequences. And in any case, I wasn't at all suggesting that".

Quentin now looked as though he had just discovered something new. "But then surely", he said, "The Mereage could also be said to be the *cause* of the trouble over the other side of the island".

"Yes, I think you are right", Sebastian said. "It could be *said* to be, by some. But then, as you know very well, we don't impose any rules on the Vicinages, do we? And the kind of relationships that the Vicinages set up with each other are not any of the Mereage's doing. We don't take anything from the Vicinages against their will. Who trades what with whom, and how, is up to the Vicinages. Who has what kind of relationship with whom, is up to the Vicinages. Because we have complete freedom here, in Pavi Bujdam, don't we? We're not like the Old World, Quentin, we are all truly free, are we not? So how can it be that the Mereage is causing the discontent over at Gsoaf, and its neighbours? Over here, where we are, there is tremendous goodwill. There is always harmony. Over there, Gsoaf is always against one of its neighbours, and it sides with one, just to be against the other. And why do its neighbours Eflmere and Ceshmere play into this? They must also be antagonistic towards each other in some way. And then they affect relations with the next Vicinages further around the mere, too". It's just that the trouble doesn't come all the way around here, where we are.

"Nonetheless", Quentin said, "If we were to improve the conditions over there, even at the expense of some of the relations and conditions over this side of the island, we might distribute harmony in Pavi Bujdam more evenly, and then after a while it might become entirely harmonious".

"Hmm", Sebastian said. He appeared to be considering. "But then we would be imposing something, both over there, and over here", he said. And doesn't imposition of any kind rather go against the spirit of freedom in Pavi Bujdam as a whole? Would it not be the beginning of something else"?

"I suppose the Mereage would no longer be what it is", Quentin agreed.

Sebastian continued now "And if we were going to do this, then we would have to take great care to make sure that all the relations between all the Vicinages were indeed perfectly equal, if we were to avoid accusations of favouritism or discrimination. I don't think being even approximately equal would be good enough. We would have to pay great and careful attention to accuracy. At the moment all the Vic-inages are very different in character. I think we would end up making them look all pretty much the same where ever you go. And who knows what small change or imbalance in the relations between any of the Vicinages around the mere, would have as an effect elsewhere"?

"Yes, there might be some difficulty in that, I admit", Quentin said.

Sebastian smiled. "I think we might have to recruit the help of Timaeus, even, because it sounds like a mathematical challenge"! Sebastian now couldn't help himself laughing.

"Well, you might possibly be right, there", Quentin said.

Sebastian continued "There is going to be the desire of what seems to be the good and the beautiful, in terms only of this distribution. And that is going to cause resentments, and perhaps poisonous ambitions, because the whole situation and arrangement, to begin with, would be one that is imposed. Which is quite different to the situation we are currently in, in Pavi Bujdam, in which we are completely free, and no one is imposing anything".

"It wouldn't have to be that way", Quentin said. He smiled broadly at Sebastian and said "We could get rid of you, and let everybody in Pavi Bujdam mutually make their own arrangements about what is imposed and how". He slapped Sebastian on the arm in a friendly way. "What if...", Quentin said, "We let everybody in Pavi Bujdam choose by majority consent, who has the Mereage"?

"I do believe", said Sebastian, "From what I have read, that some similar kind of arrangement was arrived at in parts of the Old World. I think they called it democracy. But I don't think it resulted in the kind of equality you are talking about".

"Really"? Quentin answered, surprised. "So this kind of thing has already been tried"?

"Indeed", said Sebastian. "Except that it wasn't quite as you describe. I don't think everyone was mutually making their own arrangements. I don't think, on the whole, that it was like that. Rather, I think some citizens or groups may have had some power to make their own arrangements in their own lives, but when it came to the whole, as I understand it, there were definitely impositions made by a smaller number of people who were in a position to impose, and indeed, did impose".

"How dreadful"! Quentin said.

"Well it seems the people didn't think so", Sebastian said, "Because they seemed to think that they were in control, because they chose the people at the top of the system. They had the ability in their system to cast out, from time to time, the ones who were making the impositions, according to majority opinion. And on that basis they would choose from themselves, who came next into a position of power".

"It sounds as though things weren't very stable for very long", Quentin said.

"Well, as I understand it", Sebastian continued, "There was always trouble, but things were stable enough for the system to continue for quite some time".

Quentin looked a little sad. "Hmm", he considered, "But we all know what happened in the end", he said rather quietly.

"Indeed", Sebastian said. "It wasn't like it is here, in Pavi Bujdam".

"Yes", Quentin agreed, "The situation here has been like this since the beginning of Pavi Bujdam, as far as I know".

"Yes", Sebastian said. "It is all part of the artwork created by Seraphina. Although it is, of course, a myth".

"How can Pavi Bujdam be a myth"? Quentin objected. "And anyway, a great deal of our knowledge has come from the Old World hasn't it? And what about all the books and antiques in Aumhurst? Or are you going to say that the Old World was a myth, too"?

Sebastian smiled. "Perhaps both are a myth", he said.

"But we are living here"! Quentin objected.

Sebastian, still smiling, said "Perhaps this is what it's like to live in a myth. Perhaps whatever kind of world you live in, is what it is like to live in a myth, when your world is surrounded by a mere, even if you don't know it. And let's face it, probably not everyone even in the interior of Pavi Bujdam realises that Pavi Bujdam is surrounded by the mere. Certainly, as far as I can see, many people live their lives as though it is irrelevant, or they haven't noticed it. From the interior, you can't even see the mere, unless you go up to the top of the Tower".

"So you are saying that perfect equality or relations isn't the answer then"? Quentin said.

Sebastian replied. "I would think it would be impossible, except by some extremely ruthless kind of imposition. And that in itself would imply some kind of inequality between the imposers and the imposed upon", he said. "So it would be an absurdity. Look, Quentin, you've just come back from Gsoaf, and you've spoken to them, so why is it exactly that Gsoaf cannot be in harmonious relations with both its neighbours at the same time"?

"Well, Sebastian, this is what I was saying. There seems to be a chain of harmonious relations one way around the mere all the way from Aumhurst to Ceshmere, and a similar harmonious chain goes the other way around the mere from Aumhurst to Eflmere. And somehow this means that where they meet, at Gsoaf, Gsoaf has to be part of one chain or the other, but cannot be both. That's just how it works out. For some reason, there can't be a complete circle of harmony".

"There you are, then", said Sebastian, grinning. "I said it was because of the mere didn't I?

"I see I'm not going to convince you on this one", Quentin said.

"On the contrary", Sebastian replied, "You have convinced me. I have suspected for a long time that the trouble was due to the unbroken chains of harmony going each way around the island not being able to meet up in such a way that they complete a circle of harmony".

"Well then"! Quentin exclaimed. "I have another idea".

"Do go on", Sebastian said.

Quentin proceeded to explain, "Well, we could, in theory, as all twelve Vicinages, take turns at being the puissance, and allow the Mereage to change its position, every now and then, and circulate around the island".

"We could indeed", Sebastian appeared to agree. "Then it would be rather like the hand of a clock, wouldn't it"?

"I suppose it would", Quentin agreed.

"Well as things stand", Sebastian went on, "This clock that you are proposing, by which we would have us all change places, as it were, is not ticking. We haven't yet imposed such a clock".

"No, because we don't want to impose anything", said Quentin.

"And if we did", Sebastian went on, "What would happen to the masquerade"?

Quentin looked most surprised. "What do you mean"? He said.

Sebastian continued. "Well, the masquerade takes place in no time at all, on Pavi Bujdam, doesn't it? All the clocks are stopped. And yet many masquerade things unfold in the time of the masquerade. Whilst in Pavi Bujdam, for the rest of the year, nobody pays much attention to the order of things in time. No one is really bothered about what comes before, and what comes after. Linking things to time that is other than time in Pavi Bujdam as it stands, in which the Mereage is already time-lessly where it is, could mean trouble".

Now Quentin seemed to be thinking very deeply. Then he said, beginning to sound almost as if he was in some kind of frenzy, "Perhaps this has something to do with why things as they play out in the masquerade so often seem to become so much about trouble? It is almost as if the masquerade, or should I say, masquerade time, so to speak, is the very time in which the most trouble plays itself out. I seem to remember last time even Marsilio almost ended up in prison. I say almost, because I think if I remember correctly he was only saved from it because the ogre of strange golden face pardoned him. And certainly I know that Belvoir won't even take part in the masquerade because he wants nothing to do with the play of troubles that always seems to arise there, even though he knows it's just a masquerade".

"Yes, I think you are onto something", said Sebastian. "In any case I think if you start introducing schemes of change into Pavi Bujdam, based on some new time regime, as you are suggesting, you would be introducing more trouble than already exists around Gsoaf. You might well just turn the whole of Pavi Bujdam into a masquerade all year round. As I have already said", Sebastian went on, "All trouble is due to the fact that we are surrounded by the mere, and ignorant of what is beyond it".

"It occurs to me...", Quentin went on. But then he became silent.

"What"? prompted Sebastian.

Now Quentin didn't seem to be so keen to speak. But after a moment longer he answered, "Well I was going to say that then, if, that is, I mean to say, if, that is, what I mean is... should we find some kind of disharmony in our life, individually I mean, perhaps not affecting a whole Vicinage, but perhaps just some kind of personal disharmony in something closer to home, so to speak, maybe one we don't notice every day, or don't want to notice, then we might find that impossible to overcome, in much the same way"?

"I disagree", Sebastian answered.

"How so"? Quentin replied.

"If you have disharmony individually", Sebastian said, "You certainly can overcome it. And to do so, you just have to find the Mereage of yourself, rather than living in the Gsoaf of yourself, so to speak".

"It's just that...", Quentin began again. He was obviously considering some kind of trouble or disharmony that he hadn't yet spoken of.

There was silence between the two friends, but they had been friends all their lives, and Sebastian could read Quentin well enough.

"You and Sandhya", Sebastian said, penetrating immediately to the core of what Quentin was beginning to talk about.

"Yes", Quentin confirmed.

"I see", said Sebastian contemplatively. "I wondered what this was really all about".

The two friends stood in silence for some moments, whilst the birds, oblivious to the friend's philosophising, continued to flit in and out of the courtyard, chorussing their songs of joy as they flew back and forth between the courtyard and the orange groves.

Whatever was taking place in the whole of birdkind in the orange groves around Springmere, was finding its way now into the sun-filled courtyard, even if it would only be recognised by most, as a commotion, of the feeding of young and the makings of eggs, and the avoiding of prey. But somewhere else, somewhere over the highest fence between different ways of understanding, it wasn't really that. It was something far more beautiful, far more profound.

The Springmeer birdsong was, as Sebastian had already recognised, art itself in the act of creation, an art within an art, a higher poetry, a higher art, expressed through the lower natural arts of the birds, brought to the two friends now, standing in the beautiful environment of Springmere's resonant courtyard. It was a place where there was always the possibility that Sebastian and Quentin might experience the higher art. The birds' continual songs echoed off the yellow sunlit walls, where, becoming mixed with the sunlight itself, all was part of an art of which Sebastian and Quentin themselves were a part. And Sebastian now knew it.

Quentin stirred again into speech. "Sandhya and I...", he began. "We don't meet in the bedroom anymore", he said.

"Ah", said Sebastian. "I thought that's what you might mean".

Quentin wasn't the least surprised at Sebastian's perception. He just said "Yes. That is what I mean".

"You should go to the edge of the mere together", said Sebastian. "And look out across it".

"We used to do that all the time", Quentin said. "But we seem to have fallen out of it".

"How can anyone fall out of going to the mere"? Sebastian mused, with sympathy for his friend. "Especially those who are in love".

The poetry of Marsilio's Springmere was already beginning to descend through the songs of the birds and the sunlight reflecting off the courtyard's lemon walls. Providence, as it would seem to Marsilio himself, was being brought to the two friends.

And even now a figure in a beautiful soutane,
Began to walk towards them from the side.
And now once more would Springmere bring its harmony again,
As Marsilio came to meet them as their guide.

Quentin thought on Sebastian's words but now,

The pair of meeting friends would meet the third beside their two.
Marsilio now beside them with a bow,
A deeper light upon the question surely would ensue.

"Dear friends", he smiled, "I could not help but hear,
The tenor of your conversation echoing all around".
The first two friends now greeted him with cheer,
Marsilio brings, they thought, perhaps an insight more profound.

The art of Springmere shone upon the friends,
Marsilio ever bright would find the truth within the weft.
"Sebastian's right" he said, "The mere will heal,
And from the light beyond it, will true nectar be expressed".

And so it was that the birds continued their songs in flight over the heads of the three friends, oblivious to the meanings and meters in their words. The little fountain in the middle of the courtyard continued its own musical concert of the never ending burbling of falling water, catching the sunlight in its myriads of droplets.

"When you meet", Marsilio went on to say, "It should always be for the sake of what is beyond the mere. You must surely want to know? You should try being together on the very shore of the mere, and see where it takes you", Marsilio said. "Begin on the shore of the mere, for that is the only place you should meet when you meet in the bedroom, for when your meetings in the bedroom are meetings on the shore of the mere, you will surely enter the mere together and what is beyond the mere will enter you as providence. Quentin, my friend, you are an honourable man, but without this advice who knows what will come out of the churning of that ocean"?

Quentin smiled with love for his friend Marsilio, and said "Thank you, Marsilio, I think I understand you".

"I do not doubt that you will remember when the time comes", Marsilio replied with a smile. "But in the end, it must be with the right one".

The orange groves around Springmere sang out with the songs of the birds, just as the songs of the birds came into the courtyard from the surrounding orange groves, accompanied even by the auspicious light of the springtime sun, from so far away and yet was here, where the three friends stood.

Just beyond the orange grove was the shore of the mere, and then the mere itself, shining with the same auspicious light from the faraway sun, immanent on the surface of the water, as it stretched into the far distance towards the mysterious surrounding mountains.

17

The Silver Gallop

Sandhya stood in the doorway of the beautiful master bedroom of Merehurst, looking at Quentin. Quentin was standing with his back to her, looking out of the window, across to the mere.

"Quentin you are not listening to me", Sandhya said.

Quentin turned around. "I am sorry, my dear", he said. "You are quite right. I was miles away".

"You have been distracted lately", Sandhya said. "What is it, Quentin? I know there is something. Something since you last went to Springmere".

"There is", he said. "Perhaps we should go for a walk by the mere"?

"I don't know", Sandhya replied. "Perhaps we can go this afternoon. But this morning I'm riding out along the Silver Gallop".

"With Sati, no doubt", said Quentin.

"We will be back well before lunch", Sandhya said. And with that, she went out through the door and descended the sweeping staircase down into the grand entrance hall.

Sandhya's voice echoed in the space all around as she called out to Sati, who was currently engaged in conversation with a handsome man who to all intents and purposes appeared to be a part of the household, but whose very reason for being there appeared to be to hold conversation with Sati. Conversation that asked questions like why is she not actually the Lady of Aumhurst, given that she is so beautiful? And has she ever thought about living somewhere else around the mere? And how often does she actually get to see Sebastian? And would she be interested in a forthcoming party on the edge of the mere?

The conversation was interrupted by Sandhya's voice. Sati called out in reply to Sandhya, and in a little while the two were once again walking across the cobbles of the stable courtyard to choose their thoroughbreds.

"I thought I might take Valencia out this morning", Sati said as they approached the stalls. Sandhya seemed resistant to the idea. "Would you not be better with Helios", she said, "I'm taking King, this morning. King and Helios work so well together, don't you think"?

"That's true", Sati agreed, remembering the last ride along the Gallop.

And so it was the two riders, on magnificent King and the beautiful Helios, the rarest of palominos, set off down the path from the stables to the edge of the mere.

The morning down by the water was glorious. A mist across the surface was just beginning to lift and the sun was shining through it like luminescent brush strokes on a canvas of silk. Closer to the shore vapour was lifting off the still surface of the water into the cool morning air, making the water look hot.

As the two riders reached the shore of the mere, they turned, keeping the mere on their offside, and after a short trot, the two horses broke into a canter. In the distance ahead, not yet in sight for the lay of the land, Aumhurst stood impressive and beautiful, overlooking the mere, its shoreline adjacent to the end of the Silver Gallop.

Trot broke into canter, and now the canter broke into the gallop, the two riders and their horses still side-by-side, King and Helios straining at the bit, as if remembering their last experience along this natural grandstand whose backstretch was the mere.

Eight hooves thundered across the turf, spitting out grass from their path as their muscles began to bite hard into the race. And now with even more determination their bodies lengthened and their sinews rippled, as they accelerated ahead faster and faster, with such matched power and strength that neither was likely to win by more than a nose.

Along the sparkling edge of the mere they raced with increasing vigour, but as they reached the eighth furlong both horses started pulling off course away from the direction of the gap and towards the boundary fence as if they were running wild. Wild as the wind itself that roared past Sandhya and Sati, the two steeds seemed now to be taken by demons, ignoring the reins, driven by an inner fire of their own and out of communication with their riders.

Simultaneously Sandhya and Sati drew all their strength together to assert themselves but somehow the ground of their confidence terrifyingly crumbled away from them both, as both King and Helios seemed to break free of their training and charged at the fence as if they were spooking each other like mad things, becoming all the wilder as they sensed their riders' fear.

Now the fear with Sati and with Sandhya feeds the fire,
The fire feeds the fear and stokes the madness of desire,
The steeds again the soaring glory manically pursue,
Faster faster t'ward the fence their crashing ending drew,
With hellish raw determination now at any cost,
The fence approaches oh so fast that now all will be lost.

As Sandhya and Sati braced themselves at the sight of the fence flying unbelievably and terrifyingly fast towards them, the two horses, now seemingly overtaken by some deeper primal instinct, braked suddenly to the right, throwing their riders violently into the base of the fence, which whether by providence or fortune, was a huge mound of the softest grass.

King just came to a halt, but Helios reared right up like a magnificent golden Pegasus, his eyes rolling, either in ecstasy or terror, his would-be mythical wings flaring wide and arching over Sati, as she half thought she saw them, in her dazed and delirious state.

For what seemed like a long time the universe seemed to stop. Sati groaned in shock as she felt around her body and her extremities, which thankfully seemed to be intact. She managed to call out to Sandhya, twice, but there came no reply.

Adrenaline still coursing through her veins, she forced herself to lift her body, to look for Sandhya. At first she couldn't see her, but then she caught sight of her some distance away, lying motionless at the base of the fence. A flood of strength came into her and she made her way over towards Sandhya. On reaching her she touched her shoulder and called her name. There was no response for some moments, but then Sandhya groaned and said "King and Helios, are they alright"?

Sati turned her head in the direction of the horses who were now still, but standing. "I think so", she said. Sandhya seemed to relax. And then she said "Are you hurt"?

"I don't think so", Sati said.

"Thank God", Sandhya said with relief.

18

Meeting At Springmere

The time had arrived for the meeting at Springmere. The philosophers had all come through the courtyard, past the burbling fountain and under the swooping and diving of the birds, still entering and exiting the sun-trap zone within Springmere's lemon-yellow walls. As ever, the little birds brought with them their songs from the surrounding orange groves, and this morning, it seemed, even the fragrance of the orange blossom was carried on the air into the courtyard.

The philosophers included not just the close circle of friends, but many others, too. Of course, the question of the mere was on the agenda. The Old World had done nothing to provide Pavi Bujdam with knowledge of what was beyond the mere.

The guests were assembled in the auditorium, whose interior was illuminated this morning with with a clear natural light coming in through the windows from the surrounding orange groves. The audience settled into their seats as Marsilio walked onto the stage. And then a great hush fell upon on the room as he took the stand. He began with his introductory address, in his usual manner.

"Friends, I welcome you with open arms, and am delighted that you too can be here to enjoy the embrace of this extraordinarily benevolent environment, here at Springmere, this beautiful place so magnanimously and generously given by Lord Aumhurst, my very good friend Sebastian, in whose company we are honoured to be here today".

A great applause immediately followed. The clapping then subsided and the audience waited in anticipation for Marsilio to continue. He began his speech.

"Friends, let us talk about the light of understanding. We are all in the light in some way, but there are many obstacles, and many shadows, and many different plays of light. Like the play of light on the walls of this room, coming from the orange groves. And there is also a play of light on the orange groves that comes from the surface of the mere. And all, of course, comes from the Sun".

Marsilio now walked over to the little table. He picked up the carafe and poured himself a glass of water. He picked up the glass and held it into the light coming in through the windows. It sparkled in the light. "The play of light in my glass of water", he said, "Is created from the light coming in through the window".

He put the glass back down on the little table. Addressing the audience again, he said "Every play of light is different, and every play of light is made from some other play of light. And so it is with all light of understanding. Every light of understanding is a play of light from some greater light of understanding.

"Above all, is the truly intelligible world. Not intelligible as things that must reflect light in order to be seen, such as we have here in Pavi Bujdam. But a world where everything is the light itself. This, my friends, is the truly intelligible world, and it gives rise to light that plays in the shadows of itself.

"You cannot imagine the truly intelligible world, my friends, you cannot paint a picture of it, so to speak, in your mind, based on your experience of the world of Pavi Bujdam. To do so, would be like trying to create a picture of what is beyond the mere. How can you do that, when you do not know what is beyond the mere?

"My friends, even my honourable friend Lord Aumhurst, here, would not be able to paint a picture of it, an artwork of it, unless he knew what was beyond the mere. And if he did know what was beyond the mere, and wanted to paint a picture now, of what is beyond the mere, the picture would be an image, an imitation, a reflection in his mind. Just as the persons in the gardens of Aumhurst, who stand so still, are an imitation of persons like us, who move in Pavi Bujdam. And, friends, my dear friend Lord Aumhurst, Sebastian here, although he may not realise it, has another difficulty, even if he were to try to paint that picture, of what is beyond the mere, through its reflection in his mind. For his mind itself, as with all of us here today, is but a single brushstroke, in that true picture beyond the mere. My friends, what is beyond the mere, is such a painting. An imitation of something still greater.

"My friends, we live in a world of imitation. Pavi Bujdam itself, is an imitation. This imitation, as my honourable friend Lord Aumhurst, I know, has come to believe, is the work of art of Seraphina Bassenthwaite. At least, this is how it is, according to the light of understanding our of Lord Aumhurst, here, in Pavi Bujdam. It is in the light of understanding of someone who lives as the Lord of the Mereage, at Aumhurst. In Pavi Bujdam. Lord Aumhurst himself, you see, like Seraphina herself, is as a play of light. Just as am I, and you, too. Things may be different, in some other play of light. I can assure you, my friends, that I know of others, up in the forests and hills around Aumhurst, who see things differently still. All is a play of light, coming from the truly intelligible world".

Marsilio went back to the little table, picked up the glass of water, and drank the water. Then he smiled broadly at his audience, as if he had just done something very funny. There were some murmurs of laughter around the audience, although it wasn't clear that anyone really understood why.

Marsilio now put the glass back down, looked slowly around his audience, and asked "Would anyone like to ask a question, so far"?

Someone close to the back raised their hand, and was quickly invited to speak by Marsilio.

"Yes I have a question", the person said. Then the person continued, "From what you are saying, you are more than implying that this... *truly intelligible world*, as you call it, because it is the source of our world, must presumably be a world in which there is knowledge of what is beyond the mere. Is that not so"?

"Indeed", answered Marsilio.

"Well", the person went on, "Surely knowing what is beyond the mere would radically transform Pavi Bujdam would it not? It is, after all, the greatest question that many philosophers would like to answer".

"That is so", answered Marsilio again.

"Then how is it that we can come to know this *truly intelligible world*"? asked the person. "And hence come to know what is beyond the mere"?

Marsilio answered "First, you must come to know what is beyond the mere".

Loud laughter now circulated around the audience. Some people broke out into such guffaws that they seemed to have difficulty in calming themselves.

The person in the audience who had asked the question, laughed too. "I would say that is something of a paradox, isn't it? Or perhaps a vicious circle", said the person. "I don't see how it helps us"?

"It is exactly as I say", answered Marsilio.

The person in the audience now sat up straighter. "But *how* can we come to know what is beyond the mere"? the person asked. "Should we perhaps make more effort to get the Visitors to tell us"?

"Well, as you know", Marsilio answered, "It is of no use asking the Visitors, because then you will hear all kinds of stories, even if we suppose they are prepared to speak of it, which I think in general they do not, stories of things to which you yourself have no real connection, because you have not been there, and so you will endeavour to understand these stories through your own *ways of understanding*, which will just be an imitation".

"But then how can we know"? the person insisted.

"The only way to know is to go there", Marsilio said, "However, as you no doubt know, you cannot just go there, in the same way that you might go to somewhere else in Pavi Bujdam. But you can certainly prepare to go, just as it is certain that those who do not prepare, or who are not prepared, or have no wish to even know, will certainly not be able to go there".

"I should very much like to go beyond the mere, and know what is there", the person now said.

Marsilio smiled with love. "Many persons in Pavi Bujdam might say as much", he answered. He allowed a brief, quiet pause. And then he added "Including the persons in the gardens at Aumhurst".

Loud laughter now broke out again across the whole audience. Marsilio looked around his audience with an air of surprise. "What"? he said gently. And now he looked again at the person towards the back of the room, who had been speaking. "Are the persons in the gardens at Aumhurst really so very different"? Marsilio said.

"Well they are different, yes", the person at the back said.

"Why would you say so"? Marsilio replied. Would it be because they do not move? Or because they are sculpted from bronze or stone"?

"They are different", the person replied. "They are not living beings".

"I wonder if Lord Aumhurst would agree"? Marsilio said, looking around the room for Sebastian. He found him sitting in the front row. "What say you, Sebastian"? Marsilio asked him.

Sebastian answered, "To me", he said, "The persons are most definitely being, but they are created in the image of living beings who themselves have no dependence on the persons. Whilst the persons in the garden are most certainly dependent, at least to begin with, on the living beings in whose likeness I created them".

Sebastian seemed satisfied with his own reply. He crossed his arms.

"Yes indeed", said Marsilio. "And having created them do you find they are still dependent on those whose likeness they carry"?

"Apparently not", said Sebastian. "But only apparently, I would say. If they are recognised as images of persons by any of us, then in order to be seen and appreciated for what they are, they would most certainly be dependent on us. As it happens I have often thought about this. Without us first being what we are, and seeing that they are in our likeness, they would be nothing but bronze and stone".

"Indeed so", said Marsilio.

Now someone else also towards the back of the auditorium had their hand raised. "Yes", Marsilio said to the second person. "Please speak".

The second person spoke up loudly from the back of the room. "They move", the second person said.

"What do you mean"? said Sebastian equally loudly, half getting up and turning round to look. But strangely, he didn't sound surprised.

"They change positions", the second person said assertively. "Perhaps I am not meant to say it, but they do. And I am not the only one who has seen it".

"I think you are right", Sebastian said completely unexpectedly. "I didn't suppose anyone else had noticed".

"You are not moving them yourself, then"? The second person asked.

"Moving them myself? Sebastian queried, with an air of disbelief, and sounding almost shocked at the suggestion.

"One evening during the masquerade", the second person continued, "I put my hat on one of them, the one underneath the kalpa tree at the end of the path leading down to the house, and in the morning the person with my hat on was in the middle of the rose garden".

Loud guffaws of laughter rolled around the audience. Now Marsilio entered the conversation. "Was it the same person it was on, or had the hat changed persons"? He asked serenely. He looked at his audience. "It is very important that we look into these things in the right way", he said, quite seriously.

The second person now answered. "Those two persons in particular appear to be identical", the second person said. Guffaws of laughter once again rolled around the audience.

Now Sebastian himself interjected. "Well that's because they *are* actually both the same person", he said.

"But there are two of them"! Someone else in the audience now exclaimed. "I've seen them myself". The audience roared with laughter again.

"Oh yes, there are two persons", Sebastian shouted back, "But they are both the same person".

"Ah, I think I see what you mean", said the second person. "You mean they are both images of the same person. But it's still possible they swapped places isn't it"? The audience was now rolling around with laughter.

Now another voice entered the fray. It was Amba. "Of course it's possible", she said emphatically. And now a fifth voice called out. "You can do it all the time if you are both identical", she said. It was Ambika.

Marsilio could see it was the twins speaking. "But *you* two are not both the same person", he said.

There was a moment's silence when the twins appeared to be thinking. And then, both Amba and Ambika chorused "true", together. Immediately the audience completely fell apart into mirth and the entire auditorium now rolled with laughter, although nobody was perhaps quite sure why.

Now Sebastian came in again. He was smiling now. "If the persons in the gardens are both the same person as I've told you they are, it doesn't make any sense to speak of them swapping places does it? And in any case, surely one person cannot swap places with themselves"?

"But there are two of them, so they can", Amba said.

The audience was beginning to bubble with amusement again. Marsilio held up his hands to quell the restlessness. "Alright", he said with good humour. And then smiling, he said "I think this has gone far enough".

He looked over to Sebastian. "Lord Aumhurst", he said, "I do not doubt that if you were moving the persons around yourself, or were employing someone to do it, then being honourable you would tell us now. Is it possible that your persons in the gardens are moving around by themselves"?

Looking completely innocent, Sebastian said "Well... I'm not sure what you mean by... *by themselves*", he answered. Now the audience roared again with laughter.

Sebastian laughed too. "What I mean is", he went on, "The persons are images, and it *could* be an ongoing part of the art, couldn't it? And then, if they *are* moving around while no one is looking, then any apparent volition in them, by which they might be said to be moving *by themselves*, would itself also only be an image, surely?".

Because the auditorium was full of philosophers, there were now some murmurs of agreement, but also a little more laughter, in the rest of the audience.

Now Marsilio stepped in again. "I think we should clarify the whole business of the persons", he said. He looked again at Sebastian. "Lord Aumhurst", he began, "As it happens I have heard this rumour of the persons secretly moving, or being moved, before. So it really isn't, as I already know it, just a question of hats changing position overnight".

There were murmurs of both amusement and agreement across the audience again. Marsilio looked around his audience. "And I suspect many of you here have heard these rumours, too".

Sounds of agreement washed through the audience. "We have to appreciate that the persons are a work of art", Marsilio said. "And as such, their moving around may be part of the art, too. And if Lord Aumhurst wants to arrange for that to happen, in such a way that we never see it, as part of the art, then that is his prerogative".

Somewhat amused, Sebastian now spoke up, and almost standing up, too, said emphatically "I can assure you I am doing no such thing".

"Would their moving around be part of the work of art"? Marsilio asked.

Sebastian now sat back down and replied. "If that is what we think is happening, then certainly it is also part of the art", he said. "But it is not my doing. As I said, some art is ongoing. As it happens, as you know by now, I think all of *this* is part of an ongoing art".

Marsilio waited for the ensuing babble of discussion amongst the philosophers, to die down.

"So, if, for example", Marsilio went on, "One of these persons were to find themselves in some difficulty, perhaps, for example, shall we say, they become damaged in some way, as a result of their moving, then this should not be said to be your responsibility, Lord Aumhurst, just because it is you who has created this work of art"?

"Of course not", Sebastian answered. "Not even for those whom I have created in my own image".

"And yet at the same time", Marsilio went on, "We did say that even if they are moving by themselves, as we have speculated about, then the appearance of this being *by themselves*, can only be an image, and indeed is only an appearance, because the persons themselves, are only an image".

"Yes that's what I mean", said Sebastian. "If you really appreciate that they are persons, of a kind, rather than just lumps of stone or bronze. But in all honesty, if they are moving around, or being moved around, then I cannot tell you how that is happening. But I wouldn't deny it. And in a way, I have to tell you, it doesn't surprise me".

"I don't think this should surprise any of us", Marsilio said, addressing his audience now. "After all, we don't know how it is happening, that *any of this*", he said, looking and gesturing all around, "Is arising as our experience of being, or how any of this world is arising as something that we know and experience in the way that we do. In fact, as I have often said before, this is a matter of the functioning of our brains. And precisely how or why this happens is not something that is known to science. Nor, for that matter, do most people know it as knowledge of the art of living or being. How it happens is beyond science, and beyond human art".

Someone else now spoke up from the audience. "I don't wish to disappoint you", the person began saying, "But if the persons in the gardens at Aumhurst *are* moving around, unseen, then you can be quite sure that the means by which they are moving will certainly be found, just by looking at the right time. And I would wager that somebody goes out into the gardens and moves them".

A few people in the audience now clapped.

"Perhaps you are right", said Sebastian. "But that, to me, would be part of the art, too".

"They do move overnight, there's no doubt about that", Amba said now. "If you walk in the gardens of Aumhurst on consecutive mornings, this much is clear".

Ambika now answered "I think we should try it. Why don't we camp in the gardens one night, and see what happens"?

"I think that's a very good idea", said Sebastian, "But don't expect me to join you, because I need my sleep, and I shall probably be snug in the Aumhurst Library".

There was now a low hum of discussing and conversing going on in the audience, before things began to settle down. So Sebastian spoke again, addressing Marsilio, "And now, Marsilio, I do think you should continue with what you were saying".

The audience became quiet. "Thank you, Sebastian", Marsilio said. He walked into the centre of the stage again, and looked around his audience. And then slowly he began to continue his speech.

"As I was saying", he began, "Our common *way of understanding*, or light of understanding, here in Pavi Bujdam, is based on ignorance of what is beyond the mere".

Now there were murmurs of agreement in the audience. Marsilio continued, "And as I was also saying, in order to know what is beyond the mere, we first have to cross the mere. But this is not something we can simply do in the way that we might go anywhere else in Pavi Bujdam".

Somebody else in the audience now had their hand raised. Marsilio immediately invited them to speak.

"Why is it all like this"? the person asked. "So that we cannot just sail across the mere, like we might go anywhere else. Come to think of it, why are we surrounded by the mere in the first place"?

"Well", Marsilio answered, "Just as the persons in the gardens at Aumhurst are only an image of the one in whose image they have been created, so also our own person, our own idea of *who we are*, and indeed *where we are*, is but an image or an imitation".

Marsilio paused, and looked slowly around his audience. He then said, "Pavi Bujdam, is, essentially, a myth. It is, if you like, to put it another way, a story, or a superposition of ideas, and a superposition of stories".

Somebody now called out without even putting up a hand, "It seems real enough to me"!

"Yes", said Marsilio. "Wherever you find yourself is going to seem real to you, in one way or another, if that's where you find yourself. Because that's where you find yourself. And here you are. This is where you find yourself. Allow me to ask you, my friend, how real is the masquerade"?

"Well it's real enough when we are in it", the person replied, "But it's still something we make up, by putting on costumes and masks. It's all fiction, really. It disappears when it ends".

Marsilio looked seriously now around his audience. "That is how Pavi Bujdam seems to those who are beyond the mere", he said.

Someone else in the audience now also spoke up without raising a hand. "Then why do the Visitors bother coming here"? she asked.

Marsilio retorted "Why do *you* go into the masquerade"?

"Because you can do things there that you can't do here", the person said. "Things with each other. We don't have the same fun with costumes and masks, here in Pavi Bujdam".

Marsilio replied "But it invariably leads to trouble, doesn't it? Have you ever met anyone who wasn't glad to get out of it, once they are out of it"?

The person didn't answer immediately. The truth of Marsilio's words was obvious to everyone in the auditorium. Then the person said "But why then, do we go into it"?

"You said yourself why", answered Marsilio. "But you have forgotten to mention something", he said.

"What"? the person asked.

The auditorium was completely silent. Everyone was waiting for the answer. "What happens at the very start of the masquerade, before you even go into it"? Marsilio asked.

There was a little pause and then the person answered "Well, we generally start with the maze in the gardens of Aumhurst".

"Exactly so", said Marsilio."And where did the maze come from"?

"It has always been there", the person answered. "As part of Aumhurst. Everyone knows it is as old as Pavi Bujdam itself".

"Exactly", said Marsilio again. "It is part of Seraphina's original creation. It is a place where we go, is it not, where we become separated from each other, and very often lost. And yet the thrill of it, the fun of it, of that separation, and getting lost, is what draws us into the maze, in the first place, otherwise we wouldn't go in, would we"?

They were murmurs of agreement in the audience, and then the person said "I think generally, we are also fairly inebriated by then".

Everyone in the auditorium laughed. It was true enough.

"Well there is your explanation", said Marsilio with a smile. "You said it yourself. I didn't have to tell you".

Now a third person who had been listening intently, who already had his hand raised, spoke up. "We always manage to get out of the masquerade though, don't we"? He said. "So why can't we get out of Pavi Bujdam, by crossing the mere"?

"Because", Marsilio said, "It is not the maze that stands between you and what is beyond the mere. It is the mere itself".

"Yes, but why can I not cross it"? The person asked. He was beginning to sound frustrated.

"When you come out of the masquerade", Marsilio said, "You give up the masquerade, and your costume, and your mask, don't you"?

"Of course, everyone does", the person said.

"Well so it is with the mere", said Marsilio. "To cross the mere, to go beyond it, to find yourself there, you must give up and go beyond the one who finds himself here".

The person in the audience seemed to let out a huff of breath. "Has anyone from Pavi Bujdam ever been beyond it"? he asked.

Marsilio smiled. "Pavi Bujdam has many merchants of all kinds", he said. "How would you know, unless you yourself have"? And you can be sure", Marsilio went on, "That no one can really help you in that, except someone who has been there".

The person left out another huff of breath, and said "It all sounds very confusing".

"It won't be when the time comes", Marsilio replied. "It is as I was saying at the beginning of my speech. It is all about the light of understanding, just as I described it".

19

To Catch a Person

The night was balmy and perfumed with mysterious and exotic fragrances. They seemed to flow around the gardens, over the hedges, around the corners, across the lawns, and anywhere that you might tiptoe through the dark in the attempt to conceal your whereabouts.

The masquerade was long gone, so the lamps in the gardens of Aumhurst after dark, were not to be expected. Rather, any illumination would be according to the phase of the moon, and the clarity of the sky, and perhaps the incidence of warm light from the towers and higher windows of the house, coming down into the gardens and carrying with it a certain essence of the evening pleasantries within the beautiful rooms of Aumhurst.

Tonight would become the strangest of nights. Stranger than might be imagined possible by anyone who would be adventurous enough to be in the gardens in these hours.

Sebastian was accustomed to creating works of art at Aumhurst more or less in secret, that would subsequently be exhibited to the many who visited Aumhurst. The creation of the persons had been one such work. Created in secret, they were subsequently moved into the garden one night, where they were then discovered by Aumhurst's visitors in the morning.

The persons certainly had a realistic presence about them, and whilst admired by the many who visited Aumhurst during the day, encountering them by night could be startling even for those who knew they were there.

Now, in the moonlit darkness, as Amba and Ambika silently approached the little summerhouse overlooking the slope of the West lawn, they both became aware of the strangest of etherial glows, rising up from the gardens somewhere downhill beyond the hedge at the boundary of the lawn. Positioned as it was at the top of the lawn, the summerhouse provided a superb vantage point from which to observe a good number of the persons who stood all around in the gardens. Its elevation, however, was not sufficient to see the immediately adjacent gardens just beyond the tall hedge at the bottom of the sloping lawn.

The unidentified glow had a stillness about it, it was gentle like the will-o'-the-wisp, or fireflies, but its presence was unmissable, with its greenish tint, and a mysterious, natural quality that made it impossible to explain satisfactorily with any guesses of candles or lamps, or any kind of artificial light.

Amba and Ambika entered the shelter of the summerhouse, and both stood staring at the light coming from behind the hedge. Now from their vantage point they could see it was emanating from what they knew must be a substantially wide area of ground. It was still not possible to see its source, though.

"Isn't that where the maze is"? Ambika whispered.

"I think you're right", Amba replied in a hushed voice. "Perhaps Sebastian has illuminated it".

"Can you see the maze from the house then"? Ambika whispered back.

"Not generally", Amba whispered. "I think there might be one small window though, from which you might be able to see it".

Ambika answered, still whispering, "If it is Sebastian, I wonder what he's up to"?

"Perhaps it's fireflies in the hedges", Amba whispered back.

"I think there's too much light for that", Ambika replied. "I don't

think we should go over there and look, I think we might give ourselves away".

"Agreed", said Amba. "We should settle down here, and keep watch.
If we feel like sleeping, we must take it in turns".

Amba and Ambika both watched for a while, and then Ambika said
quietly "How many persons can you count"?

"Why does the number matter"? Amba replied.

"I wondered what our chances are, of seeing one of them move",
Ambika whispered back.

"They all move at sometime during the night", Amba said.

"How do you know"?

"Sebastian told me", Amba answered, still staring straight out onto
the lawn. "He said it's rare for them to swap places, but they all move at
least a little".

"It must be someone's job to do it", Ambika suggested. "He must
employ someone to do it".

"Why, though"? Amba whispered.

"Perhaps it only happens when he knows there are people visiting
the gardens on consecutive mornings", Ambika speculated.

"Are there many visitors at the moment"? asked Amba.

"There's generally always a few, at least", Ambika answered.

The night wore on, revealing owls hooting and sometimes swooping, and mysterious movements across the lawn, that transpired to be
badgers and foxes. But as for the persons, they stood where they stood,
forever still, mysterious, murky figures, figures that in the dark were
slightly disturbing, perhaps, being indistinguishable from any other
kind of person standing motionless.

And then, after what seemed half the night, but was probably only
half an hour, some kind of larger-looking disturbance arose in the glow
of the strange light emanating from behind the hedge, in the area of the
maze. There were moving shadows thrown upwards in the etherial glow.

"What's that"? whispered Ambika suddenly, with a sense of urgency.

"Yes I saw it", Amba whispered back excitedly.

As they looked, there was definitely a moving shadow in the light.

"Someone's there", Amba whispered. "Come on", she said. And with that, she was already moving out of the door.

As fast as they could, they both made their way down across the lawn, carefully passing through its most shadowy parts, their eyes on the glow in the fast closing distance. When they reached the hedge at the bottom of the lawn they ran along beneath it and made their way to the end. Listening intently they slowly manoeuvred around the end of the hedge until the area of the maze came into view. And then, all efforts to maintain silence were lost to their gasps of astonishment.

The maze itself was aglow, and from where they were, they could see its entrance, and within it, they could see the cause of the glow. The incredible dappled pattern of the maze's hedges, like some beautiful illuminated floral fabric in contrasting dark and light, so clearly visible in the surrounding darkness of the gardens, was now manifest in front of them. Abundantly mixed in with the various darknesses of hedge foliage, through nature's own weaving into an amazing, luminous biological tapestry, was glowing foliage, the foliage itself, the leaves themselves, glowing by themselves, naturally, without any lamps or lights shining upon them, themselves living lamps as part of their own plant nature.

Amba and Ambika looked at each other incredulously. "Bioluminescence", whispered Ambika. "The Bassenthwaites own the genetics and synthetic biology labs, don't they? He must've been working on this artwork for years", she said.

"He couldn't have", Amba whispered back. "Somebody would have noticed. No, I think the luminous plants have just been planted in with the existing maze. With a team of gardeners you could probably do that within a day. And in daylight no one would know what was going on".

"That must be it", Ambika agreed. "What a strange fate for jellyfish or fungus genes", she observed. "He has an upcoming exhibition, perhaps this is part of it".

"Perhaps", Amba nodded.

As much as they looked, they could no longer see any suspicious movement in the light. There were persons placed within the maze itself, some of them on pedestals, and the head and shoulders of at least three of them could be seen eerily peering over the maze in various directions from where Amba and Ambika were standing.

"I don't see any movement", Ambika whispered quietly. They watched motionless for a little longer, but then, in complete obviousness, as bold as brass, or perhaps as bronze or stone, a luciferous figure emerged from the entrance of the maze, and walked away from them. Ambika gave a sharp intake of breath, recognising the figure she knew so well, and Amba whispered "I think that's Timaeus isn't it"?

"It is", Ambika confirmed in the quietest of whispers. "What is he doing here"?

"Perhaps we'll find out", Amba said, now barely whispering. "Let's follow him".

She was about to move when Ambika restrained her and whispered in her ear, with a sense of urgency, "Look... the person in the maze". Amba took her eyes off Timaeus and immediately looked back across the dark outlines of the three persons looming above the maze walls.

"I thought I saw movement", Ambika said.

They both continued to watch the persons intensely, and even though they both knew they were watching for movement, somehow they didn't seriously expect it, and so it was quite a shock to them both, that the person furthest from them suddenly moved. It wasn't a shifting of position of some rigid personified image, rather, what had been an entirely motionless figure with the apparent stiffness of bronze or stone, quite suddenly melted into slow but fluid motion, natural motion that betrayed the unmistakable presence of a human being. Having been stood on the pedestal, the figure was clearly dismounting from it.

As soon as the head disappeared from sight beneath the top of the hedge, Amba and Ambika together ran fast for the entrance to the maze. "Shall we split up"? gasped Amba. "One of us should stay here at the entrance. There's no other way out".

"No, stay together", Ambika answered, sensing something disturbing.

"Come on then", Amba said, leading into the maze. There was an immediate choice of two different directions. "Which way"? she said.

Ambika grabbed Amba's arm, holding her back. "We can't do it this way", she said, "Not unless you know this maze inside out. Whoever it is that was on the pedestal could get to the entrance while we're still lost inside".

Amba looked around the entrance. "You go that way, I'll go this way", she said. "And don't worry about getting lost". With that, she reached into her pocket and pulled out a large ball of thread. "I've been carrying this around for months", she said. "Every time I come to Aumhurst I have it with me, in case I get the opportunity. Now is not the time to explain though, take it", she said, handing Ambika the ball and tying the end of the thread to the middle of the hedge.

So the two of them set off in different directions into the maze, Ambika unravelling the ball of thread as she went, and as much as possible, every now and then, wedging it in to the glowing hedge. Each of them really wanted to call out to the other, to monitor their progress, and keep in contact, but managed to resist doing so.

Ambika kept walking as far as she could until she reached a dead end, and then backtracked, mentally noting that in finding her way out she must not follow paths on which there was already a double thread.

Meanwhile, Amba moved swiftly through the maze, little caring for exactly where she was, hoping for some kind of unconscious instinct to guide her.

Ambika continued to move on, unravelling the thread as she went, occasionally coming back to a part of the thread laid earlier, every so often creating a double thread, but always carefully avoiding following a double thread. But then, after some time, she came to a junction onto a path in which there was already laid a double thread both left and right. There was no other option but to turn around and backtrack on the path she had been taking. She followed it and followed it, completing a double thread as she went, until she came to a junction at a path with no thread. She proceeded to follow it.

It seemed to continue interminably, but eventually it only came to a dead end. Disappointed she turned around and followed the thread back to the junction. There, in one direction only ran the double thread she had previously laid, and in the other, the single thread she had laid whilst backtracking before turning off. She turned, and followed the single thread, creating a double thread as she was going. Eventually, after what seemed like another interminable time, the thread disappeared into an opening behind which there seemed to be an absence of light. She followed it through and found herself exiting the maze. She was back when she had started.

She desperately wanted to call out to Amba but managed to resist doing so. It occurred to her that perhaps it was impossible to penetrate the maze starting with the first choice of direction she had embarked on. The correct way in must be the way that Amba had taken, she thought. She resolved to try again this time entering by the alternative route.

Now she seemed to be making good progress, only occasionally reaching a dead end, resulting in a relatively short retracing of steps. But eventually, she simply grew weary of constantly having to unravel the ball of thread, which besides, had diminished in size now to such an extent that she doubted very much if it would last until the middle of the maze.

In an impulse of impetuousness she broke the thread from the ball, and launched the ball high into the air in what she hoped was the direction of the centre of the maze. She was hoping to provoke some kind of reaction, whether it was from Amba or someone else. She thought she heard the ball land, but there was no reaction from anyone.

So now she started moving through the maze with greater speed. She seemed to be able to keep going for some time, without reaching a dead end. Now the path she was on turned a corner and she was able to look quite a long way down the next part of the path. In that very moment a figure emerged from an opening much further down on the right side of the path, briefly crossed over the path she was on, and disappeared into an opening on the opposite side. For a moment she was transfixed in taking in what she was sure she had seen. It was only a glimpse of the figure that she had been given, but in the strange glow from the maze it had seemed to her that the figure had been in masquerade costume. She was convinced she had seen the head masked, and the glittering parts of the mask glinting in the soft light.

Now she moved fast down towards the junction, turning left into the path that the figure had gone into. It twisted and turned left and right, and before long, terminated in a small rectangular area from which there was one other exit. In the middle of the area was a pedestal on which stood one of the persons. The person was in masquerade costume.

"Come down" she said assertively. The person didn't move. The legs were not covered so she reached up and felt one of them. It was clearly cold stone. The costume had probably not been removed since the masquerade.

There are some things that happen that are, as the mathematicians sometimes say, a given. Even in Pavi Bujdam most people liked to think that most things were not such givens. For the persons in the gardens at Aumhurst everything was certainly a given. The real question about givens, is not whether or not they are givens, but who is the one given to, and who is the one giving? For when these are one, the question of whether or not something is a given, does not arise. The serpent swallows itself, beginning with its own tail.

And so it was given, for Ambika, to call now at the top of her voice, not for her sister Amba, but for Timaeus. And now there certainly was a response, from somewhere deeper within the maze, across the hedges, frustratingly still out of sight, and clearly some distance away, muffled by rows of hedges.

It was Amba's voice that called back in answer to her, but not as Ambika would have expected. Instead, her sister's voice from within the maze called "Amba"!

Ambika knew that Amba would only pretend to be her, if she was with Timaeus. But if she was with Timaeus now, she was with him alone. The maze had its reputation. Each time the masquerade began, many people would come into the maze in search of the discovery of new experiences with new partners. And in the strange glow, and strange situation, it was doubtful even Timaeus would be able to tell the two sisters apart. She had always wondered when this swapping game with her sister might tip over into something more serious.

So now there was only one thing that Ambika could do, to cut through the knot of the maze, and the unexpected play of identities at such an obviously inappropriate time, it seemed. She felt abandoned, before she had even reached the centre. What else would she do? What use would it be to try to claim her own identity by just shouting an assertion of own name? Or trying to assert the mistake or lie of another?

With greater fervour still, she ignored her sister and called out again to Timaeus.

And now there was a pause, and silence,
And by the by, Timaeus' voice came back,
Much closer through the hedges, calling her.
So she called his, a given, once again,
And he called back,
And now the frivolousness between the girls,
Having ripened to a fruit of pain,
Unravelled then and there between the sisters' separate worlds,
The ending of the games between their names.

Never again would they call each other by each other's names, confusing those who come in droves who would try to see the truth of love by studying others. Or so it seemed, at the time.

And now Timaeus appeared from around the hedging corner, notably not wearing a masquerade mask, and the two of them ran together and embraced. Ambika looked up at Timaeus, smiling, and said "What are you *doing* here"?

"What are *you* doing here"? he replied.

"I was looking for you", Ambika said.

"And I was looking for you", Timaeus replied. "I thought you would be looking for what moves the persons, so I came here".

"I thought I saw you in masquerade costume", Ambika said.

"If you did", Timaeus replied, "I'm not in it now, am I? Then even more ambiguously he said "Perhaps it was someone else, and not who you were looking for".

The couple embraced again and Ambika said "What about Amba? She's in the maze somewhere. And there's someone else, too".

"Someone in masquerade costume"? Timaeus said.

"I don't know", Ambika replied. "I saw one of the persons move".

"It's my understanding", said Timaeus, "That all the persons move".

"Not all at once", replied Ambika. "I just saw one. If they do all move, then it must be at different times".

"This is all beginning to be as strange as what happens in the masquerade", Timaeus observed, smiling.

"Oh, there are much stranger things that happen in the masquerade", Ambika said.

"They don't seem so strange at the time, though, do they"? Timaeus said. "It's only for a while, if you remember them, after coming out of the masquerade, that you can see how strange they were".

"I know", Ambika said. "Every year we come out of it and soon it is as if it was all nothing. And we forget it. And yet the next year, somehow, we slip back into it".

Is it really possible for such a conversation to continue in the middle of the night in a bioluminescent maze, without being overheard across the hedges? We should suppose not.

And what of the maze? The maze, that as part of Aumhurst, was part of Seraphina's original art. We might correctly suppose that Sebastian has embraced it and made it into a work of his own art. And that, using arts brought by the new sciences, that Seraphina might not have guessed. But perhaps did foretell after all, when she created the maze.

Sebastian himself knew the maze as an integral part of Aumhurst, passed on down through generations of Bassenthwaites. He knew it began as a work of art by Seraphina. And the same was true, Sebastian thought, of the whole circle of the lives of the friends. For Sebastian, they were all involved in the ongoing art of Seraphina.

We also know that works of art may often hide surprises,

And not to mention hidden secrets there.
So we ourselves perhaps should not be so surprised to find,
Its glowing hedges hide still more affair.

And so it was that now, around the hedged corner onto the path where Ambika and Timaeus stood, Amba suddenly appeared, still unravelling the ball of thread that she had now re-acquired, having found it where it landed. "I could hear you", she said.

"Were you with Timaeus when I called out"? Ambika immediately asked. "What were you doing? Why did you call back to me with your own name"?

"We shouldn't backtrack", Amba answered, more or less ignoring the question. "I have the route to the centre, and there's something you should see".

The three of them now proceeded to follow the thread that Amba had laid, back to the centre of the maze. The amazing maze of Aumhurst. So amazing and yet not even overlooked by Aumhurst, the great house, except by a sideways glance. The attention of the great house was rather, over the ever shining mere and towards whatever it was that was beyond the mountains beyond the mere.

Nevertheless the maze was infamous. Infamous because Sebastian claimed to be able to navigate it with ease, even in a state of inebriation. Whilst no one else amongst the circle of friends, as far as anyone could ever remember, had ever reached the centre, *except* whilst inebriated.

The general consensus had it that it was the summer celebrations at Aumhurst, a kind of carnival which invariably spread inebriation, that led to the beginnings of the masquerade every year. And rumour had it that the falling into the masquerade every summer had its beginnings always somehow in connection with intoxication and the maze.

Now as the three continued to follow the thread, they turned a corner into another path, and there, walking towards them, was none other than Sati.

"Why am I not surprised to find you here", Sati said. "The goings-on at Marsilio's speech at Springmere certainly seems to have spread an influence far and wide, has it not"?

Timaeus, in the glow of the maze, and thus surrounded by female beauty, continued on towards the centre of the maze. The four of them continued on along the winding thread, until eventually, coming upon another path, they were joined by Quentin and Sandhya. This was not the time for going into the masquerade, but the questions that naturally began to arise now amongst the group were "Where is Sebastian"? and "Where is Marsilio"?, for it seemed to them all, that they were all in the momentum of a gathering, and the bonds between them were such that it seemed inconceivable that any amongst the circle of friends could be excluded.

"Let's just get to the centre", Amba urged, and so the six friends continued on, following the thread that Amba had laid. Now as they proceeded, the glow of the maze seemed to become stronger, the twistings and turnings more frequent, and the sense of anticipation that they were approaching the centre, more intense.

The labyrinthine path at length conceded,
To a sudden turning inwards off their present course.
Relieved at last that they had now succeeded,
They inward turned together all as one to find the source.

And so they entered into the very centre of the maze, a rectangular space, semi-lit from all four sides by the luminous hedges, and immediately Amba gasped. In the middle of the space was a pedestal on which stood a person in full masquerade costume.

"That wasn't there before", she exclaimed.

Now the person moved, slowly and carefully taking off its huge, exotic wooden mask, some kind of golden ogre, which twinkled as it caught the faint light from the bioluminescent leaves. The person then stepped down from the pedestal. The person, still clothed in the rest of the masquerade costume, with its glinting braids in colours that looked strange in the bioluminescent glow, turned towards them, and there, right in front of them, was the figure of Sebastian, smiling at them. "You took your time", he said.

"Sebastian"! Several of the group exclaimed, but Sebastian held up his hands as if to quieten them. He looked at Amba. "I expect you're here to show them the gate"? He said. "Which judging by the thread here you have already found".

He turned around and walked over to the back of the rectangular space behind the pedestal. The rest of the group followed him, seeing in the glowing hedge there, the most beautifully ornate iron gate, over the top of which was positioned a brass sign, on which was engraved the name *The Gate of Arabath.*

Sebastian took out an unexpectedly large key from an even more ridiculously large pocket in his costume, and inserted it into the lock. The satisfying sounds of a working metallic mechanism chinked and clicked into the silence of the night in front of the friends. Sebastian creaked opened the gate, and standing aside, gestured to them. "Come and take a look", he said.

The others came right up to the gate, which gave access to what appeared to be a stone shaft, like the top of a tower, down which descended a spiral staircase. They peered down the stairs, which being helical - a more accurate description that Timaeus no doubt would appreciate - very quickly disappeared from view.

"Does anyone want to go down"? Sebastian jested.

"Not unless we want to go back into the masquerade", Timaeus suggested, theorising where it might lead.

"We have done that for this year, and we most certainly do not", Sati protested.

"So there you have it", said Sebastian. "Now you know".

He looked around the group and beyond. "Where is Marsilio"? he said.

"Perhaps he's still at Springmere", Sati answered.

"I don't believe it", said Sebastian. And then immediately called out into the maze, at the top of his voice, "Marsilio"!

A noise of footsteps was beginning to reverberate up the spiral staircase. The whole group of friends watched in astonishment as Marsilio's colourful magician-like figure, ever on time, emerged through the last turns of the stone steps, and out through the gate. He smiled at them.

"Friends"! he said. "I am delighted that you have discovered the location of the Gate of Arabath, as it seems to call itself, now that you are in a state that as far as I can see, is one of sobriety".

He continued smiling at the friends, whilst they just looked back at him in astonishment.

"I can tell you", he went on, "Although I'm sure you already know for yourselves, that there are many imitations of this alluring gate down there". Marsilio briefly glanced behind him at the gate, and then continued, "It seems to me that just as it is here, people in the masquerade are always becoming intoxicated in the maze and wanting to know what is through the gate". He looked back again towards the gate, and said "But of course, down there, it's all masquerade gates. And the maze is a very poor imitation of this one".

Timaeus, ever enquiring and perceptive, and keen to confirm his own theory, asked "Have you come up from the masquerade, then"?

Marsilio smiled, "I am here, am I not? And my dear Timaeus, you are perceiving well, in your suggestion that the masquerade is ongoing. And yet it is finished, is it not, as long as we are here"?

"I don't understand", said Quentin. "The masquerade happens here, in Aumhurst, does it not? And not down there"?

"But where exactly is Aumhurst, my dear Quentin"? Marsilio said. "Other than within the mere, beyond which, is that which you do not know, or understand. And have you ever entered the masquerade without first becoming intoxicated? And if you are intoxicated how do you know where you really are"?

"It's true, I suppose", said Quentin. "The festivities do always begin before the masquerade itself. It always begins with a kind of carnival, in which, I must admit there is some indulgence".

"Indeed", said Marsilio. "And it is true is it not, that the maze in the gardens in which we now find ourselves, holds certain attractions in the festival, attractions of secrecy, and opportunities of meetings and explorations in its labyrinthine pathways, of desires of the most labyrinthine kind"?

"I suppose you are right", said Quentin.

"Tell us"! said Sandhya. "Tell us what is really going on".

"Some things are a phantasy, and some things are true", said Marsilio. "Which is most true, for you"? he asked. "The carnival, the masquerade, or the peaceful harmony of living in Pavi Bujdam as you do for most of the year"?

"Pavi Bujdam, of course", said Sandhya.

"Then why do you not just stay in Pavi Bujdam? Why the carnival? Why the masquerade? Why indulge in phantasy"?

Sandhya looked at the others. "I don't know", she said, "It just happens. Perhaps it's because we feel periodically, I mean every year, that we have explored everything we can in Pavi Bujdam, everything of ourselves and each other, and our relationships, and we are looking for something else".

"Perhaps that's what the Visitors to Pavi Bujdam are doing"? Marsilio said. "Exploring something else".

"Perhaps you are right", Sandhya said.

"Then perhaps Pavi Bujdam itself is a similar phantasy, like the masquerade, but of another kind"? Marsilio said.

"I don't know", said Sandhya. "To answer that, I think I would have to know what is beyond the mere".

"Well", said Marsilio, looking around the group, and at the maze itself. "I think we have Sebastian to thank for his wonderful art, and for this beautiful glowing light from the leaves".

"Hmm...", said Sebastian, "But I think I'm not the only one who has contributed to this. Everyone present has contributed, and there is someone who is not present who is more to thank than all of us. Because she started all this, she started this art, without which our contributions would have nowhere to go".

Sebastian now moved over to the pedestal, behind which there was a box on the grass that no one had really noticed. From the box he retrieved glasses which he proceeded to hand out to all the friends. And then he took up a bottle and filled the glasses.

"I apologise for the encouragement of intoxication", he said, smiling at Marsilio. "And if I'm honest about it, I'm not sure we can ever come into the maze without it, can we"? He held up his glass. "To Seraphina, who could not be here today", he toasted.

"To Seraphina", everyone chorused.

And then Sati said quietly alone, to herself, but unmistakably, and overheard by everyone, "What makes you think she's not here"?

20

The Exhibition

Even as long ago as it was, when the persons had been created and installed in the gardens of Aumhurst, Sebastian was already experiencing an expansion of his vision of art, of what it is, where it comes from, and what it means. By now, especially after the discovery of the unusual books in the library, and the music, perhaps all left at Aumhurst by Seraphina Bassenthwaite, he was now beginning to regard the whole of life in Pavi Bujdam as an ongoing form of art. This must also be true, he supposed, of what went on in the masquerade.

He also wanted the ongoing art of Seraphina to be present within the art that he himself created, which was also ongoing. For Sebastian, in the ever expanding play of the art of Seraphina, it was all ongoing art within ongoing art, creating an art in which everything interpenetrated everything else, and everything had some kind of dependent arising on everything else. One in which, beyond the idea of what comes before and what comes after, all art forms arose out of all of art forms.

And yet everything came down from Seraphina's original art. In his vision, his beloved Sati was not only part of Seraphina's art, as indeed he himself was, and all his friends were, but Sati was, indeed, he was beginning to see, in a way, Seraphina herself, as she had come to be, within the art. And in that, his love for Sati was changing.

The day of Sebastian's latest exhibition had come at last. Exhibitions of his work were often held at Aumhurst, but this time the prestigious Ionian Galleries had offered to host the exhibition, which was to be called *Light and Logos*.

The Ionian Galleries was a beautiful venue, enjoyed during the course of the year probably as much for its architecture as for the content of its exhibitions. The announcement of an exhibition of works by Sebastian had caused great interest.

And so it was that the friends had been invited to the vernissage, and were assembled in the foyer of the Ionian, outside the first gallery, awaiting the official first opening of the doors to the special guests.

"Light and Logos", Sandhya was reading aloud, from the program in her hand. She was skimming through the written material. "I'm not sure he really says what he means by *logos*, though", she said.

Sati was standing next to her. "I think that's the point isn't it"? she said. "For Sebastian the *logos* is the sense *you* make of it".

"I doubt it has just one sense", said Sandhya. She looked at Timaeus. "What do you think, Timaeus"?

"Certainly", Timaeus answered. "The meaning of anything, after all, depends on the context through which you see it, does it not"? he said.

"Quite right, my dear", said Ambika. "It's all about the context".

Quentin was standing just behind them. "The context appears to be the Ionian Galleries, I would say", he said with a smile. The others laughed congenially.

"You're being facetious, Quentin", Sandhya replied.

"On the contrary, I think you are quite literally correct, Quentin", said Timaeus, for a moment wearing his mathematician's hat. But then off came the hat, and on went the musician's one. "But there is a higher context isn't there"? he said. Nobody answered, so he continued, "The higher context is surely beyond the Ionian Gallery, I would say, even though this venue is itself...", he said, looking around the beautiful architectural space, "Most definitely a work of art".

"Yes, Timaeus", said Quentin, smiling, "One work of art inside another, one supported and enhanced by the other". He smiled too.

Amba now joined in. "Could we, perhaps" she said, "Turn it on its head, or put it the other way around and look at the Ionian Gallery itself, in the context of Sebastian's Art? Even though the Gallery came first, of course, and the art it is displaying, by Sebastian, came second"?

"What comes first, what comes second", Ambika said, almost as if she was imitating her. "Isn't that very way itself, of looking at things, in terms of what comes before, and what comes after, just a particular way of looking at things, a particular way of understanding? Isn't there a higher way of appreciation, in which we can go beyond that"?

"Yes", Timaeus interjected, enthusiastically, "I do see what you mean. The important thing here, is that these two arts have come together, isn't it? Sebastian's, and the art of architecture embodied in the gallery. Not which came first, or which came second".

"That's really what I was saying", said Quentin. "The Ionian Galleries were here first, if you really want to talk about measuring things by the clock, but that just means the Galleries have facilitated this coming together. But then, this exhibition, the whole coming together, the whole experience of it, couldn't happen without Sebastian's art, could it? Isn't Sebastian's art facilitating it too? The two are each dependent on each other, to create what we are going to experience here".

"I think so too", Sandhya said. "In fact I think if we could come out of time altogether, and just see things as they are, we might be better off. We would be seeing from a higher perspective, I would say, one in which contexts are emerging out of contexts, all the time, if you see what I mean, like a great churning of things, contexts and experiences and meanings, and relationships, in a greater context that is beyond time altogether".

"I think there's certainly something of that, some aspect of that, in music", Quentin said.

"Well, we haven't yet seen the exhibition", Timaeus said, and looking around continued, "But it seems to me this beautiful place, the Ionian Gallery itself, is having an affect on us already, do you not think"?

"I think you're right, my dearest", said Ambika.

As they stood now admiring the space around them, the group was joined by Marsilio.

"Friends", he said smiling, "It is so good to see you all here. And what a beautiful and fitting venue this is. I wonder what we shall each or all experience"?

Marsilio too, was now looking around him at the architecture. "This is, of course, Seraphina Bassenthwaite", he said.

"We were just saying", said Ambika, "About how the Gallery and Sebastian's art are likely to work together, and how in a way they are already linked, perhaps in some unseen way, beyond this time through which they come together now, in our experience".

"That's very perceptive of you, Ambika", Timaeus smiled. And then in his usual, genteel way, said, "We didn't literally say that, but I nonetheless think that is perhaps what we meant".

"Certainly", said Marsilio. "This beautiful Ionian Galleries venue, and the exhibition indeed join hands now. And as in a dance, it is a pattern in a form of motion in which we can join hands also, and participate. And I think we should perhaps remain mindful not just of Sebastian, the Lord of this part of the dance, but of Seraphina, too, the Lady of the dance. And realise that each of us now, can perhaps become the Lord or Lady of our own dance. This wonderful dance received through these our own senses, themselves part of a still greater and more magnificent celestial dance, which with providence and prayer we might come to perceive".

"Thank you", said Sati. She touched his arm with love, and smiling, said with a sense of humour "I think through Marsilio we have completed saying grace before what we are about to receive". The others laughed in agreement. And now, as if as part of the dance, the doors to the first gallery were opened, and the group of friends were able to enter.

§

The first gallery invited visitors to walk all around the perimeter of the room, which was very large, taking in one at a time, a set of some twelve equal sized paintings, that even at first glance, seemed to be either perhaps all the same, or somewhat similar.

Sati and Sandhya stopped at the first painting. Sandhya was clearly very surprised. "It's you", she said. The painting was large. Sati was clearly the subject, as she sat in the scene, most beautifully illuminated from the side, beside her image, an easel on which was another painting, a good third of the size of the painting hanging on the wall of the gallery.

The painting within the painting, then appeared to be of precisely the same scene. And so it was that a recursion of scenes and Satis and paintings receded into one point of the painting on the wall of the gallery. Sandhya repeated herself, now more quietly, and contemplatively, as she studied the painting. "It's *you*", she said.

"Apparently not", she heard Sati reply. Sandhya turned her head now to look at Sati, puzzled." What do you mean"? she said.

Sati simply nodded towards the didactic panel beside the painting. Sandhya moved over to read it. "Oh", she said. "I see. Apparently it's Seraphina".

"Apparently so", Sati answered, a tone of disappointment in her voice.

"I do seem to remember Quentin saying you look like Seraphina", Sandhya said.

Sati didn't answer. And then she said "And I do seem to remember distinctly, sitting repeatedly for Sebastian, in a set just like *that*".

"Ah", Sandhya said, "That would explain it. It *is* you. Or rather, you are Seraphina, in the painting".

They were approached by Timaeus. "It's remarkable isn't it"? he said. "Have you seen the others"?

The three of them moved on to the next painting. At first sight, it appeared to be the same. But then Sandhya started walking back and forth between the two. "They're not the same", she said. "You look quite different in this one".

"Yes", said Sati. "I know. But look at my face and clothes in the picture of the painting on the easel. They are not the same, either".

Timaeus walked right up to the canvas and to their surprise pulled from his pocket a magnifying glass. He proceeded to examine deep into the paintings within the paintings.

"Well they're clearly all different", he said. "In some of them you are looking in one direction, in others you are looking in quite another. They are not just subtle differences. You are even wearing different clothes in each of them".

"I know", Sati said. "I remember Sebastian being very particular about it on each sitting".

"There appears to be twelve layers altogether, so to speak", Timaeus said, "Twelve distinct images of you, just in this one painting. It's what we mathematicians call a recursion". He stepped back in towards the painting, and then peered into it again. "After the smallest one there is just colour and indistinctness", he said, peering closely through the magnifying glass at a tiny point on the canvas.

"Hmm", he said, stepping away now, "It's the first time I've seen such a combination of miniaturist painting and large-scale painting".

"I don't know how he works so fast, to have produced all these", Sandhya said, looking around the gallery.

"He works remarkably fast in the sittings", said Sati, "But after that, in the studio, he said he enters a state of frenzy".

"I can imagine", said Timaeus, walking onto the next painting.

After some while, the group of friends reconvened in the middle of the gallery. During the viewing, Timaeus with his magnifying glass had been much in demand to convey information about the smallest image of Sati that was visible in each painting. They had determined that in the final painting - if it was proper to call it the final painting - the smallest image of Sati deep at the centre of the recurring images, was one in which she was wearing the same colour clothes, and looking in the same direction, as she was in the largest image of her in the first painting - if indeed it was correct to call it the first painting.

At that moment Quentin walked past. Clearly, he had overheard part of the conversation. He lent in towards them as though he was revealing a secret. "Like most of the other well established painters in

Pavi Bujdam, he does have help, you know", he said. "Other apprentice painters who work under him. They might not yet be recognised as Masters in their own right, but they are Masters in the making".

"Yes, I suppose I did know that", said Timaeus. "But I also know that he does enter the state of frenzy in his work".

"They are all beautiful", Amba said. "I think I'm feeling a little dizzy by it".

"So am I", said Quentin, sitting down on a nearby seat. Amba immediately sat down, too, beside him.

"I actually think Sebastian is a mathematician at heart", Timaeus said with a smile, looking around all twelve paintings.

"Where is Marsilio"? asked Sati.

Nobody knew.

"What does Sebastian say about it all, on the didactic panels"? asked Quentin.

"They're all the same", Sandhya said. She walked over to the nearest one, and started reading aloud to the group.

"*Seraphina Bassenthwaite* is a set of 144 paintings of Seraphina Bassenthwaite, in 12 paintings", she began.

She read ahead a little, and then continued:

> "Twelve paintings of her are included in each painting in the gallery. You may want to ask which was the first, and which was the last, of the paintings in the gallery? Whilst there may have been a first and a last sitting, there is no first or last in the paintings. The paintings in the gallery form a mandala, a circulating circle of images or situations, contexts in which Seraphina Bassenthwaite finds herself, that do not have a beginning or an end, just as the fact that there are only 12, is only a finite representation of something that to me, seems infinite. You will find that in each painting in the gallery, the primary or

largest image of Seraphina, in her whole context, appears also as the smallest in the painting opposite on the other side of the gallery. You may need a magnifying glass to verify this. They are available in the kiosk in the foyer".

"Well there we have it", Sati said. "And as we heard, this is all portraits of Seraphina Bassenthwaite".

"Not quite, there's more", said Sandhya. She continued reading. "It goes on", she said:

"You'll notice that each Seraphina has all the other Seraphinas, complete with their context, behind her. Perhaps, really, we are all like this. Even though we like to think in terms of what comes before, and what comes after. This, of course, is not all. Because the painting only shows a tiny part of Seraphina's life and context. She has a life beyond the view confined by the painting. In her life is everyone with whom she has any kind of relationship. And every one in that context, is like this, too. For a more complete picture, we would have to see in the picture, everyone, and in everyone's picture, every-one behind everyone, and in every canvas on every easel, every canvas on every easel. Alas, such a task, I could not undertake".

The group of friends remained in silence for some moments, contemplating Sebastian's words. And then a voice from across the room at the door of the gallery said "I think our dear friend Sebastian is beginning to deepen in his insight". It was Marsilio. He continued, "And I think the next gallery will be well worth the visit".

The friends moved towards Marsilio and through to the next gallery.

§

Now everyone saw the walls were covered with numerous small canvases. None of the friends could count how many, but Timaeus did carry out a private estimate, and came to a conclusion which he kept to himself.

Just inside the door, an area on each side of the Gallery wall contained just one of these many small paintings. On the wall one side of the door, the canvas was entirely white. On the other, it was entirely black. Beyond these two canvases, the number of pictures on each wall multiplied rapidly. To begin with, were canvases of stark patterns of black and white.

In the first paintings, half the canvas was white, the other half black, in numerous different patterns. Walking around the walls, the friends found the patterns on the canvases becoming more and more complex, the various black or white shapes, becoming smaller and smaller. After wandering around a little, Timaeus pulled out his magnifying glass again, and could be seen peering into the canvases. Moving around the gallery, what was once black and white, had become textured greys, on all but the closest inspection. Moving around further, the shades of greys became more numerous.

At first, they seemed jumbled, and random. But then as the friends approached the door at the other end of the gallery, the shades of grey on the canvases on each side of the gallery, began to resolve themselves out again, on one side of the room becoming lighter and lighter, whilst on the other side, becoming darker and darker. Until eventually, there was just one painting on each side of the exit door of the gallery, each with its own space on the gallery wall. One was black, the other was white.

Timaeus could be heard speaking to Sati. "I do think he is mixing mathematics with art", he was saying.

By the by, all the friends found their way to the exit door at the far end of the gallery. They wandered through, past the entirely black, and entirely white canvases, and found themselves in another gallery.

Turning to the walls each side of the entrance door to the new gallery, they found themselves looking at a number of canvases that appeared to be paintings of the previous gallery. Each, however, was tinted in its own unique colour. The overall effect of the canvases in a spectrum of different coloured tints, was quite beautiful, and almost mesmerising.

But now, as they wandered down the gallery, the canvases on display became more colourful, each in their own right, the colours became stronger, no longer a single tint, but rather, now, each painted from a multicoloured palette. And, in something imitative of the very first gallery, further down the gallery, around the wall, they began to see paintings of other paintings, in this, the same gallery.

Quentin and Sandhya began to complain of feeling confused, and dizzy, and went to sit down on the seats in the middle of the gallery. The others continued to walk around, until at length, the pictorial content of the paintings seemed to become smaller and smaller in detail, until they were looking again at large canvases of miniaturist painting, which Timaeus once again was examining through his magnifying glass.

And then Amba's Voice came from somewhere in the middle of the gallery, further away from the canvases. "Oh my goodness"! she declared. "They're landscapes and portraits", she said, looking at the paintings furthest down the gallery, "Both at once"!

Timaeus, still examining a painting through his magnifying glass, stepped back some distance, and looked around the canvas, and then walked back to join Amba. "So they are"! he said.

§

After some discussion in the middle of the gallery, the friends moved on to the fourth gallery, which as soon as they entered, seemed already crowded with visitors. But they were not visitors. The static crowd of persons were like those in the gardens of Aumhurst, except that they were not of bronze or stone, but rather, appeared to be of painted plaster, adorned with beautiful colours, often bright, often metallic or iridescent, such as usually appeared on the persons of Aumhurst during the masquerade.

The friends began to mingle amongst the persons, who already appeared to be contemplating themselves in the full-length mirrors facing this way and that, that stood all around the room, as if in the interior of some department store. And as the friends now intermingled with the persons, the judiciously positioned mirrors unexpectedly multiplied them in their number, expanding the apparent size of gallery and increasing the crowd.

As the friends spread out amongst the plaster persons, naturally standing still amongst them and beside them as they contemplated their situation, the whole gallery bloomed into the edifying scene of a quiet crowd absorbed in itself, all seemingly concerned with the painted attire of those who looked at themselves in the mirrors. It was indeed as if the whole gallery were the floor of a huge department store on which all the shoppers were entirely absorbed in the choosing of colours of adornment for their friends or themselves. The persons became the friends and the friends became the person's friends. And everyone, persons and friends alike, or so it seemed, became aware of everyone, friends and persons alike. So it was that the exhibited blossomed as the visitors themselves became the exhibited.

Eventually, though, the friends began to move and wander around, whilst the persons did not, and the temporary spell was broken. Nonetheless, the sense of a novel community experienced by the friends, continued, a community of those who moved, those who did not move right now, and those who never did move. Those who never did, being those, the persons, who were absorbed in contemplating themselves, in the mirrors. Which provided an impression of vanity, since the persons who were absorbed in their own reflections were the beings in the gallery who were most brightly adorned with the painted colours.

And so it was that the friends moved around the fourth gallery, admiring both the persons, and their gallery-wide context, played out through the reflections in the mirrors, until gradually, the moving part of the crowd evaporated away from the scene, as the friends moved towards the exit door.

On their way out, Sati alone noticed the didactic panel positioned by the exit. She read it, privately.

The persons are all absorbed in their own reflections. Those who observe, are all absorbed in the persons. The persons, all of whom are apparently, but only apparently, human, are images of those who observe. They are part of an Icastic art. So too, are the observers part of the same art, whether or not they realise it.

The art, for me, is intelligence, in action. This exhibit is just a part of it. The whole scene, of observers and persons, is a form of intelligence in action, is it not? The scene, the installation, the action here, represents the essential nature of our own mind and experience of being and relationships. My exhibit is about our life, which I see as this intelligence, in action. Intelligence, in motion. And in that moment where the motion stops, when everyone contemplates the persons, it is possible that you might get a glimpse of the Icastes, the source of this intelligence that is forever in motion. The secondary, imitating the original, is the phantasy. It is only an image of the original, and yet thinks it is the one who observes!

Sati contemplated the words. This was very Sebastian, she thought. She looked around the gallery one last time. She noticed that she had not seen Marsilio enter or leave the exhibit. He must have been ahead of them, all the time, she thought.

§

On entering the fifth gallery the friends were met with a black curtain not far inside the room, all the way around the perimeter, and from floor to ceiling. There appeared to be no opening through the curtain, so the friends walked around it, until they reached the other end of the gallery. And there was an entrance through into a darkened space in which nothing was visible, but for a little line of lights disappearing into the interior. The opening was partially covered by a curtain, making it all the more difficult to look in.

The curtain entrance was attended by an usher, who made sure to tell everyone that the entrance into the exhibit was to be "one person at a time".

"But the persons are all in the other room", Amba jested.

"It makes no difference", the usher said flatly, either indifferent to her joke, or simply not understanding. "One person at a time", he repeated, as if he had been privately practising the phrase so much that now his confidence in it was unshakeable. Amba assumed he had no knowledge of the persons so many of which Sebastian had now created, or at least, no knowledge that they were widely known by those who knew Sebastian's art, as *the persons*.

"Which person is going to go in first, then"? she said, turning to the others.

"When I go in I think I should like someone to accompany me", Ambika said, tauntingly "How do we know there's not a Minotaur or something, in there"?

"It makes no difference", the usher said, in precisely the same tone of voice, "One person at a time".

"I'll volunteer to go first, if we like", Quentin said. For the first time the usher said nothing, but held the curtain aside as Quentin entered. Then the usher said simply "Follow the lights".

Quentin disappeared into the interior and the usher closed the curtain.

"If we hear screaming I'm going in", Sandhya joked. She was half expecting the usher to make his "it makes no difference" speech again, but almost to her disappointment he remained silent.

It seemed quite a long time before Quentin re-emerged. When he finally did, he smiled at the others, and said "It's amazing, and beautiful", gesturing for someone else to make the journey.

They went in, one at a time, in accordance with the usher's instructions, not one of them, having emerged, giving any clue as to what they had experienced inside. Finally, it was Sati's turn.

As soon as the usher closed the curtain behind her, she was engulfed in blackness, all but for the line of tiny lights leading into the interior.

Intrigued, she followed the lights. As she approached the end of the path she realised she was walking towards someone else, as she saw walking towards her, a pale, barely visible figure, strange, in the lack of light, but obviously, her intelligence told her, an image of herself. It was her reflection in a mirror. It seemed to her momentarily as though she was walking towards her own ghost, which was walking towards her.

She walked right up to the mirror and touched it with her hand, somehow to confirm what it was, even though the greater part of her knew this was unnecessary. And then, surrounding her, feint, tiny dawn-like beginnings of light, light that seemed to her to be of infinitely many colours, very, very slowly, gradually, began to arise all around her into such a gentle ocean of resplendent, subtle scintillations, that it was as though she were at the centre of a vast diamond, illuminated from some far-off prism-refracted light.

She soon felt as though she had been transported from the gallery, seemingly upwards and upwards into some vast space all around her, for the distance into which she found herself now looking, seemed, even in the very low levels of light, to be extending into a far-off infinite space, an invisible distance in which the colours merged and faded into a faint, misty, whitish blue hue. It reminded her of looking out across the mere in those early morning weather conditions that would sometimes come, in which it was both misty and clear light at the same time.

Now as the light levels gradually began to rise in the darkness still surrounding her, the scene all around, which had, to begin with, been a glittering wash of feint colours, somehow began to differentiate within the blackness into myriads of indiscernible smaller patterns, facets within iridescent rainbow-coloured facets, as though the infinite diamond was now manifesting its infinite facets in the darkness all around her, gradually revealing some scintillating truth of itself.

As the infinitude of sparkling lights brightened more, within that patterning she began to see the emerging of an endless crowd, receding far, far away into the distance, further than she could see, more of Sebastian's persons, she supposed, until she began to realise she supposed wrongly. For now as the illumination began to rise to its fullness, something was emerging through the numberless glinting species of colours in their collective glass-like quality. In a kind of immeasurable psychological power of their effects, through some hidden moment inherent in their mixings, she began to realise she was surrounded not at all by a multitude of persons, but by endless reflections of herself.

At first, she only felt it, sensed it, until she instinctively moved her arm, only to see the entire crowd move their arms. Like the rising sun across the glistening mere, on those misty mornings when the last wisps of mist have lifted, a new clarity was coming to be, as the innumerable images of herself were all around her, looking in all directions. It was a strange, cosmic-like population of her self, vaster than vast, spreading out all around her, receding into infinity, a far-off infinity of nothing but her own selves disappearing into obscurity, where she in all her multitude finally merged and disappeared faintly through a strange, inexplicable, inexorable curvature of light that no orbit of her mind could truly grasp or overcome.

Briefly, but only very briefly, as the slowly rising light levels transiently reached their zenith before slowly but surely diminishing again, she became ephemerally aware that she was standing in a magnificent hall of mirrors, that must be enclosed within the blackness of the curtains. Again, it was as though she had been transported, but transported now into some dream of herself, within the covering of the curtains, beyond which was her true life.

She stood and watched, to the last, until the final faint glimmerings of luminousness sank into oblivion, and she was once again surrounded by the blackness. Filled with wonder, and wanting to repeat the experience, but unable to, she at first stood for a while, and then turned to the little line of tiny lights leading to the way out. She followed them slowly through towards the curtain, and now, faintly illuminated within the curtains, on a stand to the side of her, facing her, she found the didactic panel for the exhibit. She leaned towards it and looked harder at it. It was blank, all but for the name of the exhibit, which read *Indra's Net*.

2 1

The Seventh Gallery

The sixth and final gallery of the exhibition was, at first sight, more conventional. Seen from the doorway to the gallery the illumination of the whole room appeared to be emanating from the paintings themselves, perhaps because they were spotlighted with some secret calibration of colouring, whilst no other lighting was so obviously visible. Every canvas seemed to subtly glow, inviting attention, even from a distance.

The friends walked into the room and spread out. Timaeus approached one of the paintings that for unknown reasons seemed to attract him more immediately than the others. He stood and studied it. At first he wondered if it was going to be more play on the idea of infinite recursion, as he had seen previously. He had seen that it was a self portrait of Sebastian, standing in front of a large canvas, and in the act of painting.

Timaeus' eyes moved to the content of the canvas within the painting, half expecting it to be a scene of Sebastian standing, painting on yet another canvas. But it was not.

Instead, he saw that it was a scene of the masquerade.

Further down the gallery Amba too, stood absorbed in a painting, another, different scene of Sebastian standing, again in the act of

198

painting on yet another canvas. She too, was studying the picture on the canvas within the painting. She too, had seen that it was a picture of the masquerade.

Timaeus contemplated the masquerade scene, which seemed to pull his attention involuntarily further into it, like some kind of visual magnetism, into all the various and strange activities of the many brightly coloured characters busily engaged in its surreal-like charade.

Something struck him strongly about it, as he looked, something not quite right, and yet obviously purposeful in the context of the painting. The appearance of the brightly coloured costumes was certainly masquerade-like, and true to precisely the kind of costumes that he was familiar with, at masquerade time. Most of the characters in the crowded scene, as was always the case in the masquerade, wore masquerade masks. But conspicuously, and no longer true to the life of the masquerade, there were depictions of some people he knew, including himself, clearly, personally identifiable because they were inexplicably not wearing masks.

Puzzled, he took a step further in towards the canvas to take a closer look. He saw that in the detail, where he himself appeared in the painting, he was clearly looking at Amba who was some distance away from him, his gaze clear and intent. He wasn't sure how he knew it was Amba, but he was sure. Amba was also maskless in the scene, and she looked back at him, her eyes fixed on him, across a sea of interacting masquerade figures, who, dancing and arguing, and conversing, and carrying out commerce, playing musical instruments, chasing and flirting and engaging in all kinds of bawdy activity, seemed oblivious to the maskless ones amongst them.

He felt as though he was somehow reading the painting, but without really knowing what it was he was reading. And now he began to wonder why it was that he had felt so sure that the one looking at him across the crowd in the painting, was Amba, rather than Ambika.

For some reason he looked down the gallery and saw Ambika standing there, absorbed in another painting further down on the same wall. He had just caught sight of her as she was briefly turning to call over her shoulder to Amba, who was a little distance away, clearly wanting to share with her something she had seen in the painting.

"What is it, Ambika"? Timaeus overheard Amba say, as she crossed the room towards the painting. The two women were now staring into the painting, one of them pointing to a detail. Timaeus turned and looked back into the painting in front of him. Now he noticed that within the masquerade crowd Ambika was indeed also present in the painting, but well off to the side of the crowd, unmasked, and hand in hand with with another unmasked figure whom he now realised was unmistakably Sebastian. He hadn't really noticed him before because the body of the figure was mostly obscured. He was leaning out from behind a bush at the edge of a forest. He undoubtedly seemed to be pulling Ambika behind the bush with him.

Timaeus instinctively looked down the gallery again, and there was Amba, still staring into the painting, but Ambika was now nowhere to be seen. As he looked across to the other side of the gallery somebody touched his arm. He recognised the way it was done; it was a gesture that Ambika frequently used. He turned around to see her there, smiling at him. "You should come and see this", she said, guiding him down towards the other painting. "Ambika just showed it to me", she said.

In response to her calling her sister by her own name, Timaeus said "There's no need to do that", quite matter-of-factly. He continued, "There's no one else here. Besides, I thought you said you and Amba had stopped doing that now". They had reached the other painting. Amba had clearly overheard them and now turned away from the painting towards them, smiling, and said to Ambika, "I don't know what he means, do you Amba"?

Timaeus didn't really understand the need for the name game, but ignored it. He was used to it, if growing a little weary of it. "So what's going on in here then"? he said, looking at the painting, partly to distract attention away from the name game, which he found rather tiresome.

The painting was similar, but different to the one he had been looking at. He looked carefully at the depiction of the masquerade. He started to become more and more absorbed in it, until he felt Ambika touch his arm again. And then with his attention briefly distracted away from the masquerade, he immediately saw Ambika on the other side of him, and realising it was Amba who had touched him, quickly turned back to see Amba still with her hand on his arm.

For some reason that was inscrutable to himself he put his hand on hers in the manner he was accustomed to, with Ambika. Her eyes were on his but then she looked sideways to the painting and nodded towards it. He took the cue, and looking at the painting saw that whilst it did in a way, still look like the masquerade, it now looked more like a forest, a beautiful forest, of a crowd of mature, straight trees, of a woodland carpeted with spring bluebells. And in a few more seconds, he noticed some of the dark boles of some of the trees, had leaning out from behind them, carnival-costumed figures.

He couldn't understand why there was something poignantly beautiful about it, and lost all caring and consciousness of how the transition had taken place, whether it was in his own mind, or on the canvas. This was probably one of Sebastian's pareidolia paintings, he thought to himself. He squeezed the hand still on his arm, and with a brief look sideways saw that it was Ambika standing there. It seemed completely natural and almost irrelevant, if also slightly symbolic in some way that he was not fully conscious of, that she was in full masquerade costume, apart from the absence of mask.

Quentin was now behind them, saying "There is something in the paints that Sebastian uses". And then Sati was there. "Perhaps it's the way he mixes them", she said.

Timaeus agreed, and looked around the painting for more clues. There was nothing unusual, but he became aware that the others beside him had now turned around and were looking away. He turned round to see what they were looking at.

Quentin was surprised at Timaeus. He had been waiting for this moment for a long time, and after all, Timaeus literally already had Amba on his arm, and who knows what else they might get up to? "There's no need to look", he said abruptly. But it was too late, and he knew it. Quentin was already looking at the mirrors on the opposite wall of the gallery.

"These are wonderful paintings", Sati was already saying, walking towards them. Then she noticed Marsilio laid out, asleep, on one of the seats in the centre of the gallery, in full masquerade regalia. "What is he doing in costume"? she called back to the others.

"Have you not been to the seventh gallery"? Quentin immediately answered. "It is entirely an exhibition of masquerade costumes". He started walking towards the central seats. "Perhaps it's not Marsilio", he said authoritatively, looking at the figure laying on the seat. A few moments later he stopped at the seat and stared at Marsilio. "It's a mannequin", he said triumphantly.

Sati was upset. "Who put him there"? she said.

"You should be more careful", Sandhya called out from further down the gallery. Everyone knew, that everyone knew that Sandhya had just come from the seventh gallery. "There are horses of fire in there", she said, her voice shaky. With that, she started taking off her masquerade costume. She now frantically pulled it off, ripping it when it resisted her, and threw it down the gallery towards the others. "You can take up the mantle", she cried.

Timaeus was continuing to study Sebastian leaning out from behind the bush, pulling Ambika towards him, and catching a temporarily vivid impression of what seemed to have been a daydream, stepped back from the painting murmuring "The seventh gallery".

Marsilio's voice was behind him. "There is no seventh gallery", Marsilio said.

Sebastian was in the middle of the room saying "I'd like to show you how it is done, if I may"? He was surrounded by a number of large and attractive pots of paint. "Come", he said, gesturing to Sati and Quentin to examine the contents. Each of them came over and each looked into one of the pots, becoming immediately stationary, seemingly frozen in time, completely enthralled with the content. They looked rather like the persons in the gardens of Aumhurst.

"And now", Sebastian announced triumphantly, "The seventh

gallery"! and pulling back the curtain with a theatrical flourish, revealed a number of similar pots of paint forming an island around which stood mirrors, entirely encircling the pots. Timaeus could see in the illusion of the images in the mirrors countless reflected pots of paint extending in all directions out to infinity, away from the centre, and yet all enclosed within the black curtain. Sebastian began mixing the paints in the centre, and as he did so the colours spread and mixed infinitely outwards in the reflections of reflections, towards a horizon that shone like the mere around Pavi Bujdam. And then out of his mixing Sebastian produced a masquerade costume which he put on. Laughing aloud he then jumped over the pots and into the reflection, whereupon infinitely many Sebastians in masquerade costumes disappeared in every direction.

§

On both walls of the gallery were just paintings. There were no mirrors. The paintings were those that were there when they had come into the gallery. Timaeus looked up from the seat in the centre of the gallery, on which he was laying. Ambika was holding his hand. "You fainted, my dear", she said. "You looked as though you were dreaming".

"I think I was going into the masquerade", Timaeus said.

"Perhaps you were trying to, my dear", Ambika said. "But you cannot do it from here. You know how it must be. We only ever go into the masquerade after getting lost in the maze in the gardens at Aumhurst.

"I wasn't deliberately trying to", Timaeus said.

"I don't think any of us ever are, really, are we"? Ambika said.

"It was one of Sebastian's paintings that did it", Timaeus replied.

"Ahh yes", Ambika answered. "He does seem to have created a masquerade in the paintings. I think you got lost in one of them". She smiled. "It's his fault".

"Actually", Timaeus answered, "Quentin told me that Sebastian himself thinks that everything he does with his art is really part of Seraphina's art. So perhaps we have Seraphina to blame", he said, smiling too, now.

"Perhaps no one is to blame", Ambika said. "After all, it's Sebastian who maintains the maze, isn't it? And he seems to fall into the masquerade every year, along with all of us doesn't he? And in any case, even if it is all part of Seraphina's art, as he says, even if *we* are all part of Seraphina's art, whose art is Seraphina"?

22

Gossip

King, the swift steed of Merehurst stood ready on the beautiful bright turf of the greensward that goes down to the edge of the mere. In the full thundering of the bells in the folly tower, on the monthly meeting of the Merehurst ringers, he stood, eyes alert. Perhaps aware in his own inexplicable way, of the mathematics of the plain hunt that rang out from the tower.

In a passing moment of silence from the folly, Helios, the beautiful palomino, golden in the Sun, sure of hoof and nobly ready, the one and only one who taking flight on wings of courage might Divine frenzy invite, stood now beside King, amidst the grandsire of the bells.

Sati speaks gently to both horses, and chooses King.

Now upon the saddle fast she rides,
Towards the Silver Gallop and to Aumhurst she makes haste,
Having heard the story of the nights:
When she herself at Merehurst stays, at Aumhurst she's replaced.

Never was entanglement at Merehurst her intent,
By accident alone it seems to her,
That she had fallen fast and entered into things undreamt,

And only now can see the poison lure.

The messenger the keeper of the mews,
Himself by accident he claims had spilt the secret,
And now the cup turned over doth confuse,
Its contents runs like blood from all that's pure and true and sacred.

So Sati rides as never has the Silver Gallop seen,
Like frenzied fire but is it the Divine?
Her purpose true now having seen from higher in her being,
Her courage now must challenge fate's design.

Fate above nature, nature's force,
Helios charges now along the mere a golden flame,
Fate itself empow'red to change fate's course,
To now resolve on Sati's love its purpose to reclaim.

Through the gap at boundary's fence Helios gives his lot,
And faithfully he races to the last,
That Sati might prevent in time the sealing of the knot,
Unsnarl Lachesis' thread that has been cast.

What human dramas must unfurl from causes out of sight,
In Pavi Bujdam there begin as naught,
But deep within the masquerade are played out every night,
Such trials from Sati's story will be wrought.

At last dismounted from the steed approaching Aumhurst's doors,
Sati rushes in and to the scene,
She flies the stairs and galleries to all the upper floors,
And bursts upon the pair to intervene.

Sebastian stands the brushes in his hands.
Amba sits enrobed in silk.

The fearful thread is broke; the stable keeper's yarn no longer fits.

"What is it my dear"? said Sebastian, looking round from the newly wet canvas.

Sati sat herself down on the chair just inside the door. "I thought", she began, breathless, "I thought...", but she just continued breathing in silence.

"You thought you were still in the masquerade", Sebastian said, perceptively, turning back to his painting. There was a moment's silence, then he said, while continuing to steadily brush the paint, "No matter, we all do it from time to time. Don't think anything of it".

"I thought...", Sati said, for the third time, but she still didn't finish.

Amba, remaining perfectly still in her position, still looking in the direction she had been told to look by Sebastian, said "I thought... I was Seraphina once. But I think that's more likely to be *you*, Sati, isn't it? Judging by the portraits on the walls, here".

"It's *art*", said Sati, getting her voice back.

"Yes I know it's art", Amba replied, "As is *this*. But *they* are said to be portraits of Seraphina. Those who visit Aumhurst think they are. Some might say it's the art of deception".

Now Sebastian interjected. "It is not I, who am deceiving anyone. What you see you see yourself", he said dismissively, continuing his painting.

"So you admit they are of Sati"? Amba said.

"I do no such thing", Sebastian replied.

"They do look genuinely old", Amba said, prompting for more information.

"The ones on the walls of Aumhurst, they are genuinely old", Sebastian confirmed.

"How can they look so like Sati"? Amba prompted again.

"You should ask Sati that", Sebastian answered, still painting. "Not me".

Amba took the cue. "What say you, Sati"? she said.

"I say they are not Seraphina", Sati answered.

"So they *are* you"? Amba exclaimed with a vague tone of triumph.

"I didn't say that", Sati said. "I said they are not Seraphina. Which they are not. Because they are just an image. They are works of art, made in imitation of her".

Amba was not impressed. "Yes, of course", she said, "Of course they are just images. They are paintings. They are art. They are an artistic imitation of her. But they are still images of *her*. Or are they really images of *you*", Amba said.

Sati replied calmly, "Who is Seraphina? Who am I? Who are you"?

Sebastian paused in his painting, and still contemplating the canvas, said "We're all images".

"But Sati, you look like her, and she looks like you", Amba said, insistently.

"Ah", Sebastian said, "Yes, but that's down to the artist, isn't it? And perhaps I too, am just an image of Seraphina's"?

Sebastian now stepped away from the canvas and put down his brush. He looked at Amba. "As I see it, Seraphina is the artist", he said. "I have been seeing this for some time now. I think you all know this. She is behind all this, you know. Our whole life in Pavi Bujdam, I mean. She is said to be the architect of Aumhurst and the Mereage, and probably the whole of Pavi Bujdam, I know, but I know there is more to it than that. I think everything here is her ongoing art, Aumhurst, Merehurst, all the Vicinages, all of it. Including me. And even the art I myself create, only happens because first of all I am here, in all this, so as I see it, even my art, is in a way, her".

"Yes, yes, yes", said Amba, "That's all very well, but then what kind of person or being is Seraphina, if she is able to create all this"?

"What kind of person or being are you"? said Sebastian.

"What do you mean"? Amba said.

"I mean", Sebastian replied, "Who are you? Are you really so different to me? Isn't that just a way, through some means, that Seraphina has painted herself into the picture, in different ways"?

Amba looked a little bemused. "So you're saying now not just that

Seraphina is somehow the artist behind all this, but that we're all somehow Seraphina herself"? she said.

"Well", said Sebastian. "In a way I am saying that. But we have to stop thinking of her as a person, in the way that we are used to. And you have to understand that all these paintings of Seraphina, around Aumhurst, are only images. They are only representations. Actually, I think, if she ever really did exist here, in Pavi Bujdam, as some ordinary ancestor of mine, rather than being just a myth, then I think that Seraphina Bassenthwaite was an image, too. An image of the real Seraphina, just as we are".

"But we're not all female, are we"? Sati said.

"Certainly not", Sebastian replied. "But our gender is only what we are being in the image, isn't it? It's not the original. We must find the original".

"But I like being female", Sati said. "I think both our genders, and the fact that we are different, are really important. I wouldn't want to be neutralised".

"Neither would I", Sebastian replied. He was, Sati thought, now beginning to show signs of the frenzy. He went on "But perhaps it is only by the merging of the two that you can discover something that is beyond both". Sebastian now seemed to be even more inspired by the frenzy. He continued "Perhaps each is just a different image of the mere itself. And perhaps in their merging is the image of what is beyond the mere".

"What about Sati, here"? Amba said. "Why is she the only one that actually looks like Seraphina"?

Sebastian shook his head. "What do you mean, she looks like her"? he said. "Surely what you mean is that she has a likeness to the image of Seraphina that is in the old paintings, that's all. And as I said, that's only an imitation, an image. Nobody knows what Seraphina looks like. Not if you understand what or who Seraphina really is, in the way that I am saying".

"But isn't that what an artistic image is meant to be, Sebastian, if it is a painting of a person, isn't it something that looks like them"? Amba said.

Sebastian looked surprised. "How would you apply that to the paintings by Picasso, in the Old World exhibition in Ionian gallery"?

"You artists always say things like that", Amba replied. "Anyway, if all this is Seraphina's art, whatever kind of being you are saying she is, then whose art is Seraphina"?

"Perhaps there is another beyond Seraphina", Sebastian replied.

"Well, whoever that is", Amba said, "Would have to be beyond the mere, that's for sure. Because I don't see them here".

"Quite right", said Sebastian.

Sati, who had so far been sitting quietly, still on the chair just inside the door, now spoke up. "So you think I'm just an image"? she said abruptly.

"No", said Sebastian. "That's not really what I'm saying. You are more beautiful to me than any image. And I think you know that. Why else would you have imagined what was happening in your imagined masquerade, just now"?

Sati didn't answer.

"What about me"? Amba said quietly. "Am I just an image"?

"It is exactly the same", Sebastian replied. "We all are, if you're talking about persons. So is Sebastian Bassenthwaite. Just like the persons in the gardens, but in a different way".

"And what about the rest of me, then"? said Amba, almost sadly.

Now there was a click and the door creaked open. Everyone looked over to the door, and saw Belvoir entering through it, carefully carrying a silver tray and fresh coffee for everyone. He walked across to a small Old World table, set down the tray and began to pour the coffee, all, as usual, without saying a word.

"Belvoir"! Exclaimed Sebastian. "Good man".

Much to everyone's surprise, Belvoir poured himself a coffee, too. And then to their even greater surprise, he spoke.

"I'm afraid as I approached the door I couldn't help overhearing your conversation a moment ago", he said gently, as was his way. He looked directly at Amba. "And I thought Amba sounded a little dismayed", he said, as though he was about to offer her some spiritual advice, as well as the coffee.

"Please, Belvoir", said Sebastian, gesturing to an Old World chair. "Do sit down". He was expecting Belvoir to say something more to Amba.

Belvoir sat down on the chair and stirred his coffee. After some moments he spoke again in his characteristically gentle voice. "I have always very much admired the persons in the gardens", he said. "They are a beautiful work".

"Thank you, Belvoir", replied Sebastian, "And I appreciate your acknowledgement".

"The persons are absorbed in their own world", said Belvoir, almost dreamily. "Much as *we* are". He then proceeded to drink his coffee, slowly, as though he had completed what he was going to say. Everyone else's attention remained on him. There was the distinct feeling that he had not yet finished what he was saying. After a little while, he put down his cup, and turned to Sebastian. He began speaking again.

"I was wondering", he said, "If Belvoir might venture to propose an idea concerning the persons"?

Sometimes speaking of himself in the second person, like this, was a characteristic of Belvoir. Marsilio often did it, too. And since entering the room, Belvoir was doing what Sebastian had always known him to do, on the previously rare occasions when he had the privilege of entering into philosophical conversation with him. He appeared to be randomly changing the subject of whatever philosophising or discussion was taking place.

Belvoir had come into the room saying he had overheard their conversation, seemed to be about to offer Amba some wisdom, and now they seemed to be talking about something completely different. But Sebastian knew Belvoir well enough not to be misled. Sebastian knew Belvoir's way, and he knew of no-one with greater depth and powers of penetration.

"You wanted to propose an idea about the persons"? queried Sebastian, endeavouring to keep Belvoir talking.

"Yes", Belvoir answered. "As part of the work of art that the persons are", he went on, "I think it is well known, is it not, that the persons move"?

The others laughed loudly. "Yes, I think that's well-known by now", said Sati. "Especially after the meeting of the Academy at Springmere".

"Well I was wondering", Belvoir continued, "If on the next full moon, some of the persons might like to move down to the edge of the mere, so that they may be seen looking out across it. I think such a thing would carry an important message as a work of art".

For a moment Sebastian seemed to be absorbing what Belvoir had just said. Then he suddenly said, "What an excellent idea"! He shook his head in astonishment. "Why did *I* not think of that"? he said. "It would say so much. And I think it would go down well with all the clans".

"It might certainly promote more interest in what might be beyond the mere", Sati said. "And perhaps, because the clans all have their own beliefs on what is beyond the mere, each would think it is about them".

Amba looked unconvinced by the idea. "You don't think people will think it vain"? she said.

"Why should they think it vain"? Sebastian said, puzzled.

"Well", Amba said, "It could be seen as a sort of deliberate drawing of attention to the fact that Aumhurst overlooks the mere, as a kind of self-congratulation on our privileged position here".

"Yes I would be inclined to agree", said Sati. "I do see what you mean. The whole social hierarchy of Pavi Bujdam does, after all, most definitely rise upwards from the interior outwards. Those who live around the mere, or indeed, overlooking it, are undoubtedly more privileged".

Now Belvoir spoke again. "But it wouldn't truly *be* vanity, would it"? he said. "It would *be* about the mere".

"Belvoir is right", Sebastian said. "I don't think it would create disharmony. I really don't think the ongoing harmony that has existed in Pavi Bujdam since time immemorial can possibly be on the basis of appearances, or what anything *looks like*. It's something much more fundamental to Pavi Bujdam. Is that not so, Belvoir"?

"I think", Belvoir answered, "There is a book in the library, here, a book on the downfall of the Old World, that talks about what it calls the play of appearances. I was wondering if you were familiar with it"?

"I can't say I am, Belvoir", Sebastian said, aware that Belvoir was doing it yet again. He was branching off onto some other subject. He wondered how he could now ever get back to the original subject they had been discussing, before Belvoir came through the door.

Sebastian went on "There are plenty of books in the Library on the downfall of the Old World, but I can't recall any book that talks about a play of appearances".

Belvoir continued, "I would be happy to show you, when next we meet in the library. It argues that the Old World became a world entirely running on the principle of concern with appearances, the creation of appearances, and the attempt to control the destiny of the world through the manipulation of appearances. I mention it only because it is perhaps a suitable answer to your question".

"My question"? Sebastian queried, having now forgotten what he himself had said.

"Indeed", Belvoir answered. "You asked why people should think it vain, if Aumhurst placed its persons looking out over the mere. And as Amba and Sati suggested, it would be because they might become resentful about the hierarchy in Pavi Bujdam".

"Oh, yes", Sebastian said. "That's right".

"And you said yourself", said Belvoir, "That the ongoing harmony in Pavi Bujdam doesn't exist on the basis of appearances, or what anything looks like, did you not"?

"Yes, that's right", Sebastian said.

"But we are ourselves, in thinking about putting the persons over-looking the mere, are now becoming concerned with appearances as the cause of disharmony, are we not"? said Belvoir.

"Yes, I suppose we are", Sebastian agreed.

"So it seems", Belvoir continued, "To sum up, that we are concerned with disharmony arising in the people of Pavi Bujdam, as the result of appearances. Even though the ongoing harmony in Pavi Bujdam is not as the result of appearances. So, although we might want to draw attention through your art, to the mere, and the question of what might be beyond it, that is to say, by moving the persons so that they look out across the mere, we will think it better not to, because it will create an image, through which disharmony might arise in the people".

"I think that is what we are saying", Sati said.

"And is it not so", Belvoir continued, "That the image we are talking about, is the image of the persons looking out across the mere, and that we are truly putting them there for a good reason, and not for vanity"?

"That's right", Sebastian said.

"So it is agreed, is it not", Belvoir went on, "That disturbances or disharmony can arise through an artistic image, even where there is no ill-will or vanity, in the cause of the image"?

The other three all agreed.

"I suppose you might call it a misunderstanding", Sati said.

"Indeed", Belvoir said. "It always arises because different people have different ways of understanding".

"Exactly so", Sati said.

"And for those who understand the image of the persons looking out across the mere, in terms of the importance of the mere and the question of what is beyond it, the image does not appear vain or disharmonious, does it"? Belvoir asked.

"We'll I don't think it does, no", Sebastian agreed.

"So we must ask ourselves then, must we not", Belvoir continued, "Whether it is really the art form itself that is disharmonious, or whether the cause of the disharmony, is elsewhere"?

"Yes I think we should ask that", agreed Sati.

"Hmm", said Sebastian, "You mean that the actual cause of the disharmony is perhaps in the one who is looking at it, and becoming disturbed by it, you are saying"?

"Precisely", Amba now said. "I don't disagree. But surely it would be more judicious, would it not, if we sacrificed the art, in order to stop the disharmony arising, in those in whom it might arise"?

"Yes, I suppose you are right", Sebastian agreed. "Perhaps it would be better to avoid any possible, additional disharmony. Who knows, we might end up disrupting the whole balance of Pavi Bujdam? Perhaps we should not, after all, put the persons looking out over the mere. Perhaps that would not be such a good work of art".

Now the door clicked again and Quentin's voice was now heard. "That's the first time I've heard you holding back, as an artist"! he said to Sebastian with a wide grin. Closing the door behind him he walked across and joined them. "May I"? he said, gesturing towards the coffee.

"Please do", Sebastian said.

"What's all this about you censoring your own art, Sebastian"? Quentin asked. "For fear of upsetting people? I don't believe it. What's brought about this change"?

"We were just saying", Sebastian said, "It is possible to create images in art that might cause discontent or disharmony".

"So what"? Quentin said. "And only in some people, surely? I say that's their lookout".

"But we should all care about each other, shouldn't we"? Amba objected.

"What do you say, Belvoir"? Sebastian asked.

Belvoir looked earnestly at Sebastian. He said "I say that first and foremost we should love. And I say that devoting a work of art to the mere and its importance, and to the message that in truth, what we are really looking for is knowledge of what is beyond the mere, is an act of love. Even when we do not know what is beyond the mere, this much should be clear. But if we are not attracted by the mere, if we have no concern with what is beyond it, if it is only our business in Pavi Bujdam that concerns us, then even this much will not be clear to us. And we may then just have to be judicious, as Amba has suggested. Some people might even call that compassion. But to me, that is a mistake".

Belvoir looked at Amba and smiled. "I don't really think that Amba is disinterested in the mere, is she"?

"I would certainly like to know what is beyond it", said Amba. "But I think I might also be afraid of upsetting people".

Sati said immediately. "When I look out across the mere, I've always felt that way about it. And I think I would not hold back in showing how important I think it is".

Belvoir continued, "If we don't recognise the importance of the mere, and what might be beyond it, then we are likely to become lost in fickle images and appearances. It might seem to you all", he said, "That it is only in the masquerade that you fall into images and imitations of things, and masked identities, and become over-concerned with them, but I can assure you that even here, in ordinary life in Pavi Bujdam, we live in a world of images and imitation, and we become lost in that, because we do not know what is beyond the mere".

"Yes", Amba now said. "I think I see what you mean. You mean that even life here, now, in Pavi Bujdam, is in its own way, a kind of masquerade, but of another kind? I've sometimes felt that, too".

"That is what I am saying", said Belvoir. "And so it was, no doubt, also in the Old World. But have you not ever noticed how even when you are completely immersed in the masquerade, there is a part of you that sometimes, somehow, knows it's only a masquerade"?

"Of course", said Sebastian, "Because our true life is here, in this Pavi Bujdam, and not in the masquerade one.

"Perhaps", said Belvoir. "But can you see that perhaps here, too, in Pavi Bujdam, there is a part of us that might already know in some way, what is beyond the mere, and knows that this, here, now, in its own way, is like a masquerade. And therefore perhaps not your true life."

"That is exactly how I sometimes feel", Sati said.

"How can we come to know, for sure, what is beyond the mere"? Sebastian said.

Belvoir looked at Sebastian, smiled, and said "I suspect you already know". For a moment Sebastian thought that perhaps Belvoir had been down to the Harborage, and had seen the Satya Vajra, but then Belvoir went on to say "Judging from what I have heard about your recent exhibition at the Ionian Gallery".

Sebastian replied, "I do intend to find out what is across the mere. But how I come to do it may not be what you are thinking, Belvoir".

"How can we know what is beyond the mere"? Quentin now said, seeming to be pressing Belvoir harder, for an answer.

"Mirrors", Belvoir said. "We see images of ourselves in mirrors do we not? To see our self, we need a mirror".

"I would agree with you there", said Sati.

Belvoir held up his hand again now, as if to say "wait". "If you want to know what is beyond the mere", he said, "Then you need a mirror in which to see your self. And just as the persons in the gardens at Aumhurst are to us, images, or an imitation, so also our own person is an image or imitation when seen from beyond the mere. This is how it is. And so through the mirror, we can see our own person as an image, which is also how our own person appears from beyond the mere".

"I understand", said Sati. "It is rather like how the masquerade and our masquerade selves, in all those costumes, and masks, seems to us, now. But what is this mirror, that we need"?

"It is the mirror provided by love", Belvoir said.

"So where can we find this mirror"? Sebastian said.

"Where do you find your love"? Belvoir answered.

Sebastian looked at Sati. Quentin and Amba were looking at each other.

Belvoir went on, "And then eventually, when we come to understand the image, then we have a new way of understanding, and we even begin to know without doubt what is beyond the mere".

And now Belvoir finally seemed to complete his great celestial circle, as perhaps Marsilio would have seen it, through which he had been moving ever since he came into the room, and once again, his attention was now on Amba.

He turned to her. "Amba", he said, addressing her with a great love that everyone in the room could feel, "*You* are not just an image, are you"?

Amba looked at Sebastian. "I think Sebastian would say my person is", she said, looking at Sebastian. "In fact, he said so".

"But not you"? Belvoir said.

Amba now looked at Belvoir steadily, and said with great certainty, "I'm not just an image, no".

Belvoir now turned to Sebastian. "Sebastian", he said, "Sati is your mirror", and now turning to Sati, he said "And Sati, Sebastian is yours".

He then lent back in his chair. "Look into your mirror", he said, "Find what is beyond the mere".

Finally, he then turned to back Amba, and said "And Amba, whose mirror are you, and who will be your mirror"?

23

✦

Jenkins' Coppice

Timaeus walked along beside Ambika,

Again around the circle by the stalls in Pavi market,

Past oils and gold and silver and amrita,

And fragrances with diamond charms and glittering rings and garnet.

The Sun was smiling down on them,

and as they walked past the stalls selling humorous gifts, Timaeus, feeling its warmth and light, said to Ambika "You were saying, if I remember, last time we were here, about the energy from the Sun, and about stories of time and place and love, were you not"?

"I'm not sure what I said about time", Ambika replied. "Certainly I might have been speaking of the ocean of streams of stories of love and beautiful places. But it seems to me that they are above time, and above the whole idea of what comes before, and what comes after".

Timaeus answered, "From what I experience with music, there seems to be a higher place that it takes me to, like that, beyond any idea of what comes before, and what comes after".

Ambika replied "Yes, I do know what you mean. Music has that power, too, with me".

Timaeus looked at Ambika as they continued to walk on, and seeing her now, in such unselfconscious beauty, so relaxed in the light of the Sun, like nothing that could be touched by gross senses, and yet so palpable that in the deepest part of him he knew he longed for her with the whole of his natural being, he said to her "I'm sorry my dear, what was it you were saying"?

"You listen to my words", she said, "And then you forget them, and think the meaning in them has come from you", she said.

"Do I"? he said.

"Yes", she replied, "And it is probable that I do the same".

"Do you"? Timaeus said.

All the recent talk of finding out what might be beyond the mere was having its effect on Ambika. Whether she was making sense was another matter. It was almost as if she was in a more confused kind of frenzy. "It seems to me", she said, as they walked on, "Perhaps this is right, as long as the one we are speaking of who sees the true meaning in the words is not the Timaeus or Ambika who thinks they do not know what is beyond the mere".

Timaeus laughed at his own inability to understand her words, which he was convinced no one else would have done. "Now you have certainly lost me, I think", he smiled, "It sounds to me as though you are in some kind of frenzy, already".

They walked on a little further, Timaeus contemplating what she had said. And then he said "I think there is a difference between understanding words, and understanding where you are, or where you are coming from, so to speak, as you are speaking the words".

"Now you have lost *me*", said Ambika. "Perhaps", she said, "Perhaps all of it, here in Pavi Bujdam, and who knows, perhaps even beyond the mere, perhaps for all of it, *in the beginning was the word*, whatever the word is, or was, before it even became or becomes what we know as the word".

"Perhaps you are right", Timaeus answered, in good humour, still without following what she was saying. But he nonetheless found himself saying more, probably more out of what he was used to in the flow of things in their philosophical conversations, than out of any real understanding. "And if that is so", he began, "It must also be true in the masquerade, must it not"? It seemed to him, an appropriate thing to say, whatever her meaning.

"I think you are right", said Ambika, but now not really being sure whether he was right or not. It was as if their philosophising had taken off by itself, leaving them both behind, in search of some blindfolded flight towards nowhere in particular.

They walked on together for a little while, continuing past the gift stalls, until Ambika said "It is your birthday soon, is it not"?

"I believe so", Timaeus answered.

"I wondered if you would like to move in to the next ring of stalls, and I will catch you up in a few moments"? Ambika suggested.

"Yes of course, my dear", Timaeus said, and turned through the gap in the stalls, towards the next concentric circle.

Ambika walked a small way back towards one of the stalls on which there was something that had caught her eye, that she thought might make a suitable birthday present for Timaeus. She had been examining the wares on the stall for some time, when she heard the stall-keeper say to her "My goodness! There are two of you"!

Ambika immediately looked up and saw her sister beside her, also examining the wares. She was wearing riding dress, apparently having ridden to the market.

"Are you having the same idea as me, for Timaeus"? Ambika said.

"No, I think I've changed my mind", Amba said, "I will see you a little later", she said, and moved away. Some time later Ambika herself found she could not make a decision on any of the gifts, and so she went through the gap between the stalls, in search Timaeus.

She could not find him anywhere, so after some further searching around another couple of the concentric circles of stalls, she returned to the gift stall. The stall-holder immediately said to her "Your sister and the gentleman were here just a moment ago, looking for you. They said if they cannot find you, they will meet you back at Merehurst".

This didn't seem too inconvenient for Ambika, since she had already arranged to ride out with Sandhya and Sati today, from Merehurst to Jenkins' Coppice.

§

Quentin leaned out of the window from the upper storey of Merehurst, and watched the couple approaching the house. Behind him, from the other side of the room, Sandhya said "I have arranged to ride out again today, with Amba and Sati".

"I think you should", Quentin said, his voice entering the room from outside the window.

Sandhya said "I suppose you'll be rehearsing the dancing again today, with Isabella won't you? Or will Diotima be there too"?

Still leaning out of the window, Quentin replied "Not today. And if you were inferring something about Isabella, I'm just rehearsing with her, for the performance, that's all, it's nothing more than that. You should be pleased. After all, it's your idea".

"Well you'd better come up with something good", Sandhya said, and then she turned and left the room. Quentin watched the couple below continue to approach the house, so he turned and left the room, walked along the gallery, and descended the stairs.

By the time he reached the bottom of the stairs the housekeeper had already let the couple in, and now seeing Quentin, announced "Ah, Quentin, we have visitors. Ambika and Timaeus have arrived".

"Thank you, Bellamy", Quentin said, and showed them into the Observatory Room, which was a little further around the hallway, with grand bay windows overlooking the mere. Positioned in front of the beautiful, wide, sweeping window, were two telescopes, one each side of the window bay, one modern, one antique.

"That's a beautiful specimen", Timaeus exclaimed, seeing the Old World telescope on the right. He walked up to it, admiring the beauty of the brass, and the engraved patterning on its substantial stand. Like the modern telescope on the other side of the window bay, it was directed somewhere out over the mere. Seeing the lens cap over the eyepiece, Timaeus asked "Do you mind if I take a look"?

"Not at all", Quentin replied. "Help yourself. It's currently looking at one of the islands, where I think there is some rather interesting wildlife. But do, by all means, reposition the telescope, if you wish to. I think you'll find it has been beautifully restored, by the way, and the image is very good".

Timaeus looked through the telescope making noises of approval.

"Would you excuse me if I take Ambika away for a moment"? Quentin said. "There is some music for Sandhya's project that I wanted to show her, and discuss".

"Of course", Timaeus said rather vaguely, whilst now peering intently through the telescope, out to the mere.

Quentin took her hand, and led her out of the room. He closed the door behind them and without letting go of her led her around the corner back into the hallway. As soon as they had turned the corner he took her other hand in his, and simply said "Amba".

"You know it's me then"? she smiled.

"How could I not"? Quentin said.

"I swapped with with Ambika in the market", she said. "And for some reason, Timaeus either hasn't noticed or he is choosing not to say anything. He does that sometimes".

"Amba", Quentin said again, "I don't know why you still play that silly game so much with your sister. But I'm glad you did. And the thing is... Well I think you know Sandhya and I have not been together for quite some time".

Amba nodded silently.

"I just want you to know...", Quentin said. "Because I do feel that way about you".

Amba smiled, her eyes shining like the light of the mere, and said "And I you. You could have said sooner, you know".

§

The door to the Observatory Room clicked open. Sandhya came into the room, and seeing Timaeus clearly absorbed in the view through the telescope, said "Oh I'm sorry, am I interrupting"?

Immediately, Timaeus looked round from the telescope, and exclaimed "Sandhya, how nice to see you. No, not at all, do come in.

Quentin said he was happy for me to use the telescope, and I was just watching the fishing boats".

Sandhya walked over to the telescope, and said "May I have a look, too"?

"Of course", Timaeus said, "After all, it is your telescope"! he laughed.

"Not mine, actually", Sandhya said quite flatly, "It's Quentin's and he never lets me use it".

"I can't believe that", Timaeus said with a smile.

Sandhya began to observe through the telescope. Then she said "Oooh, look at this", inviting Timaeus back to the eyepiece. She moved her head to the side, but remained close to the telescope.

"My goodness", Timaeus said, then he laughed a little. "I imagine they think they can't be seen"?

"Well clearly they are bathing in the mere, let me have another look" Sandhya said, moving her head gently against his. Timaeus with equal gentleness moved his head a little to the side to give way to her request. She looked down the telescope briefly, and then turned towards him. "Merehurst has a private beach, you know, have you ever seen it"?

"No I haven't", Timaeus answered.

"It's secluded and even from the mere is hidden behind Holm Island, which of course is part of the Merehurst estate".

"How interesting" said Timaeus, with his usual amiableness.

Would you like to see it"? Sandhya asked.

"Certainly", Timaeus said, in his accustomed, polite way.

§

Having already been to the horses, Sati walked side-by-side with Ambika, away from the stables and towards the back door of Merehurst, looking for Sandhya. They were keen to begin their ride out together to Jenkins' Coppice. Once through the door, they saw Bellamy.

"Bellamy, have you seen Sandhya", Sati asked. "Yes", Bellamy replied, "I think she's gone down to the beach".

Sati turned to Ambika, and said "What is she up to? We arranged to ride out".

"Let's go back to the stables and get the horses", Ambika said. "I'll

ride down and see if I can see Sandhya. You can go on towards Jenkins'
Coppice and we'll catch you up".

Back at the stables once again, Sati chose Helios, and Ambika chose
King. Both horses knew well the way to and from Jenkins' Coppice,
which was a favourite with the riders, second only to the routes along
the mereside.

Jenkins' Coppice was ancient and extensive, and despite the name,
was a mix of vast, dense coppice, and great mature, dense woodlands,
often without clear boundaries between them. Great areas of the woods
were remarkably indistinguishable, with a vast network of paths that
twisted and turned through both wild woodland and coppice, a veritable challenge to anyone who wanted to try to memorise the lay of the
paths. Only the horses themselves seemed to know their way around
the paths reliably, and it was their knowledge that riders usually called
upon in order to find the way in or out of the Coppice.

Sati, on Helios, the magnificent palomino, set out at a walk, and
then a trot. Ambika, on King, took the winding path down towards the
beach. After just the first two turns of the descending path she was able
to see sideways through a gap in the trees, down the bank to the winds
of the path ahead of her. And there, she recognised, was Sandhya, to
her surprise not on horseback, but on foot with Timaeus.

For a short while she watched them walking side-by-side, until she
saw Sandhya suddenly swing round and step in front of Timaeus. They
seemed to be talking for some time, and then she put her hand up and
touched his head. Ambika felt in no doubt about the nature of what
was going on. She nudged King, and galloped off back up the path.

Once at the top of the path, instead of turning off towards Jenkins'
Coppice, she headed straight for the front door of Merehurst. She tied
up King, and entered the house.

Merehurst, like Aumhurst, was almost labyrinthine. Being also the
work of Seraphina Bassenthwaite, although very different in character
to Aumhurst, its soul seemed to resonate with the creative spirit of
anyone who had the privilege of coming to know it. The house now
seemed to Ambika, to resonate with her intention to find Quentin, but

not in a way that was helpful. There were great and small rooms on every floor, and numerous passages, hallways and galleries connected by a large number of minor staircases. All of which slowed Ambika's progress in searching the house.

Eventually, she came across a gallery with heavy, floor-to-ceiling tapestries along its walls, and headed towards a door through which she could hear muffled voices. She listened outside the door for a moment and recognised one of the voices within as Quentin's. He seemed to be deep in earnest conversation. And then she heard what was unmistakably her sister's voice.

The conversation seemed to pause, and she momentarily contemplated entering the room. Then, as the door handle clicked and began to turn, without time to think she quickly stepped sideways and hid herself behind the nearest tapestry. She heard the door close and footsteps moving away from her down the gallery. She was certain they were her sister's, and not Quentin's. When the footsteps were clearly some distance away, she slowly and very carefully peered out from behind the tapestry, looking down the gallery. She saw her sister, also, like herself, in riding clothes.

As her sister disappeared around the corner, Ambika carefully emerged from behind the tapestry, but paused before going into the room. She had already hatched a plan. She waited a little longer, and then opened the door.

On entering the room she saw Quentin looking out of the window. "You were quick" he said, turning around. "And"? he said.

Ambika smiled at him, and held out her hand towards him, inviting him to come out of the room with her. "I want you to come and see this", she said, "And I have something I want to tell you".

To her surprise he said gently, with a smile, "What have you done with Amba"?

Ambika was taken aback. "How long have you been able to tell us apart"? she said.

"Do you think it is possible to love one of you and not tell you apart"? he said.

Ambika found herself saying "Do you think it's possible for someone to love us both even though knowing the difference"? She didn't really know why she said it. It just came out.

To her surprise Quentin came straight back with an answer. "Of course it is", he said. "But not truly, without knowing what's beyond the mere".

"So I assume you know about Sandhya and Timaeus then"? Ambika said.

Quentin laughed. "Ambika", he said, lovingly, "Sandhya and I have been apart for quite some time, you know. I can see you are worried about Timaeus, but I can assure you I know both Sandhya and Timaeus well enough to know that what you are suggesting is ridiculous".

Ambika was silent for a moment, and then just said, "Really"?

"Yes, really, Ambika", Quentin affirmed. "I can tell you that she has a tendency to frenzy in which she loses touch with the common way of understanding things. In the frenzy the ropes are broken, as it were, and she becomes like a momentum of music that the musicians playing it can't keep up with. And it's not that I think when that happens, her way of understanding things is not the right way. On the contrary, I think it is right, and I think it is actually the more common way of understanding things that is the mistaken way. When she's like that you would probably be confused by her behaviour. Most people are. Timaeus won't be misled, I'm sure".

Quentin looked firmly at Ambika. "Look", he said, "You must know Timaeus well enough, surely? I don't think he will ever become part of that kind of frenzy. I'll wager he's not engaged in the way that you think he is".

Ambika walked towards Quentin and put her arms around him. "Thank you", she said.

Quentin held her, and at that moment Amba appeared in the doorway.

"What are you doing, Amba"? Amba said from the doorway.

"Oh Ambika", Ambika said, "I'm saying thank you to Quentin".

Ambika let go of Quentin, and said "I have to fly", and with that, she left the room in a hurry.

Now upon the saddle to Jenkins' Coppice,
Ambika races purposeful upon the faithful King,
There amongst the trees to find her peace,
In sweet knowledge that she will once again Timaeus win.

§

Timaeus and Sandhya came to the kissing stones on the edge of the path, that looked down upon the beach. "The kissing stones", said Sandhya, gesturing towards the three large stones that seemed to be defying gravity by supporting each other at their tips. "Kissing stones are usually two", she said, "But these are three".

Timaeus regarded them quizzically, and said "Interesting. They do seem to be defying gravity, don't they"?

"They do", Sandhya agreed.

"But then", Timaeus said, "I'm sure if you did the calculations it would all work out".

"It doesn't look as though it would take much to send them tumbling though, does it"? Sandhya said. "Although it might be exciting to experience falling into the mere from a kiss", she said.

"Have you ever fallen into the mere"? Timaeus asked.

"Not once", Sandhya said, "Although recently I fell by the mere. I was thrown by King". She momentarily remembered the exhilaration. Something like a strange, liquid fire began to stir in her system, as she thought about it, and she said "Shall we ride out to Jenkins' Coppice"?

"I haven't been on horseback for a while", Timaeus said, politely as ever, "But yes, of course. Thank you for the invitation".

And so the two together to the stables went their way,
To choose the trusty steeds that they might ride,
And finding there no King or Helios Sandhya guessed the tale,
And so chose Dionysius for her guide.

They raced to Jenkins' Coppice all the way,
But once within the woods a careful amble they must tread,
The labyrinth-like paths they must obey,
Enjoying every bole and burr and bower each step ahead.

The bliss of nature thick at hand through thickets they must wind,
The moss-greened limbs and toadstools by the way,
The silent secrets of the birds disturbed by humankind,
The luscious glades within where they might stray.

The turning this way first then turning that,
Towards the stream they roam betwixt the twigs and branches low,
Ducking down whilst still in saddle sat,
The faithful horses even here their way they seem to know.

And now Dionysius neighs aloft and Sandhya feels the cause,
Timaeus follows close but now away,
His noble steed in turning fast aside his rein ignores,
The frightened horse now off the path does stray.

Sandhya calls, Timaeus hears and answers,
But now their separate paths apart together they must ride,
Through coppice move like labyrinthine dancers,
To dodge the stream-side bog and meet together by the by.

Timaeus now alone moved through wild woodland, allowing his horse, Socrates, to lead him, confident in the steed's knowledge of the woodland. He moved from wild woodland back onto a neat path through dense coppice, a narrow bridle way that snaked around with yellow-brown curtains of coppiced trees on each side of a carpet of fresh green grass. The yellow-brown curtain of thousands of layers of millions of small branches with endless thickets of young growth, gradually changed into a green darkened by greater shadow, as he followed round a tight curve that opened up into less dense coppice on a wider path. And there, riding on King, was Ambika coming towards him.

The two horses greeted each other, as did Ambika and Timaeus, Timaeus kissing Ambika's hand as a knight of the round table kisses the hand of Lady.

As love that once begins to cross the mere,
Doth withstand the plays of masquerades and follies all,
So through the woods they hold each other dear,
Timaeus and Ambika from the frenzy never fall.

The horses walk on. The couple move in silence, listening to the birds whose paradise is known not to birds themselves but to the pair. Whose silent motion through the greenwood is like some concentric air around a space Divine from where the beauty of the bird song falls into the bodies of the birds in the thickets of the coppice.

And by the by, through their spiralling, in a small clearing they chanced upon another pair, Sati riding Helios, and Sandhya upon Valencia. Surrounded by the ecstatic songs of the birds and embraced by the green circle of trees, the four riders exchanged their experiences, and in the dappled light under the Sun-dripped leaves, they came to know new experiences from their exchanges.

Timaeus and Ambika, flushed with a new idea, felt together the pull of Springmere, and without further hesitation decided to ride back for the joy of its yellow walls and courtyard, which somehow had entered their one heart and seemed to be calling for them.

Sati and Sandhya, together inflamed by Sandhya's love of the frenzy, wanted nothing more but to ride for the Silver Gallop. And so they did. Through thicket and through greenwood, through wildwood and clearing, until at last they reached the only true stretch within the Coppice, now like a grandstand stretched before them.

No greater temptation could there be, Helios and Valencia knew it well, and now the spring of joy is sprung as both the horses break away from their confinement in the coppice, and soaring into their own frenzy gallop side by side towards the oak tree and the fork.

Sati closes in towards Sandhya, and both feel the equine frenzy as the oak tree flies towards them,
They cannot cross upon each other's path.
Helios flies one side, Valencia to the other,
And now the two diverge yet still are driven by the charge.

Away they race with no more sight of other,
The gallop and the frenzy all the more,
Past glades and paths and parts of golden swards,
Past copse and spinney each without the other each towards,

Their separate transformation of the frenzy,
Till at last from narrowing path the gallop must subside.

Valencia all but halts and walks towards the narrow clearing,
Sandhya there between the branches sees,
A bright-robed figure move betwixt the stripy barks appearing,
And knows it is Marsilio in the trees.

His horse snorts and moves. He emerges from behind the edge of the spinney and sees Sandhya. His countenance is evanescent, his voice is quiet. "We should ride back to Merehurst", he says. And so they do.

Past copse and wildwood Sati races till at last she slows,
And now with Helios walking comes upon,
A narrow clearing there which in-between the branches shows,
Marsilio 'twixt the stripy barks appearing.

His horse snorts and moves. He emerges from behind the edge of the spinney and sees Sati. His countenance is evanescent, his voice is quiet. "We should ride back to Aumhurst", he says. And so they do.

Back at Merehurst Sandhya asked Marsilio why he went to Jenkins'

Coppice. Marsilio said "Why do any of us do anything? We are, you know, just part of a stream of stories, within stories, within stories. One story, you know, can lead to many images of itself. And they go on, after they have been set in motion, in the thing we call time. Which is just another story. You, Sandhya, are part of my story, and I am part of yours. As I am part of many other stories. Which are all part of me. And all of us here are part of a story set in motion by Seraphina. I can even appear in different stories, within my own story".

"Who else's story am I in"? Sandhya asked.

"You will be in someone's", Marsilio answered. "But I can see you are only partially in the continuation of Seraphina's. Whilst I am wholly in hers, and hers is in mine".

Back at Aumhurst Sati asked Marsilio why he went to Jenkins' Coppice. Marsilio said "Why do any of us do anything? We are, you know, just part of a stream of stories, within stories, within stories. One story, you know, can lead to many images of itself. And they go on, after they have been set in motion, in the thing we call time. Which is just another story. You, Sati, are part of my story, and I am part of yours. As I am part of many other stories. Which are all part of me. And all of us here are part of a story set in motion by Seraphina. I can even appear in different stories, within my own story".

"Who else's story am I in"? Sati asked.

"You are in Sebastian story", Marsilio said. "And he is in the continuation of Seraphina's. And you and I are alike, Sati. We each appear in different stories, within our own story".

"How does it all fit together"? Sati asked.

"Even Seraphina is a continuation of someone's story", Marsilio said. "She is in your story, and she is in my story, but she is also in someone's story in which there is no Marsilio or Sati, and never was".

"Where does she come from? Whose story is she in"? asked Sati.

"Ah", said Marsilio. "Where do you suppose all stories come from"?

"I suppose from the one who thinks them up", said Sati.

"And who is that one"? Marsilio asked.

"I don't know", said Sati.

"Sati, my beautiful love", Marsilio said. "Who is your mirror, and whose mirror are you"?

"Sebastian", Sati said without hesitation.

Marsilio touched Sati's hand gently, with love. "Look into your mirror", he said. Find the tap root of your love. And remember it is a mirror you are looking into. Find out what is beyond the mere, and who it is".

24

The Mere

We would be mistaken if we thought that everyone who lived around the mere on the most harmonious side of Pavi Bujdam, was always in harmony and creatively inspired. Marsilio, being an astrologer, would say it was a matter of celestial influences, and that melancholy might come to anyone.

In Marsilio's terms, it would be extremely rare for all to fall under adverse conjunctions and aspects at the same time. But then, in nature, even in Pavi Bujdam, the rare is not the impossible. Everything, after all, in the first place, only comes to be because it is a possibility. All being and existence is the play of possibility.

And so it is that Sebastian, Sati, Quentin, Amba, Ambika, Timaeus and Sandhya, one day, sat round in a circle, facing each other, in one of the beautiful upper rooms of the Harborage, overlooking the mere.

"I just don't know" Sebastian said. "I don't know what's happened".

"Does anybody have anything to say"? Ambika said. "Timaeus, what about you"?

"I'm afraid I seem to have dried up", Timaeus said.

"Sandhya", Quentin said, "What about your project"?

"What project", Sandhya asked.

"The music, from Seraphina, and what about the dance"? Quentin replied.

"Yes, what about that"? Sebastian said.

Sandhya sighed. "I don't know", she said. She looked melancholy. "It would seem I've lost interest".

"Well, shall we ride out today"? Amba asked Sandhya, hoping to break the negative spell.

Sandhya sighed again. " I don't think so", she said.

Sati stood up and walked over to the window. She stood still, staring out at the mere. The rays of the Sun sparkled through the prisms of the window, flooding down onto the floor of the room, bathing it in the unmistakable light of morning. It did seem full of promise, but the promise of what?

No one stirred.

And then Sati, still with her back to the group, looking out of the window, said "I've got it. I know why".

"It's the mere isn't it"? Sebastian said. He had already thought so, for some time.

"It's the mere", Sati said, echoing him. "It doesn't come from us. It comes from the mere".

"What does"? said Quentin.

"The philosophising", Sati said. "It comes from the mere, not from us".

"But we philosophise *about* the mere, do we not"? Amba said.

"I know", said Sati.

"It makes sense to me", Sebastian said. "I would dare say we *are* the mere, philosophising about itself".

"I see", said Quentin.

"Do you"? said Sandhya, sceptically.

"I see it too", Amba said, at last a tone of enthusiasm in her voice.

Now Timaeus spoke up. "I must confess I don't see how that can be", he said. But then he paused, and seemed to be inspired, and said "No, I think I've changed my mind. I mean, I don't see how, but since you looked at the mere just now and said what you said, we already seem to be philosophising again don't we"?

"I don't think I am", said Sandhya, still sounding melancholy.

Sati was still standing looking out of the window towards the mere. Now she turned around and faced the group. "You don't understand", she said. "I think we need to go to the mere. It's no good thinking about it. We need to experience it. We need to know it".

"You're right", Sebastian said. "We need to be immersed in it".

"Who is willing"? Sati asked. Six hands were raised into the air. The seventh, Sati's, was now raised also. "I too", she said.

§

It was a pleasant path down to the mere. A little further around the shore from the Harborage a sandy beach stretched between two rocky outcrops, forming a little cove. It was the perfect place for bathing, for entering the edge of the mere, whether just for refreshment, in the long heat of the summer days, or for others, in search for the meaning of the mere to show itself. Which, perhaps by Grace, it might, to those whose deepest longing was to know more of the mountains on the horizon and perhaps even of beyond.

The friends stood on the sandy shore, mesmerised by the calm expanse of the mere, looking at the emerald and green umber islands in the blissful sun, and their reflections in the water. It seemed to be inviting them in, almost intoxicating them with its beauty, the islands seeming to be places of deep and peaceful pleasure just waiting to be reached, as if they were already alive in the hidden potential and joys of the mere and wanting to share them.

"Some say the water is salty", Sebastian said. "But it's not saltwater is it"? he said dreamily and enigmatically.

"I think you'll find it is", Timaeus said, with surprise, and giving Sebastian a quizzical look.

"I've heard some say it's wine", Ambika said.

Amba laughed. "I think they might be intoxicated themselves, first", she said.

"I don't think so", Ambika replied. "Because I've heard others speak of it as milk".

"It doesn't look like milk to me", Timaeus said.

"I don't think that's what they mean", Ambika replied.

"What do they mean then"? Timaeus said.

Ambika smiled. "They're speaking figuratively", she answered. "When you think of the effect it has on us", she said, "Then I think it is an ocean of milk".

"Well, I think I've lost you there", Timaeus said.

"No", said Quentin. "I think she's right. People do speak about the mere in strange ways", he said. "I've even heard it said by some of the clans that the mere is like a loom that weaves the threads of destiny".

"I think we make our own destiny", said Sebastian, staring out at the mere. "But anyway, who wants to come in"?

All the friends now threw aside their different coloured robes and ran as one, splashing into the Sun-sparkled droplets of the mere's edge, falling into its water with a joy that all the joys in Pavi Bujdam combined, could only ever imitate. Perhaps as an image, or a painting. A painting perhaps painted from colours that mixed with skill might seem to make the light of the sun or a fire. But mixed too much might also lose their lustre, and become the umber of the Earth or the dark of the night. Whilst within the winey, briny waters of the mere, their brilliance hidden there, gives the kind gift of undivided light to those who through the arts and through philosophy must live.

Now all the friends are in the water, sending concentric ripples out across its otherwise still surface, the water playing with the light both far and near, the light playing with the water.

The light across the water always plays and dances here,
Inviting who would rest from all desiderata,
And float within the liquid crucible,
And sink into the beautiful.
For all is here transmuted when,
Surrendered to the power known by few,
That sweet Divine exchange brings light to all anew,
And maketh more the fullness of the coming home again.

Who among the many who betroth the mere loves whom?
Who is the perfect love created from the womb?
When love itself before the womb doth come,
From far beyond beyond the mere?
And farther still it cometh from,
It playeth as a light within the mirror,
That we might come to wake and know through love like this,
The love beyond the farthest mere the light of endless bliss.

Naked in the truest flesh all seven friends entwine,
Their persons now dissolved in harmony Divine,
The stories all arising from the mere,
The matter less, the light the more,
The more the all that all adore,
In innocence they play and make their twine,
That maketh now the cloth that makes their loves in time,
So through their loves the real to make by spinning forth the wine.

25

La Primavera

Springmere was just right for the performance, Sandhya had said. It was to be outdoors, and the orange groves all around provided the perfect backdrop for it. They had found the ideal grove, facing South towards the orange trees, soft underfoot, and shaded by a canopy of oranges and orange blossoms.

Now Timaeus sat himself comfortably to the side of the scene with his twelve-stringed lyre. The fragrance of the orange blossom was all around him as he sat close by the trees, engaged in tuning the lyre.

Amba, Ambika, and Sandhya, dressed in flowing, diaphanous white gowns, hardly concealing their bodies, held hands in a circle, practising their entrance into the scene. With them, was Diotima, the dancer who frequently came to the meetings of the Pavi Academy at Springmere, who lived a little further around the mere.

Sebastian, now suitably rehearsed, dressed in red, and equipped with a caduceus in his right hand, awaited his entrance on the East side of the scene, stage right, which was to the left of Marsilio and Belvoir, who were sitting in the audience. The East side, stage right, left of the audience, Belvoir had said, would be the side representing original wisdom.

Quentin now arrived at the gathering, accompanied by Isabella, another dancer who also lived further around the mere beyond Aumhurst and Merehurst, close to where Diotima lived.

By the by, all the participants were in costume, and ready to enter the dance. Diotima, now dressed as Venus, looked radiant, and almost madonna-like. She stood between the orange trees behind centre stage, ready to enter onto an elevated position.

Isabella, the youngest, looked beautiful in her flowing robe, the very picture of a nymph, Chloris, they had decided to call her. She played perfectly the part. Like all nymphs, she was a created being, alive in the forest, but like all nymphs, not knowing who she really is, and unaware of the origins of the forest and its creatures, and its ways. Isabella waited, stage left, ready to enter from between the trees on the Western side, to the right of the audience.

Behind her, waited Quentin, most impressively dressed in blue and grey-blue as the West wind, Zephyr, his cloak and headpiece swirling around and above him. The West wind, who would blow all stories ultimately towards the East, but who coming from the West, and not the East, must enter the forest in ignorance.

Also waiting in the trees, ready to enter in front of Isabella, at precisely the right moment in the dance, was Sati. She was stunningly dressed in flowing, floral fabric, and garlanded around her neck and over her hair with flowers. The company of performers called her Flora.

Sandhya herself, together with Amba and Ambika, now hand-in-hand again, also waited to make their entrance before Sebastian.

When everyone was in position, the little audience including Marsilio and Belvoir proceeded to applaud, as the cue to begin the performance.

Timaeus began playing the music passed down by Seraphina and found by Sebastian, which now came to life on the strings of the lyre, and filled the scene with seemingly celestial harmonies in the rhythm of the three-by-three of the *tempus perfectum*, sufficient to spellbind the little audience.

And now began the dance,

The first upon the scene,
Three graces to enchant,
Sandhya arm in arm,
with Amba and Ambika,
They circling spin the charm,
Upon the Western three,
Who soon upon the scene,
Will enter through the trees.

Together with Diotima, the three graces, Sandhya, Amba and Ambika, all dancing most elegantly to the music, emerged from the trees, surrounding Diotima hand in hand, with a dance that circled round and around her, orbiting her with her beautiful Venus attire. Then they were temporarily breaking open their circle one by one and reforming it again, leaving Diotima standing in her elevated position centre stage at the back of the scene.

The dance took the three graces stage right of Diotima, who raised her right hand in a gesture of her continued participation in their dance, even though she was no longer within their circle.

Circling and cycling in beautiful weaving of infinite stories of love,
Three by three the dancers move their way upon the ground,
The stories in the tapestry, the music in the sound,
Weaving in and weaving out the thread there to explore,
An interweaving there of songs and stories from before.

The three graces continued to circle in their dance, in the same position in the scene, as some commotion at the Western side, stage left, took place through the trees.

From the trees there, Isabella leaped into the scene, dancing a dance of agitation and disturbance. Through the same entrance she was immediately followed by Quentin, entirely blue in his magnificent Zephyr costume. They continued to dance a duet together, the choreography depicting conflict, and the turbulence of a hunt and capture.

On its conclusion, the couple came to rest with Quentin holding Isabella, who was looking back at him in fright. As soon as their duet came to its conclusion, two more figures entered into the scene.

Between the nymph Chloris, played by Isabella, and Diotima who was still standing elevated as the glorious Venus, Sati emerged through the trees into the scene, in her fabulous floral attire, whilst Sebastian, far stage right, turned elegantly into his position, and facing East, raised his caduceus to the sky.

Sati, as Flora, now danced around Isabella, whilst Isabella, as the nymph, maintained her contact with Quentin. Sati's dance took over now from Isabella's, dancing a dance now of changefulness. Dancing the rhythm of three by three. And as Marsilio watched he saw Sati's transformation of Isabella's Chloris, into her floral self. And he was sure of something else he saw also.

She was with child.

Meanwhile, the three graces continued their circling dance, turning under each other's hands, and exchanging positions, with such beautiful ensemble that it was like a vision of an eternal exchange of love in some single, triple being, that had somehow broken free from her celestial orbit and had come down to Earth, into the orange grove, where the three now danced their hypnotic dance.

As the performance continued, Marsilio observed the three graces, with their translucent, diaphanous robes, flowing over their bodies, and he noticed something, whilst Sandhya and Ambika were facing each other as the circle rotated. He leaned towards Belvoir, and spoke to him quietly, saying "Is it not so, would you say, that both Sandhya and Ambika are with child"?

Belvoir simply nodded.

Marsilio leaned back again, but no sooner had he done so, that on looking at the other women, he was overcome with the conviction that everywhere he looked, they were with child. For a moment he thought perhaps it was an effect of the music and the dance, on his perceptions. He was sure it must be. He leaned again towards Belvoir, about to speak to him, but this time, as he moved, his own movement seemed to be in time with the music, and it seemed to him that he was himself, part of the dance. He leaned back again to his chair, the movement once again following the music, seemingly inevitably.

He could now not take his eyes off Diotima, a veritable vision of the beauty of Venus herself. She seemed radiant, almost haloed. She was looking directly at him, or so it seemed, with an expression of both perfect serenity and some secret, deep knowing. He could not help but continue looking at her, and whilst still absorbed in her beauty he caught in the periphery of his vision what seemed to be another small being above Diotima, and also, above Sebastian's caduceus a cloud that somewhere in his comprehension he knew, as in the way of dreams, to be a cloud of ignorance, that somehow, Sebastian was holding back from entering the scene.

As the music rounded off into a cadenza, and finished, all the performers became momentarily frozen in time, the transportation of mind that Marsilio had been experiencing receded, and he found himself looking once again, just at the company of performers. He now thought he was, after all, mistaken about them being with child.

Only the branches of the orange trees, with their leaves, oranges, and orange blossoms, were above the performers. And in another couple of moments the whole company had dissolved from their suspended positions, flowing into a line in front of the audience, together now with Timaeus, holding hands, and bowing.

The audience applauded enthusiastically.

§

In due course the performers were changed out of their costumes, and joined Marsilio and Belvoir for a discussion inspired by the performance.

"How was it"? Sandhya began.

"My dear friends, it was wonderful", Marsilio said. "Your rehearsals have been well worth the while. How did the idea come to you"?

"It came from you", Sandhya said. "From what you have said, over the years. And then somehow, when I came across the music that Sebastian found at Aumhurst, it started to bring everything together, into a kind of meaningful whole".

"Ah", Marsilio said. "That makes sense. And I can see that it is a scene of springtime. Indeed, a *story* of springtime".

"Come on Marsilio", Sebastian urged, "Give us your appraisal, give us a speech on what you think of it"!

Marsilio laughed. "Well", he said, "It is a story of the West wind, our dear friend Quentin here", he said, smiling at Quentin. "Hunting for nymphs, in the forest, no less, as did so many of those who came to be in the forest when it was very young. But everything leads into something else, does it not? And so I see the nymph becomes none other than Flora, a metamorphosis, no less, and so the forest itself becomes Flora's. It is the expression of herself, her springtime, the blossoming under Venus... or should I say, the first Venus"?

The others listened intently. Marsilio continued "For there are two Venuses, the higher and the lower. And if Mercury assists in our maintaining harmony and peace through piety, prudence and justice, justice, I say, which is not something received from the force of the world, and from hierarchies of human power, but rather, which is simply to give to the world what is owed to the world, and to give to God what is owed to God, then we can heal the past and live in the present. For only then, through the lower Venus who comes as Flora, the Venus of the corporeal seed and its flowering, we can realise the higher Venus. For it is none other than the lower Venus who becomes pregnant with the means for the higher Venus to be realised. That very means is ourselves. For it is through the lower Venus that we come into being, and so the lower Venus is herself the very means through which, in wisdom, the higher Venus is realised. And that is why I say to you, my friends, find your mirror, look into your mirror, and find what is beyond the mere".

And at that, Marsilio finished speaking, and the others contemplated what he had said.

"Pregnant, you said", echoed Sandhya, now seeming to take on again the expression she had worn during the performance.

"Does that have special meaning for you"? Marsilio asked.

"I have become so", said Sandhya.
Quentin looked at Sandhya. *"Pregnant*? I didn't know", he said.
Sati, without forethought, said "Whose is it"?
Sandhya remained silent.

But now the persons seated all around,
Seemed to be as if by transmutation all as One,
Their thoughts exchanged and now no longer parts,
But joined in ranks to share the more profound.

Their ways of understanding meet and weave,
The threads of each entwined as but one cloth,
The weaving of the one from cloths undone,
To bring to light a greater sense of one.

The loom it moves and now weaves by itself,
Betwixt the friends it spreads the cloth by stealth,
Implanting seeds unseen into the mind,
That things that never were they seem to find.

And so it is that Sandhya takes the thread,
And seems to them a pattern to embed within the cloth,
That now the loom doth take and must repeat,
As now she looks around the group and now she deems to speak.

"I wanted to", Sandhya said.
"You wanted to become pregnant"? Quentin answered. "But no one
in Pavi Bujdam becomes pregnant except during the masquerade".
"I wanted to", Sandhya reasserted.
Amba now said "So how did you manage it, if I can put it like that.
Who was it"?
"I had help", Sandhya said.
"Clearly", Amba replied. "Who was it"?
"It was Belvoir", Sandhya said.

"Belvoir"? echoed Quentin, Sebastian, Ambika, and Amba, altogether, incredulously.

They all looked at Belvoir, who showed no reaction whatsoever.

"So this wasn't in the masquerade"? Amba said, knowing that Belvoir never took part in it.

"No, I told you", Sandhya said. "It was here, in our ordinary time in Pavi Bujdam. The clocks were going. He glanced at me".

"He *glanced* at you"? Sebastian said.

"Yes", Sandhya replied. "That's how it happened".

Everyone was silent. No one seemed able to respond. And then before anyone had time to decide how to respond, Sati said "Me too".

Sebastian looked at Sati in astonishment. "You mean you believe her"? he said.

"Yes", Sati said. "It happened to me too".

Sebastian looked at her for an extended moment, and then looked around the group. "And is there anyone else this has happened to"? he said.

Now Diotima spoke up. "Yes, me too", she said.

"What are we to make of this"? Sebastian asked Marsilio, who had been sitting quietly, like Belvoir, showing no reaction.

"We must always ask the right question", Marsilio said.

He turned to Diotima and said to her, "Diotima, was it Belvoir who glanced at you"?

Diotima looked at Marsilio perfectly innocently, and said "Oh no. It wasn't Belvoir".

"Who was it"? Marsilio asked.

"I don't fully know", Diotima answered.

"Well I think", Marsilio said, "If we are seeking to improve our way of understanding, it would be most prudent now not to continue with any speculation. Rather, I think we should ask Belvoir himself".

At last Belvoir spoke. "The truth", he began, "Is that Sandhya and Sati have indeed most probably been impregnated through my glance, and as far as they can see it, in this moment, they are telling the truth".

The others seemed shocked. Marsilio however, appeared unmoved. He simply said "I think there is more you need to tell us, Belvoir".

So Belvoir continued. "Their impregnation is not what they think", he said. "It is not their having come to be with child, in Pavi Bujdam, if indeed they are truly with child as they say".

"How so"? Sebastian asked.

Belvoir continued. "Is it really the glance of Belvoir"? he said, "Or the glance of God? It would appear even the glance of Belvoir sometimes instills the kinds of memories we have indeed this morning seen played out in the performance. But of course the performance was only an image, an imitation, a representation. And if they are indeed with child, then I say that even this, is in any case only an image. Indeed, I can tell you, Belvoir himself only exists as an image".

"I think we need to investigate more", Marsilio said.

"If I might ask some questions"? Belvoir said.

"Of course. I think you should", Marsilio agreed.

Belvoir now looked at Diotima, who had looked so magnificent and madonna-like in the performance, and said "Diotima, if I may, can I ask you the if child you say you are with, is the result of intercourse with someone here, in Pavi Bujdam"?

Diotima answered, "If a glance is the intercourse you refer to, then yes, certainly. But otherwise, no".

Now Isabella spoke to the group for the first time. "I want to come forward", she said.

"Ah", Marsilio said. "Now I see more people are coming forward".

"Coming forward"? Amba, Ambika and Quentin echoed.

"Forward"? Timaeus echoed too. "*Coming forward*? Coming forward towards what, precisely"? he asked. "It sounds to me as though we are still in some kind of performance, and people in the audience are coming forward towards the stage at the front. Who are these people on the stage, that's what I want to know. And who are these people who are coming forward? What's the difference"?

"What is this performance the audience are watching? said Amba. "Why are they watching it? That's what I want to know. Perhaps, whatever the reason is, is the reason why they need to come forward". And anyway, why is the audience still the audience, why don't they all *come forward*".

Now Ambika said "It sounds as though we are still in the masquerade".

Marsilio held up his hand to quieten everyone. "You have something to tell us, Isabella"? he asked.

"Me too", she said. "It happened to me too". She looked at Quentin and said "Quentin glanced at me. And now I am with child".

Belvoir turned to Isabella and asked "Isabella, you are indeed worthy of any man's glance. But may I ask you, have you ever had intercourse with someone here, other than a glance, by which I mean, have you had intercourse of a corporeal kind, perhaps in the masquerade"?

Isabella blushed and shook her head.

"But you say you are with child"? Belvoir said.

Isabella nodded.

"Perhaps", Belvoir said, "If I might venture to suggest it, none of you are with child at all. But perhaps you wish to be. Perhaps it is even that you wish to be without knowing or seeing that you wish to be. Perhaps you wish for it here, rather than in the masquerade, which is where, as you know, becoming with child always happens".

"I don't want to be with child", Isabella said.

"Perhaps you are not with child", Belvoir said. "And perhaps...", he said, looking briefly at Marsilio, "Anyone who might have looked upon you and thought you were with child, when you were in the performance, was at the time, for reasons unknown to themselves, deluded by the wonder of the performance, and therefore sympathetic to your thought".

He turned and looked at Marsilio. "What does Marsilio think"? he asked.

Marsilio answered, "Marsilio thinks it true that perhaps this is some cloth of belief that has spread amongst us, perhaps due to some aspects between the planets. Is it really possible for someone to become with child, through a glance"?

Belvoir thought for a moment. Then he said, to everyone's surprise, "Of course".

"How so"? Sebastian asked again.

"Not with a glance of the human kind", Belvoir said. "You have to understand the nature of the glance. When you are painting...", Belvoir continued, "Is it not so that sometimes what you put into the picture is the result of just a glance at the picture"?

"Yes", Sebastian replied, "But it's not the glance itself that brings it about. There has to be the artist".

"Of course", said Belvoir. "But who is it that puts the idea into the artist"?

"It comes to me", Sebastian said.

"And would this be so all the more, if you were in the Divine frenzy"? Belvoir asked.

"Of course", answered Sebastian.

"And might it be", Belvoir went on, "That you might paint an image of yourself into the picture"?

"That indeed has happened", Sebastian said.

"And is it not for this very reason that it is possible for an artist to give birth to himself, or herself, in the art, as part of the art, through the art"? Belvoir asked.

"Of course", Sebastian replied. "But what the artist gives birth to, as you say in that way, would only be an image of the artist, not the artist herself or himself".

"Indeed", said Belvoir. "But I only say this by way of illustration. Nonetheless, what appears to be life in the image, is an image of the life it has been made in the image of, is it not? Such as when you created the persons in the gardens at Aumhurst"?

"Speaking as an artist", Sebastian said, "That's true. But actually, I have thought for some time now, as I think you yourself may have just suggested, that everything here in Pavi Bujdam, myself included, is essentially the work of Seraphina Bassenthwaite. And that we are an ongoing part of the art that she started". Sebastian looked at Sati. "Perhaps she has indeed painted herself into the picture", he said.

"I can understand what you are saying", said Belvoir. "But Seraphina, as the artist, is not really the One from which it all begins, is she"?

Amba spoke up now. "This is precisely what *I* was saying, Sebastian", she said. "I don't think the mere or the island of Pavi Bujdam is the work of Seraphina".

"Perhaps not", said Sebastian.

"Indeed", Belvoir said again. "Perhaps the mere and the island are part of the work of a still greater artist"?

"Perhaps so", said Sebastian. "But then who is the original artist? Is it God? I have to ask you because I know you are a theologian".

Belvoir shook his head. "The original artist is she who gives birth to the first art", Belvoir said. "And every other artist is he or she who creates or gives birth to more of the art. Either by the artist putting his seed into that which already exists, just as he himself is the result of seed, or by the artist giving birth to more continuation of the art, just as you intuit of Seraphina".

"So who is the first artist"? Asked Sebastian.

"She is the first mirror, and the beginning of all the mirrors", Belvoir said.

"What do you mean"? Amba now said quickly before Sebastian, who was about to ask the same question, had time to speak.

"She is all of the art", Belvoir said. "And I would say, that to the One from whom she comes, all this art is but a mirror".

"How do you know this"? Sebastian said.

"Have you never seen me in the masquerade, then"? Belvoir asked. Sebastian thought he was about to change the subject again, as was often his way.

"You never come into the masquerade", Sebastian confirmed. "And before you came here, you were a monk".

Belvoir almost looked surprised. "Have you never seen monks in the masquerade"? he asked.

"I have", said Sati. It was generally more or less impossible to remember details of the masquerade, but everyone knew that it happened, and there were certain things about the masquerade that one could remember. Sebastian had no clear image, but nonetheless, he too felt sure that there were monks in the masquerade.

Belvoir continued "The masquerade appears to be in Pavi Bujdam, indeed, it takes place at Aumhurst, does it not, except that things are different then"?

The friends nodded and agreed.

"And in the library there are books about the Old World, in the Library in the masquerade", Belvoir continued, "It is just that in the masquerade practically no one is inclined to read books, very much, because everyone is too busy following more basic desires. But nonetheless, I can assure you, the books are there. And if you want to go to the library now and see if these books I am about to speak of, are there now, and you cannot find them, and you are not in the masquerade, then this will tell you something about the nature of the masquerade".

Belvoir continued "In any case, I can tell you that the books will tell you that there is a place in Pavi Bujdam called Arabath, and that the people there have a name for this first or original artist. They call her Tiska".

"Arabath"? repeated Sati.

Now Timaeus spoke up too. "So there *is* a place called Arabath", he said. "And it is in the masquerade".

Now Ambika spoke. "But it was only the gate to Arabath that we saw, and it wasn't in the masquerade", she said. "We saw it in the maze, indeed, but when we saw it in the maze, we weren't in the masquerade after all, were we. I think we were not intoxicated"?

"Yes", Timaeus agreed, "What we saw in the maze was only the Gate to Arabath. But did I not say at the time that it was a way into the masquerade"?

"It was indeed the way in", Marsilio said.

Now Sebastian, already tired of all this talk about the gate to Arabath, said "But I still want to know, how would it be possible for the original artist, no matter what his or her name is, to make a human being in Pavi Bujdam actually with child, through a glance, as you said would be possible, Belvoir".

"Did I say that"? Belvoir said, looking as though he was struggling to remember. "I don't think I said that, did I? he said, looking at every-one else.

Sati said "I think you just said it was possible for someone to become with child, through a glance".

"Ah yes", Belvoir agreed, "That would be it. Of course it is possible", he said. "But not through a glance from the artist, as you quite rightly pointed out, Sebastian".

"Then how"? asked Ambika.

Belvoir said "I say it is the original One, the Source, who merely glances at the art, and by doing so sows within it the seeds of His image".

"I still don't understand", said Sebastian. "How would it be possible even for the original One, that you speak of, to whom you say the orig-inal artist appears as if she were a mirror, how would it be possible for this original One to make a human female actually with child, without that One being the human father who impregnates her?... which would mean by Him first becoming a part of the art himself, and becoming a human being, which must begin by him being a child in the womb? It seems to me to be a circular kind of paradox".

"It is", said Sati. "It's like asking which came first, the chicken or the egg"?

"I think not", said Belvoir. "What if the child in the womb were the One Himself"?

"How can that possibly be"? Sati said.

Belvoir answered "It is perfectly true to say that the child in the womb may be the original One, even as the original One remains unchanged and untouched by his image, who appears in the art, as the child in the womb. We theologians even have a name for this. It is called the immaculate conception. And the original One, we call God".

"How can that possibly be though"? Amba objected. "After all, you and Sebastian seem to be saying that the world in which there are mothers and wombs is the ongoing art of the original artist. And I think you said that the original artist comes after the original One. So the child in the womb, as an image in the art, must surely come after the original One".

"Indeed", said Belvoir. "You were paying great attention. But if you remember we are saying that to the original One, the original artist is but a mirror, and the art is to extend the art and create more art in an eternal continuation of the art. This is why we theologians say that really, there is only God, and that everything is God. Even though really, God takes no part in the art, except through the original artist".

Sati now seemed to be in some kind of frenzy. "Aha", she now said, in an animated way, "Indeed, I think I see it now. It is like Sebastian's exhibition. In the fifth gallery. The original art is just to create many mirrors". She thought for a moment. "Perhaps infinitely many".

"I can see you are on fire, Sati", said Marsilio. "Do continue, please".

"Well it seems to me", she said, "That the continuation of the art, perhaps by some means that we have not yet talked about, continues eventually in some way that no longer clearly and obviously is seen as a reflection of its source. In a way it becomes dependent on itself for its propagation, even though really, it is still all created as a reflection of its source, through these mirrors".

Belvoir smiled. "You have done well", he said. "It is of course only part of the story, and perhaps at some later time we can look into this more, but you have done very well indeed".

"What is the rest of the story"? asked Sebastian, eagerly.

Belvoir leaned towards him, and said encouragingly, "Find out".

"How"? said Sebastian.

"Find what is beyond the mere", said Belvoir.

26

Architecture

In Pavi Bujdam, just as also in the Old World, many believed that certain places, including those of human architecture, had their origins as described by myth. This was certainly true in the cases of the Tower of Pavi Bujdam, and Aumhurst, together with other revered places in Pavi Bujdam, and even, as it happens, the Pavi market.

How anyone comes to believe such things is of course a matter of the mind of the believer. But so too, is the alternative belief by many, that all such places are merely the creations of human beings, working for political or commercial purposes.

As the secrets hidden in the pages of some of the books in the library at Aumhurst had recently revealed to Sebastian, perhaps the truth can only be found in the architecture of minds themselves. Just as much as the truth was sometimes symbolised, for some, in the architecture of the buildings, in the revered and holy places.

But by the way of things, the architecture of most minds in Pavi Bujdam was such that few would be motivated to do such things as to try to get to the top of the Tower of Pavi Bujdam. That was largely left to the leaders of the clans. And most people who would come to visit Aumhurst, were never really motivated to truly try to understand

Sebastian's art, let alone seek out consultation with the kind of books in the library of Aumhurst, that Sebastian read.

On the contrary, in Pavi Bujdam the architecture of the mind in most people was something moulded by upbringing and experiences. It depended on the clan, if a person belonged to a clan, and the Vicinage in which a person lived.

Once the foundations of a building have been laid, and the walls erected, then even before the volume of the building is sealed through the adding of the roof and the closing of the spaces in the walls, with doors and windows, changes to the building can be difficult to achieve. Where change does happen, it invariably involves disruption and disturbance, and sometimes destruction.

The architecture of the mind may go on extending and improving itself, without such disruption, disturbance, and destruction. But then it never fundamentally changes. To let more light into a building that has been built too dark, to allow observation of the rising and setting of the Sun, or of the firmament, from a building that has been built in an unsuitable way, will invariably require disruption, disturbance, or destruction. The same is true of the architecture of the mind.

And so it was that Pavi Bujdam accommodated all kinds of architectures, both of buildings and minds, variations that fell into the twelve principal Vicinages, and the relations between them. And somehow, overall, for Sebastian now, all this, all the architecture of Pavi Bujdam, even the arrangement of the Vicinages, was beginning to represent for him, something in the mind of Seraphina. And then, once or twice it had also occurred to Sebastian, that perhaps Seraphina's mind was in some similar way, represented by the mere.

Across the Vicinages was the mix of the clans, each of their own collective mind, together with its corresponding architecture of ideas. Thus, as Sebastian saw it, the whole of Pavi Bujdam was an architecture of sorts, an architecture of minds, an architecture of ideas, and beliefs, existing within the architecture that had been brought into being by Seraphina Bassenthwaite. Perhaps, one might even say, by the architecture of her mind. Sebastian, by now, regarded her as the architect of it all. And in a way, he regarded everything and everyone in Pavi Bujdam, as being her. At least in the same way that a self portrait is the artist.

But in Pavi Bujdam, all this architecture was surrounded by the one mere, that could be seen from anywhere around the coastline of Pavi Bujdam. You didn't have to live in one particular Vicinage, or belong to any particular clan, in order to come to know the mere.

One day, Sebastian found himself alight with the idea of giving another exhibition, of paintings of the view of the mere from the different Vicinages. Then it occurred to him that he might also consider different views of the mere as seen by the various different clans. And he soon then came to the idea of seeking out other artists, from within the clans, and from the different Vicinages, who might like to exhibit their own images of the mere, in the exhibition.

So it was that the exhibition of paintings of the mere by the various clans, in views from the different Vicinages, came to be. It was during the creation of this project, that Sebastian noticed something remarkable about all the various pictures that came to be offered for the exhibition.

He had set up identical galleries in three of the Vicinages around Pavi Bujdam, at Aumhurst, Gsoaf, and Phrygia, forming an equilateral triangle between them. Various images of the mere were hung in the three galleries, and moved around between the galleries in order to try to arrive at the best arrangement.

Sebastian could not help but notice how similar were the images of the mere, in paintings submitted from any one Vicinage. This was even though each Vicinage was home to artists from all the clans, and each clan and its own traditional way of depicting the mere. Not only that, but the various paintings looked quite different when hung in the galleries of each of the three Vicinages.

To begin with he thought it might just be an effect of the light, which because the Vicinages were facing in different directions out over the mere, was different at any given time of the day. But then he realised something more interesting was going on.

Each of the clans used their own, limited pallet of colours to paint the mere. Each had a different idea of what the mere looked like. But then, also, as the paintings were moved from gallery to gallery, the image of the mere as it appeared in each painting, took on a different appearance.

And so it was that Sebastian came to believe that the architecture of Pavi Bujdam, as originally conceived by Seraphina Bassenthwaite, not only affected how any one of the clans had come to see the mere in their own view, but it even affected how anyone might perceive an image of the mere, by any of the clans, according to where they were in Pavi Bujdam. It seemed to Sebastian that all these things were interconnected.

He became even more convinced that Seraphina Bassenthwaite must have had overall knowledge of the mere, or a way of seeing it, beyond anything possessed by anyone in any of the clans, in any of the Vicinages of Pavi Bujdam.

Each of the clans had their own understanding of the mere, their own myths about it, their own beliefs about it. All of the Vicinages had their own view of it. But what was it, Sebastian wondered, that Seraphina knew?

He had gone back to the great library of Aumhurst, and had started searching in the books of the clans. He had begun to see emerging patterns that were common to all the clans, and he compared their beliefs to what he found in the architecture of Pavi Bujdam. But he could not solve it.

Eventually, one day, he found a book in the library called *Arts and Architectures*. It was a large volume, all in impractically small print, requiring a magnifying glass in order to read it, of the kind that Timaeus now frequently used. At first Sebastian thought this book was not going to offer anything of any particular interest to him. But then, going back to it several days later, there, in the text, he found the name Seraphina Bassenthwaite. Looking through the magnifying glass, as soon as his eye passed over it, it leapt out at him.

He read on, and to his amazement, her name was part of a mythical account. This was the first time he had seen a written account of the mythology of Pavi Bujdam. As Sebastian went on to read, he found that Ezequiel Bassenthwaite was the first Lord of Aumhurst. And that was where the mythology began. Ezequiel was the son of the great sculptor Maximilian Bassenthwaite. But Maximilian was himself said to have been born from Seraphina, the greatest artist in the universe, and the wife of the great dancing emperor Rhuz, famed for his immortality.

Maximilian had created the most beautiful alabaster sculpture ever seen, of the female form. He then fell in love with his creation. Naming her Saraswati, he prayed to Venus to bring her to life, which Venus duly did, by bringing Maximilian and Saraswati into her own dream of life, which she was dreaming along with the other planets.

Maximilian then had a son by Saraswati, who was Ezequiel. Seraphina then created all of Pavi Bujdam as a home for him, and so it was that he became the first Lord of Aumhurst. Ezequiel then had a daughter, Sati, who eventually married Rhuz, the great dancing emperor famed for his immortality.

One day, Sati's father Ezequiel, came into a serious disagreement with Rhuz, and so when Ezequiel was creating the first spectacular masquerade at Aumhurst, he shunned Rhuz, by not inviting Rhuz and Sati, his own daughter, to the masquerade.

Failing to remember that he himself was the offspring of Maximilian and Saraswati, who had been brought to life by Venus, and that Maximilian had been born from Seraphina, the first wife of Rhuz, he did not see that everything he created for the masquerade had come through Seraphina. So his plans fell apart, instead, creating chaos and disorder.

Sebastian read on, and there was more.

Sati was angry with her father, Ezequiel. So angered was she by Ezequiel's rejection of her beloved husband Rhuz, that she had gone to the masquerade anyway, uninvited. And she had killed herself in front of everybody. The description of her death was extraordinary. She had sat down in meditation, in front of everybody, and had drawn her consciousness upwards from her navel, to her centre, and then up into her throat, and then to the position between her eyebrows, whereupon she gave up her body. Sebastian noticed that she didn't, however, disappear from the narrative. Rather, in the continuing narrative she was then referred to as Seraphina.

Sebastian had never heard of anything like it, before. He didn't really know what to make of it. But one thing was clear. Seraphina was regarded as a mythical figure, a kind of goddess in the origins of Pavi Bujdam, but it was also believed that she was the architect of the actual buildings, buildings that still stood today.

Of course, he knew, Marsilio or Belvoir would probably say that Pavi Bujdam even today, was a myth. But somehow, this find concerning Seraphina seemed to lend weight to his already developing belief that she was somehow behind everything.

It was from then on, that the nature of his painting began to change. He now began painting more abstractly. What he was putting on the canvas seemed to him, to still be images, for all their often apparently completely abstract nature, and indeed they were sometimes more like abstract images of things or people in Pavi Bujdam. But now they were more symbolic in nature. They weren't symbols of anything that could be explained. They seemed to him, to stand as experiential symbols in themselves, of the experience itself that he had, when immersed in the painting. And it stood for some experience beyond both the experience of the painting or anything in Pavi Bujdam that had inspired it.

Sebastian's discovery of the myth also meant that the enigmatic connection between the Sati he knew, and the Seraphina he knew *of*, had just got stronger. Somehow, he began to really see Sati as Seraphina, and Seraphina as Sati, just as the portraits in Aumhurst suggested.

27

Meeting in the Woods

Behind Springmere, off the edge of the orange groves, and up onto the hill, was extensive woodland. Unlike Jenkins' coppice, it consisted all of tall, large and mature trees, and only some individual trees were occasionally cut down to provide large timbers. The woodland stretched all the way up the hillside over many acres, with occasional clearings on one side that looked down over the mere. In springtime, beneath the trees, there would always be there a sea of the most beautiful purple and ultramarine bluebells, and their very presence seemed to sing of the wonder of nature, the enchantments of the trees, and the true, eternal meanings of things.

The paths up through the woods twisted and turned, branching every now and then, but eventually, all paths led to the crown of the hill. There, at the top of the hill, was a horseshoe clearing, the open side looking out over the mere.

The woods were usually a place of stillness and silence apart from the ever present birdsong and the occasional sudden disturbance of undergrowth from a startled deer. On the days when the Sun shone over the mere towards the woods, the light combined with the reflected light from the mere, and would enter the woodland through the dark vertical lines of the trees at its edge. This would play tricks with the light, at certain times of day even creating the illusion of two suns obscured by the woods. The dappled dual light would play on the leaves and on the forest floor, as the calls of the wood pigeons, and in springtime, cuckoos, echoed from the boundaries.

One morning Sandhya and Sati were riding up through woods, on King and Helios, the two horses walking side-by-side.

"What will happen about Merehurst"? Sati asked Sandhya. "Now that you and Quentin are no longer together"?

"We rather thought we would develop it", Sandhya answered.

"How so"? Sati asked.

"We thought we might turn it into a Centre for the arts", Sandhya said.

"Will you and Quentin continue to live there"? Sati asked.

"Probably, for the time being", Sandhya replied. "It's certainly big enough. And we both still love it. Quentin seems to be happy with Amba, and I myself, have, shall we say, someone in mind".

"Have you"? Sati said, intrigued. "Can I ask who"?

"All in good time", said Sandhya. She looked ahead up the path, and said "This part isn't too steep, is it? Shall we canter for a while"?

The horses broke into a canter along the length of the path up to the next clearing overlooking the mere. "Look, it's beautiful"! Sati exclaimed as they arrived. The mere was stretched out beneath them, shining in the sun as it so often did, the islands of the archipelago adorning its surface like a bounty of emeralds studded into a great silver ring. It spread away from them, disappearing into an indistinct distance which itself faded into a blue haze, above which rose the line of seemingly luminescent grey-blue mountains.

"It does make you wonder doesn't it"? Sandhya said.

"What"? Sati replied.

"What's beyond it", Sandhya said.

Sati didn't answer, but continued looking out over the scene. And then there was a rustling in the woods behind them, and from between the trees emerged Timaeus, riding Socrates from the stables at Merehurst.

"Good morning"! he greeted them. He walked his horse over, to join them overlooking the mere.

"I was just telling Sati", Sandhya said, "That we are probably going to turn Merehurst into a Centre for the arts".

"An excellent idea", Timaeus said.

"Does Sebastian agree"? Sati asked.

"He thinks we should make it a centre for the sciences", Sandhya replied.

"Why can't it be both"? Sati said.

"Indeed, why not"? said Timaeus. "Merehurst would be well suited to it, I think. Merehurst is not like Aumhurst, with its Old-World style and furnishings. It seems the right environment for both the arts and sciences. And in any case, the division seems to be dissolving doesn't it"?

"That's what I think", agreed Sati. "Only the other day Sebastian was saying how glad he was that in Pavi Bujdam so many of the sciences have become an art, and that it has allowed him, as an artist, to create art through the sciences and the new technologies. Although I have to say, though, other than the maze, I don't really know what it was he was referring to".

"Shall we move on"? Sandhya said. The others agreed, so the three of them went back onto the path and continued up the hill, through the woods. The path wound on and sometimes steeply upwards, pleasantly bounded both sides by the mature woodland. By the by they reached another clearing.

"Let's look at the mere again", Sandhya said, turning off the path into the clearing. The three of them came off the path and went into the little clearing which was noticeably higher than the last, providing a magnificent view of the mere.

"Look at that", said Sati, gazing over the scene. "It looks as though you can see the mountains more clearly from here", she said. The three friends were taking in the view, occasionally pointing out to each other something they had spotted on the islands, or some vessel out on the water, when there was a rustling from the bushes behind them. Sati turned around and saw Sebastian on the beautiful Arab Plato from Aumhurst's stables, coming towards them.

"Sebastian"! Sati exclaimed. "I wasn't expecting to see you up here today", she said.

"Nor I you", he smiled.

"Greetings, sir", Timaeus said. "A little while ago we were talking about what might happen to Merehurst", he said.

Sebastian looked out over the mere, and breathed with delight at the view. "Oh yes", he said, and turning to Sandhya said "Have you thought any more about doing some of the sciences there, Sandhya"?

Sandhya said "Well we were wondering if it might be a good idea to do both sciences and arts there, given that so many of the sciences now are turning into arts, anyway".

"Well I think that's an excellent idea", Sebastian said. "What do you think, Timaeus"?

"I have thought quite a lot about it recently" Timaeus answered, "I mean, about the connection between the sciences and the arts".

Now Sandhya said "When I was out riding with Ambika she told me you had developed quite a lot of ideas about that at the Institute".

"Yes, that's right", Timaeus said. He carried on looking from island to island, enjoying the view.

"Well go on then, tell us what you think", Sati said.

"Yes I'd like to hear it", Sebastian said.

"Well", Timaeus said, "I'm not sure it would be of any interest".

"I'm sure we are all keen to hear", insisted Sandhya.

Still surveying the scene over the mere, below them, Timaeus said "Well, let me put it like this. The sciences rely on the way in which nature is consistent, in her behaviour, don't they"?

"Quite true", Sebastian said.

"And that's possible", Timaeus went on, "Because nature herself is governed by mathematics and numbers, is this not so"?

"Indeed it is", Sebastian said. "Go on".

"Well I think", Timaeus began again, "That many of our scientists don't really understand what is going on with themselves".

"What do you mean"? laughed Sati.

"Well, what I mean is", Timaeus continued, "That there is not a great deal of understanding in the sciences themselves of why there should be this reliable relationship between nature and mathematics, to begin with. In fact, if the truth is to be told, having discovered that there is this relationship, it seems to me, the scientists now are rather like magicians. They have learned how to do nature's tricks".

"They're not just tricks though, are they"? Sati said.

"In a way they are, I think", Timaeus said, "Because in a way, nature is a kind of magician, in the way she has created the world, and indeed us. Although I must admit I got the idea of looking at nature in this way, from Marsilio".

"That doesn't surprise me", Sati said, smiling.

"Anyway", Timaeus went on, "The scientists, having learned the tricks, now create new tricks. And there is of course, great value to us, in many of the tricks that they are now able to perform. So they now consider themselves to understand our world, and who we are, and where we come from. But really, they don't understand, I think. They certainly still don't know what is beyond the mere. Really, they have just come to understand the tricks of nature. And they are confusing their understanding of the tricks, with understanding the magician, and the magician's stage, and the magician's audience, and why the whole show has come into being, in the first place".

"I see what you mean", said Sandhya. "I shouldn't think it really matters much to the scientists, though, as long as the scientist can find out how the tricks of nature are done, and then utilise that knowledge".

"Quite so", Timaeus agreed. "But imagine if we did have a better understanding of what is really at the root of the relationship between numbers and the tricks of nature. That itself might have an impact on the way our science can develop, especially in those sciences that are already becoming arts. When I talked to Marsilio about it, you see, he not only spoke of nature as a magician doing tricks that the scientists can learn to do, but he also referred to nature as the great illusionist.

And that seems to raise the question of who the illusionist is, and why the tricks are being done".

Sebastian said, "Actually, in some of the art that I create I do sometimes feel that there is some mathematical form in it".

"It seems to me", Timaeus said, "That all mathematical form is a kind of architecture of relations between numbers. I feel that numbers are somehow the basis of the whole show, so to speak. I really do think it's all down to numbers".

Sebastian's horse snorted rather loudly, almost as if in disapproval.

And now another much louder snort was heard from behind the trees on one side of the clearing. Everyone looked around to see who was there.

Coming through the trees, riding the beautiful black horse, Pythagoras, was Quentin.

"My dear Timaeus", Quentin said, having overheard the conversation and now grinning, "I, being a musician, happen to think that music is the basis of this whole show in which we are living. And I also suspect that music is also the basis of numbers".

Sandhya laughed. "Surely you mean the other way around, don't you"? she said.

"I most certainly don't", Quentin said. "I mean it the way round that I said".

"You think music is the basis of numbers"? queried Sati. "You think that music is somehow behind what mathematicians think about"?

"That's what I said", Quentin confirmed.

Sebastian joined in again, saying "I could also say I think art is the basis of mathematics", he said, "But on what grounds would any of it be true"?

Now Timaeus spoke again. "I'm not sure there are any grounds at all, for such a claim", he said. "But Quentin, you do seem very sure of yourself, I must say. And I wonder why"?

Quentin smiled. "Ah", he said, "Well, as it happens, I have just ridden down from the Stone Circle. And I happened to come across Marsilio while I was up there, who was also out riding. And we started to talk about philosophy, and it was something he was saying that made me think it".

Sati laughed. "Ah well", she said, "If we want to hear the truth I suggest we make our way up to the stone circle".

"I would be very happy to come back up there with you", Quentin said. The friends turned around their horses and began to make their way back to the path.

But now two more voices chorused together from the within the trees. "So would we", they called out in unison. Everyone looked and saw Amba and Ambika, riding two beautiful steeds from the Aumhurst stables, Boethius and Parmenides.

And so now the seven friends proceeded to follow the path further up the hillside, towards the stone circle, the penultimate viewpoint over the mere before the very summit of the hill.

As they ambled up the path, they struck up a philosophical conversation concerning the soul. Timaeus said that he didn't see why there was any need to talk of such a thing, and that it was more important to talk of experience.

Ambika answered him saying, "I think all our experiences are parts of stories of experience, and like many stories that we hear or actually experience being a part of, you don't necessarily know what the end of the story is until you get there. And when you do get there, it may be that you realise everything else but where you are now, was just a story. And perhaps where you are now is just part of the story".

Amba said, "Why shouldn't the soul be something you experience"?

"Indeed", said Sebastian now. "I think there is probably lots of talk about it, without it being talk of experience".

"Well then, you see", Timaeus said, "I don't think you are contradicting me, are you? He smiled, quite pleased that their current philosophising was somewhat lighthearted and easy-going.

"What kind of experience are we talking about"? asked Sati.

"I don't know", Quentin answered, "But I agree with Timaeus that if we are going to talk about things at all, then it should be on the basis of experience, and not just belief".

Both Amba and Ambika now enthusiastically voiced their agreement together.

"I say the same thing about what is beyond the mere", Sebastian now said. "I think we don't need beliefs about it, I think we need to know. I think we need to go there". Sebastian sounded strangely serious, now, to the others.

"Well I think", said Sandhya, "That it's like love. I think it's possible to believe that you love, when you don't really love, at all. Just as when you do love, you don't need to believe it".

"Good point, Sandhya", Sebastian said in approval, and then Sati said "Yes, Sandhya, I agree".

"Well I think", said Timaeus, "That it would be a good thing to raise such questions with Marsilio".

"Agreed", said Sebastian, "But perhaps even more so, with Belvoir too".

"Absolutely", agreed Sati. "Especially now that, for some reason, these days, he seems to be more open to talking about things".

"Yes", Ambika said. "How is it we have managed to get Belvoir to speak so much, these days"? she mused.

"I think", said Timaeus, "It happened when Sandhya and Sati, and oh yes, Diotima too, it happened when you all believed he had made you pregnant by glancing at you". Timaeus grinned.

"That's true", said Sebastian.

The path became quite steep, making their progress slower now, and as they approached the area of the stone circle, the trees became very dense, making the path quite dark. But then as they approached the opening from the trees onto the clearing, the stones were immediately visible. Their ancient presence was palpable.

As the seven friends walked their horses up to the Stone Circle they could see the unmistakable figure of Marsilio, in vivid red, the costume he always wore when people thought of him as a magician, sitting in the centre, his horse beside him.

As soon as he saw them he smiled, saying "Greetings, friends! What delightful providence that you are all here. Come into the Circle, and join me! You can dismount from your horses, they won't leave the Circle".

The horses came into the Circle but Sati said "I think Helios might have a different idea".

"Trust me", said Marsilio, "I can assure you he won't leave the Circle". Trusting Marsilio, Sati got down from her horse, as did the others. They went and sat in a circle, surrounding Marsilio. The horses all stood serenely, cropping the turf.

They sat for a while, the beautiful, shining expanse of the mere with its hundreds of islands, stretched out beneath them in the backdrop to the Stone Circle, until Sati said "We were just saying that when we speak of the soul we should speak of experience, rather than belief. And I myself have a question I wanted to ask about that".

"Ah", said Marsilio. "Indeed. But then I wonder why you have come to the Stone Circle"?

"This was my idea", said Timaeus. "Because I knew you were here. You and I were talking a little earlier about science, and numbers, were we not? And you were saying, if I remember, that there is a kind of music behind the way numbers work, and behind the way nature creates her tricks that the scientists come to understand"?

Marsilio smiled. "Indeed", he said. "Most of the scientists can't see it, because they don't take into account the play of numbers, or the mathematics, that is going on in their own heads, that they are not aware of".

"Why are they not aware of it"? Timaeus asked.

"Because it is in their brain, in the way their brain is working, and in general, they don't take their own brain into account in their understanding", Marsilio answered.

Ambika said "Some of them who are studying the brain, do study the mathematical structures in the brain, surely"?

"Yes", said Marsilio, "But when it comes to beauty, and the good, and that which we love most, and especially when it comes to our ignorance of what is beyond the mere, they invariably presume that these all come from the things they understand, rather than seeing that what they understand still comes from what they don't understand".

"Do you mean", Timaeus said, "That mathematics itself comes from our ignorance of what is beyond the mere"?

Before Marsilio had a chance to answer, Sebastian said "But we do know what is beyond the mere in a way, don't we, because we know what is in the heavens".

"Indeed", said Marsilio. "But if we knew what is beyond the mere we would have a very different understanding of what it is we are looking at in the heavens."

Marsilio now turned to Sati. "You are looking very beautiful today", he said.

Sati smiled. Marsilio continued, "This is of course because you are indeed very beautiful. To me, this morning, you are the very picture of love, the very picture of beauty. And I trust that by my saying this, and by my looking at you in this way, that you have not become pregnant in the wrong way"?

Sati smiled and said "I think that kind of frenzy has gone".

"Then why have you come to the Stone Circle in search of answers to questions about the soul"?

Sati looked at Timaeus. "Timaeus said you were here", she said.

"Indeed I am here", Marsilio answered. "But questions of the soul are much deeper than questions about the magical tricks of nature. Such as the tricks through which our own bodies arise. And, indeed, our brains. What is nature, as the scientists speak of her, but a word, a name? The magical tricks of nature are only possible because of where nature comes from. Nature is not the highest. Above nature, is where nature comes from. Things go far, far beyond nature. Nature herself is beneath fate, and fate is beneath Providence. We can speak of nature here, but my dear, beautiful Sati, if you want to ask questions about the soul then we are not in the right place. If we ask them here, we are likely to start talking about theory, like the scientists, rather than about experience. So let us not ask such questions while we are here".

"Where should we be then"? Sati asked, seeming now to be glowing with innocence and beauty.

"I myself, as you know, am sometimes a magician of sorts", said Marsilio, "As we all are, whether or not we are aware of it. Sati, most beautiful one, you ask questions about the soul. And for that, we need the help of the white magician".

"Who is the white magician"? Sati asked.

"Well, Belvoir of course", answered Marsilio. "And I have no doubt we will find him within the ring of trees at the top of the hill".

28

The Bluebell Wood

Further along the route up the hill from the Stone Circle, towards the summit of the hill, where there was the ring of trees, the path passed through Jubilation woods, famed for its vivid, violet-blue bluebells.

Here it is the seven friends must pass,
Passing through the sea of violet-blue within the grass,
Betwixt tall trees all reaching for the Sun,
Serenely reaching upwards through the woods towards the One.

To reach the top the hooves must pass through thickets and through thorns,
As all around the path the blue adorns,
Spreading to infinity it seems a sea of blue,
Through dark dense wood where trees grow straight and true.

A blackbird calls a sweeter song that ringeth all around,
Through golden silence cuts the sweetest sound,
And from the fissure what was caught within the net flies free,
As from the forest Indra comes to thee.

The treading of the hooves through woodland wild,
Ascending from the plane below where all remain beguiled,
They seek someone within the sea of blue,
That stretches out around the path towards the truth of who.

The shadows 'twixt the trees are plays of light,
That loves to play within the play that makes the darkness bright,
So shadows might from shadows then reveal,
The shadows that from light are made which then reveal the real.

And so betwixt the trees above the blue the sun shines through,
That brightness through the darkness can be true,
So from the shadows light may dance above the blue so bright,
And lead across the blue towards the light.

When all the friends ascend the bluebell wood,
Then through the sea of blue the woodland path leads where it
should,
And should it come to pass it leads beyond,
Then there will be the finish and the breaking of the bond.

The bond that keeps the dwellers on the plain,
And draws them back towards the plain to dwell there once again,
Unless the path across the violet sea,
Is passed beyond the highest ring and sets the traveller free.

And so it was that the eight joyous explorers of the beautiful Jubilation woods wandered upwards along the winding path under the trees,
surrounded by the glorious carpet of the bluebells. A sea of violet-blue
so beautiful that even the insects and the unseen snakes who slithered
in the undergrowth knew, somewhere, even in the shadow of their
unknowing being, its magnificence.

"This is where I can really feel my soul", sighed Amba, "In a place
like this".

"I too", said Sati. And now the others too, in a quiet music of agreement, voiced their accord, as the horses walked on through the bluebells, faithfully carrying the friends upwards towards the summit of the hill and the ring of trees.

Amba began to ride beside Quentin, Sebastian began to ride beside Sati, and Timaeus began riding beside Ambika.

They even begin to hold hands, across the pairs of horses.

"I only wish Augustus was here", Sandhya found herself saying aloud.

"Ah... so", said Sati, "I wondered who it was. You were keeping that quiet. But I thought it might be".

"Augustus from Knolmere?" asked Ambika. "According to the rules of the Mereage he is next in line to Aumhurst".

"I know", Sandhya said.

29

❦

The Tree Circle

At length the sea of violet blue all around them was diluted with green grass and white flowers, and the spaces between the trees increased. Now in front of the friends, along the path, came what looked like a clearing at the crown of the hill, except that there in the space was the unmistakable ring of trees.

The horses walked on in silence towards the ring, Marsilio now leading the way. One by one they entered the circle between the trees, and now the friends dismounted from their horses. Across to the side, stretched out into the distance was the mere, studded with its islands, all now far below them.

As Marsilio had promised, there, in the centre of the circle, was Belvoir in his white habit, the hood covering his head, his hands meeting invisibly inside the sleeves, standing still as though he was a statue, or perhaps another one of Sebastian's persons.

He turned around to face the friends. "Ah"! He said. "The Pavi Academy comes to Belvoir, I see! Well, welcome to the ring of trees".

At Marsilio's suggestion everyone now sat on the soft, tufty grass around Belvoir. "I think...", Belvoir said, "...That nobody comes all the way up to the Tree Circle unless they are in search of something. And usually they are seeking things of the soul".

"I have a question", Sati said. "But first, I should like to know why you are the white magician".

"I am a magician, am I"? Belvoir smiled. "What has brought you to that conclusion"?

"That is how Marsilio referred to you", Sati replied.

"Indeed"? Belvoir said. "Well that would be because Marsilio is of course the red magician. Or so he thinks. But I can assure you that Marsilio is no magician. And neither am I. It is nature herself who is the magician".

For a few moments, the friends sat in the circle, with Belvoir at the centre, saying nothing, as the birds in the forest all around continued their singing.

Then Sati said "I should like to know about Seraphina". She then turned and looked at Sebastian. "Because I think Sebastian has become obsessed with her", she said.

"Who is Seraphina"? Belvoir asked.

"She is the architect of Pavi Bujdam", Sati said.

"Yes I know that", said Belvoir. "But who is she"?

Sati remained silent for a moment. "I don't know", she said.

"But you look like her", Sandhya said, as if she was sure this was a qualification for knowing more about Seraphina.

Again, Sati remained silent for a moment. And now she just said "I know".

Now Amba spoke. "Is it possible that you, Sati, are her"? She said. "I mean, in the same way that Sebastian's persons in the gardens at Aumhurst are all really the same person"?

"I don't know", Sati said. "I think that's what I'm here to find out".

"But you are seeking things of the soul, are you not"? Belvoir said.

"If you really want to know", Sati said, "I feel it hurts my very soul that Sebastian is putting his attention in that direction, in the direction of Seraphina, rather than in my direction".

Sati had no idea that this was what she was going to say, but nonetheless, she found herself saying it.

"Does it really hurt your soul"? Belvoir asked.

"Yes", Sati answered.

"How do you know"? Belvoir asked.

"Because I can feel it", Sati answered.

"How do you know it is your soul you can feel"? Belvoir asked.

Sati didn't answer.

Now Sandhya decided to interject. "I once thought I felt the same way about Quentin", she suddenly said. "But now I know something else".

"You can't possibly know how I feel", Sati said.

Now Amba unexpectedly joined in. "I once thought I felt the same way about Sebastian", she said. "I mean, because of Sebastian and you, Sati".

Sati looked backed at Amba, pointedly. "I already knew that", she said.

"And I also thought once", Amba went on, "That I felt that way about Timaeus, because he was with Ambika. And I don't mind saying so now, because I don't anymore".

Now Quentin spoke to Amba. "Well I know how I feel about you", he said.

Amba turned to Quentin and took his hand. "And I feel the same about you", she said.

Timaeus now joined in and turned to Ambika, and said, "Well I know how I feel about you, Ambika". Ambika squeezed his hand and said "And I you".

Now at last it seemed to be Belvoir's turn to speak again. "And yet it is only you, Sati, who looks like Seraphina", he said. "You, who are with Sebastian, the Lord of Aumhurst".

Sati nodded.

"Perhaps then", Belvoir continued, "We shouldn't be paying too much attention to your likeness to Seraphina".

"I think we should", said Sati. "Because since I look so much like her, is it me that Sebastian really wants to be with, or is it her"?

Belvoir gave her no answer. Instead, he just looked at Marsilio. "And Marsilio", he said. "What of you"?

Marsilio answered earnestly "I love all of you, as my very soul".

Belvoir smiled. Then he said "But Sati said her soul hurts".

Marsilio replied "I think perhaps she does not truly know that".

"I know what hurts", Sati objected firmly.

Now Belvoir looked at her. "But Sati, as I asked you before, how do you know it is your soul"?

Again, Sati was silent. "Where is my soul"? she said.

Sebastian, who had been quiet, now spoke. "I think I know where my soul is", he said quietly.

Sati heard him. "No doubt you will say it is beyond the mere"? she said, looking at him. "Since you are always thinking about that. Because that's where you think Seraphina is".

Belvoir now looked straight at Sebastian, and said "Do you know what is beyond the mere"?

"Actually, I think I do", said Sebastian.

"Have you been there"? said Belvoir.

"Not exactly", said Sebastian.

Belvoir answered "Then you do not know. But I suspect, from what I have come to know about you, that you are determined to find out".

Sebastian made no answer.

"I think he thinks Seraphina is there", said Sati.

"No", Belvoir said. "Seraphina, if she is anywhere, is here. It is just that the Seraphina you all speak of, that by all accounts and by the portraits in Aumhurst, our beautiful Sati here is certainly the spitting image of, did know what is beyond the mere".

"That's what I have been saying all along", Sebastian said. "And I think all this is her work of art. Including my work".

"No", said Sati now. "I am your work, and you are mine, don't you see"?

Belvoir now smiled and seemed very pleased. "Sati is correct", he said.

Timaeus now joined in. "I think we are none the wiser then", he said, "Because we don't know why Sati looks like Seraphina, or what this means. And as far as I can see, from what has been said, Sati does not know whether or not it is her soul that she is feeling. Although, I would say, if there is a soul, then I would certainly like to think that is where I feel my love for Ambika".

Belvoir said "I can assure you, Sati, what hurts, if it hurts, is not your soul".

"Then where is my soul", Sati asked.

"Across the mere, of course", Sebastian said.

"You would say that", Sati said. "Because that's where you think Seraphina is".

"No, I don't", Sebastian answered. "Because Belvoir said she is here". He turned to Belvoir. "But I think", he said, looking at Belvoir, "Belvoir knows what is beyond the mere. Just like Seraphina knew".

"I certainly do not know what Seraphina knew", Belvoir answered.

"Who in Pavi Bujdam does know then"? demanded Sebastian.

Belvoir remained silent.

"I want to know", Sebastian said, sounding demanding again, most unlike his usual self, "You know what is beyond, Belvoir, and I am the Lord of Aumhurst, so tell me".

Belvoir still remained silent. Then he said "You will have to find that for yourself".

Sebastian was now in a kind of frenzy that the others had never seen before in him. "Give it to me"! He demanded of Belvoir. "Give me the knowledge"!

Belvoir looked over his shoulder, through the ring of trees, and towards the ridge. Everyone else followed his gaze. The ridge stretched away from the summit of the hill on which they sat, a sharp edge, like the upward, facing edge of an axe, at first, for some considerable distance, descending in height somewhat below the hill, but then rising again, to snake its way, upwards, and upwards and upwards, ever upwards, way above the height of the Tree Circle, up and up, steeper and steeper, towards the rocky peak in the distance.

Sebastian was quite sure he knew why Belvoir was looking up there. "The hermit", Sebastian said.

Belvoir looked back again, and at Sebastian, and simply nodded his head.

"I suspected you might know", Belvoir said, "When you said you thought you knew what was beyond the mere".

"Who is the hermit"? Sati demanded to know.

"I want to go and talk to him again", Sebastian said.

"But who is he"? Sati said.

"Some call him Pythagoras", Sebastian said.

"They say he is a Visitor", Belvoir said.

"Why has he not returned to his own land"? Sati asked.

"He withdrew, instead", Belvoir answered.

"How does he survive up there"? Sati asked.

"The people from Schisma take him food", Belvoir answered again.

Sebastian was already on his feet. He was looking up at the peak. "I'm going up to find him", he said.

"It looks too dangerous", Sati objected.

"It is too dangerous to take the horses", Belvoir said. "The ridge has to be taken on foot. Unless you go up the side of the hill. Those who want to go, need to leave their horses here".

It soon became apparent that nobody wanted to be left behind.

30

The Hermit

The first part of the ridge was easy, but nonetheless not kindly. A very real sense of danger was always present, as the path was narrow, rocky, and each side fell sharply and steeply away, down and down as a sea of small rocks and loose shale.

The friends passed along it in single file, in silence, the only other life they could see being the occasional eagle, high above them, soaring silently in the purer air. After the path started to climb again, it proceeded for a long time without too much difficulty, but little by little, its steepness increased, and it began to wind left and right into steep rocky domain in which its course ahead could not even be seen until close upon it.

Everyone moved carefully up and up on the path, higher and higher towards the peak, until eventually it was not possible to proceed without using hands also, to assist in the ascent. Each side of the path the view was magnificent, the plains below with tiny villages, and behind them, when anyone was brave enough to turn around and look at it, an incredible view of the vast expanse of the mere, stretched out towards the mysterious blue-grey horizon.

Eventually the path wound around to the opposite side of the peak, so that the mere was temporarily no longer visible. A little later the friends found themselves quite suddenly and unexpectedly stepping between boulders onto a small rocky plateau, on which was growing, seemingly incongruously, a number of small, rough-hewn trees. On one side was a number of cave-like openings into the rock. And there, sitting on quite a large, flat, smooth slab, on the side overlooking the mere, was the bearded hermit.

As the friends silently approached him from behind, quietly stepping across the plateau, the hermit made no sign of movement. They all came up onto the flat slab, and sat down on it, while Belvoir approached the hermit. He slowly lowered himself into a position beside the hermit, and began a slow, quiet, wordless chant. After a while, it became apparent to the rest of the friends that both of them were chanting. And then there was silence again.

Now, quite suddenly it seemed, the Hermit rose to his feet, and turned to face the others. His hair was matted and he was clothed only in what appeared to be ash. At first, he stood absolutely still, his eyes closed, and then he opened them and looked around the group. And then he spoke.

"Who is the one called Sati"? he asked.

Sati stood up.

The hermit spoke a word, perhaps of surprise, perhaps of something else, in a language that nobody recognised. Then he said simply "It is true then. You are beautiful".

Sati didn't move or say anything.

Now Belvoir said "She has a question about the soul".

The hermit sat down again, this time facing the friends, and beckoned to Sati to come and sit beside him. She walked over to him and sat. The others moved too, gathering closer around.

For what seemed like a long time, the hermit just looked at her. Then he said "How did you come to be in Pavi Bujdam"?

"I was born here", Sati answered.

"No one is born here", the hermit said. "Everyone is born in the masquerade".

"That's what I mean", said Sati. "But everyone born in the masquerade has their place in Pavi Bujdam also, don't they? I mean, as I understand it now, we all must somehow be pushed out into Pavi Bujdam through the gate of Arabath, even though we don't remember it"?

The hermit answered "Only as long as you are born in the masquerade. And to those beyond the mere, Pavi Bujdam is no more than a masquerade. And to those beyond those, it is the same again".

The hermit's words struck Sebastian hard. He could not remain silent any longer. "I knew it"! He said, "There's another mere! Isn't there? Beyond the land beyond our mere? If we are like the masquerade to them, then what is on the other side of their land"?

"Since you already suspected it, you are intelligent", said the hermit. "You perceive well".

"But no Visitor has ever mentioned another mere", said Sebastian, "Why not"?

The hermit answered "Of course not. When the Visitors are here, they are here. Do *you* always remember what is beyond the masquerade when you're in the masquerade"? The hermit then said, even more pointedly, "Or rather, is it that you get immersed and lost in the masquerade"? The hermit raised his eyebrows questioningly, in a way suggesting he already knew the answer.

"Yes, that's true", said Sebastian. "We do all become rather lost in it, for a while. But surely, for the Visitors, when it's time to go back, the Visitors who are here must remember their own land"?

"Of course", said the hermit. "As *you* remember the Pavi Bujdam you live in for most of the year, when you come out of the masquerade. But when you are in the masquerade, do you ever mention it"?

"That's true", said Sebastian, "It doesn't even seem to come into anyone's mind".

"But what of the mere that surrounds the Visitor's land"? Sati asked. "Do they not also wonder what is beyond *their* mere"?

The hermit laughed. "You are intelligent also", he said. "And how do you think they are viewed by those in the land beyond them"?

The hermit laughed again, and went on, "And each land with its own idea of the world of which it is a part", he laughed. "Just as you have yours", he said, "And no doubt a different one, when you're in the masquerade".

"How many meres are there"? Sebastian asked.

"How many do you want there to be"? the hermit laughed again. "Some say seven, like seven planets. It's easier that way. But what is the point of trying to limit the limitless to a limited understanding"?

"But if it all goes on and on, then what is the point"? Sebastian sighed. "What is the point of us trying to know what is beyond just our mere"?

"The point is to know", said the hermit.

Sati said "If there are more meres beyond the ours, then what is beyond them all"?

"Beyond them all", the hermit answered, "Is a land they call the land of no land, and beyond that, is the cause. Some say that is a mere, too".

The hermit then gazed at Sati as though she had been transfigured. "Most beautiful one", he said, looking at her, as if in amazement, "To me, it is clear from your beauty, indeed, that you yourself are really just a Visitor here".

"But I was born in the masquerade, like everyone else here", Sati said, "Except, I suppose, the Visitors".

The hermit looked straight at her. "Then why have you come to the peak, to speak with me, if you are not seeking to find who you really are, and where you really come from"? he said.

"I came because I have a question about the soul", Sati answered.

"Indeed", said the hermit. "Why else would you come here? What else can your question possibly be, but this? But what else can there possibly be to say of the soul, if it is not who you really are, and where you really come from"?

Sati stood in silence, taking in what the hermit was saying.

The hermit went on, "You say you were born here, but do you actually *remember* your birth in the masquerade of Aumhurst"?

"No, it's true, I don't", said Sati, "But then nobody remembers their birth, do they"? she said.

"How do you know that"? asked the hermit. "Are *you* everyone"?

Sati didn't answer.

The hermit said "As it happens, many people in Pavi Bujdam do say they remember their birth, but what they remember is their imagination. However, I think you, Sati, will remember your birth, and not just in your imagination. I can see it in you. And when you do, you will realise what your birth in the masquerade really was, and that you were not born there".

Sati looked at Sebastian. "Well I know one thing", she said, "It's only by my being here, that I can be with Sebastian".

"You are lovers"? The hermit said. "You meet together"?

"I think we are true friends, also", Sati said.

"It's true", Sebastian said, looking at Sati.

"Do you meet at the edge of the mere"? the hermit asked pointedly, "Rather than just for the sake of meeting together? Or perhaps, knowing the people of Pavi Bujdam as I do, meeting just for recreation, or for the sake of society, or what society thinks is the purpose or meaning of such meeting"?

"I think we do", said Sebastian, and Sati nodded.

"Hmm", said the hermit. He looked seriously at Sebastian. He seemed to be studying him. "I know you from when I first came here", he said. "You make the persons in the gardens of Aumhurst, do you not"?

Sebastian nodded.

"What is your name"? The hermit asked. "I have forgotten".

"Sebastian", Sebastian said.

"Ah yes", the hermit replied, "You are indeed the one who has currently inherited Aumhurst. The artist. The Lord of Aumhurst no less".

Sebastian nodded.

"And your work is of course all part of the work of Seraphina", said the hermit.

Sebastian felt a stirring within himself, at the hermit's words, reflecting what he had already been thinking himself, for some time. "So this really *is* all the work of Seraphina"? Sebastian said, feeling vindicated. "Including my work? It's her work, ongoing, now that she has gone, isn't it"? he went on.

"Gone"? Said the hermit, surprised. "But you are here aren't you"? said the hermit.

"I certainly am", Sebastian replied.

"Then of course she has not gone", the hermit said. "You yourself, this one you call the Lord of Aumhurst, this one you call Sebastian, and whatever else you like to call him, you said you meet with Sati, did you not, and who is it that Sati looks like?" the hermit now said, looking briefly up to the sky.

The hermit now looked at Sati. "The persons in the gardens are a good imitation", he said. "But this doesn't necessarily mean that Sebastian knows what they mean", he smiled.

"I think they are all of the same one", Sati said. "Sebastian has never said who". She turned to Sebastian. "Are they a representation of you"? she asked, "A representation of your soul, perhaps"?

Sebastian didn't answer, but the hermit, still looking at Sati said "You speak of souls before you truly know the mere, what is beyond it, or really what you are doing. What do you know of the soul"? he said dismissively.

Sati and the hermit just looked at each other.

Now the hermit continued, and gently said "Souls are not separate, Sati, they live mutually within each other. They are one, they are each other's mirror. And the souls of lovers who live and love by the truth of the mere become as complimentary as the souls of eternal friends. And the joining of two souls in such friendship is not any less than the joining of lovers. And as lovers you should see what flowers from who join themselves truly in search of what is beyond the mere".

The hermit looked sternly at Sebastian and Sati and said "And they must still search for what is beyond it even if they find themselves as Lord and Lady".

Now Sebastian spoke again. "The persons are not the only sculpture work I have done", he said. "I have another sculpture that is not displayed in the gardens", he said. "Sati is the only one who has seen it".

The hermit remained silent.

"You mean the one called The Lovers"? Sati said to Sebastian.

"Yes", Sebastian confirmed.

"I think it's beautiful", said Sati, "But some would say it's not the sort of thing to display publicly".

"Perhaps you should put it on display in the gardens", the hermit said. He continued "Or perhaps better still, put it overlooking the mere".

"How can I come to truly know what is beyond the mere"? asked Sebastian.

The hermit seemed to snort. He seemed dismissive. Then he said "Only the knowledge of what is beyond the mere will bring that knowledge to you".

The hermit then appeared to be speaking to both Sebastian and Sati. "See the soul of each other, as a step towards knowing your own. If there is sufficient love, it is possible. It might be easier for you to see the soul of your partner than it is to know your own. You may only discover this when you think you have lost them".

"Am I going to lose him"? Sati asked, looking sadly at Sebastian.

"Not if you come to know the secret of the mere", the hermit answered. He then stood up. He pointed upwards beyond the cave entrances. From the side of the cave entrances another ridge extended away, rising steeply upwards for a long way, to yet another, still higher peak.

"The Unknown One will come to speak with you when the time is right", he said. And with that, the hermit simply stood up, and withdrew into one of the caves.

Later that week, all the friends were saddened by the news coming from the village of Schisma, that the hermit had died. They heard from the villagers who took food up to him, that shortly before he died, he had said his work was now completed.

31

Delusion

Once again it was the most beautiful morning at Aumhurst. Sebastian stood, looking upwards and around the azure sky in amazement. This was the certainty he had been waiting for. Here again was the depthless infinity of diamond-clear blue, once again without even the merest hint of cloud, and not even the slightest sign of any breeze.

The mere stretched out before him, once again like a finely polished mirror, the deep green of the islands immaculately reflected within it.

§

The previous evening had been beautiful, with the friends gathered to watch the sunset from Merehurst. Now Timaeus stood looking out of the great bay window overlooking the mere. "It's perfect weather", he said. In the bright, early morning sun the day seemed to be charged with a powerful potential, an energy of adventure. He turned to Ambika and said "Sebastian will be going out on the mere today. From the calculations, I think 11 o'clock will be about right. We can watch him from the observation tower. It's something he's been working on".

"What has he been working on"? Ambika asked, slightly curious.

"If you come and look, you'll see for yourself", Timaeus answered.

"Is this the Satya Vajra you are talking about"? asked Ambika, unexpectedly.

"You know about it"? Timaeus asked with great surprise. "Did he tell you? I thought he was keeping it a secret until the trial today".

"Sati knows about it, of course", Ambika answered. "Or did you think Sebastian keeps secrets from her? I don't know if she knows about him going out on the mere this morning, though. She never mentioned it to me".

"Well, do come and watch from the observation tower at eleven", Timaeus said.

"I will", Ambika replied. "Provided I'm not going to watch him kill himself. Sati said something about speeds and a death zone"?

"Oh yes, of course", said Timaeus. "But that's all in the old standards. Things have moved on. I can assure you it's perfectly safe".

Ambika didn't seem very convinced. "Sati didn't seem to think Sebastian was totally confident about it", she said doubtfully.

"He just doesn't trust the calculations", Timaeus said. "I do".

§

Amba walked into the courtyard of the Merehurst stables. She saw her sister there. "Are we riding out today"? She asked. Ambika didn't answer her. Instead, she just said "Did you know that Sebastian is going out on the mere today"?

"No", Amba said, nonchalantly. "But he often does that. What of it"?

"He will be in his new vessel", Ambika said. "The Satya Vajra it's called, apparently".

"A new project"? Amba queried.

"It breaks all previous speed records across the water's surface, as I understand it", Ambika said. "I think he has some crazy idea that he can reach the opposite shore of the mere".

"What about the storms"? said Amba.

Ambika looked up and around the sky. "What on a day like today"? she said. "I'm sure he would've taken that into account, anyway. I imagine if they form, he will just come back".

"Well I hope he knows what he's doing", Amba said.

Ambika smiled. "I think Sebastian always knows what he's doing", she said.

§

Quentin looked at Amba in surprise. "You mean he's going to try to get across the mere using a machine that he's built"? he said incredulously.

"It's not a machine", Amba laughed, "It's a boat. It's called the Satya Vajra".

"A boat is a machine, isn't it"? Quentin said.

Amba went on, "Timaeus seems to know all about it. Apparently this boat is capable of previously unheard-of speeds. I know Sebastian seriously thinks he can make it to the other side of the mere. Timaeus is going up in the observation tower to watch, at 11 o'clock".

Quentin shrugged his shoulders. "Well I think we had both better be up in the observation tower to watch also, then", he said.

§

Sandhya was walking back from the stables when she saw Bellamy by the fence, talking to one of the horseman from further around the mere. The stable keepers and the horsemen, as she and Sati knew well, tended to be conduits of gossip. Thinking nothing of it she entered the house and went into the boot room. Shortly afterwards Bellamy came in too.

"Morning Bellamy", Sandhya said. "Catching up on the gossip were we"?, she joked.

"Not really gossip" Bellamy said. "Just some proper news now about the rumours last night".

"Rumours"? Sandhya asked.

"About the strange lights over the mere at Gsoaf", Bellamy said.

"Just a mere storm, wasn't it"? Sandhya said.

"Yes, it turns out it was", Bellamy replied. "But it was unusual, after all, apparently".

"In what way"? Sandhya asked, finishing tidying the outdoor clothes and rearranging the various garments.

"Apparently it's spreading around the mere from Gsoaf", Bellamy said. "Both directions, apparently", he shrugged. "They don't usually do that. I know they move, but I've not heard of them spreading out in both directions around the mere before".

Sandhya frowned. "No, nor have I", she said. "It's not coming across the mere towards Pavi Bujdam is it"?

Bellamy laughed. "Oh no, nothing like that", he said. "But eight of the Vicinages have already reported sight of it, I hear. I think we will get a view of it too, before long. If it continues, the whole of Pavi Bujdam will be surrounded by it".

Sandhya raised her eyebrows. "Interesting", she said. "We'll look out for it".

§

The Old World clock in the hall chimed 10:30. Quentin walked along, opening doors, looking for Sandhya. There was no sign of her, so he turned the corner and made his way towards the South wing and the observation tower. Then he heard Sandhya's voice calling him from behind.

"Quentin"! She called. "Have you seen Sati, we're meant to be riding out this morning"?

Quentin turned and called out "Last I heard was that she had gone over to the stables". Then as an afterthought he shouted "We're going to watch Sebastian go out on the mere, in his new vessel, from the observation tower. It should be worth seeing. Do you want to come up and view, instead"?

Tired of shouting, Sandra walked the length of the passageway towards Quentin. She looked a little puzzled. "What are you talking about"? She said. "Why do we need to watch? Why is it going to be especially worth seeing"?

"He's going out on some new speed vessel he's created", Quentin said. "The Satya Vajra I think she's called. She's capable of unheard-of speeds, I'm told, and he seems to think he can make it all the way across the mere. And back again, presumably", he smiled.

Sandhya's face looked sickened. "Do you think Sati is at the stables"? She said.

"I'm pretty sure that's where she is", answered Quentin. "Why"?

"Quentin", Sandhya said with urgency, "There's a freak mere storm. Ask Bellamy out about it". And then before Quentin had a chance to answer, she ran off down the passageway.

Sandhya raced over to the stables as fast as she could, and arriving breathless, she saw Sati, preparing Helios for riding.

"Go" she screamed. "Go to Aumhurst! You have to stop Sebastian! He's going out on the mere on the Satya... whatever it's called, and there's a freak mere storm coming".

"What"? Sati said, still taking in what Sandhya had just said.

"The storm is going to completely surround Pavi Bujdam", Sandhya said. "And Sebastian might not know about it".

Now alarmed, Sati understood, and said "Should I go on King? Isn't he faster"?

"No. Take Helios, he's definitely faster", said Sandhya.

Now Sati was already up and on Helios, and galloping fast away. They were soon on the path and then up onto the Silver Gallop. And once again, Helios, the magnificent palomino, was racing the length of the Gallop, alone with his rider, fully sensing her frenzy, now no longer the thrill of the challenge, but some unfamiliar force driving harder into his sides than he knew to be Sati's usual way. Helios gave his all as they hurtled towards the gap in the boundary fence, seemingly faster than ever before. Sati's grip on the reins was firm this time, the gap was the way and the only way. And through it they flew together, a united, charging engine of flying turf and billowing dust.

Onto the path to Aumhurst they galloped, even faster now, the gap behind them, Aumhurst looming ahead, and Sati made the decision to branch off to the shoreline path, the direct route to the Harborage, despite its looser surface. The charge along the path sent clouds of dust high into the air, which would have seemed to any observer as if there was some deliberate and reckless destruction of the path taking place.

The little fence to the area of the Harborage offered no impediment to their determination, Helios jumping it with the ease and grace of a golden god, a final flight of Pegasus-like glory before the reins were ruthlessly tightened and Sati's hand was gripping his mane to break the fury.

Sati was down from Helios and running down the steps and into the already open door of the boathouse. Breathless she stopped, and looked, and there was the Satya Vajra, in the water, poised, silent, and stationary, behind the opened doors to the mere. But Sebastian was nowhere to be seen.

§

Sebastian had lowered the telescope and now looked out across the mere. Everything looked perfect and clear. It was the last, final check before trying for the opposite shore. He checked the time. It was almost eleven. The perfect launch time. He needed to get back down to the Harborage. He left the Observatory, and decided to ride back down on the more scenic old path, even though the new one was easier and perhaps only two minutes ride, rather than the three minutes down the older windy path.

§

Sati walked up to the entrance of the Satya Vajra, and there on the side, was Sebastian's final checklist. The last item written down was a final check of the mere through the telescope. She rushed outside and back onto Helios, galloping him up the new path to the Observatory. She raced inside the building, and up the stairs, and called "Sebastian"! But when she reached the telescope, again, he was nowhere to be seen. She walked over to the telescope and looked through it. There was no sign of any movement on the mere. Then she heard a noise like she had never heard before, and she realised it must be coming from the Harborage below. It must be the Satya Vajra.

She hurtled herself back outside and onto Helios, and raced him back down the path to the Harborage. As she reached the building, she saw the Satya Vajra already a good way out from the shore, moving like a missile away from Pavi Bujdam.

As she stood, watching in dismay, suddenly there were hooves and horses thundering towards her from the fence. It was Sandhya and Quentin. "You didn't stop him"! Sandhya shouted.

Sati just fell down onto Helios' neck and sobbed.

§

The journey back to Merehurst was accompanied by much peering out onto the mere, in vain. It wasn't possible from the level of the mere to ascertain the whereabouts of the Satya Vajra. Once at the top of the observation tower at Merehurst it was possible through the its telescope to still see the plume rising up from behind the Satya Vajra, identifying its position. But then, it wasn't long before at the same time, the expanding mere storm started coming in from both directions around the mere.

Continual flashes of light within the storm all the way across its width, illuminated the dense purple cloud as the two ends of the storm approached each other like the closing of some vast theatre curtain. Timaeus was looking through the telescope when he remarked that it looked as though the storm seemed closer to them than usual, perhaps only three quarters of the way across the mere, and that it looked as though Sebastian was already beyond it, through the remaining gap, and further away from them. But he couldn't be sure.

In what seemed like no time at all the two ends of the storm rapidly approached each other, and then they met, completing a wall of dense, dark cloud and bright flashes, and there was no more sign of Sebastian. No one was sure whether he had escaped from the storm by passing through the gap, or whether it had swallowed him up.

Sati was unresponsive to anyone's attempt to talk to her. Timaeus tried to console her that Sebastian would probably be fine, and after the storm would be able to come back and would be quickly out of the zone of the mere storms. But there was no hiding the tone of concern in Timaeus' voice.

§

The people of Pavi Bujdam were used to mere storms coming and going. No one expected any mere storm to last for a whole week. But it was for a whole week that Pavi Bujdam was encircled by the strange, dark ring of the storm, with its ceaseless flashes illuminating from within, the cloud, or fog, or vapour, or perhaps the turbulent rising up of the waters, or whatever it was that mere storms seemed to consist of. The prolonged presence of the storm gave rise to much debate and speculation, a minority of the scientists who observed the storm through telescopes, insisting, according to their already held opinions about mere storms, that it was not, in fact, a weather storm, at all. When pressed for alternative explanations they seemed to favour the idea that the appearance of the storm was a play of light, some kind of mirage brought about by the atmosphere over the mere.

At night the ring around Pavi Bujdam glowed and flashed relentlessly, most of the time in a strange, deep, purple hue, sometimes highlighted with blues and greens. By day it continued less spectacularly, with sunshine and clear blue skies extending over Pavi Bujdam as if the rest of the weather was intent on ignoring the storm, if indeed, that is what it was. But Sebastian didn't return. He was gone, whatever the nature of the storm.

By the end of the week most of the friends were coming to terms with the idea that they had probably lost Sebastian. Every day at the same time they would convene at the top of the observation tower of Merehurst to observe the storm and the point where Sebastian had last been seen.

Then, on the last day of the week the friends, including Marsilio, had met at the top of the observation tower, and Amba was looking through the telescope, when everyone heard her say excitedly, "Something is happening"!

They took turns to look through the telescope in rapid succession, and last of all, it was Marsilio's turn. "I can see the mountains again", he said, "The gap is widening". Just as the storm had closed its circle, so it was opening again, from the same place. As the gap widened, the intensity of the darkness seemed to lessen, and the distant mountains became partially visible all around.

Now Sati was watching through the telescope, when she said "I can see something"! Quentin quickly looked through the telescope, and exclaimed "It's the Satya Vajra! It's coming back through the gap"!

Sati took the telescope again, and said "It is! It's him! Unless the

Satya Vajra is driving itself"! The plume from the rear of the craft was clearly visible and it was heading through the gap back towards Pavi Bujdam like a missile.

Now the rest of the friends took brief turns at looking through the telescope, and there was much excitement. Marsilio, however, had walked over to the opposite window of the tower. Despite their pre-occupation with watching the progress of the Satya Vajra, the others heard him say "There's someone riding on the path towards Aumhurst".

"Who is it"? asked Sandhya.

"Somebody in white" was Marsilio's simple reply.

"Is it Belvoir"? asked Ambika, already walking towards the window. She peered down out of the window and said "I don't think it is". Sati came over to look, too, and agreed that it didn't look like Belvoir.

By the time the Satya Vajra had passed through the gap and left it considerably behind, the entire ring of the mere storm had all but faded into ordinary looking light cloud, and all the distant mountains were visible again. It was agreed that shortly the friends would all ride over to the Harborage at Aumhurst, to meet the arrival of the Satya Vajra, and as everyone hoped, Sebastian.

§

Once everyone had arrived at the Harborage, there was no clear sign of the Satya Vajra, so it was decided to take the horses up to the Observatory, where the view out over the mere would be much better. Once in the Observatory, they found the telescope already lowered to look over the mere, and there was a good view of the Satya Vajra, its plume rising up behind it. Shortly afterwards the vessel became clearly visible without the use of the telescope.

Everyone watched as it approached on a dead straight line towards the Harborage, the plume following it all the time diminishing in size as the craft was slowing. And now it was possible to hear the strange sound of the craft as it approached closer in the direction of the Harborage. Confident now that the arrival would be safely made, the friends were about to take once more to the horses, to ride down to the Harborage, when Sandhya exclaimed that she could see somebody already down at the water's edge.

"Who is it"? Sati asked, coming over to look. When she got back to the window, it was clear that it was the figure in white that she had seen when they were in the observation tower at Merehurst. "Come on"! She said, "Let's get down there"!

Everyone arrived back at the Harborage to find the figure in white already standing on the moorings, obviously awaiting the arrival of the Satya Vajra. Sati was about to approach the figure, when she was restrained my Marsilio. He seemed now to recognise the figure. "It is most prudent to wait", Marsilio said. "It is the Unknown One".

Eventually the Satya Vajra came steadily into the moorings and pulled up to a halt. The canopy opened and Sebastian jumped out. He didn't seem to be in any way unusual. Sati ran up to him and put her arms around him. The others took turns to embrace him.

At last Sebastian had a chance to speak. Much to everyone's surprise he simply said "Well there we are, it seems to be possible".

"What happened"? Quentin said. "How have you managed for a whole week"?

"What do you mean"? Sebastian asked, puzzled.

Quentin slapped Sebastian on his arm. "You've been gone a whole week"! he exclaimed.

Sebastian looked more puzzled. "The storm only lasted about an hour", he said. "I've only been gone a few hours"!

It now seemed that everyone tried to speak at once. And then into the perimeter of the hubbub stepped the Unknown One. He was dressed in a white robe, similar to the one worn by Belvoir. Much to everyone's surprise he addressed Sebastian with what appeared to be a reprimand, almost as if he already knew him.

"What is this nonsense"? He demanded. "You want to know the truth about the mere"? he said sternly. And then looking at the Satya Vajra, he said disparagingly, "And you think you can find what is beyond the mere with *this*"? Waving his hand towards the vessel, as if to dismiss it like an annoying feather.

"You", he went on, "With the keys to the tower", he said, "Behaving like all the others"! He looked at Sebastian steadily. "What on earth did you think you were doing"? he demanded.

"I believed it had to be possible to cross it", Sebastian said. "And it is".

"You haven't crossed it, you are deluded", the Unknown One said.

"But I have crossed it and seen that the mountains are a mirage", Sebastian said, "I've been up to the shore, almost".

"Nonsense"! The Unknown One declared. "You have not left Pavi Bujdam. The mere you have crossed is still part of Pavi Bujdam. You can go up to the stars and to infinity in your machines, and you still would not have left Pavi Bujdam".

"I don't understand", Sebastian said.

"Clearly", the Unknown One said.

"I for one would like a better explanation", Timaeus now joined in, in his inimitable way, indirectly addressing the Unknown One. Ambika immediately pulled on Timaeus' arm as if to try to quieten him.

The Unknown One saw Ambika's gesture, and smiled at her. "I can see that you are wise and beautiful", he said, "And you are perfectly correct in thinking that an explanation is not the answer".

"Nonetheless...", Timaeus insisted.

The Unknown One held up his hand in front of Timaeus as if to say, "patience", and pointed to the Satya Vajra. Then he looked at Sebastian. "Why did you call this the *Satya Vajra*", he asked. "Do you know what it means"?

"It means Weapon of Truth", Sebastian answered.

"A weapon against what"? The Unknown One asked.

"The mere"? Timaeus ventured, only half seriously.

"The mere is not your enemy", the Unknown One said. "The mere is your friend. The weapon, if you have one, is in you, not in your technologies and your sciences. The required weapon is simply your weapon against delusion, like *this*", he said, pointing to the Satya Vajra. "You should continue with your art", he said to Sebastian, "And leave the science to the scientists, until such time that they become knowledgeable artists and their science becomes their medium".

Even as he was speaking, the Satya Vajra was becoming lower in the water. It started to list, first to one side, and then to the other. Clearly, some damage had been sustained. And now its integrity could hold no longer, and it became obvious that she was sinking.

Everyone just stood and watched in silence, as the vessel disappeared under the water with a burbling sound, and sank to the bottom by the jetty. When they looked away and around again, the Unknown One was gone.

Marsilio turned and addressed the group. "Let us not be dismayed, but let us learn from our adventures", he smiled. "For all of life on Pavi Bujdam is an adventure, after all. And perhaps we would do well to remember that as Marsilio sees it, all our adventures fall under the adventures of the stars, which is where we truly are beyond the imitations and the image we call Pavi Bujdam. And so too we ourselves, if we could but know it, are already truly beyond that which is already much closer to us than the stars, which is the mere".

"It is just as the hermit said", Marsilio continued. "Many years ago I spoke with him. But now he is not here, it is for me to pass on what he said. Beyond Pavi Bujdam is another land, and another mere. And beyond that, another and another. The hermit named seven, but said they were really innumerable. The land and its mere beyond us, is far more beautiful than here. And beyond that, is another, still more beautiful. But each one has its own idea of the world, you see. Indeed, each one has its own idea of the universe. We cannot pass from here to another, in the way that Sebastian tried with his Satya Vajra, still within the Pavi Bujdam idea. Unless we are already a Visitor then we cannot pass to another land, beyond the mere, except by taking part in the masquerade".

"The masquerade"? objected Sebastian, incredulously. "But the masquerade is just the masquerade. It's just something we fall into each summer, because we are looking for new experiences and new relationships. It's what one does, isn't it? And no one in the masquerade really considers the mere", Sebastian said.

Timaeus laughed. "I agree", he said. "I don't think anyone even ever thinks about the mere, at least not in that way, not when they are in the masquerade", he smiled.

"Indeed", said Marsilio. "It is true of most. But it's not true that no one does. There are those who do".

"Do *you*"? Sandhya asked. "When you are in the masquerade"?

"I do", said Marsilio.

"What about Belvoir"? Sati asked. "He seems to know what is beyond the mere, and yet he never takes part in the masquerade".

"It is not that he has never taken part in the masquerade", Marsilio answered. And I am sure he will do again one day", Marsilio continued. "And I have no doubt that he will cross the mere after taking part in the masquerade, the next time he goes into it".

"It seems absurd to me", Timaeus said, "That we cannot cross the mere from here, and yet we can, if we take part in the masquerade. It doesn't make sense. At least, not to a mathematician".

Marsilio answered "When we cross the mere as a result of our taking part in the masquerade, it is because we no longer see things in the way we ordinarily do in Pavi Bujdam, but rather we see everything as the Visitors see everything, which is how things are seen once you have crossed the mere. It is similar to how you regard the masquerade now, which is not how it seems to you when you are immersed in the masquerade".

Sandhya sighed loudly. "Well it's all very strange and rather too wearisome for me", she said. Then she looked at Sebastian. "What surprises me", she said, "Is that you, Sebastian, thought it not sensible for me to try to jump the boundary fence on the Silver Gallop, whilst in the fury of the frenzy, and yet you thought it sensible for yourself to try to cross the mere".

Marsilio said "There is nothing sensible about either". He looked at both Sandhya and Sebastian. "Both are the result of a kind of frenzy", he said. "And when it comes to it, what it takes to cross the mere, in one way or another, is always going to be beyond what is sensible".

Sebastian looked bemused.

Marsilio continued, "The situation is, Sebastian, precisely as the

Unknown One declared when he was here. You have not truly crossed the mere today, or over the last week, or over the last few hours, whichever way you want to look at it. You only tried to cross the water in the first place, because you were deluded by Seraphina's art. The illusion she has spun has worked on you without you realising it. You cannot find Seraphina beyond the mere that you appear to have crossed today, because that mere, is only the one in her art, it is just an image. All this, as you correctly suppose, everything of Pavi Bujdam, is the art of Seraphina. It is all just images. But find yourself, and you will find Seraphina".

Marsilio looked sideways towards Sati, and still talking to Sebastian, he said "Or find Seraphina and you will find yourself".

"I do understand now", Sebastian said. "I made a mistake, that's all".

Whether or not he did understand, Marsilio doubted.

"We all make mistakes", Marsilio said. "When we are deluded by Seraphina's art". He turned to Sandhya. "And it would be a mistake", he said, "My dear, beautiful Sandhya, to try jumping the boundary fence on the Silver Gallop. However, I think it perhaps possible that if you did know, in the moment you tried it, what is beyond the mere, then you may be able to jump the fence while you are in that frenzy. But take careful note, beautiful one, I don't think it would be in your command, as Sandhya, in Pavi Bujdam, to do so".

"I think I understand", said Sandhya hesitantly, thinking about Sebastian's recent exhibitions, and her experiences there.

Sati, suddenly now looking extraordinarily innocent, then said, "Am I in the image of Seraphina, as part of her art"?

"Ah...", said Marsilio. "No one can deny that, can they"? he said. "Not if they have seen the portraits at Aumhurst. But there you have me, my beautiful Sati", he said, looking at her with the greatest love. "You are certainly a most beautiful part of Seraphina's art. But if you continue to ask questions like that, you will soon be asking questions that I cannot answer for you. Because we are all images, here, in this art. And as Sebastian has come to thinking, there is a way in which a work of art may have many, many artists. All of whom, are images themselves, in a still higher art. So Seraphina is not the only artist. And even Seraphina herself, I can tell you, is an image. Everyone in Pavi Bujdam knows her as the architect of Pavi Bujdam, but she is not the only one".

Marsilio looked around the group of friends. "Just as Pavi Bujdam is not the only land. And our mere is not the only one". He now looked at Sebastian, and said, "And just as Sebastian here, could not possibly create all the wonderful works of art that he does, without all those who also contribute to it. His teachers, and those who make the materials that he uses, the beautiful things in Pavi Bujdam that he paints, and even all those here, to whom he knows he will show the art, who themselves are part of his inspiration to create his art".

Marsilio smiled at Sebastian with love, and said "And just as Sebastian could not have made the Satya Vajra without the new sciences and technologies that he used in order to make her".

Timaeus smiled too and said "And indeed someone called Timaeus who helped with the calculations"!

"Perhaps it would be better if you had not", said Ambika, sternly.

Marsilio gave Timaeus a friendly slap on the arm. "If you hadn't", he said, "We would never have learned what we have learned today".

§

And so the Saga of the Satya Vajra comes to end,
The play of stories playing out their way,
And we to further things beyond the mere our way must wend,
To wildwood and to forest go to play.

32

The Unknown One

"Amba where are you"? called out Ambika.

"I'm still looking for the path"! Ambika's voice echoed back through the dense woodland.

But looking for the path, indeed looking for any path, was proving more and more difficult.

Timaeus' voice could now be heard from somewhere further away in the woods, "I haven't found anything yet", he called. The hoof prints on the soft ground betrayed the direction he had taken.

"Sebastian! Where are you"? Sati called.

"I'm always with you, even if you can't see me"! Sebastian called back.

Quentin's horse now reared and then refused,
No further into thicket and to wildwood will explore,
He stands his ground his rider not amused,
But makes it clear to Quentin he will forward go no more.

Quentin calls "Parmenides is stuck! He will not move"!
Amba's Voice calls back "Then turn around"!
Progress through the wildwood now impossible will prove,
For all the friends they cannot make more ground.

Such was the confusion in the wild forest of untamed nature up the hill beside the path on the higher ridge, beyond the Circle of Trees. To find the Unknown One by this route was proving to be a futile idea.

At last Sati called out, intending her voice to be heard by everyone, "Turn the horses around! Let's go back"! she shouted.

All the friends turned around their horses and began picking their way back through the confusion of narrow passing places and possible paths, brushing past overgrowth and heading back towards clearer paths and better progress.

One by one, their paths once again converged on each other, and once again the friends became a united group.

"I don't know what we were thinking", Sati said, as the horses picked their way carefully back down the ridge to the Circle of Trees. "Marsilio did say this was no route for horses".

Eventually they came back to the Circle of Trees and Sandhya said "I know! Let's ride back down to the mere, and let's go over the side of the hill, let's go down the Green Sweep"!

"Good idea"! called Sebastian, already on his way in that direction.

All seven friends emerged from the side of the wood at the top of the Green Sweep. There before them, extended from as far left as they could see, to as far right as they could see, and stretched out as far as the horizon, was the shining mere, with the countless little islands dotted within it.

The Green Sweep lived up to its name. In bright lemon green it swept downwards as a sheer sweep of limy green lush grass, the steepest slope at the top, the incline becoming less and less as it swept smoothly and invitingly down and away towards the edge of the mere. So far down it went, and yet the gentle smoothness of its great curve made the drop look easy, and it seemed to be calling to them to take the plunge. The free expanse of it, the sheer spaciousness of it made it the most inviting grass slope that ever was, to both human and horse.

After the impossible struggle of trying to pass through the band of forest on each side of the ridge beyond the Circle of Stones, it openly promised the pent-up power of the horses freedom of movement at last. It promised self expression, and the joy of the gallop, all enhanced by the natural downward pull of gravity, or was it really a pull towards the mere?

Who could possibly stay at the top of the Green Sweep, looking down onto it, and out towards the scintillating mere, and not give in to the temptation to plunge downwards onto its deliciously continuous curve, its fresh, wide, sloping space, onto that luscious lime-green grass, and accelerate effortlessly under gravity into the shining light and gorgeous expanse of the glistening mere? What an experience it would be!

The horses and their riders stayed temporarily stationed, poised for a moment at the top of the Green Sweep, like a cavalry awaiting sight of the enemy, breathing in the magnificent view over the ecstatic expanse of the bright green slope. Then Sebastian said "I have a strange feeling".

"What is it, my dear"? asked Sati.

"I don't know", Sebastian replied, "It's almost like a premonition of some kind, similar to how I feel sometimes when we are about to go into the masquerade, and yet we are not".

"None of us are intoxicated or anywhere near the maze", Sati observed.

"No", agreed Sebastian. "That's true".

And then, without warning, Sandhya suddenly broke rank, almost as if into battle, riding away from the group, her horse pounding down the brightness of the steep slope into the joy of the gentle curve below, out and away, and down and down towards the full extent of the gorgeous green and the light of the mere. She could not help but let out a whooping scream of elation.

Taking the cue, the others now broke what little formation they had, and poured down the hillside like an outward spreading equine flood of ecstasy, bearing up a full party of human delight. With whoops and cheers, all being was now abandoned to the joy of the race, the sheer thrill of the gallop downwards under the pull of gravity. Straight towards the bright and happy meeting of the Green Sweep with the shining mere.

Their downward momentum turned into a madness of speed along the final, flat extent of the curve. They jubilantly raced on across the wonderful, sun-drenched, green grass, laughing like children.

But now a darker band in front was seen, something along the edge of the mere that from the height of the Green Sweep no one had noticed.

It was a massive growth of weed of some kind, blocking their passage to the mere, and more than one of the friends noticed that it seemed to be growing and entangling itself in itself in front of their very eyes. It was like a living thing with its own movement, and yet it was only weed.

Now they could all hear a thundering of hooves off to their right, as suddenly, there, racing along the edge of the mere towards them, this side of the weed, was Marsilio, dressed, as was often his way, as a red magician.

As they continued to gallop towards the weed, they could already see it was the most incredibly entangled mass of growth they had ever seen. So tangled was it, as a knotted mass of nexus and plexus, that its very substance seemed secondary to the shapes and patterns and impressions that were visible in it. As the friends gazed at it they saw in it, as if it were a canvas of some kind, all kinds of ideas and images that drew their attention.

Becoming more and more drawn into it Sandhya eventually shouted "It's some kind of artwork, I think. And look at that! Who would have thought it? There's a picture of me"!

"No", shouted Quentin, "It's a picture of me"!

"No"! Amba called out, "It's a picture of me"!

"What *is* this stuff"? Sebastian tried to shout out to Marsilio, now almost disgusted by it but somehow even partly amused by its plexus-like texture and tangles of knotted threads, that now at closer quarters he could see was woven into some kind of false fabric or tapestry of logic.

Now Marsilio's magnificent white horse, still racing and with far too much momentum, brought him sideways headlong into the group causing the frightened horses to scatter hither and thither, with much neighing and rearing.

"Steer clear of it if you can"! called Marsilio. "Its mindweed".

"What will it do"? Sati called.

The red magician answered "If you are not careful it will feed on you and make whole cities out of itself".

Timaeus had now made his way to the side, and called out to the others. "I think I've found a way through"! he shouted triumphantly, brandishing a sword capable of cutting a Gordian knot.

"Where did you get that from"? demanded Ambika sternly. She was quite shocked to see her gentle and genteel Timaeus brandishing a weapon.

"I'm not sure", said Timaeus, "But on reflection I think it might have come out of the mindweed", he shouted back. Nevertheless, he was already in the act of bringing down the sword fast in a great arc that whistled through the air onto the immensity of tangles in front of him. The line of the weed split in two at the cut, recoiling temporarily in billowing balloons of beguiling counterargument, that ordinarily, someone like Timaeus might have been drawn into, had he still had a weapon to brandish. But now, the sword itself had turned to weed in his hand, and Timaeus shook it out of his grasp, with disgust.

"What on earth is driving this stuff"? Amba was shouting from a little further along the mere. She had already tried to take her horse through it, and the weed was now entangling itself around the horse's legs. Sebastian came charging over towards her on his trusty steed, shouting "Don't get involved"!

Amba was still trying to withdraw her horse from the weed, an effort that turned into a grotesque parody of dressage, the horse lifting his feet high but hopelessly in the attempt to free himself from the grippy weed.

Ambika, now close upon the weed herself, could feel warmth coming from it. Amba saw her sister reaching out for the weed and started shouting to her "Come away from it"!

But it cares about me"! she called back. "I can feel its warmth, it loves me, and look at it, it's so sweet. It's so kind, and gentle, it's so spiritual. If only we could all love each other like this, and protect the weed when we are all in the masquerade together. After all, we are all in this together".

Meanwhile Quentin seemed to be affected in somewhat the same way. He was looking at the weed and saying "I like it like this, it's like we are children or babies but adults at the same time. But more like a child or a baby". Now he too, reached out for the weed, saying "Hey baby, I love you baby, I love you baby, will you be mine"?

Marsilio, now charging towards Quentin and Ambika, noticed that they had both now suddenly fallen asleep on their horses with their arms around their horse's necks. "Wake up"! he called out urgently, and seeming to draw upon some magical strength from his red costume, pointed at them. Hearing him, they immediately sat back up in their saddles, turned their horses around, and attempted to gallop away.

Sebastian was just wondering what to do, to try to free Amba from her predicament, when suddenly and unexpectedly the weed seemed to wither and withdraw. Amba's horse was set free, and now a gap opened up within the barrier of the weed, which then widened sufficiently that all the friends could pass through, closer to the edge of the mere.

Straight in front of them, right by the edge of the mere, they could see the white-robed figure of the Unknown One, standing with his back to them, looking out across the mere. The eight friends now approached the Unknown One, and dismounted from their horses.

Realising that events had just taken a turn that was somewhat reminiscent of being in the masquerade, Marsilio regretted being dressed as a red magician now that they were in the presence of the Unknown One. For all his wisdom, for the first time in his life he felt it was silly.

The white robed figure slowly turned around, away from the mere, to face the group. He looked at them with disdain.

"Do you truly know what you are doing"? he asked, his eyebrows raised.

"I don't think we do", Marsilio said, confident that the ludicrousness of their whole fiasco spoke for itself.

"Then why do you persist in thinking that you are the doer"? said the Unknown One. "When it is clear that you cannot succeed in directing the course of events as you would wish".

"Sometimes it works out", Quentin said.

"And so you presume that to be the result of your will"? said the Unknown One. "And what when it doesn't work out? No doubt you presume that not be the result of your will"?

"Well..." Quentin said, thoughtfully.

"A little selective, don't you think"? said the Unknown One. "I think even your scientists might agree to call it cognitive bias".

"That's perfectly true", Timaeus said, surprised. Then he noticed a little of the weed was left on his clothes. He pulled out his magnifying glass and began examining the weed closely. "It looks the same whether or not it is magnified", he announced loudly. "But I'm reluctant to examine it too closely, because the last time I did that with one of Sebastian's pictures in the exhibition, I think I became rather lost in it".

"It's time to let the mindweed go", announced the Unknown One. All the friends stood and watched as all the weed seemed to be blown into the mere, where it floated out and disappeared under the water.

"Everything goes back into the mere eventually", the Unknown One said. "Because everything comes out of the mere".

At that moment the deepest rumbling imaginable began coming towards them from somewhere over the mere. As the friends looked out over the water they could see the sky darkening in the far distance.

"It's a mere storm", Sati said. As they stood and watched, a great length of the horizon before them darkened to a deep purple hue. Now blue and sometimes red flashes of intense light started to appear from somewhere behind the obscuring veil of purple turbulence. As they continued to watch, the surface of the water far away appeared to be bubbling up as if it were boiling. There were churning clouds of colour and light above the mere, rising and falling with gigantic motion in some great dark, massive convection, looking as though it was pulling the water from the mere up high into the clouds. Then as the vapour came down again from the clouds, back into the water, it seemed almost to be creating fire in the water.

As the booming sound continued to come towards them, the friends all saw that the curtain of the storm appeared to be getting higher and wider.

"That's unusual", Sandhya said.

"Very unusual", Timaeus agreed.

Now Ambika, in disbelief, quietly said "It's because its coming towards us"!

"No I don't think so, they never do that", Sebastian said. It's just getting bigger isn't it"?

Now Amba and Quentin and Marsilio, all in one chorus, confirmed "It's coming towards us"!

Somehow, the friends expected the Unknown One to turn around to look at the storm, but he didn't, he just stood where he was. The booming sounds became louder and louder, the flashes of light brighter and brighter, with different colours now becoming visible within them, as the storm grew bigger and bigger.

The water of the mere behind the Unknown One was now agitated. Further out they could see chaotic turbulence. The storm was still a long way off, but had come closer to Pavi Bujdam than any mere storm that had ever been seen. Now in the presence of the storm the light over the mere in front of them dimmed, so much, that if they had turned around they would have seen the Green Sweep no longer in its beautiful bright green colours, but now in the semi-dark, subdued into dusky grey and umber, together with all its surroundings.

The already choppy waters of the mere became even more turbulent, and now the friends started to see things coming out of the water. At first, there were fish, which they didn't find surprising, but then there were birds, then crocodiles, and then books, and then buildings, and then, it seemed, the whole of Pavi Bujdam with all twelve Vicinages, and then even the Pavi market, together with gemstones, amulets, talismans and cintamani stones.

Timaeus saw numbers coming out of the mere, Quentin heard the most beautiful music emanating from its depths, and Marsilio saw such things as Seraphim, Angels and even demons. Sandhya and Sati together saw Helios rise out of mere, on golden wings, and Sebastian saw Seraphina coming out of the mere. Whilst all the while, Sati saw Sebastian coming out of the mere.

And now the friends watched in astonishment as the mere itself came out of the mere, so that the mountains behind it were visible behind the storm, which also came out of the mere, and for the first time all of them could see further than the mountains around the mere. And then as they eagerly looked to see what was beyond the mere and its surrounding mountains, keen to see what was there, the masquerade came out of the mere.

The masquerade was full of trouble. Troubles and trials and tribulations. And there was much wailing and gnashing of teeth. In the masquerade they saw Pavi Bujdam, but not as the Pavi Bujdam they all knew and loved. Everyone in the masquerade wore masks, and when they looked at the masks they not only saw the mere, they saw the masks were made from meres coming out of meres, and Pavi Bujdams coming out of Pavi Bujdams, in an ever circulating churning of what seemed to be a great mere. And beyond it was Pavi Bujdam, but as they had never seen it before. Breathlessly beautiful, they saw it surrounded by its mere, and out of its mere was coming a mere.

Beyond that mere were the best and most beautiful surrounding mountains that the friends had ever seen, surrounded by the best of all meres. But as that mere and its surrounding mountains came out of it, the mere that came out was the best and most beautiful mere that they had ever seen. And out of that mere came the most beautiful mere of all, which was the best of the best of all the meres, and there within it, was the best Pavi Bujdam of all. And then they saw that the best Pavi Bujdam of all was surrounded by the best and most beautiful mere of all meres, and out of it was coming by far the best and most beautiful of all meres.

As Sati watched she felt somewhat as she often did when she was coming out of the masquerade, but much more so, and she could now see the Unknown One standing by the edge of the mere like nothing more than a little reflection in a mere within a mere.

Now the storm seemed to recede, and as Sati watched,

The vestige of its former coloured hue,
Faded into wider azure blue.
And now again she saw the one unknown,
But now no longer was he there alone.
His former figure now she sees becomes,
A multitude of many, many ones.

Even to Marsilio the Unknown One now seemed to take on the appearance of a white magician. Who had now become many white magicians. Infinitely many white magicians, all along the edge of the mere. White magicians dressed entirely in white. The Unknown One was no longer one, or so it seemed. There were many of him, all along the edge of the still churning water.

No longer there alone but one of many,
His actions though of one were one of plenty,
The multitude of white magicians there,
A seeming endless line along the mere.

The Unknown One, or the white magicians, now produced a golden chalice and turned once more away from the friends, and facing the mere, the friends saw him stoop down to scoop up some water from the mere.

As he stood up, holding the chalice high up in front of him, as if in a toast, he turned around towards the friends, and smiling, declared, "A human life"! All the friends saw a few droplets of the water spill from the chalice like little droplets of liquefied light, scintillating in the sun, or a countless myriad of little droplets of liquefied sun, scintillating in the one light of the Unknown One, bright in white all the way along the edge of the mere.

Amba thought she could see in every one of the droplets the whole of Pavi Bujdam and the mere, and her sister, Ambika, and Quentin too, but whether it was within the drops, or reflected from the mirror-like surfaces of the drops, she did not know.

Now the Unknown One smiled and laughed as the one chalice was now being passed from one white magician to the next, the Unknown One grinning and laughing all the time, passing and passing, from one figure of himself to an apparently other, the single, shining, golden chalice.

The one golden chalice continued to be passed and passed on, a separate thing, handed from one white magician to the next, sometimes one way along the line of the white magicians, sometimes back along the other way. It seemed like some kind of mad game.

Sebastian watched the play of the Unknown One as the white magician who seemed to be enjoying himself as so many white magicians, seemingly in some kind of dance, the passing back and forth of the golden chalice all part of the dance. Sebastian himself was now standing as rigid as a soldier awaiting the next order, and he fancied now again that he could feel the turning of the Earth's mass around itself, under the cosmic blue sphere of the sky.

If the persons in the gardens at Aumhurst had been here facing the mere, they too, would have seen the play of the white magician, as the whole line of white magicians, seemingly without beginning, and without end.

But where the persons stood in gardens all around,
Unable by themselves to change their ground,
To look upon the mere was far beyond,
Such freedom from the limits of their bond.

Sebastian himself and Sati too,
Spellbound by the white magicians who,
Were passing back and forth the chalice gold,
Became entangled in a mind of old.

And seeing there the chalice seeming true,
It seemed some white magicians vanished too,
And then some more but still the chalice passed,
'Till only now a few remained at last.

The chalice still it passed along the line,
As white magicians vanished all the time,
Until at length magicians only three,
Ensured between themselves the cup would be.

Timaeus now considered on the play,
The chalice being passed along the way,
For it would seem that being separate fare,
When three more vanished it would still be there.

That chalice from the white magician came,
The water though therein it could not wane,
If all the ones should vanish once again,
The chalice or its contents must remain.

Or so Timaeus thought.

Now the Unknown One, still appearing as the remaining three white magicians, spoke again, pointing to Sebastian and Sati.

"So it seems you do not truly know what you are doing", the Unknown One said. "I think we have established that. So the next question is, do you really know who you are"?

All three white magicians now roared with laughter and moved around each other pointing hilariously at one another, almost as if accusing each other.

The third white magician who now held the chalice, wiped his eyes of the tears of laughter, and stepped forward to put the chalice purposefully on the ground, and then he himself stepped back in line with the other two white magicians. He then looked at Timaeus, as if he had been able to read his mind, and gestured for him to come and take the chalice. Timaeus, for some reason unknown himself, declined.

All three white magicians now looked at the chalice and laughed heartily again, occasionally looking towards the friends almost as if in sympathy. All three of them now pointed towards the chalice on the ground in front of them, and all the eyes of all the friends remained on it, watching carefully. But there was another pair of eyes, too.

Seeing now the cup a pure white swan,
Upon the mere did watch and float along,
All eyes were on the chalice on the ground,
The white magicians laughed and moved around,
And one by one they vanished without sound,
One moment there it was and there it shone,
The next no longer was for it was gone.

And so it was that with the vanishing of the last white magician, the disappearance of the Unknown One, the chalice vanished too, even though it had appeared to be something separate from him.

"Perhaps nothing is really separate from anything else", Timaeus thought to himself.

Sati, watching the proceedings, thought to herself, "He's gone.

"He took his chalice yet all else is here,
All else that manifested from the mere.
Perhaps the greater chalice is the mere,
And if I vanished too all I hold dear,
For me might seem then not to cease to be,
But rather all would always be as me".

Nobody heard her thoughts.
The friends all just stood, as if nothing had happened.

As birds above the mere are flying free,

Yet none seen there without the mere could be,
So too is nothing seen without the mere,
Nor even mere is seen without the seer.

How many does the Unknown One become?
There is no limit, limitless is he,
For nothing is without the Unknown One,
No golden goblet, water, he or she.

In seeing of the truth and all the seeing,
No ways of knowing as a separate being,
Through thoughts and understanding ever come,
Of being that which knows the Unknown One.

First must come the being of the One,
The white magician's tricks are then unspun,
The magic of the mere itself unfurled,
In Joy of being nothing in the world.

33

Et In Arcadia Ego

At last the time had come. The time Sati had been waiting for. The end of her current story and the beginning of a new one.

§

What marvellous means is this by which the golden palomino,
The horse called Helios beautiful and strong,
Will take his rider Sati with all virtuousness of Zeno,
Towards the truth of Seraphina's song?

§

Sati was grooming Helios in the stables at Merehurst, when she heard footsteps. Turning around, she saw Sebastian standing at the door, looking at her. Something obvious in his demeanour told her there was something very important that he was going to say.

She stopped her work and turned around to face him. She didn't need to say anything. She just stood, looking at him, waiting for him. Just as she had been waiting, all this time.

"I want you to be at Aumhurst with me", he said.

"I live there don't I"? Sati said, staring at him. "I'm often at Aumhurst with you. I was there last night, wasn't I"?

"I want you to be the Lady of Aumhurst", Sebastian said.

For a moment there was silence in the stable. Then Sati quietly answered "Then I will". Her gaze softened. "You took your time", she smiled.

She heard Helios move. And something in his movement caught her attention, but she didn't turn around.

"So we have to go back into the masquerade, don't we"? Sebastian replied.

"I know", Sati said.

"And we have to go under the Sun, and not under the moon", Sebastian said. "Will you come and meet with me at the entrance to the maze at midday, and hence into the masquerade, with this plan"? He asked. "Will you, Sati, take this step"?

"I will", said Sati. And then she said, "Will you, Sebastian"?

"I will", said Sebastian.

After Sebastian left, Sati, still facing the door, and still taking in what had just taken place, heard Helios move behind her again. But it was a large rustling noise that she was not familiar with, and it caused her to turn around. There she saw, or thought she saw, for a moment, Helios sidling away from her, but with a look of approval.

She met his eyes and attempted to read him. She knew he was communicating with her, and she with him. Somewhere between them was a love she didn't understand. Perhaps it was love beyond all understanding. And in the next moment, as Sati saw him, he reared up with outspread wings, completely capturing her in his countenance, while Sati stood transfixed. When he came back down, his hooves clumping back onto the straw, he was again the Helios who was familiar to her, an extraordinary but wingless yellow palomino.

§

Once more upon the Silver Gallop flies the yellow Helios,
Towards the meeting at the promised place,
So now it is the couple can at last their union realise,
And bring them more towards the light of Grace.

§

Once Helios was safely stabled at Aumhurst, Sati made her way to the maze. She was struck by how different it looked in the middle of the day, compared to how she last encountered it in the dark. The leaves and the foliage all looked the same. As she approached the entrance, there, already waiting for her, was Sebastian. Just as she had been waiting for him, all this time. They joined hands, and soberly made their way through the maze towards the centre, and there, as before, was the gate to Arabath, but now already open.

In no time they were in the masquerade again. Now once again there was Sebastian as the ogre of strange, golden face, and Quentin, his snub-nosed blue servant, moving through the beautiful gardens of Aumhurst but no longer with ambiguous intentions. The play of the masquerade was now different in Aumhurst. Or was it even Aumhurst? Perhaps it was Merehurst? Who could tell?

It might well have been Merehurst, for there in the orange groves, where the birds fly above, was Sati, the most beautiful of all damsels now become the most beautiful of all Ladies, together with Sebastian now of such strange, but beautiful, golden face, that he was no longer an ogre, and more a Knight.

And there, too, in the masquerade itself, was the mere. The mere of water, or brine, or wine or milk, according to whoever described it, or however it was viewed, and from where it was viewed. And wherever there is a mere beyond a mere, all must surely anyway be a milk of radiance from the greatest splendour. And in its churning it might become all kinds of things. It might even become Pavi Bujdam and its mere, and every land and its mere beyond it. And even the moon might come out of the churning of that ocean, and perhaps even a masquerade from the moon.

The masquerade mere had always been there, in the masquerade, but no one had ever really noticed it. Until now. There was always the mere, always. It always was, and always will be.

And if it could speak it might well say "Around Pavi Bujdam, I am, and around the masquerade each year, I am. And around every masquerade within the masquerade, I am. Forever so it was, forever shall it be. Even in Arcadia, and in the garden of love, around the *fête galante* in the *fête champêtre*, I am. Yes, even in Arcadia I am".

The mere is everywhere, and everywhere it declares itself to those who can see. Just as even in the Old World, somewhere through the gate of Arabath and within all the masquerades within the masquerades, there were poets there, who could see it everywhere. And just as there was once even an Old World artist who declared it in his painting to be so. And the poets who could see the truth of Seraphina's imagination would pay homage to it. For it is carved upon the very tombstones in the garden of love where the flowers should be.

For there beyond the mere is where our joys and our desires,
No longer falsely bound are they by blackened priestly briars.

So now within the great celestial dance,
The couple dancing turn upon the mere beneath their feet,
Becoming then the mere themselves at once,
And entering there therein within the waters they will meet.

And now within their dance upon the winy milky mere,
That they might in the masquerade reveal its higher sphere,
Through Sati's beauty naked yet beneath a veil of silk,
So each the other leads in love towards the mere of milk.

Yet there toward the mere before their eyes they see the weed,
Of mere imagination impregnated with the seed,
And there within the weed they see another mere is made,
Within this weedy world there is another masquerade.

On within the masquerades within the masquerades,
The couple now must go to find their forests and their glades,
To find the *fête galante* within and break the dream that binds,
The pow'r within romance that keeps away the weed that winds.

There within they find again their forest and their grove,
Wherein within their bodies there to each they must betroth,
For even there the orange blossom smells so sweet in spring,

Where Sati from her former nymph her wisdom she must bring.

Above the Venus of the scene a cherubim there flies,
Who being born from seraphim brings treasure to the wise,
Whilst deep within the masquerade within the masquerade,
Entangled by the mindweed there a poorer bind is made.

His arrow now released it strikes Sebastian through the heart,
Who now must bring his knowledge to the living of his art,
Whilst Sati being Seraphina's own no more apart,
Must find the truth within as she is struck by Cupid's dart.

§

Now providence doth shine upon their way,
Their fate together now they will obey,
As Sati finds the one she loves is higher,
For her true love is Seraphina's Sire.

Sebastian is none other than that one,
Through whom himself together they must bring,
The play of light upon the mere unspun,
Their purpose now fulfilment of that ring.

The symbol then he gives upon her hand,
Their masquerade lives now in new found land,
As Aumhurst's Lady Sati is in place,
In Pavi Bujdam there she lives in grace.

Sebastian through the *fête galante* must charm,
As through the grove with Sati on his arm,
They walk beneath the oranges and birds,
Whereon to Sati now he speaks the words:

"My love of thee who brings for me the light,
The one true Self that we may find tonight,

I long for thee as who I hold most dear,
Beyond this world the bliss beyond the mere.

Our differences and separations play,
Like ripples on the mere there every day,
Each its own in part but all of one,
Dissolved again when all is said and done".

§

And so we see a secret has emerged:
When all the play of separation's purged,
The play in time of separate ones plays on,
Whilst all the time the timeless one is One.

As all the friends as twelve do play their part,
They each dance forth through Seraphina's art,
And so it comes to pass in Aumhurst's grange,
That each through all the others must exchange.

And so we ask is Quentin Sebastian's kin?
Or Augustus is he too a half sibling?
A brother half of Sebastian and Sati too?
As Sandhya is Sebastian's sister true?

If Sati's love is Seraphina's Sire,
Yet Sebastian is the one she doth desire,
Whilst both come forth through Seraphina's art,
Then who doth Sati love in her true heart?

Seraphina's art begins as love,
And then becomes illusion from above,
A spacious light in which the senses play,
That then becomes the forming of the way.

Through more entangled fate it comes to be,

That deep within the weed disharmony,
Will play itself throughout and through the rings,
A game of myth as worlds about it brings.

And only when we from the myth awake,
Will then the strife the play of rings doth make,
Give way to knowing true the Source of all,
From whence all love doth come before the fall.

So when the friends to Belvoir go in need,
Of hearing forth the truth beyond the weed,
Beyond the masquerades the truth of us,
He gently smiled and then he answered thus:

"An evermore expanding play of love,
From one true Self is shone from tales above,
And all whom we have loved or ever may,
Shall take their part within the worldly play".

34

Helios

"And so it was", said Gautama, "That Augustus, with Aedesius and his friends sitting around him, by the fire, came almost to the end of his storytelling. Augustus sat back and rocked a few times in his rocking chair, smiling. The fire crackled. The long case clock ticked its mellow, leisurely seconds in the world of time on Pavi Bujdam, so different from the time in the masquerade. Aedesius and his friends came out of the spell of the story as if they were awakening from a dream. Aedesius put together his hands and said 'Obeisances to you, Augustus, for you have have told us everything we wished to know about Sebastian and Sati, and Pavi Bujdam, and the secrets of the mere. Please tell us now of the adventures of your good self, and Sandhya, and how you came to be Lord and Lady of Aumhurst. Please continue'. Augustus smiled, and looking around the friends, answered 'Aedesius, dear one, and all of you friends, how can I tell you? For our adventures are only just beginning. And it is easier for us, than it was for Sebastian and Sati. We make progress so much faster. All we have to do is to make sure that we don't ever forget the importance of the mere, and that it is our destiny to discover what is beyond it'".

And with that, Gautama began his final narration, in the voice of Augustus:

When those who still within the masquerade,
Bravely go beyond its false parade,
They also pass beyond the gleaming mere,
To change its playing slowly year by year.

And so it is a masquerade must change,
To bring the mountains quicker into range,
For those who would beyond the mere to go,
To quickly pass beyond the weedy foe.

The mountain in the middle of Pavi Bujdam was, after all, just a mountain. Even though erected on top of it was the Tower of Pavi Bujdam. The clans held to the idea that the higher you can get up the tower, the further you can see. And it was perfectly true, up to a point. But it did not usually reveal what was beyond the mere.

Occasionally, though, when conditions were just right, unknown to anyone in Pavi Bujdam, except to those who actually discovered it, you could in truth see beyond the mere from the top of the Tower. But you could never do it just by sending a drone up, as Sebastian tried. Just as you cannot get across the mere using technology, except in appearance only, as Sebastian also tried.

To see across the mere from the Tower, is of course to see whilst still standing with your feet in the Tower. But across the mere is across the mere, and what is beyond all meres never did depend in the least on Pavi Bujdam and its Tower.

And so it was that Sandhya and I, Augustus, have never been to the Tower, but the very next summer after we entered Aumhurst, in the masquerade, Sandhya and Augustus, (whom I, Augustus, shall speak of as though separate from who I am), having inherited the key to the Tower, were wandering together through the forests and groves of Merehurst as it appeared in the masquerade these days, on the slopes of the hill that goes up to the Circle of Trees, and beyond, to where the hermit lives, and beyond still, to the Unknown One, at the Beacon, from where the view is all around.

Hand-in-hand they wandered, free in the delight of their bodies thinly veiled in translucent chiffon as they delighted together on the lawns under the leaves, and occasionally entered the beautiful forest where they started to become intoxicated with its nature. And in their wanderings through the delightful groves situated between the unexplored parts of the blissful forest, they found themselves promenading together in the most beautiful *fête champêtre*, in which there were many paths to explore.

And as they walked together underneath the leafy bowers, their bodies free beneath the chiffon, under the joys of the songs of the birds, and in the soft, dappled light from the Sun streaming through the trees, in rest from their adventures and dalliances, they came across another couple walking on the path towards them, the gentleman elegantly dressed with a top hat, and the lady carrying the most beautiful parasol, from which she enjoyed shade from the powerful sun.

The couple stopped to greet Sandhya and Augustus, and asked "We would like to go to the top, to the Beacon. Would you be so kind as to tell us the right path that should we be taking"?

Sandhya and Augustus, knowing well the hill, greeted the couple and replied with the easy answer they also knew well, saying "At any junction you come to, you will find that you can go perhaps straight on, continuing on the level, or perhaps you can choose to go up or down. If the opportunity is there to go up, and you choose to go up, you will go up. There is no right or wrong about it. All the paths meet at the top. If you want to get to the top, if you want to find the Beacon, just keep going up".

The elegantly dressed couple thanked Sandhya and Augustus, and continued on their way. Sandhya and Augustus smiled at each other, happy to have been of help. And then Sandhya heard a noise coming from the clearing in the trees behind her. A noise she recognised, without really knowing how, or why.

She turned around, and there, in the clearing, was Helios. Augustus,

I, still beside her, was looking the other way. I should of course have been looking at her. Helios seemed to be looking at her with approval. She felt somehow, in a way that she couldn't understand, that he was telling her something. And somewhere inside her she had the strongest feeling that she was about to embark on a magnificent adventure, far greater than the conquering of the boundary fence between Merehurst and Aumhurst.

Indeed, here she was, in the Merehurst of the masquerade, already as the Lady of Aumhurst. And she was determined that she would put that privilege to good use. Not for the advantages that it gave her in Pavi Bujdam, or indeed, in the masquerade. But to find what is beyond the mere.

What that boundary fence between Merehurst and Aumhurst was meant to symbolise now, she couldn't remember or imagine. But that was how things were, in the ever present symbolism of things in the masquerade. She looked at Helios, and Helios sidled away from her and looked at her. She was sure it was a look of approval. And then silently he reared up, wings spread wide, before clumping back down again onto the turf of the clearing.

Postlude

"And so Augustus", said Gautama, "Came to the end of the story he was telling, of Aumhurst, and Sebastian and Sati, and Sandhya and himself, and how he and Sandhya became the Lord and Lady of Aumhurst, after Sebastian and Sati had disappeared from Pavi Bujdam. And he was finished of all his storytelling".

Pythagoras and his friends stirred out of the spell of the story as if they were awakening from a dream. However, Pythagoras, still wanting to know more, said "Obeisances to you, Gautama, for everything you have told us. Nevertheless, there is still something about the meres that I don't understand.

"In the stories you have told us, of the stories told by Augustus, in Pavi Bujdam, you have spoken of the mere around Pavi Bujdam. But as I understand it, this mere and many other meres are all in the interior of Puvk Paradisa, where we live. So what of our own mere, around Puvk Paradisa? Please be so kind as to tell us of the land beyond the mere around Puvk Paradisa, and of what is beyond that".

Gautama smiled to the friends in compassion. "You are indeed very astute", he laughed. Then he answered:

"There is another land beyond our mere,
That facing us is shining like a mirror,
A place that has no place but has a sea,
That causes all the meres within to be.

To cross the sea you first must find the source,
Inspired beyond by Seraphina's horse,

For there beyond is Seraphina's Sire,
Still more beyond and guardian of the higher.

For when the guardian sleeps the meres are rife,
And when the guardian wakes there is the life,
The life that shines for all and needs no more,
And yet that life is yet another door.

Before the door the meres are all around,
Yet yonder two more meres are to be found,
Arcadia there itself is shining bright,
And there upon its mere an island white.

It shines forever more before the water,
A splendour long before King Thestius' daughter,
With many names we say Pavi St Veda,
The glorious isle above the fate of Leda".

"Obeisances to you, Gautama", said Pythagoras. "Such stories you have told us, that we are now intoxicated by their energy! As we are now swooning with what you have told us, we would very much like to be part of these stories, and to experience them, and so before we try to reach the island of Pavi St Veda, or even ask you more about the fate of Leda, I think we should all like to cross the meres in the interior of our land, in search of Pavi Bujdam, Aumhurst, and its masquerade. We should very much like to become Visitors to that land! Having heard and learned so much from your stories, perhaps we can bring something of worth, to its people".

Gautama laughed. "Dear ones", he said, "All these stories are energies, growing and dissolving, all forever in each other, in the churning of the meres. All are forever exchanging, and eternally recreating, in Seraphina's art of whatever eternally remains. All come not from your Gautama here, even though they are all my stories, but from Pavi St Veda, from the eternal exchange of love in the Presence of the One beyond all meres, who glances at the meres and enters all as the Way."

"Before we go, I have one last question", said Pythagoras. "Please tell us who Seraphina is, and why she creates this art, and how and why she paints herself into her picture".

"My dear friends", Gautama smiled, "She has painted herself into her picture in order to fulfil her aspiration to realise the truth of herself, and become one with her lover, from whom she, as the great artist, has never really been separate, or other than.

"And so it is that all those she has created in her art, and all those and everything they create in their arts, and what they create, too, and then what they create, too, without end, forever and ever, shall contribute to these, our Pavi lands, and even to our Puvk Paradisa here. Here, in what eternally and infinitely remains from her first art, her exchange of love with the One. And thus she and her lover remain forever in the blissful forest together. We call her Seraphina, because she becomes the Lady of Aumhurst".

"But who then, is the Lord of Aumhurst"? asked Pythagoras.

"It is good that you ask", said Gautama. "Because you yourself, may one day find yourself as the Lord of Aumhurst, especially now that you are determined to go into the masquerades. You must find the answer to this for yourself", Gautama said, now looking round all the friends, and not just at Pythagoras. "But you will not be able to do it without finding what is beyond the mere".

Here must end the story of the friends,
Their myth and their philosophies no more,
But from that island white it still descends,
In countless other ways the waves meet shore.

The crashing surf it churns the sand of mind,
That each mind sees according to its kind,
The empty play upon the surf of time,
As though it knows the reason and the rhyme,
According to the way of me and mine.

But only when the sand itself is gone,
Beneath the mere on which the Sun is shone,
Does all beyond the mere reveal itself,
As all within the mere that is yourself.

Brian Capleton is an alumnus of Wolfson College Oxford, The Royal College of Music, Trinity College of Music (now Trinity Laban Conservatoire of Music and Dance), Dartington College of Arts, and Keele University. He holds a Doctorate in music and a Masters in Performance and Research. He was a lecturer at the Royal National College and worked for many years in the field of music performance and musical instruments. He currently lives in Cornwall and writes both fiction and non-fiction.

Other titles include *Ekanta*; *Śiva's Brainchild*; *The Nonsense Play*; *Being and Brain*; *Circles, Myth and Imagination*; *Beyond Naivety* and numerous books in the field of music, musical instruments and musicology.